THE DEVIL'S ACOLYTE

THE DEVIL'S ACOLYTE

Michael Jecks

headline

First published in 2002
by HEADLINE BOOK PUBLISHING

10 9 8 7 6 5 4 3 2 1

Cataloguing in Publication Data is available from the British Library

ISBN 0 7472 6920 3

Typeset in Times by Avon Dataset Ltd, Bidford-on-Avon, Warks

Printed and bound in Great Britain by
Mackays of Chatham plc, Chatham, Kent

HEADLINE BOOK PUBLISHING
A division of Hodder Headline
338 Euston Road
London NW1 3BH

www.headline.co.uk
www.hodderheadline.com

For Janice and Jim –

the good and not-so-good fairies!

Glossary

A scullery adjoining the western end of the abbot's refectory...	**Abbot's Lodging**
	Acolyte
	Alms
	Almoner
	Calefactory
	Cellarer
	Cloister
	Commission of Array

Glossary

Abbot's Lodging
A separate building in the western wall of Tavistock's monastic plot.

Acolyte
The term denoting an inferior church officer, usually an assistant or sometimes a novice.

Alms
Donations of food, or money, or clothing to the poor and needy, for example beggars at the Abbey's gates or the lepers living at the Maudlin.

Almoner
The monk whose duty it was to distribute **alms** to the poor.

Calefactory
A room in the convent set aside for relaxation. Here, the monks could sit with a mug of ale and let their aches and pains drift away.

Centenar
In the King's **Host**, the officer in charge of a hundred men.

Coining
This was the process by which tin was assayed or tested. It was taken to a coinage town (e.g. Tavistock), where it was weighed, a corner was chipped off and checked, and the amount of tax due was called out and paid before the ingot was stamped ready for sale to one of the waiting pewterers. We know that there were five such coinings per annum at Tavistock in 1303.

Commission of Array
The feudal **Host** was available to the King for his wars. As a matter of duty, all able-bodied males aged between sixteen and sixty were inspected by the Commissioners of Array, and the best taken, in theory.

Dorter   In practice, like so much of medieval life, corruption was rife. Monks' dormitory.

Frankpledge   Every boy over the age of twelve was expected to swear an oath that he would keep the peace himself, but he also had a duty to prevent others from being fractious. By the terms of this pledge, if a crime was committed, the whole community was penalised.

'Gardy Loo!'   This was the cry of *'Gardez l'eau!'* or 'Watch out! Water!' which housekeepers roared before emptying their chamber pots into the street. See **kennel** below!

Host   Under ancient feudal law each man in the kingdom must arm himself with those weapons suitable for his status, and present himself whenever called. These men, whose attendance was based upon their loyalty to their master, whether it be the knight, his lord, or the King himself, had to serve a set number of days, usually living off the land, and then might return home.

Indentures   Because the **Host** was growing unwieldy and insufficient for a task such as the defence of assets in France, for example, **indentures** were gradually introduced. An indentured man could expect board and lodging, pay while fighting, a uniform and other perks. A contract was written and then torn in two, one half kept by the lord, one by the serving warrior. The **indentures** were the tear-marks in both halves which could later be matched to prove the validity of either half.

Kennel This was the large gutter which ran down the middle of a street.

Layrwyta In the days when all peasants were slaves, their owners were reluctant to see too much breeding. Children were an expensive overhead. One way to prevent expense was to fine women who were sexually incontinent; thus the **layrwyta** was a tax on children born out of wedlock.

Medarius The Abbey's monk who purveyed mead, ales and wines for the community.

Morning Star A simple but deadly weapon, consisting of a club with nails hammered into the top.

Receiver Towns with their own markets raised considerable sums of money. **Receivers** were responsible for collecting up all the money owed to the town, and for keeping a true and accurate accounts. As with so many offices in medieval times, this post was widely open to corruption.

Reivers An old term for the thieves, blackmailers and murderers who commonly raided on either side of the Scottish Marches. Often, little wars were begun as a direct result of their predations.

Reredorter Behind the dorter, the communal toilets.

Salsarius The monk who was responsible for looking after the monastery's stock of salted meats and fish, so important during the winter months.

Shavaldour During Edward II's turbulent reign many men decided to take what they could without reference to the law. Shavaldours were marauders who raided and robbed all over Durham and the area of the Marches. Many knightly outlaws proliferated at this time, and weren't to be brought to heel until Edward III launched the Hundred Years' War and gave them a new, and more profitable, focus for their energies.

Stannaries The name given to the districts where tin was mined and smelted. Men living there were exempt from local laws because they were the King's own. They answered only to the Stannary Courts and the Stannary Parliament.

Undercroft The name given to the vaulted cellars beneath the Abbey's buildings; used for storage.

Vintenar A commander of twenty men-at-arms in the King's host.

Cast of Characters

Sir Baldwin de Furnshill Once a Knight Templar, Sir Baldwin is Keeper of the King's Peace in Crediton. He is known to be an astute investigator of crimes.

Simon Puttock The Bailiff of Lydford, Simon is responsible for law and order on the moors, under the watchful eye of the Warden of the Stannaries, Abbot Robert Champeaux of Tavistock.

Hugh Simon's servant. Hugh is a moorman and understands Dartmoor and its folk.

Sir Roger de Gidleigh The Coroner of Exeter, responsible for investigating cases of sudden death over a substantial area of Devonshire.

Abbot Robert Champeaux Of all Tavistock Abbey's Abbots, Abbot Robert was probably the most influential in his day. Taking on his post with a debt of some £200 in 1285, he soon made the Abbey profitable. One of his inspired ideas was to buy the Wardenship of the Stannaries.

Augerus Steward to the Abbot himself, Augerus is responsible for the Abbot's stores and seeing to his master's private needs.

Gerard New to the Abbey, Gerard has been tempted into thefts by older, unscrupulous men.

Mark This monk is **salsarius** at the Abbey (see *Glossary*).

Peter	Once a monk in a northern Priory, Peter came south after being attacked by Scottish marauders, and was grateful for Abbot Robert allowing him to live in Tavistock as **Almoner**.
Sir Tristram de Cokkesmoor	The King's Commissioner of Array, Sir Tristram has the responsibility of recruiting men for the King's army.
Joce Blakemoor	**Receiver** of the tin at the five coinings held at Tavistock, Joce is an important local man within the Burgh.
Walwynus	Also known as Wally. An unsuccessful miner, Walwynus has spent the last few years eking a living from his smallholding while trying to locate another seam of tin.
Ellis	A barber. Monks are not allowed to bleed themselves, and all abbeys need a barber to open veins, as well as removing teeth and ensuring that cheeks and tonsures are neatly shaved.
Nob	Originally from the north of England, Nob runs a local pie-shop with his wife, Cissy.
Cissy	Wife to Nob, Cissy is also the unofficial aunt to all those young women who need help with their social lives or children.
Sara	Widowed while young, Ellis's sister has recently become pregnant and is in need of a comforting shoulder to lean on.
Hamelin	The miner who took over Walwynus' works, Hamelin is sorely troubled by his lack of success. His wife and family are in dire straits, but he can't find the tin he needs.

Emma Hamelin's wife is desperately worried about her youngest son, Joel, who is showing signs of malnutrition.

Rudolf von Grindelwald A Free Swiss from the Forest Cantons, Rudolf has come to Dartmoor with his wife Anna and family to buy tin, for he is a master pewterer.

Anna Rudolf's wife.

Welf and Henry Two sons of Rudolf who have joined him on his trip to Devonshire.

Hal Raddych One of the old school of Dartmoor miners, Hal is a near neighbour to Wally and Hamelin.

Author's Note

The story of the Abbot's Way is one of those ancient tales which are all but impossible to validate. It's true that many of the books which include the tale make the legend sound almost feasible . . . but not to a truly cynical mind. For one example, look at the little booklet *Dartmoor Legends Retold – vol. II* by T.H. Gant and W.L. Copley, published by Baron Jay.

I picked this story as the start point for my novel because it offers an attractive amount of detail – the name of the Abbot of Tavistock of the time (Walter), the fact that there was a dispute with the monks of Plymstock Abbey (I changed this to Buckfast because I can find no record of an abbey in Plymstock) and the name of the leading protagonist, Milbrosa. However, lest there be any doubt, I personally do not believe that the legend as retold here has any historical validity. It is a curiosity, nothing more.

In some ways this story shows the extreme difficulty of being accurate when you are writing historical works. While it is possible that somewhere amongst the old Abbey papers a record of the event exists, I seriously doubt it. If such a record was there, the keen eye of Professor H.P.R. Finberg would have spotted it years ago, and he would have gleefully reported it in his superb history *Tavistock Abbey* (Cambridge University Press, 1951).

The way that history, or much of it, has been passed down through the centuries is not by means of researched and authenticated material, but by word of mouth. Stories which once bore a shred of truth are now so embellished and distorted that the man behind the myth of Robin Hood, for example, would be hard put to recognise himself, just as the Dark Ages warlord King Arthur (if he ever existed) would be astonished to hear about Camelot and his Knights of the Round Table. Word-of-mouth stories *were* subsequently written down, of course, and then were copied out by others and used as 'historical' documents. In this way we learn of the flight of Brutus (not the assassin) from Troy and his eventual landing in Devonshire, where he wrestled with and beat the indigenous population of giants, thereby taking over the entire kingdom of England, Wales and Scotland. That story, originally invented by Virgil, appeared in many monastic histories after Geoffrey of Monmouth first penned it. Subsequently, when King Edward I needed a justification to lay claim to Scotland, his spin-doctors hit upon the idea of following up this Roman concept. If the original men to arrive on Albion found a single, discrete political unit which they conquered, the logic said, the island always had been one entity, and still should be; thus the King of England was obviously the King of Scotland and Wales.

The Scots disputed this. Then, as now, they distrusted the 'spin' or propaganda emanating from Westminster. This claim, and the Scottish rejection of it, was to bedevil Anglo-Scots relations for hundreds of years, until the Scots agreed to let the English share their Royal Family in 1603 (James VI of Scotland; James I of England).

So what of the Abbot's Way itself?

We know that hundreds of years ago a series of stone crosses was erected in southern Dartmoor. At some point it was given the name of the Abbot's Way. This could have been because the Victorians noticed that it ran from the Abbey at Buckland to the Abbey at Buckfast – but others have disputed this. R. Hansford Worth points out that many tracks across the moors were well-defined long before the monasteries were built. The path from Buckfast to Nun's Cross is unmarked by crosses – although they could have been stolen, of course. In his book *Worth's Dartmoor* (1967) he proposes that if the Abbot of Buckfast *did* sponsor a new path, it would have gone by Holne over the Holne Ridge to Horn's Cross. From there it went over Horse Ford on the O Brook to Down Ridge (where there are two crosses), on to Ter Hill, and then to Childes Tomb via Mount Misery. After a cross west of Fox Tor Mire, it led to Nun's, or Siward's, Cross. After this section, the route follows more closely the way marked on modern Ordnance Survey maps.

Now, I cannot claim any great knowledge of this part of the moor, but I rather like Worth's methodology: seeking out and following the line of all the crosses – and, of course, there were more of them in his time. And those which had gone in Worth's day were still sometimes remembered by his contemporaries (who had themselves dug them up to use as gateposts), so for the purposes of this book I have assumed that Worth was correct. If you look at the map of the area, it is very noticeable that on the route suggested above, between Buckfast and Nun's Cross, you pass nine stone crosses; by following the route marked as the 'Abbot's Way' on the map, you pass two. If the Abbot's Way was marked by crosses, which route is more likely?

If you wish to follow in the footprints of the story, I would recommend Eric Hemery's excellent *Walking Dartmoor's Ancient Tracks* (Robert Hale, 1986). Like me, Hemery prefers Worth's route rather than the curious one given on the OS maps. And don't forget to buy the Dartmoor Rescue Group's book on walks in Dartmoor, because it gives excellent advice on all aspects of walking. Most of all, enjoy the feel of the moors. There are few places in our crowded little island where we can really see how things would have been, hundreds of years ago. Dartmoor has changed in many ways, but as you stand at Siward's Cross and gaze south and east, it is easy to sense the millions of people who have tramped past here over the centuries, through rain and sleet, frozen to the marrow, undernourished and desperate, and weighed down by overwork.

I only hope you don't feel the same as them!

Michael Jecks
Dartmoor
July 2001

Prologue

When they sat down in the old man's room on that Tuesday evening, it was the scar that initially held them all spellbound, rather than his stories.

The room was only small, the fire resting in a slight hollow in the middle of the floor, and the novices seated around it. The Almoner hunched forward, his elbows resting on his knees, his head moving from side to side as he studied each boy. Gerard the young acolyte felt a shudder of revulsion pass through his frame as Brother Peter's gaze passed over him. In this dim light, the Almoner looked like a demon viewing his prey. Gerard almost expected to see him sprout wings.

Away from the fire there was no light at this time of night, and the wind was gusting in the court outside, making a curious thumping as it caught ill-fitting doors and rattled them in their frames. This dismal sound was accompanied by the constant rumble and clatter of the corn mill next door; its low grumbling made itself felt through Gerard's bony buttocks as he sat on the floor.

Gerard gawped at the Almoner's terrible wound, knowing he shouldn't, fearing that at any moment, the man would look up and catch him at it.

Old Peter was aloof mostly, far above the novices in his supreme authority, yet most of them rather liked him. He rarely had to raise his voice to command their respect, rarely had to offer them the strap; he could keep them obedient and quiet through the mere force of his will. Yet Gerard didn't much care for Brother Peter. Not now. And the lad was incapable of averting his eyes.

Even as the Almoner turned his gaze from them to the fire, his thin head nodding, his lip curled ever so slightly at the sight of the novices, as though it was hard to imagine that so pathetic a bunch of young males could have been selected from the length and breadth of Devon, Gerard fixed on that hideous mark, wondering anew how painful it had been.

Even after four or five years, Almoner Peter's wound glowed in the firelight, a livid, six-inch cicatrice that began beneath his ear and ran along the line of his jaw to his chin.

It must have hurt like hell, Gerard told himself as the Almoner began his story. Most men would have died after receiving such a blow; it said something about Peter's powers of endurance that he had not only survived it, but had managed to teach himself to talk again, even with his jawbone shattered and no teeth on that side. The boy shuddered as he imagined a heavy blade shearing through *his* flesh, *his* bone, *his* teeth.

Old Peter enjoyed talking, particularly when he was relating tales like this one. Gerard could see his eyes glinting, reflecting the sparks from the fire as the logs settled. To Gerard tonight, he looked mean and malevolent, cunning and cruel. It wasn't Peter's fault, it was the acolyte's reaction to the threat he'd been given. He kept darting nervous looks at his neighbours: any one of them might be the agent of his ruin, simply by seeing him going about his business. Not that any of the novices looked too bothered right now. They were all busy listening open-mouthed to the Almoner as he related another of the old legends.

'Aye, it was a miserable winter's day, when Abbot Walter set off for Buckfast, many years ago now, and Abbot Walter had a long, hard way of it. Strong of character, he was. Brave. Off he went, aye, him with none but his advisers and a few clerks to take notes, and all because of an argument between Tavistock here and the Brothers at Buckfast.'

The Almoner paused and stared about him, mouth slightly open, tongue noisily burrowing at the gap where his teeth should have been. He often did this, as though it was an aid to thought, but Gerard privately believed that it was an affectation, one which Peter had cultivated to repel novices.

'Aye, Abbot Walter was a good, holy man. He lived as the Rule dictated, and he expected his monks to do the same.' He glowered at the boys as though expecting modern youths like them to dispute the justice of Abbot Walter's attitude. Shaking his head he stared into the flames before continuing gruffly.

'Like you, they were, some of them: always wanting more ale and wine and meat than they needed. And when the Abbot was gone, the bad ones among them decided to make the most of his absence. One in particular, there was – an acolyte called Milbrosa, learning the ways of the chantry, a happy, cheery fellow with a winning manner and an open, honest face, the sort of man who finds it easy to make friends. Bold, he was, and disrespectful – always prepared to make jest of older monks. He scoffed when he was told that his levity would lead to punishment – if not in this world, then in the next.

'Aye, he behaved like many of you would. When a cat dies, they say that the rats will dance and sing, and that's how Milbrosa and the younger monks were when Abbot Walter left. Before his packhorse had even crossed under the Court Gate, Milbrosa led a few of his friends down to the undercroft beneath the Abbot's lodging, and there they broke into a barrel of his best wine.'

There was a subdued intake of breath. The novices listened intently, utterly absorbed as he spoke, not because his strange, slurred speech made him difficult to understand, but because Peter seemed to take an almost sadistic pleasure in seeing how badly he could terrify his young audience. And the youngsters loved to be thrilled by his fearsome tales.

His voice dropped, and all had to lean forward and strain to pick up his words as he said grimly, 'You can imagine it. Five monks all vying to swallow more than any other, like so many Scotch gluttons set loose to pillage a tavern!'

Gerard could hear the hot fury in his voice, and he saw a small gobbet of spittle fly from Peter's lips. It flew through the air, falling with a short hiss into the fire. Yet when he lifted his eyes to the old monk, Peter's angry mood had flown. He was contemplatively tugging at a thread of his gown.

'Aye. Drunks. A terrible thing. Milbrosa was the worst of them. He'd have emptied a whole pipe on his own if he could. They guzzled their fill, getting horribly, beastly drunk, befouling themselves, spewing and retching, and yet returning to wash away the taste, drinking more and more, forgetting their divine duties, ignoring the bells calling them to Mass, not attending the Chapter meetings. It was a terrible thing. Terrible.

'But they couldn't remain besotted for ever. After some days, they gradually stirred themselves among the wreckage and filth they had created there, and when they saw what they had done, the appalling truth of their crimes broke upon them like a thunderous wave smiting a ship.'

He sat with that characteristic twisting of his features as he imagined the scene in his mind's eye. Gerard wondered whether the hideous grimace was in truth nothing more than a relaxation of his face – it was the nearest the Almoner could come to a smile since the Scottish reivers he so detested had attacked him and left him for dead.

'You can just see it, can't you? There they all were, bepissed with terror in the undercroft. They had stolen from the Abbot, and stealing is a terrible sin. But worse, they had taken his favourite wines! What more evil crime could a man commit? There they lay, moaning and groaning, waiting for the earth to open and swallow them, or for the ceiling to fall and crush them. That would be preferable to their pain . . . or living with the shame of their sins!'

Gerard shivered. '*The shame of their sins,*' he repeated to himself. The boy knew instinctively that Peter was thinking of *him* as he spoke those words, because Peter had guessed he was a thief; he had seen Gerard at night, and later he had warned him, telling him to confess his crimes and stop his sinning. The Almoner's scowling features had petrified the boy – although not so much as the man who had ordered him to steal just once more, or be exposed to the Abbot as the thief he was.

'They set themselves to with a will,' Old Peter resumed. 'All went to the Chapter meeting and confessed their guilt – not that they needed to. Their brother monks were well aware of what had been done, and Milbrosa's enemies were pleased, because they hoped this would be an end to him. But Milbrosa was no fool. He knew that he could avert the Abbot's anger if he simply replenished the stores, but he had no money with which to purchase good wine. Like all of us, he had taken the vow of poverty.

'What could he do? No more than what he did. First he cleaned the undercroft with his friends; they scrubbed and washed and scrubbed again until all the flagstones were shining and clean. Perhaps that would deflect the Abbot's rage when he heard of their drunkenness at his expense. When their master returned, they must endure his chosen punishment, but that could be days away, Milbrosa hoped, and in that time anything could happen. Perhaps by some miracle he would see a way through the problem.

'But once a man has submitted to an orgy of dissipation and fed the beast within him, it is hard for him to forego the pleasures he has enjoyed. Thus it was with Milbrosa. He craved more wine. Only used to ordinary ale like a monk should be, the heady stuff he had stolen had created a thirst he couldn't appease.

'It tore at him, this lust for wine, but how could he assuage it? Sunk deep in gloom he went to the *frater* and ate a meal with friends. They tried to persuade him that his sole hope was to pray to God for peace and await the Abbot's return. He should submit to his master and accept whatever penance the good Abbot Walter should impose upon him.

'Perhaps he would have listened to them and recognised the good sense in their words, but then travellers arrived, and in among

them, walking with them for security, was a messenger. Abbot
Walter had, he told them, completed his business and was
travelling by ship to the Abbey's possessions in the Scilly Isles,
far to the west of Cornwall. He would not be coming straight back
to the Abbey.

'It was enough! Instead of going to the altar and opening his
heart to God, this drunken, foolish sot went down to the undercroft
again with his friends. Instead of praying for help, they worshipped
their own gluttony with another barrel of wine. But this time,
when Milbrosa awoke, his head pounding from the alcohol, he
realised that he and his friends were truly lost. The theft of one
barrel was a foul crime deserving of punishment, but for this
second offence the penalty must be severe. Milbrosa might even
be exiled to the Scillies. Glancing about him at the bloated figures
of his friends, he acknowledged that their only crime was to have
followed him, and he was racked with guilt.

'He was still drunk, the fool, but he didn't realise it. In his
drink-bleared mind he thought he was wide awake and
sober. Many a sotten oaf believes himself sensible and clear-
thinking when he is thrown from his tavern, and Milbrosa was
like them. He was no more sober than a peasant at the end of
harvest when the last of the cider barrel is gone, aye, and it was
while he was in this state that he thought he saw a way out of his
shame.'

Almoner Peter's voice dropped again, and he studied his
audience still more keenly. 'He left that undercroft, my lads, and
stole silently and secretly to the court. Once he was there, he
hesitated. It was night-time, and although the weather was chill
and ice lay all about him, the moon showed him that the whole of
the Abbey was asleep. Alas! If only his Brothers had woken and
realised the vile crime he was about to commit! His breath hung
in the air like a feather, and he shuddered; he thought from the
cold, but no. It was his soul rebelling against the evil of his deed.
Aye, the Good God tried to send him sense, to persuade him that

his sins were none so foul yet that he should lose his soul if he prayed for forgiveness, but he was deaf to God's entreaties!

'For in the silence of that evil night, Milbrosa made his way to the Abbey church, entered, and walked to the chest, where he removed some silver plates and took them away with him.'

There was a gasp, and the old monk nodded grimly, acknowledging their horror. 'Imagine! He actually dared to go into God's house to plunder God's own silver. Milbrosa must have lost his mind. He ran from the church, and secreted the plate beneath his bed, before returning to the undercroft and drinking himself to oblivion. At last falling into a troubled sleep at the side of his friends, he tossed and turned. Dreams came to him, as the Saints called to him to return the plate and save his soul, but to no avail. Saint Rumon himself, our patron saint, beseeched him to take back the plate and sin no more, but Milbrosa heeded none of them and pelted headlong to his doom.

'The next morning he woke with a head still befuddled and as soon as the keeper had opened the gates, he collected the silver and made his way to the moors. There he found the travellers among whom the messenger had mingled, and offered them the silver if they would pay him for it. They agreed, for they had no idea that the stuff was stolen from the church, and before breaking his fast, Milbrosa had a full purse. He returned to the town and met with a merchant, who consented to send the money with a message to the Abbot of Buckfast asking for fresh supplies of wine, and then he made his way to his bed and flung himself on to it, wallowing in crapulous relief that he could again replenish the Abbot's stores.

'But when he awoke hours later, he realised what he had done and he was riven with anguish. Sober once more, he knew that he had committed a mortal sin. If an ordinary man were to steal from the church he would be named felon and would wear the wolf's head; any man could execute him, and justly. Milbrosa was secure from that for he was a monk and could claim benefit of clergy, but his crime was nonetheless so foul that he could expect a terrible retribution when the Abbot returned.

'There was nothing else for him to do. He went to his friends and told them what he had done. Head hanging, penitent as only a true sinner can be, he begged them to help him, but one by one as he appealed to them, they told him that they couldn't help. How could they? None of them had any money. They couldn't go and buy back the silver.

'It began to look as though Milbrosa would after all be forced to confess his guilt to the Abbot and submit to whatever punishment he was given. It was plain enough that there was no way of recovering the silver.

'But then one of his friends had an idea. Or maybe it was Milbrosa himself who mentioned it. Whichever it was, surely the devil himself put the idea into their heads.'

Peter's voice dropped into a hushed monotone. There was no fidgeting among the boys in front of him, only an appalled silence. Gerard could see the whites of their eyes, their mouths open, fearful as the Almoner reached the final shocking chapter.

'A voice suggested that they should go and beg money from a tin-miner. It said that there was this man who worked alone out in the wastes, a Jew – this was long before the Jews were thrown from the kingdom – and he was known to be wealthy. Milbrosa needed no second bidding. He proposed to march straight to the tinner's house and plead with him for money.

'As good as his word, he packed his scrip with a little bread and set off. His friends, alarmed by his demeanour, went with him.

'It was a good step, many miles from here. You have all seen the road that leads to the moors. It starts at the riverbank and climbs steeply, and once you have left the farming country, once you have passed through Walkhampton you are in it, but I daresay not many of you have climbed that way?'

On hearing the chorus of denials, Peter sniffed. 'When I was a lad, I walked to meditate and pray. I used to cover twenty miles

each day when my Abbot allowed me, and since coming here
from the Northern Marches, I have already walked many miles on
the moors, yet you haven't even crossed the river, I suppose. Oh,
aye, you modern youths are a feeble lot compared with my peers.

'The road goes up and up until you feel as if your knees will
crack. That was how Milbrosa felt, for he was pushing himself on
as quickly as he could. He *had* to have money to buy the silver
back from the travellers! When you breast the hill, there is a flat
plain, and then you must pass on to the ancient cross called
Siward's, or Nun's Cross, which marks the border of the moors.

There it's much more soft and rolling,' Peter told his audience,
'with a few rocky outcrops in the distance, and heather and grasses
that hide the clitter. There are boulders strewn about all over the
place, and if you wander from the beaten track, you are forced to
scramble up and down all the way. It is a broad, grey land, harsh
and unwelcoming. There are no trees, they are all gone, and when
Milbrosa stood on the edge of the moors that day and gazed
before him, he thought that this could be the ends of the earth. It
looked like a place blasted by God's wrath. The only signs of
civilisation were the fires rising from tin-miners' homes and
furnaces and the occasional pits dug all about, or the great heaps
of spoil where miners had tipped rubbish from their work. It is a
foul, chill, unwholesome land, especially in the depths of winter,
with the freezing winds blowing in your face and piercing your
robes. Milbrosa felt his courage fading as he stared ahead. His
hangover was severe, his head felt as though it had been cracked
open by a bill, and his belly wanted to spew up the vast amount of
wine he'd drunk. Aye, he was a most unhappy monk.

'But with all his friends there he had no choice but to carry on.
They walked eastwards along the rough tracks and paths until
they came to the turn which led to the Jew's house and took it,
going cautiously now, for there were many mires up there, great
deep pools of bog in which a man could fall and disappear for
ever.

'At last they found the house. It was one of those rough miner's dwellings. Ah, but you haven't seen them, have you? intrepid lot that you are! It was a narrow, low place built of granite, with the walls protected from draughts by piling earth against them and letting the grasses grow. The roof was of timber, with turfs thrown atop to stop the rain seeping in. When you live so far from other people, you can't always get straw to thatch, but grasses will keep out the worst of the wet.

'There was no one there, but as they opened the door and gazed at the empty little hut, they heard the clop of hooves and a man's voice, and there, behind them, they saw the Jew, leading a mule.

'Milbrosa was struck dumb at the sight of the man. His mule was heavily laden; he must have been about to set off on a journey or perhaps was just returned from one, and Milbrosa felt sure this was a bad time to be asking him for favours. Aye, but although *he* was unwilling, his friends and companions urged him forward. If he was to save himself, they pointed out, he must gain the man's favour and win a purse to rescue the silver before the Abbot returned and learned of his crime. They thrust him forward, and he stood shivering in the cold before the Jew, twiddling his fingers and licking his lips nervously.

' "What is it?" the old Jew snapped, for he was only just returned from the coining at Ashburton, and his legs were tired.

' "Master," Milbrosa said hesitantly, "we are but poor monks from Tavistock, and we must beg for our food and drink. Have pity on us and give us some of your money."

'This man might have been a Jew, but he was no fool. "Poor monks? You have an abbey to live in, with great estates all over Devon, and more wealth than I could dream of. Look at my poor rude hut. I must live in that, and my only cup is a wooden one, whereas you drink from silver and pewter. Look at my bed, a palliasse of heather, while you sleep in good cots of timber with mattresses strung from ropes for your comfort. My fire is mean and smoky, while you live in warmth with roaring hearths and chimneys to draw away the fumes. For my living I must scrape and dig, while all you do is kneel and sit. Surely *I* should beg alms from *you*?"

'Milbrosa didn't want to dicker with him. He threw out his hands in appeal. "Master Tinner, we have nothing. Our buildings are God's, our house is His, our beds are His. Our duty is to serve Him, and sometimes we needs must ask for more from the people whose souls we save and preserve, so that we do not die of cold and hunger."

'Now this Jew was a kindly man, and truth be told, he had plenty of money. His mule was heavy with a chest of it because his workings had been fruitful and he had sold plenty of good tin at the coining. He was of a mind to help this young monk, but even as he bent his head to pull some coins from his purse, Milbrosa found himself looking again at the mule.

' "Master Jew, your mule looks heavily laden. Are you off to the market?"

' "Just back from the coining, aye. I had to buy provisions."

'Milbrosa turned back and saw the heavy coins filling the Jew's purse. He looked at the mule and noticed the chest. It was enough. He picked up a rock from the ground at his feet while the Jew was peering into his purse, and suddenly Milbrosa slew him, striking with his rock until the Jew's head was crushed like an egg trodden underfoot.

'His friends had stood incapable of moving with the horror of it, but now, with the Jew's brains spilled on the moor, they took Milbrosa by the arms and pulled him away, calling to him, fearing he had become mad, thinking he was so distraught by his crimes that he had lost his senses. Yet he hadn't. Oh, no. The clever, evil fellow smiled at them and said, "Friends, release me! You don't realise what you are doing. You see me here and think I am mad because I killed that Jew, but hear me out.

' "That man lying dead is not worthy of your concern. Wasn't he a Jew? Who need fear for a man such as him? He was not one of God's chosen, for isn't it known that all Jews renounced Christ and worship the devil? They are damned. How else could they have demanded that Our Lord be executed on the cross? Surely it is obvious that to kill a Jew is no more heinous than to squash a fly?"

'The mad fools who were his friends were appeased. Although they knew that their companion had committed another grave sin, they permitted him to sway them with his words. And then, when some were yet wavering, he said this: "And it is fortunate for us that I have killed him, for look at the chest on his mule! It is heavily laden. It must be filled with money. Look at his purse, that too is massy with coins. We might take both and use them to retrieve our silver, and yet have enough to purchase more silver, to the greater glory of God, to place on the altar in our church. And if there is some spare, we can buy ourselves wine."

'That was enough for this greedy band. Eager hands tore at the mule and now Milbrosa took command. First he washed his hands of the Jew's blood, and then he ordered that the body should be carried some little way to a mire and thrown in, and thus their crime would never be discovered. They loaded the Jew's body on to the mule, and the patient creature carried its master to his grave. When the monks had hurled the Jew into the bog, the mule too was killed and pushed in, for Milbrosa had no taste for being accused of stealing it. At last they returned to their booty, and picking it up, made their way homewards, confident that no man would ever know of their crimes.

'The travellers were content to sell back the silver, and Milbrosa and his confederates soon recovered the plates and had some shillings besides, so when they were once more in the Abbey, they bought wine to celebrate.'

Almoner Peter's eyes met Gerard's and the acolyte felt his heart thunder. 'Soon afterwards snow fell, and they were pleased that no one would be able to learn of their crimes. It covered the country with soft, clean powder and hid everything. To celebrate their success in concealing murder and theft, Milbrosa and his friends visited a low alehouse and drank some of the shillings which they had left over from their theft. In such a way can the weak fall prey to evil,' he intoned.

A young fellow of some eight or nine years, whose eyes, Gerard considered, ran the risk of rolling from their sockets, gasped, 'So their crimes were never discovered, Almoner?'

'Of course they were discovered, you poor dolt! How else do you think I could be telling you the tale if they weren't?' Peter rasped.

'The men had all but consumed their wine when a messenger arrived. He was from Buckfast, he said, and the good Abbot there had witnessed a miracle in the church. The bells had been rung to declare the wondrous event, but he asked that Milbrosa and his friends, since the Abbot was still abroad, should join him in a great feast there to celebrate the honour that had been done to the monastery.

'Nothing loath, for the opportunity of participating in the festivities was as agreeable to them as ale would be to a blacksmith on a summer's day, they set off with the messenger. Up the hill there,' Peter said, pointing eastwards, and their eyes gazed at the solid wall as though they could look through it and see the group of monks toiling up the path beyond the river, 'he took them, always in front, always a little beyond them, his head cowled and hidden. It was terrible weather, cold and gusting, and there was the smell of snow in the air. Milbrosa was happy that the guide knew the moors so well, but he began to grow concerned when a mist came down. Still they strode on, their heads bowed, their hands clasped, the thought of the fire at the Abbey helping to draw them on.

'The mist grew thick and their steps faltered. None could see more than a few feet in front of them, and they were forced to walk close together, but still their guide led them on, until at last Milbrosa shouted to him, demanding that they should find a place to rest. The guide didn't answer, but bent his steps northwards, and the monks stumbled along after him, muttering bitterly and complaining about the cold.

'They didn't have to worry about it for long. No. A low hovel appeared ahead of them and, their hearts bursting with relief, they hurried forward. Suddenly the mist cleared, and they could see where they were.

'Milbrosa gaped. This shelter, this rude dwelling to which the guide had brought them, was none other than the Jew's home. Here, before the door, Milbrosa could see that the place where he had struck down the Jew was still marked with crimson, which seeped through the snow as though a cauldron of blood boiled beneath it. He felt his tongue cleave to the roof of his mouth, and he called to the guide in a voice that was suddenly hoarse. Then the guide turned to face him, and Milbrosa felt his heart lurch in his breast as the man lifted his hood.

'The monks screamed as one. Their guide was the Jew. His head was crushed and his eyes were dead, his tongue protruding, and even as he raised a finger to point to Milbrosa, his face melted away, and the monks could see that this was the devil himself, come to fetch them to make them pay for their crimes! Milbrosa and the other monks were lifted up by demons, their screams heard by the miners who lived all about there, and carried off to hell, where they yet burn, hundreds of years later.'

Peter sat back, eyeing his audience with satisfaction. One of the boys had given a little yelp of terror as he came to the climax, and the Almoner nodded sagaciously. 'So that was why the Abbot's Way came to be marked out.'

'I don't understand,' Gerard said, and he spoke for them all.

'After the disappearance of the monks, the Abbot of Buckfast refused to believe the tales of devilry. He had invited them to celebrate a miracle, and thought that his messengers and the monks must have lost their way in the mists, and had fallen by accident into a mire. No one would dare to stand against the

Abbot, especially not in defence of the Jew, no. So the monks were prayed for, like any lost souls who go missing on the moor or who disappear at sea, and to try to prevent it happening again, the Abbot decided that there should be way-markers to help travellers. He had great moorstone crosses planted like trees all the way across the moor, avoiding the dangerous mires and taking a good direct route from Buckland to Buckfast, so that in future monks and other travellers would be safe.'

One of the boys relaxed visibly. 'So there wasn't really a ghost or the devil. They just drowned in a bog.'

Peter looked up at him, and his eyes narrowed into grim slits. 'You think that, boy? You don't believe in the devil? Perhaps you will go the same way as Milbrosa. He scoffed at dangers and took risks because he didn't truly believe. Now you know what happens to men who laugh at the Rule, to felons dressed as monks. No man may know of your sins, but God does, and the devil too. He always takes his own. There is no escape. You may enjoy a short period of pleasure, but sooner or later, you will be found out and taken away like Milbrosa.'

He leaned forward, and his voice became a hiss.

'And if that happens, my cockies, may God have mercy on your souls!'

The Almoner's words struck at the children like a lash, and when the bell tolled for their beds, Gerard could see that they were relieved to be released from him. Rising with the others, Gerard was about to walk out with them when he felt his sleeve caught by the old monk's hand.

'So, did ye like my tale, boy?'

Gerard jerked his arm away. 'It made them think.'

'And what of you, lad? Did it make *you* think?'

'Me?' Gerard tried to laugh lightly, but as he left Peter's room, he could feel those eyes on his back, as shrewd and far-seeing as a hawk's, and he knew fear again. If he stopped thieving, he could be maimed, just as Peter was. Augerus had hinted as much, pointing to Peter and asking whether Gerard wanted to look like him. That was the alternative to continuing his stealing, Augerus meant, and the casual brutality of the threat left Gerard feeling sick.

Now, with Peter warning him to stop, he felt as though everyone knew about his stealing.

Earlier on that same grey and overcast Tuesday, Hamelin had been working in the cold mizzle. Groaning, he slowly stood upright and stared out over the moors with the exhausted gloom of a broken man.

'You all right, Hamelin?'

'Christ's Ballocks!' he murmured, leaning on his old spade. 'How could a man be well in this, Hal?' His tongue reached up to the sore lump in his gum. It was painful, hot to the touch, and he couldn't speak too loudly because the swelling hurt like a cudgel-blow with every movement of his jaw.

'Poor bastard!' Hal, older and, to Hamelin's eyes as cragged and tough as one of the dwarf oak trees from Wistman's Wood, dropped his pick and walked to his side. 'You'd best get a man to pull that tooth. Your whole cheek's blown up.'

Hamelin gave a non-committal grunt. Although he was grateful for the sympathy he had no money for treatment.

The last tooth he'd had pulled had cost nothing; it had been done by another miner, a brawny man with thick, stubby fingers and no sense. He'd grabbed Hamelin's jaw and jerked it down, then shoved the large pliers in and squeezed tightly before trying to drag the tooth out. That tooth and the one next to it had both broken off, leaving Hamelin in agony for weeks until the abscess which had grown beneath had finally burst, flooding his mouth with foulness. The mere memory of that was enough to put Hamelin off the idea of going to another tooth-butcher.

'That barber, Ellis, he's supposed to be good,' Hal said after a while.

This was true, but Ellis was a professional and wanted money in return for his skill, and Hamelin had nothing. Anything he did have, he should save and give to his wife. Emma needed the money for food, for her and for their children.

Hal shrugged his shoulders and returned to his tool. 'You should pay that Ellis a visit when we go to Tavvie for the coining on Thursday.'

Hamelin nodded slowly. Gazing about him at the scatterings of soil with the leat tumbling down its narrow way in the middle, he felt the desolation of the place sinking into his soul and infecting him with despair.

Hamelin was not born and bred on Dartmoor. His father had been a serf who had run away from his master in Dorsetshire and made his way to Exeter, where he had lived for a year and a day without being captured, thus securing his freedom. Hamelin had been brought up as a poor freeman with no training, for his father couldn't afford to apprentice him, and yet he had managed to make himself a small sum of money by hard work. Then his little shop burned to the ground and he lost almost everything. All his spare money was tied up, but he was lucky, so he thought, that at least he had loaned cash to a local man who was plainly wealthy enough to repay the debt with a good rate of interest. Except he wasn't. He had gambled the lot away, and then he went to the Abbey, so the debt couldn't be enforced.

That was why Hamelin had hurried to this desolate place. Cold, wet and grim, he had a loathing for it that bordered on the fanatical. He had come here determined to find a rich lode of tin. From all he had heard in Exeter, it was easy. You walked about until you saw traces of the tin-bearing ore in a riverbed, and then traced the river back upstream until you found the source. You might have to dig a few times, exploratory little pits designed to see whether you had the main line of the tin, but that was it. It had seemed incredible to Hamelin that everybody didn't run to the moors to harvest the wealth that lay beneath the soil.

But after six long years of intensive searching, after wearing through spades, after all but breaking his back moving lumps of moorstone and trying to bale water from pits he was trying to dig, he felt as though it was all in vain. Luckily Hal had taken him under his wing. Apart from Hal's friendship, the only wealth he had found was Emma. She was the only source of joy in Hamelin's life. The children he was fond of, but they were a continuing drain into which all his money was tipped, while Emma, with her smiling round face, was a comfort to him.

He had met her on one of his journeys to the Stannary town of Tavistock years ago. She had been serving in a pie-shop, and he had bought one pie, and then stayed there for the rest of the day, chatting and teasing her. He had adored her from that moment. It was something he had never thought could happen to him, but she was kind, generous of heart, and made him laugh; and he seemed to make her as happy in return. Soon they betook themselves to a tavern and drank, and that night they fell together on her bed. Within a week they were wedded, with many witnesses watching at the church door.

That happiness was blessed with children, as the priests liked to say, but Hamelin spat on the idea. *Blessed*! How could children be thought of as a blessing? They needed food, and that meant money. Hamelin had nothing. The children stared at him with their sunken eyes, their swollen bellies, each time he went to see them, every few weeks, and when he saw his lovely Emma and how wizened she had become, he felt as though his heart would burst. She was broken down with toil, her back bent, her face aged beyond her years. As he took his leave-taking to return to the moors he had grown to detest, she hugged him and kissed him and wept a little, as did he as his feet took him up the steep hill towards Walkhampton, over the common, and on to the Nun's Cross at the edge of the Great Mire. Yes, he wept too, for the life that he should have been able to offer his wife. If he still had his money, he'd be able to, as well.

Injustice! That was what tore at him. If he'd not made that damned loan to the bastard who'd fleeced him, he'd be able to support his family. Instead, he was out here, stuck in the middle of this hell-hole.

From his vantage point at the top of Skir Hill, he could look all along the small valley that pointed northwards. His house was a huddle of stones, almost invisible among the clitter, with its thick layer of turf for a roof. It was small and smoky, but at least it was warm in the winter, which was more than other miners' places. His home was not too bad – but it was this desert all about which appalled him. It was as though he had been convicted of a crime and punished with exile in this hideous land, all alone but for the occasional traveller passing by. If he could only get at his money, he would be safe, but even the lawyers he had spoken to had laughed at the idea of appealing a monk. Who wouldn't balk at the prospect?

He felt crushed by the unfairness. Today the sky was a grey blanket that smothered his soul. There was no pleasure here, only despair, he thought.

A sparkle caught his eye, and he frowned, peering north-westwards. There, on the track that led from Mount Misery towards the Skir Ford, he saw a tiny group of people and carts. Travellers. It was tempting to go and speak to them, but he had work to be getting on with. Perhaps today he would find a rich seam, maybe enough to buy food for his wife and children.

Or maybe he would find a purse of gold, he thought cynically, and returned to his work.

Chapter One

When the messenger found Bailiff Simon Puttock, some few days after Brother Peter's story-telling, the Bailiff and his servant, Hugh, were watching the routine of Tavistock's coining. Simon was doing so with more than his usual care, after the fiasco of the previous couple of days.

It was all because of his blasted daughter, he told himself again. She had no consideration for others. Two days ago, when he was due to set off for Tavistock, she had disappeared without telling him or Meg, his wife, where she was going. When he realised that she had been gone most of the morning, he nearly went out of his mind. It was all very well for Meg to point out that she herself had gone for walks with men when she was fourteen and fifteen, as Meg had probably been more mature in nature and outlook even when she was Edith's age; and in any case, boys today weren't the same as when Simon was younger. They were less respectful, less well-behaved, more likely to ravish a beautiful young girl like his Edith. The little sods.

As usual when she came back, there had been an almighty row. She couldn't understand, Edith sulked, why her parents should be so over-protective. She wasn't a child any more.

That was when Simon saw red. He bellowed at her and was near to thrashing her for her insubordination and lack of regard for his and her mother's feelings; if he hadn't been due to travel here to Tavistock, he would have done just that. He knew his neighbours all believed that women needed a beating now and again, and Simon was a source of amusement for his tolerance, but that day his daughter had gone too far.

Just when he had wanted to set off early, the arguments and wailing and weeping had held him up, and he gathered up everything in a rush, stuffing it any old how into the bags on his packhorse. His servant helped moodily – for Hugh was always grumpy when there were voices raised against his favourite, little Edith. Simon then gave his wife one last hurried kiss before throwing his leg over his mount and setting off at speed. Hugh desperately hopped along at the side of his own pony, trying to hold it still long enough to clamber atop. After so many years of riding alongside his master, he was less like a sack of sodden oats in the saddle these days, but that didn't mean he enjoyed the experience, and he still eyed horses as nasty, vicious creatures whose only pleasure was to unseat him as soon as possible.

Simon had been forced to wait while his servant caught up, as Hugh refused to urge his horse on to what he considered a dangerous speed. If they had set off when Simon had intended, they would have had plenty of time, even allowing for Hugh's slower pace, but as it was, with Edith's little performance delaying their departure, he hadn't bothered to check the things he had packed.

Yes, Simon considered. It was all his daughter's fault.

He could remember his mood as he arrived at Tavistock, as black as the clouds in the sky, brooding on the ingratitude of daughters in general and his own in particular, with Hugh scowling bitterly on his own little mount and answering only with a grunt whenever Simon spoke. A tedious, wet and miserable ride it had been.

However, it was as nothing compared with the grim realisation which struck him that evening before meeting his master, Warden of the Stannaries, Abbot Robert Champeaux. Simon had gone through his belongings once with a general lack of concern, still affected by the scene that morning, but then he had paused and gone through his things more urgently, searching each bag with care for the little felt sack which contained the coinage hammer. It wasn't there. Racking his brains, Simon vaguely remembered seeing it on top of his bags on his chest in his solar. It must have tumbled off as he snatched everything up.

If *that* realisation was terrible, having to go and see the Abbot himself was worse. The latter was a cheery fellow, red-faced, with a thin grey circle of hair fringing his bald pate; there was no need for the good Abbot to have his tonsure shaved by the barber every so often. His fair complexion held a tracery of little burst veins, and his nose was mauve, but his voice was as loud and enthusiastic as ever as he welcomed Simon with a heartiness that was entirely unfeigned.

'Bailiff, come in and sit down. Sorry not to have been here when you first arrived, but I have only just settled back myself. I have been over at Buckfast meeting my brother Abbots and talking about the costs of our Benedictine House at Oxford.'

His eyes left Simon and slid across to the window. When Simon followed his glance, he saw a deer trotting through the trees and slipping down to drink from the river. The Abbot was a keen huntsman, and Simon knew that the sight of a deer so near must have been sorely tempting. Abbot Robert's fingers tapped impatiently on the arm of his chair. 'We were kept talking for hours about finance, when the whole matter could have been agreed in moments. Why people insist on talking around and around in circles when they could be . . .' He gave a slight cough and seemingly reminded himself of his duties. 'Tell me, how was the journey from Lydford? And how is your lovely wife?'

All through the casual small talk, Simon was edgy, waiting for the right moment to broach the subject of the hammer. He took the proffered wine, drank deeply, answered his host's searching questions about prisoners in the gaol and about a boundary dispute between two tin-miners' claims at Beckamoor Combe, and then, when he saw the Abbot's eyebrow raised in enquiry, he confessed his error.

'*You left the hammer at your house*? God help us, Bailiff, how could you be so careless!' The Abbot swallowed hard and gave him a long hard stare. 'This is not the sort of behaviour I expect from you, Simon. You are my most trusted servant. You have failed me, and that is a great sadness to me. I had—. But no. Enough.'

Simon squirmed. He hated making mistakes. Robert Champeaux was a kindly, generous-hearted man, but his years as Abbot had not been easy. When he was originally elected in 1285, thirty-seven years before, he had found the Abbey finances in a disastrous state and had been forced to borrow two hundred pounds, but since then he had, through careful management and scrupulous care, been able to rebuild the monastery's fortunes. Lands which had been lost were now regained, at Ogbear and West Liddaton; he had marvellously improved the farming and taken up new fisheries; while by his purchase of the Wardenship of the Stannaries he had brought in still more money which he had spent helping to found a House at Oxford in which Benedictines could study, and building the new church here in Tavistock. And even after doing all that, Simon knew that Abbot Robert had been able to save plenty. His Abbey had grown to be one of the wealthiest in Devonshire.

Robert Champeaux was not the sort of man to leave a vital tool behind. Nor could he understand how someone else could. It was not mere anger that darkened his brow as he stared at Simon, but genuine incomprehension.

Although the Abbot wasn't avaricious for his own purse, Simon knew he wanted to leave Tavistock on a sound financial footing. Stupidity like this could endanger his legacy – and that was why he was intolerant of such lapses.

'You had?' Simon prompted him automatically. 'You said, "I had"?'

'Nothing. I shall have to consider. You have many duties already. Such as, sending a messenger to fetch the hammer before the coining,' Abbot Robert said pointedly.

That was two days ago. Simon had ridden back yesterday with his servant as a foul-tempered companion. At his house he found

Meg instructing two of their manservants in redecorating their little solar. She loved their house, and had recently had a new wall of timber panels installed to separate off a little store-area from their parlour. Now she was having the walls whitewashed and the wood limed in preparation for the likenesses of saints to be painted on them.

'I thought Saint Rumon *here* and Saint Boniface *there*,' she said. 'To remind us of Tavistock, where you have been so fortunate and Crediton where we were so happy.'

The sight of her smiling face made him pause and stand in the doorway for a long moment.

Before moving here they had owned their own farm outside Sandford, near Crediton, where they had been content, and afterwards, when they had lived a short time in quarters at Lydford Castle itself, neither had been happy. The grim stone block was cold and hideously uncomfortable, not at all like their old home, and because of her unhappiness Simon had searched for somewhere else. Soon he found this little cottage with the enclosed garden and ample room for themselves and their servants. Although Meg had been pleased with their place near Sandford, this one had attracted her from the first moment she saw it. Perhaps it was a reaction against the castle, or maybe it was her joy at giving birth to their first son Peterkin, who later died, to their joint despair, for she had begun to plan for the improvement of it as soon as she had arisen from her bed.

Seeing him, she had fussily hurried the two men from the place, and then stood before him smiling. 'You wanted this?'

He took the hammer from her.

'I found it this morning as soon as the men moved the chest to paint the wall,' she chuckled. 'Will you be in trouble?'

'Not if I get it back for tomorrow,' he said. 'If it's late I could be fined. The last man forgot it once, I think, and he was fined three shillings.'

The smile was wiped from Meg's face at the thought of so much money being taken. 'That's terrible. Surely Abbot Robert wouldn't do that to you?'

'Forgetting it could have led to three hundred miners milling about in Tavistock, all demanding that their metal should be coined, all drinking steadily until they were of a mood to riot,' he said drily. 'You haven't seen the damage that ten happy miners can wreak after a few quarts of ale, so you can't imagine a hundred angry miners on the rampage after a couple of gallons each. It doesn't bear thinking about! So yes, the Abbot will fleece me as best he might if I don't get this to Tavistock quickly.'

'You must have been very distressed,' she murmured, putting her arms about him.

'I was.'

'And now you have to leave again. So sad.'

She had turned her head from him, so that her cheek was against his breast, and he could smell the lavender in her hair. He stroked it, kissed her head and let his hands wander down her back to her waist. A shiver ran through her body, and then she stood back and slowly began to undress. 'You don't have to leave immediately, do you?'

It was while he was giving himself up to a pleasantly erotic recollection of the occasion, that the procession arrived.

There was a sudden quietness among the bearded, scruffily dressed miners. Up until then Simon had been aware of the rumble of low voices and the clatter of pots and trenchers as the girls from the local alehouse filled pots and served pastries. Not now. Suddenly the marketplace was silent, and when he looked up, he saw the Steward's men roping off the centre, the crowds being pushed back by servants.

When a space was cleared, the King's beam was brought out and adjusted, the Controller and Weigher carefully checking the machine with their standard weights, which were solemnly unsealed from their box while the whole crowd watched intently, witnessing the fact that there could be no cheating here. It was in the interests of the miners that the metal should be fairly weighed. All were to be taxed against the measured weight of the tin that they had brought, and until the miner paid the tax on his ingot, he could not sell the metal.

When all was prepared, the Assay-master sat at his small anvil, his hammer and chisels ready, while the other officials took their seats facing the beam where they could have a clear view.

The Receiver, a short, dark-haired man with the face and belly of a glutton, stood and called the crowd to witness the coining, and porters began bringing up the marked ingots of tin. Some were well-formed, neat rectangles of metal, but many were rougher, marked by their moorstone moulds' irregularities. These heavy blocks of one or two hundredweight were placed on the scales and the true weight was shouted out and noted by the three clerks to the officials. Each ingot had the mark of the owner stamped upon it, and the name was called out at the same time, checked with the register held by the Receiver.

Simon knew of him. He was called Joce Blakemoor, a local Burgess, and Simon had never liked him. He seemed too smooth for the Bailiff's taste.

The Assay-master, a slim, wiry man with the dark hair and features of a local, was chiselling chips from the first of the ingots and seeing that the metal was of the right quality. In front of him was a grim-faced miner with a filthy leather jerkin over a patched linen shirt, so heavily stained that it looked like worn leather. His lower face was hidden entirely by a thick, grey-speckled beard, and his head was covered by a hood, which gave him the appearance of peering out shortsightedly, rather like a suspicious snail. He watched the Assay-master with a keenness that told Simon he must be the owner of the tin, hoping against hope that his coinage wouldn't be too expensive. Simon knew the man. It was old Hal Raddych.

There were many witnesses, from miners, to locals, to several strangers who Simon thought must be pewterers and agents. People from all over the country wanted tin.

One in particular caught his eye – a tall, well-made man with oddly-cut clothes. He was no local, Simon was sure. When a red-headed youth in a Benedictine novice's garb bumped into him, he swore, but not in English or French. The youngster was profusely apologetic, and the man smiled and nodded.

Simon was leaning against a pillar and viewing things, his servant scowling ferociously at all about, for Hugh detested crowds, daring any cut-purse to try his luck, when the messenger reached them; it was to the noise of the stamps hammering the King's arms into the ingot that Simon received his summons.

'I must go to the Abbot *now*?' he repeated, bellowing over the din, and as he spoke the noise suddenly stopped. By coincidence, the assaying of one ingot was complete, and the bill of weight charged against Hal Raddych was being scrawled on the bill sheet. Once the tax was paid, the tinner could sell his metal, so there was a short period of expectation while the interested merchants and pewterers' agents witnessed the bill being signed, and it was into this void that Simon's voice roared.

Every head in the place was turned to him. Ashamed, he wanted to scurry away like a rat, but he didn't wish everyone there to see how upset he was at having to pay a fine, for he was sure that was the reason for the summons. The Abbot had decided to fine him for his incompetence and stupidity in forgetting the hammer, even though he had brought it here in good time. When he glanced about him, he saw that Hal Raddych was staring at him. Behind him, Joce Blakemoor too was watching him keenly.

Seeing him only made Simon irritable. 'Damn the man's eyes,' he muttered, squaring his shoulders. 'I hope he gets blinded by a chip from an ingot!'

It was only much later that he came to wonder whether the expression he had seen in Blakemoor's eyes was less amusement at Simon's plight, more fear for himself.

* * *

Joce Blakemoor's expression hadn't been missed by Walwynus, either. Wally was watching as the tin was gathered up and weighed, the metal gleaming in the sun where the Assay-master had chiselled off a corner.

A few yards away was the slightly gaunt figure of the Abbot's Steward, Augerus. Wally nodded to him and tilted his head, and Augerus nodded. Wally didn't like the man, but he was useful, he thought as he made his way to a table outside a tavern. There he held up a penny for the host, and when Augerus arrived, the landlord had already brought two pots of strong ale.

'You wish to sit?' Wally asked.

'For a moment, friend,' Augerus said gratefully. 'My Abbot is returned, and he's had me rushing all over the place, cleaning this, sharpening that, preparing his writing reeds and tablets . . . Ah! Life was so restful while he was away.'

'I heard you had a good evening in the tavern,' Wally said.

Augerus shrugged contentedly. While the Abbot was out of the town, he felt free to indulge himself, and it was good to relax with a few ales and a friend. 'You have it?'

He watched as Wally produced a small lump wrapped in material, bound with a thong. 'Here.'

Augerus pulled the knot free and glanced down at the pile of coins.

'You want to count it?' Wally asked.

'No. But it's not much for all the effort.'

'You know our friend. He's not generous,' Wally said easily. There was little point, in his mind, explaining that instead of a fifty-fifty cut, he had taken four-sevenths of the money – eight shillings out of fourteen instead of seven. Augerus was expecting a full half, but Wally felt justified in awarding himself more. He took much of the risk, after all.

Augerus grunted discontentedly. 'I'd best be back.'

'Aye, well, see you later.'

'I may have something then. A pewterer is in the Abbey.'

'Not tonight. There will be too many wandering about the town drunk. Leave it till tomorrow. I'll warn our friend.'

Augerus nodded and left. Soon Wally rose, and as he walked from the alehouse, he saw her again: Sara, the girl with the anxious eyes, as he had thought of her. Yesterday evening, when he had been hanging around outside Joce Blakemoor's house, idling there for no particular reason, he had seen the girl rush up to the Receiver's front door and hammer on it. An attractive little thing, Wally thought regretfully. Of course, she was far too good-looking for the likes of him, with her fine red gown with embroidered flowers at the hem and her silken fair hair shaken loose from her wimple and floating about her shoulders as the breeze caught it. She looked beautiful in her apparent distress.

The door had opened and Joce's servant had appeared, glanced quickly up and down the street, and then fixed upon the girl with evident trepidation. Wally wasn't surprised, for all knew that Joce was a vicious bastard to his servant. Wally couldn't hear a word spoken, but he saw the servant disappear inside, then Joce himself came to the door and held out a hand wordlessly to the girl. She took it with obvious relief and entered the house with him. Wally left soon afterwards, musing on the sight.

Now he could see her in daylight, she no longer looked so worried. Since going to Joce, she had obviously lost her concerns, and Wally was pleased. She was a lovely thing, a delight to the eyes, with a smile that many men would die for, and an easy manner, friendly and outgoing. Perhaps more outgoing than she should be, he considered, bearing in mind her visit to Joce's last night. It had been painful to see her in such distress. Now her joy chimed with his own pleasure. The monk Peter had made him the happiest man in Tavistock.

'Sara!' he called.

She turned on him a smile so radiant that he felt as though the clouds had parted and the sun burst forth with renewed vigour.

'Hello, Wally. You're looking well.'

'Not so well as you, I'll bet.'

'I am happy today,' she said confidentially, swinging her hips so that her skirts swelled and billowed, as if she was dancing to a tune only she could hear.

'Why?' he asked. 'Have you found a shilling at the roadside?'

'I can't tell you,' she said, still happily swaying. Then she stopped, stepped forward to him, laying a hand lightly on his forearm, and leaned up to him, saying breathily, 'But it's wonderful!'

As quickly as she had moved forward, she retreated through the crowds, leaving him with a bemused smile on his face. She wasn't really his sort, he told himself, but even so the feeling of her breath upon his skin had sent his entire face tingling, and he wished that he was married to someone as impulsive. Wally touched his lips with a feeling almost of awe, unaware of the dark and bitterly resentful eyes of Ellis, the barber, who spied on him from a short distance away.

Ellis had witnessed Wally's brief conversation with Sara, and from where he stood, slightly behind Wally, it had looked as though she had leaned up to kiss him. In public! Full of misgivings, Ellis pushed his way through the crowds after his sister.

He had never married. There hadn't been an opportunity. His trade was his life, apart from his sister, and although he had never known the joy of fatherhood, of watching a wife of his own grow great with a baby, seeing her face alter, glowing with that inner warmth as she became aware of the life within her, he had seen other women in the first flush of pregnancy. Sara had been like that when she was married, bearing her children. And now she looked that way again.

It was not until she had reached the far side of the market square that he caught up with her. 'Sara, what are you playing at?'

'Nothing! What's the matter with you?'

'I saw you out there, looking up at him, all moon-eyed. Have you been bloody stupid?'

'Let go of my arm,' she said, snatching her forearm from his grasp. 'Leave me alone, Ellis.'

'You haven't been foolish, have you?'

'No. I have been very sensible,' she said with a flash of fire in her eyes. 'I have found a man to love, and who loves me.'

'And have you slept with him?'

She stiffened, then smacked a hand across his cheek. 'That is *my* business, and none of yours, Brother!'

'You have, haven't you?' he said dully. 'And now you're pregnant.'

'Just go away, Ellis.'

'I know who it is.'

'I don't care! He'll marry me.'

'*He'll* never marry you, you fool.'

It was the first time in days that the agony of Hamelin's ruined tooth had faded to a dull ache, and now, after the abundant stream of strong ale that Hal had bought him, he felt as though his mouth was almost normal. If only his tongue would keep away from his teeth. He seemed to keep biting it accidentally.

He moved somewhat precariously from the tavern's door to go and watch the coining, grabbing at a rail here, a fence there, breathing loudly, but with a happy smile on his face. 'Where's the coining, friend?' he asked of a man near the market.

'Right in front of you! Christ, you're as drunk as a monk!'

There were other men all about, and some began to laugh at the sight of Hamelin's state.

'Look out, he'll spew over us all.'

'Not Hamelin, eh, fellow? Hamelin could always handle a few pints.'

'So can many – but they all fall over just as heavily!'

'Even bloody monks. The Abbot's Steward and his friend Mark

were here last weekend, and pissed as rats in cider! Jesu, it was hard to get them out the door, they were swaying so much.'

Hamelin frowned. He could hear voices, but he was finding it hard to focus. Perhaps he ought to go and find his wife. Her rooms weren't far from the market. He could go and talk to her. Apologise for his failure. She might soothe him a little. If only he hadn't drunk quite so much . . .

'The Steward was almost unable to talk, he was so far gone. Mark had to help him through the door, and you could hear the two of them roaring and laughing up the road.'

'Aye, well, the Abbot's away, isn't he? It's rare enough that the monks get a chance to have a drink. Poor bastards! I'd go mad, locked away in that place like them.'

'Doesn't sound like they're too securely locked up, does it?'

'Yeah, well, every once in a while they get let out.'

Hamelin tried to speak, but phlegm in his throat threatened to choke him. When he had coughed a little, he said, 'You mean that thieving shit Mark was out here last weekend? If I'd known, I'd have killed the bastard!'

There was a sudden silence. His voice had been louder than he intended. Not that he regretted it. He'd be damned if he'd apologise for cursing the man who had robbed him of his wealth. Mark, it was, who had taken Hamelin's money, then gambled and lost it all. And by simply taking on the tonsure, he had evaded his debtors. 'The bastard!' he repeated.

'You should keep your voice down.'

'Who's that?' he demanded truculently, peering at the man who had joined him.

'It's me – Wally.'

'Ah! Oh, Wally. Yes. You're a friend, you are. What are you doing here?'

'I don't really know,' Wally admitted, jealously eyeing the tinners. He should have been up there, selling his tin. If his mining had succeeded, he would have been, instead of earning money by thieving. Ah well. He was alive, and that was the main thing. 'Come on, Hamelin, let's get you somewhere safe.'

'Can't go home like this. Wife's got no money. Youngest is ill. Can't let her see me like this.'

He was a dead weight on Wally's arm, and Wally staggered. Then he saw a bench, and led Hamelin to it. 'Lie down on that,' he puffed.

Hamelin was reluctant to do so, explaining that the sky was turning around and around, and that people were staring at him, but eventually Wally managed to settle him, and soon he was rewarded with harsh rumbling snores.

That was when he returned to watching the coining.

There being a slight pause, Joce and other officers were refreshing themselves with wine. At that point, Wally caught sight of Sara again. She hovered on the edge of the crowd, a hand up as though to wave, her attention fixed eagerly on Joce's face. Then she called to him softly, her face still excited and joyous. Wally thought he'd never seen such a lovely girl, not since the Scottish woman.

He heard her call out, saw Joce stiffen, saw the Receiver's face alter subtly, that cruel sneer spreading as he turned and strode towards her. The man spoke for a moment, and then guffawed, while Sara's features seemed to crumple. Suddenly her eyes had regained that appalled expression of the previous night, and her hand went to her mouth.

Wally felt his spine turn to ice.

'Stupid bitch! Thought because I'd rattled her once, I'd marry her!'

Wally could hear the harshness of the braggart's voice. Sycophantic colleagues all about Joce chuckled as he spoke. Even Brother Augerus was there, Wally saw.

'She asked me to marry her. Well, anyone would promise that, for a chance to lie with her. So I did. But Christ's Blood, only a stupid strumpet could believe in an oath like that! Marry *her*? I'd as soon wed a whore from the tavern. She's a good slut, though. I've only once before enjoyed one more, and that was years ago in the north.'

Wally stumbled away from the market, feeling physically sick.

Somehow he had made an appalling mistake. The man with whom he had worked, with whom he had shared so much, was gone, and in his place was this new character, a man whom Wally should have detested and scorned – or slaughtered. The words, 'years ago in the north,' kept ringing in his mind. There was only one girl Joce could have meant by that. Suddenly Wally knew he hated Joce.

Wally leaned against a door and stared dully back the way he had come. He needed a drink, he thought, and then remembered the state of Hamelin. No, he'd go and get some grub instead. There was the pie-shop nearby, and he headed to it with feet that were suddenly leaden.

At the shop, he was welcomed by the scruffy cook.

'Hello, Nob,' Wally said distractedly, and bought a small, cheap meat-pie.

'How's it going?' asked Nob cheerily.

At first Wally scarcely heard the amiable enquiry; he was too taken up with his feelings towards Joce. Wally and his pal Martyn had worked for the Receiver for a long time. Admittedly, he was a man of careless violence, but had proved a good ally – and was a useful fellow when it came to disposing of stolen goods. When Wally had first met with the greedy Augerus at the Abbey and found in him a man who might be able to arrange for trinkets to be stolen, Joce was the natural man to fence the goods. He might not pay the best price, but it was adequate, and the profits split between Wally and Augerus were enough to live on frugally.

But all this time Wally had never realised that Joce could have been the man who killed the girl. She had been raped, then murdered, and for ages Wally had suspected that it was Martyn who had done it, but now he wondered if Joce had been the guilty one, the killer of the woman who had saved Wally's life.

His belly was full of bile, but he made a conscious effort to act naturally, to listen and chat as Nob spoke. He didn't want to appear distraught. If he was to have revenge on Joce, he must seem innocent. How to hurt Joce, though? That was the question that nagged at him now.

'I don't understand how monks and farmers get so much from the ground,' he said, forcing himself to speak conversationally to Nob, 'All of my vegetables wither as soon as I plant the buggers.'

Nob gave a sympathetic grimace. 'It's a hard life on the moors.'

'Aye. Down here there are women, ale and warm houses,' Wally agreed. Out in the street, he bit into his pie and, when he looked up, he saw his young friend hurrying back towards the Abbey, his ginger hair flaming in the wind. 'Gerard!' he shouted, and the lad stopped, staring about him with confusion.

When he caught sight of Wally, a smile spread over his face. 'Oh, it's you! Are you here for the coining?'

'I was, but the sight of that arrogant oaf standing there so self-important makes me want to puke,' Wally said.

'Yeah, well. I have to get back,' Gerard said, his eyes going to the church tower, gauging the time.

It was then that Wally had the idea that would cost him his life. 'Wait! Do you have two minutes?'

'Not really. I've got to—'

'Two minutes to avenge your sins, Gerard? That's all it will take,' Wally said.

Gerard eyed him doubtfully. There was a brightness in the other man's eye that was almost like madness. 'What are you planning, Wally?'

Chapter Two

The messenger led the two men back to the Court, and Simon was about to bend his steps towards the Abbot's rooms, when he was surprised to find that they were going over to the cloister itself.

'The Abbot's not in his lodging?' he enquired.

'No, Bailiff. He's in the undercroft. This way.'

Simon grunted. The lad who accompanied him was clearly not yet a Brother, although he didn't look new to the monastic life. He was probably in his mid-teens, a gangling youth with dark hair and a very pale complexion. Not someone who had spent his childhood on the moors or in outdoor exercise, Simon thought. A wealthy boy would have been out hunting, riding, practising with lances, swords and daggers. Some fellows, who were less likely to inherit their fathers' estates because of older brothers, could be pale and weakly-looking, because they were trained up to be academics, lawyers or priests, but this boy had more the look of a serf's child. His hands were calloused from heavy work. For all that he possessed a kind of boyish awkwardness, with his loose build and clumsy gait, Simon could see that he was no weakling. His shoulders were broad enough, and his arms looked as though they might have a certain sinewy strength.

'Here?'

'Yes, sir.'

Simon pushed at the door. He recalled this place only too well from a previous visit. Then he had thought that his friend Baldwin could die in there. Something about the memory stirred him, and he felt the hairs stand up on the back of his neck. He was glad to know that Hugh was behind him.

The undercroft was a great long room, smelling strongly of fresh wine and preserved meats, but with the ever-present scent of rats. The ceiling was quite high overhead, well-built with neatly fitted stones mortared together to form the vaulting, and it needed to be because in this room were many of the stores for the brethren, and the barrels were stored on top of each other in ranks. Light entered from narrow windows set high in the walls, and the shafts lighted the motes of dust which perpetually spun and danced. Flies and beetles droned through in their search for food, and occasionally struck a cobweb, making it shimmer and vibrate until the fly was wrapped in spider silk.

'At last, Bailiff. I wanted to show you this,' the Abbot said.

His voice was rough with anger, and Simon was about to bow his head to accept whatever punishment his master deigned to hand down, when he realised that the Abbot was pointing to a barrel not far from the door.

'Look at that, will you?' the Abbot grated. 'I had these barrels brought here from Boulogne myself. I was told about the vineyards by a Brother Abbot in Guyenne, ordered the wine once it was ready, paid for the transport, everything – only to have some thieving cretin drink the lot!'

The Abbot wasn't alone. As Simon approached, another monk stepped forward, a tall shape who stood with his head bent. As soon as he spoke Simon recognised the curious wheezing tones of Brother Peter. No other monk at Tavistock had such an obvious speech impediment.

'My Lord Abbot, perhaps there was simply a mistake? Isn't it possible that the wrong barrel was broached before, and now it is clearly empty when it should be full because your own Steward served you from the wrong barrel?'

In answer the Abbot jerked his head at an anxious-looking clerk. 'Well, Augerus?'

The Abbot's Steward was a pale-skinned man with deep-set blue eyes in a long, fleshy face and a nose which had been broken and only badly mended. He had a thick, bushy beard, but his upper lip was clean-shaven. A foolish-looking fashion, to Simon's mind.

'No, my Lord Abbot,' he answered. 'I wouldn't have touched this barrel. I know which I am supposed to open, and you yourself told me that this was a special one, not to be broached until Bishop Stapledon came to see you.'

'Quite right!'

'When would this wine have been taken?' Simon asked.

'When do you think? You remember I told you I was only recently returned from seeing my Brother Abbot in Buckfast? It is an arduous journey, not one to be undertaken lightly. I only ever go there when there is a good reason, and I do not hurry to return.' A glimmer of a smile softened his features for a moment. 'The hospitality is good, and my Lord Abbot has a good pack of raches.'

'Did you realise it had been stolen as soon as you returned?' Simon enquired.

'No. My Steward has only now discovered that an entire barrel has been emptied behind his back,' the Abbot said heavily.

'I see. And when did you last check this barrel, Augerus?'

'When the Abbot was away. Since his return I've been too busy, what with restocking and seeing to my Lord Abbot's needs.'

There was an almost frantic eagerness in the man to persuade Simon of his innocence, and the Bailiff was inclined to believe him – especially since there was no sign of a break-in.

'Well,' Simon said, crouching at the barrel, 'it's definitely been broached, and there's little left. From the puddle on the floor, I'd say they used a plug, not a tap. If you open a barrel by knocking in a tap to force the bung out, often you'll get no waste. Then as you turn the tap, you may get some drips, but look at this lot!' He waved his hand at the damp stain on the stone flags. In the cool, still air, little had evaporated. There was no way of telling how long ago the wine had leaked.

'Whereas if you shove a bucket beneath and push the bung out, only stopping the flow by pushing a plug into the hole, you always lose a great deal,' the Abbot acknowledged caustically. 'I think I was aware of that, Bailiff. So what does that prove?'

'That your Steward is innocent. He wouldn't be so crass as to waste this much wine; he'd have used a tap.' Simon saw Augerus throw him a grateful look.

'I see your point,' the Abbot grunted.

'Can you suggest someone else who might have done this terrible thing?' Brother Peter asked. There was a strange note in his voice and Simon eyed him a moment before answering.

Peter's dreadful wound seemed to shine in the gloomy light of the undercroft, and not for the first time in the years since Simon had first met him, he thought that a wound like that would have killed anyone else. The pain and horror of such a shocking blow would have finished them off, or the wound would have got infected. Peter was very lucky to be alive, Simon thought – or exceptionally unfortunate, forced to go through life with a blemish that made him repellent to men and women alike.

It was especially tragic, because he looked as though he had been a handsome fellow once – tall, strong-looking, with those square features and a high brow. Not now. He had adopted some odd little mannerisms too, Simon considered, such as talking with a hand near his face as though to conceal the wound, and his habit of turning his face slightly, so that it was away from those to whom he spoke.

Simon wondered whether he would want to live with a hideous mark like that ravaging his features. He concluded that he would have preferred death.

'I am suggesting no one,' he said finally. 'I wasn't here.'

'It must have been someone from the town,' Peter said briskly. 'No monk would dare – or bother. We all receive our daily allowance, after all.'

The Abbot was gazing down at the barrel. 'Whoever it is, I will pray for him that he should give up his career of felony. Perhaps he will come to me and confess his theft, and if he does, I shall pray with him.'

And issue a highly embarrassing and shaming penance, Simon added to himself. He liked Abbot Robert, and respected him, but he knew that the Abbot would look harshly upon anyone who could dare to steal his favourite wine. It would rank as foully as stealing his best mount or rache in the Abbot's mind.

'Bailiff, come with me. Peter, please arrange for this mess to be cleared. At once!'

'Yes, my Lord Abbot.'

The Abbot swept from the room, his habit rustling the leaves and twigs along the floor. Simon and Hugh hurried after him.

'So, Bailiff. The coining is proceeding apace, I trust?'

'It was when you called me.'

'My apologies for dragging you away,' the Abbot said drily. 'I am sure you would have wished to remain to observe such a thrilling sight.'

Simon said nothing. It was very rare for him to hear the Abbot sounding so . . . so petulant.

His master stopped and looked about him, then he motioned to Hugh to leave them and crooked a finger to beckon Simon to his side. They were alone in the space before his lodgings, and no one could overhear the Abbot's words. 'Bailiff, I apologise for asking you here. It is important that you tell no one outside the Abbey what you saw in there. You understand me?'

'Of course. But why?'

The Abbot gave a dry, humourless chuckle. 'Sometimes when one wishes to spread gossip it is necessary to have the right person overhear it. No!' he said hurriedly, noticing Simon's offended expression. 'Not you, Simon. There was another man there in the undercroft who may choose to repeat what we said.'

'I see.' Simon assumed that Abbot Robert expected either his Steward or Brother Peter to chat about the discovery to other Brothers, and noted the fact. He would not confide in either, he decided. 'What now? Do you wish me to seek the thief?'

'No, no,' the Abbot said hurriedly. 'There is no need. This is abbey business, and outside your sphere. Surely the guilty party is a monk who sought wine for himself.'

'And took an entire barrel?'

'It would not have been easy. No matter. The knowledge that I have shown *you*, the well-known and feared enquirer after the truth, a man known for his integrity, will drive the thief to panic and confession.'

'So you wish me to do nothing? You merely hope that the monk who did this will tell you of his own accord?' Simon queried.

The Abbot gave him an odd, measuring look. 'My friend, I know you have many other pressing responsibilities. I wouldn't want to load more work on you.'

'My Lord Abbot, I can easily . . .'

'Bailiff, this is an abbey matter, not something for you to worry about. Please give the matter no more thought.'

Oddly, when the Abbot left him a short while later, Simon for the first time since he had met the Abbot, was left with the impression that the man's words were less than entirely honest.

Brother Mark could easily have been a tavern-keeper if he hadn't joined the monastery. He was a cheerful, rotund man, with the ruddy complexion, multiple chins and expansive belly that so often seemed to go with the position of *salsarius*, the monk responsible for the preserved fish and flesh. His rumbling bass voice could often be heard as he went about his business in his dark, cool undercroft; singing hymns sometimes, but more commonly, when he thought that no one could hear, or when his ebullient nature got the better of him, he sank to saucy little songs that shouldn't have been heard outside the lowest alehouse.

When, looking up, he saw the Bailiff, he picked up his long leather hose to coil it and called out a cheery greeting. 'Godspeed, my friend. And how are you this perfect morning?'

'I am well, I thank you,' Simon returned, but it was hard to speak with his teeth clenched.

Mark glanced after the Abbot. 'Don't worry about him. He's a good man, even if he can be a little acerbic at times. We've all caught the lash of his tongue on occasion.'

'It's not that. I just . . .' Simon wished that Baldwin or his wife were here. It was impossible to talk to a monk. As the Abbot himself had said, the Brothers were incorrigible gossips.

'Come into my chamber, Bailiff. I have some wine that will ease your soul. Come!'

Simon followed him to a pleasant room near the Water Gate which was filled with the odours of his trade: spices and smoked, curing meats.

'A good location, eh? Views all over the court from here, so I can keep my eyes on whoever may come into the Abbey, and if they look dangerous – why *phit*! I can be out of the Water Gate like a scalded cat! Hah! We got one last week, too. Some damned mange-ridden beast that kept getting into the garden and shitting in the beds. It's ruined the carrots. We have had the seedlings springing up all over, instead of in our usual careful rows, because this cat kept digging and scattering all our seed. Always looked for the softest soil where the choicest crops had been placed. Anyway, we caught it last week, trapped it in a box, and then tipped boiling water over it as we let it go. You should have seen the thing run!'

Simon sat at the monk's bidding and took a cup of wine from him. 'Thanks.'

'My pleasure.' Mark already had a massive goblet filled, and Simon noticed his hand shaking as he picked it up. Mark enjoyed his drinks too much, he thought.

Simon said, 'I much prefer dogs. They are at least loyal. You know where you stand with a dog.'

'Absolutely. Cats can be useful for removing vermin, but most of the time people don't make them pay their way. They just leave the beasts to roam, and feed them with choice cuts of meat. Madness. All it means is, the blasted things come to my garden and ruin it.'

He sat nearby, on a stool that gave him an uninterrupted view of the great gate. 'No matter. I would wager that I need not worry myself about that cat. I think it will have learned its lesson. You see? This place is calming. You sit here, and all your fears flee. It is a sanctuary. Safe from all worries: sexual, social and financial. Here, only your personal service to Christ and God matter.' Taking a great swallow of his drink, Mark cocked a bright, gleaming eye at the Bailiff. 'So, was it the thefts he asked you about?'

Simon coughed. 'Is it common knowledge?'

'Oh, Bailiff, of course it is! We have no possessions here, no money, so our only currencies are food, drink, and gossip. What else could we have? And when my good friend Augerus learns something, he naturally shares it with me because I have the same lust for gossip, but I also have the job of looking after food and drink. With whom else would Augerus wish to come and discuss the thefts, if not with me?'

'You keep saying "thefts", not "theft". I have only been told of the stolen wine. Has anything else been taken from the Abbot's stores?'

'Aha!' Mark shot him a look. 'Maybe I should hold my tongue.'

'Why? If there have been other wine barrels emptied . . .'

Mark chuckled. 'Bailiff, if the Abbot had other *personal* items of his own stolen, don't you think he would have sought help before now?'

Simon mused over that. He did not believe the Abbot to be so self-centred as to ignore other thefts and only seek the thief when he was himself the victim; but then Simon considered the boldness

of one who dared break into the Abbot's storeroom. Maybe Abbot
Robert thought that a man so fearless was more of a threat than a
mere petty thief?

'What other things were taken?'

'Oh,' Mark smiled, 'I think you should ask the Abbot himself
about that. It's nothing to do with me. All I know is gossip.'

Simon drank some more of the excellent wine. 'Perhaps
you could tell me then who you *think* might have been responsible?'

Mark cocked his head. 'I probably could, but that would mean
breaking one of the cardinal rules of gossiping, wouldn't it? I'd
never hear another word from anyone, would I? No, I think you
should seek your thief all alone.'

'At least tell me this: did you hear anything after dark any night
in the last week or two?'

'Well, there are always odd noises. That blasted cat, rats, wood
settling, men wandering to find the privy . . . But I can say this, I
have heard nothing out of the ordinary.'

Simon looked into his wine. 'If someone had been stealing
from the Abbey, what . . .?'

Mark hastily crossed himself. 'Stealing from here, Bailiff? God
forbid that such could be done! Holy Mother Church should be
safe from the depredations of felons.'

'Yet it is a fact that outlaws will often rob churches. There are
rich metals and fabrics inside. Could someone have done so here?'

'*No*,' Mark said with emphasis. 'I would have heard if someone
stole from the Abbey itself, and I have heard nothing of the sort.
And I assure you of this, Bailiff,' he added, jabbing a finger
towards Simon's chest. There was no mistaking his seriousness.
Simon noticed with amusement that even the shaking had disappeared: rage had overwhelmed his alcoholic tremor. 'If I heard
of someone doing such a thing, taking candles or plates or
cloths from the church, I would denounce the thief immediately.
Immediately!'

'As a religious man should,' Simon noted. 'Yet you are aware of something.'

'True,' Mark said heavily, and slumped in his seat before looking up roguishly. 'But that's not to do with stealing from the Abbey itself. It is the taking of unnecessary wealth. Jesus taught us that God's bounty means all should have enough, didn't He, and that men should give up whatever they don't need for the good of the less fortunate. Perhaps this is a case of that nature!'

Simon sipped his drink. Mark was the sort of man who would hoard a secret to his bosom like a diamond, because in this environment the only currency was knowledge. However, Simon had the impression that he was sincere in his religious protestations. There were stories of men who robbed from the wealthy in order to support the poor. Could someone in the Abbey be behaving in that way?

Ah, well. It was nothing to do with him. The Abbot had told him to leave the matter alone.

As he thought this, he saw Mark watching him. There was a brightness in his eyes which spoke of more intelligence than Simon would have guessed at from his conversation.

Simon considered. 'So you think that someone taking money from another, so long as it was put to good use, would be justified?'

Mark set his head on one side. 'Perhaps. Provided that nobody was hurt. And that the stealer did not take it for personal advantage.'

'You are toying with words now. Surely if someone takes something, that is theft and there can be no excuse. A felon is a felon.'

'There are some crimes which are worse than simply attempting to enrich oneself, Bailiff,' Mark said sternly. He slurped at his wine. 'The man who actively does harm to Holy Mother Church is himself lost. There are some . . . But there! One has to point out the error of people's ways, and hope that thereby one can save their souls.'

'I have no idea what you are talking about,' Simon smiled.

Mark returned it with a grin that was both cheeky and tired. 'I think perhaps that is for the best, Bailiff.'

The Bailiff grunted, and they spoke of other, less weighty matters for a while, until Simon had drained a second cup and left Mark with thanks for his hospitality.

The *salsarius* watched him go, his lips pursed. There were things he would have liked to have said to the Bailiff, but he daren't, not yet. Perhaps later, once he had spoken to that thieving devil, the miner Walwynus.

There was no excuse for a man who stole from an Abbey. Yes, a thief who took property or money from a rich merchant and then distributed the wealth among the poor, thereby achieving Christ's aim of sharing out the world's riches with those who needed it most, allowing each man his own piece, that was honourable. But not when the profits were kept to enrich the thief.

Wally had willingly participated in stealing from the Abbey, taking things from guests, purely for his own profit. That was evil. It could only lead to harm in the long run, ruining the Abbey's reputation. As soon as people learned that the Abbey had allowed it to go on, they would think again before donating funds; travellers would go elsewhere, and the Abbey would sink into the mire of speculation and foul, irreverent gossip.

Mark wouldn't let that happen. He knew about Gerard, and he knew that Wally somehow acquired the goods from Gerard. It was Wally who made the profit. He must have forced the boy to steal for him. Mark would deal with the lad himself later.

It was time for Wally to pay for his impiety, for his crimes and his greed.

The Swiss stood at the edge of the crowd while the coining went on. It wasn't the biggest tin market he had ever seen, but the number of ingots were breathtaking, and he watched with the hunger that only another craftsman can comprehend.

Rudolf von Grindelwald was a master pewterer, and the sight of so much top-quality material was making his fingers itch. He wanted to get his hands on the gleaming bricks of solid metal. To refine the tin, smelt it, mix in the proper quantity of lead and create beautiful plates, cups and mugs. He could do this, for he was an expert.

The process of purchase here was straightforward. Each of the miners stood anxiously while their tin was assayed, and then they had to pay their fine before offering it for sale. That was simple enough. Rudolf could follow that, although his understanding of the rough, rolling language here with its curious local dialect and odd words, made it all but impossible for him to make out a single sentence.

It was maddening. There were pewterers and agents from as far away as London and even Venice, but they could converse with these grubby, leather-skinned moormen. Rudolf had travelled here with his family to buy, but how can a man buy when he can speak none of the local language?

Although he attempted to offer money for metal, the miners eyed him askance, and when Rudolf tried to push his way in among a knot of buyers who had encircled the first few miners to haggle over the price of their tin, he was rudely shoved out of the way.

It was enough to drive a free man to draw his knife, and he almost did. Only the sober reflection that he was in a foreign country where the law would hardly miss one Swiss, made him leave it in its sheath.

In disgust, he spat at the ground and walked from the main square. There was no point in being here, watching while the choicest ingots went to other dealers. He would find the tavern where his son Welf was drinking the strange-tasting English ale, and sample some more himself, before they made their way back to their camp at the outskirts of the town. Later, perhaps, he might find a man with tin to sell, after the initial rush had died down.

Tomorrow they would set off again, back to London.

Entering the alley in which the tavern stood, he found the sun was immediately shut off by the tall buildings at either side. Only a narrow streak of sunlight hit the wall on his left, struggling through from the roofs above. It was a narrow lane, this, with a good-sized kennel in the middle for the rubbish and faeces of men and beasts. Rudolf passed a sow rootling in scraps of waste, then had to follow the lane in a broad sweep around a large house. As he did so, he saw a figure drop from a window high in the wall. Rudolf grabbed at his knife again, stunned. Surely this man had just robbed a house! He was about to leap forward when another man appeared in the window above, a large sack in his hand.

Giving an inarticulate cry, Rudolf sprang forward, catching the first fellow before he could bolt. One brawny arm went round his waist while the other, holding his knife, went to the fellow's throat. Only then did he see the tonsure.

'*Bruder*!' he grunted, and instantly pulled his blade away. 'Brother, I am sorry.'

The lad was up and gone like a rabbit when the hound is after it. There was a clattering noise, and Rudolf found himself staring up at a swiftly falling sack. Too astonished to move, he gaped in horror as it struck him. He tottered, and then a man appeared at his side and grabbed the sack.

'You threw that at me!' Rudolf declared with rage. He was still in shock, and feeling bruised. The sack had been heavy, full of sharp objects.

'Friend, I am sorry, it fell from my hand.'

'You are a thief!' Rudolf said. The stranger's accent was at least easier to understand than the miners' dialect.

'No! Wait! You have scared off my companion. He'll be at the Abbey now, but let me explain before you do anything.'

'Explain? You steal from a house. There is nothing to explain!' Rudolf thrust his hand into the sack. To his amazement, it was filled with fine pewter: plates and mazers and bowls were rattling together inside the bag, haphazardly intermingled. 'You are a felon.'

'No. I have rescued all this. Please – let me explain.'

The man's face was filled with fear, and looking at him, Rudolf guessed that he was in no danger from him. A criminal he might be, but Rudolf had seen stronger-looking girls. And better-fed ones, too. That look made him waver.

'Come, you have me,' the man said persuasively. 'What harm can it do for us to have a bowl of wine and talk about this? I shall explain everything.'

As he spoke, Rudolph heard other voices calling. A group of local men had entered the passage, and now stood eyeing the thief and Rudolph with grim-faced suspicion.

'Wally? Are you all right?'

'Look! That foreigner's got a knife to him!'

Rudolf's companion grinned. 'I'm fine.' Then, more urgently, 'Quick! Let's get away from here. And put that knife away, in God's name! Do you want us both to hang?'

Chapter Three

Early that Friday morning, Hamelin woke with a shock as the tavern-keeper began rolling casks through his doorway. After sleeping all afternoon and night on the bench in the open air, Hamelin's body had stiffened. His joints and muscles wouldn't work, and he didn't want to see what the world looked like anyway, so he lay back with his eyes screwed shut, trying to ignore the row until it was impossible to do so any longer.

When his eyes met the daylight it felt as though someone had slammed a ten-pound hammer against his head and he snapped them closed again. Someone must have rammed a woollen mitten in his mouth, he thought, but then he reasoned that it was only his tongue, swollen and befurred. Gradually he dared open his eyes again, and his skull seemed on the brink of exploding. The pressure was awful. His tooth was now only one part of a whole chorus of agony; his head felt like a boil which was ready to be lanced; and Hamelin would have been glad enough to provide a blade to any kindly soul who would be prepared to use it. Death had to be preferable to this.

It was only after he had drunk two quarts of water that he could think of making his way back to the mine. From the town, the hill looked utterly insurmountable, but the miner knew from bitter experience that the only cure for his particular malady was exercise. He'd feel a lot worse before he improved, but once the sweat began to pour from him, his recovery would be on its way. And then he saw old Wally up ahead, and he tried to shift himself to catch up with his neighbour.

'Wally?'

The other miner's face almost made him feel refreshed. Wally had been brawling: his left eye was closing, and he had a cut lip. Fresh blood had dripped onto his shirt. Hamelin was tempted to ask who he had fought, but Wally's face didn't encourage an enquiry.

Wally shot him a look, then grunted, 'You're up early, Hamelin.'

Hamelin gave a sour grimace. 'Nothing much to keep me. No bed, no money. What else could I do?'

'What of your wife's bed?'

'Hal bought me some beers and I had to sleep it off.'

'It was me put you on your bench,' Wally said shortly. He was preoccupied with his suspicions about Joce and what the man might have done to Agnes, all those years ago. He felt the weight of the coins at his belt. He could leave the area, he told himself. Go somewhere Joce wouldn't think of looking for him. When the Receiver learned that his pewter had been stolen, he would go insane with rage – that much Wally knew. Wally also knew what sort of a devil Joce could become when the mood took him: he had seen it happen before. Yet he didn't want to run away with this money. It felt unclean, like the thirty pieces of silver which Judas was paid. It would be better for him to give the money away, all of it, and build a new life elsewhere. At least he had deprived Joce of it; that was a comfort.

'You, was it?' Hamelin grunted. 'Nah, I didn't want to go to my wife when I was in that state. I'll go and see her later. We'll know then.'

'Know what?' Wally asked. He wasn't in truth very interested in Hamelin's stories of woe, he had his own trials to cope with, but talking took a man's mind from trudging onwards and the length of the journey.

'My boy,' Hamelin said hoarsely, and then the words stuck in his throat.

It wasn't as though he was hugely fond of all the children; Hamelin loved his wife, and that took all the love he had in his soul, but there was something pleasing about Joel, his youngest. He was an affectionate child, mild-tempered compared with some of his siblings when they had been his age.

To Wally's astonishment, Hamelin began to sob.

'Christ Jesus! What's the matter, man?'

'It's Joel. He's dying. I don't think he'll be alive when I next see Emma.'

That same afternoon, Ellis the barber sucked at his own teeth while he studied Hamelin's. It was calming to remind himself that he still had almost two thirds of his own teeth in place when he looked into other men's mouths.

This was not going to be an easy one. He could see that right from the start, and was tempted to reach for his little leather sack filled with the tiny beads of lead which he had once bought from a plumber. This was his personal 'sleep-maker'. That was what he called it, and it invariably lived up to its name, sending off any man against whose head he directed it, and yet this one had such a thick skull, Ellis was a little anxious about using it. He would have to give a hard blow to make an impression on this miner's head.

'Well?'

The growled question from the man with the obscenely swollen cheek made Ellis decide quickly. He reached behind him and took his wine flask from the table. 'Master, it will be painful, so first drink this. It is a good, spiced wine and will soothe your spirits.'

Sitting in the chair, the man grabbed for it and upended it. Soon his Adam's apple was jerking regularly up and down. He would finish the whole skin, Ellis thought – but it scarcely mattered. The wine had been very cheap and the miner had paid in advance.

'Ellis?'

The soft voice came from his room at the back of the little chamber, and Ellis glanced over his shoulder. He could just make out his sister's form in the darkness of the room and, excusing himself, he left his patient to his drinking and went into her, closing the door behind him.

'Sara, where in God's name did you get to?'

Now that he was closer he could see that her happiness and confidence of the previous day was gone.

'Don't be angry, Brother,' she begged, and the quiver in her voice told him that she was close to tears.

He sighed and poured himself an ale, eyeing her resentfully. She had always possessed this fragile quality. Ellis was small in stature, but had the strength of corded leather in his thin arms; his sister had the same build, but with none of his strength, either physical or mental.

'Come, lass, it's not that bad,' he said gruffly.

'I . . . I have been a fool, Ellis.'

'No more than usual, I daresay. Well? Are you going to admit that you've been screwing around?' he demanded bluntly.

That was when she began to sob, and she gradually told her story.

'I slept with him, yes, but he swore he'd marry me, and that was why I went to bed with him, to cleave him to me. He made his promise, Ellis.'

Ellis thought of Wally's expression after she had left him in the crowd the day before. 'You can't trust the words of men like him.'

'I went to him as soon as I realised I was with child,' she continued, not heeding his words. 'I went to see him, and he took me in when he heard what I said, he took me in and gave me his oath there and then, making us man and wife, and then he sealed his vow by taking me to his bed again, and I stayed there with him until yesterday morning.'

'I saw you with him,' Ellis grated. His face was growing red with anger that a man might dare to molest *his* sister.

'But when I spoke to him yesterday afternoon when he was with his friends, he laughed at me and said I was no more than a

Winchester goose, a common slut. He denied our marriage, Ellis. He rejected me and laughed about me with his friends. I heard him. He denied me! Oh, my God, Ellis, what am I to do?'

'I'll see to him,' her brother said tightly. 'Leave him to me.'

'Oh God, no, don't do anything, it'll only make things worse! I have to try to sort it out myself,' she wailed. 'God! What will I do? I thought I had a wealthy husband, someone who could protect me and the children . . .'

Ellis would have commented on the wealth of a man like Wally, but kindness made him mute when he saw her despair.

'Instead I shall be known as a whore, and insulted in the street!'

It was some little while before Ellis could return to the miner, and when he heard the man shouting for him he rose with a sense of bone-weariness mingled with anger that this miner Hamelin should interrupt his grim contemplations.

He climbed to his feet and walked back out into the chamber, and there he produced his pliers with a cruel flourish, pleased to see the fear leap into the miner's face. A man could brave a sword or dagger in a street, and yet grovel like a coward before the barber's tools, he reflected.

'Don't worry,' he said, taking away the wineskin and walking around behind his patient. 'This will hurt you much more than me.'

His sleep-maker struck the man's head like the clap of doom, and Ellis stood gazing down at the slumped figure for some while before he could bestir himself to remove the offending tooth. He was still thinking about his sister's words. Although he had hoped he was wrong, she had admitted that she was pregnant. She hadn't said who the father was, but he knew. Oh yes, he knew!

'The bleeding bastard,' he said to himself, before gripping his pliers again and opening the snoring Hamelin's mouth.

* * *

Hamelin reached the door of his house in Tavistock some short while after dark. It was quiet as he entered the alley, and he felt that was good. If there had been bad news, he would have been greeted by cries and wailing. Instead, as he walked in through the door, he could see that Emma was so far from being distressed that she had fallen asleep with Joel in her lap. The other children were curled on their palliasse, the dogs on their old rags next to them. Hearing the door, one small dog opened an eye and wagged his tail, before falling to scratching himself conscientiously. Fleas meant that much of his coat had already been pulled out by the roots, and he was bald in many places.

Hamelin smiled at the dog. All was well in his world. He had a sore head, and a bloody mouth, true, but his son was alive, his tooth had been pulled – thank God! – and he'd had an enormous stroke of luck today. Emma stirred, and Joel grunted in his sleep, and it was that which woke her. Startled, her face showed terror for a moment, but then relaxed, her hand going to her heart. That brief shock made Joel begin to sniffle and wail, a low moaning noise that grew, and Emma grabbed him up and rocked him, the little stool on which she sat squeaking and cracking under their weight.

It was some while before she could settle him again. She rested Joel in a small crib, and stood, stretching her back. When she turned to face him, her apron awry, her tunic stained and faded, Hamelin thought she was the most beautiful woman he had ever seen. The warm firelight was kind to her, smoothing out the wrinkles and lines of worry, while emphasising the soft curves of her body. She pulled the hair from her eyes and smiled almost shyly, accepting his hand as he pulled her down onto a rug near the fire, lifting her skirts and parting her legs. Afterwards, when his breathing was calmer again, he kissed her.

'It's good to have you back here again, love,' she said simply.

'How is he? I couldn't stay away, not knowing.'

'No better, I think. We need good beef broth or an egg. Decent nourishing food,' she said with quiet sadness. Her emotions were worn away with sorrow after so long. It was as though she was already in mourning for her dead child.

Hamelin felt his heart lurch within his breast, and taking a deep breath, he rolled over on to his back. 'I had expected to come here and find him dead.'

'I know. There's nothing more we can do. If he dies, it's God's will.'

They held each other silently. They knew too many children who had succumbed to wasting diseases or who had suffered from that hungry illness over winter when their teeth became loose and their gums bled. Sometimes the teeth would fall out and the child would slowly die.

'I have brought money,' Hamelin told her tenderly. 'There's no need for you to go without for a long while.'

'Money?' Emma sat up sharply. When she saw her husband's eyes gleam as they took in her bare breast, she hastily pulled her tunic across and gathered it together with a fist. 'Where did you get money? There was nothing for you at the coining yesterday. How did you come by it?'

'Calm down, woman,' he commanded, and with a hand he gently forced her fist to open, so that he could cup her breasts. 'I sold my debt.'

'Who to? No one would be stupid enough to buy that!'

'One man was – Wally. He thought it was a good deal and paid me cash for it.'

'Wally? Where would *he* get money?' Emma scoffed. 'He has no more than us!'

Hamelin could almost feel her body cooling, as though she suspected that he was a thief. 'Come, love, I haven't killed anyone. We were walking back to the mines today when he asked me why I was so glum, and I told him about Joel. He already knew about Mark robbing us. He said, "Injustice is terrible. Let me buy the debt to save your son's life." '

'Wally never had two farthings to rub together.'

'I know,' Hamelin said. 'But maybe he got lucky.'

'You swear you haven't robbed anyone?' she demanded.

'Of course not. All I know is, I have a purse full of coins for you.'

Emma felt herself wavering. She would hate to think that he could have robbed someone – but the thought of money was horribly attractive. It meant life for her child, freedom from fear for a while.

Hamelin was speaking, and she forced herself to listen. 'It was odd this morning. I had walked back to my camp, and I saw that fat bastard Brother Mark up there. He was having an argument with Wally. I could see them clearly – it sounded as if he was giving Wally instructions or something. Then old Wally went off eastwards while Mark turned back towards Tavvie. I was coming back here myself – to get my tooth pulled and to see you – so I set off a little while after, just to annoy him. Mind, he kept going at quite a pace without looking over his shoulder even once.'

'He's allowed on the moors, isn't he?' Emma said flippantly.

'I've never seen him up there before, though.'

'Forget him.'

'How can I?' he growled. 'He ruined us.'

'But you say Wally might have saved us?'

In answer, Hamelin grabbed his purse from his belt on the floor beside them and, opening it, tipped a pile of bright copper coins amounting to several shillings over her breast. Then, kissing her nipples, her throat, her chin, he said, 'Do you believe me now? I got money for you and the children. What's wrong with that?'

Emma opened herself to him again; after all, if he said he had come by it fairly, it wasn't her place to doubt him. They *needed* the money, no matter where it came from.

* * *

Hal Raddych had also returned to their camp on that Friday morning. He was tired, and his head ached a little, but less than it should have, after drinking so much the night before. Hamelin had already been there, wandering about like a man in a daze, but Hal thought his tooth must be troubling him. It was merely a relief to see him go.

He didn't comment when he saw the mess their timber-pile was in. Hamelin was in no mood for listening to more instructions at the moment. Hal would wait for a better time. It was the store of wood that he and Hamelin needed for their works. As he was always telling Hamelin, it was important that stores were kept in an orderly manner. Letting good wood lie on the damp soil of the moors would ruin it and lead to wastage. Grunting to himself as he surveyed the collapsed heap, he shook his head, then set to rebuilding the stack. It looked as though Hamelin had grabbed a balk from the bottom of the pile and let the rest simply collapse. Slapdash as ever, in Hal's mind. A sloppy miner was a miner who would die as his mine fell on him.

If Hamelin didn't mend his ways, Hal would have to find a new partner, he thought to himself irritably, noticing that a hammer, too, had been carelessly left to sink part-way into the mud.

He didn't notice the small handful of nails that were also missing.

On the following Monday, Simon was woken by an agitated voice. He opened his eyes and recognised the red-headed acolyte he had seen at the coining.

'What the . . .' he demanded, pulling his cloak back over his nakedness before rubbing his tired eyes.

The night before, he had been invited to a feast with the Abbot in celebration of the successful coinage – they were several thousandweight above the previous coining and the Abbot was delighted with his profits – and Simon's head was naturally more than a little woolly. He felt fine, he told himself, but at the moment

he wanted water rather than food. There was a faint odour of
vomit in the air, and he wondered fleetingly whether he had been
sick over himself, but then he focused again on the red-headed
novice.

'What's your name, boy?' he growled.

'Gerard, Sir Bailiff.'

'Well, Gerard, you must learn that, in future, when you come to
the room of a man who has enjoyed your master's hospitality, you
should bring a pot of water or wine.'

He looked about him. This room was the main chamber for
respected visitors – the servants and lower classes must sleep in
the stables or out in the yard itself – and Simon stretched
contentedly in the bed. For once he had been able to sleep alone.
Usually when he came to the coinings, he was forced to share his
bed.

This morning the chamber was quiet. There had been several
guests the night before, but they seemed to have gone already.
Most of the beds were already empty; only one still had an
occupant, a yellow-faced, rather dissipated pewterer, who lay on
his back, breathing in heavily, then puffing out gusts with faint,
but now Simon could concentrate, deeply annoying, popping
sounds. At the side of his bed was a small pool of vomit. Simon
wrinkled his nose.

'Doesn't matter what you eat, there are always peas and carrot
in it,' he muttered.

'Sir, the Abbot . . . I mean . . . Oh! Sir, I am . . .'

Stifling a yawn, Simon looked up at the lad. 'Don't be flustered,
just speak slowly and clearly. My head isn't all it has been.'

'Sir, the Abbot asked me to call you because Wally has been
found dead on the Moors.'

Fast asleep on a bench in the adjoining room, Hugh had a rude
awakening when his master roared in his ear to rouse himself, and
then booted him off the bench and on to the floor.

Simon stormed from the chamber, and his eruption, and the

hasty slapping of Hugh's boots on the flooring, woke the yellow-faced pewterer in the bed across from Simon. A scrawny man in his early thirties, he yawned, scratching at his thin beard and groin. Then he stood and walked to the window, gazing out through the branches of the tree that grew outside, and then, since all was silent, he returned to his bed and idly thrust a hand beneath the mattress, pulling out a leather satchel. Opening it, he rootled about inside for a moment, but then his face sharpened with the realisation that something was wrong. He emptied his satchel onto the bed, staring down at the contents with shock, his eyes dark with suspicion.

That the man was dead was not in question. Just the smell was enough for Simon's belly to rebel. He had to swallow hard. Grabbing at the wineskin dangling from his saddle, he took a good gulp to wash away the bile. Hugh, on his pony at Simon's side, reached for the skin, but Simon irritably slapped his hand away. His servant didn't need it – or rather, there was a priority of need in which Hugh came a long way below his master.

His guide was Hal Raddych, the stern-looking miner Simon had watched at the coining. Below his hat's brim and above his bushy beard, his left eye peered out intelligently enough, although his right had a heavy cast that made it confusing to speak to Hal face to face. He was reasonably wealthy, compared with other miners Simon had met, a steady man, honest and reliable, who worked with Hamelin not far away.

As Stannary Bailiff, Simon had grown to know most of the miners on the moors, and he thought that Hal was as fair-minded a man as could be found. Many weren't. The harsh life of the miner seemed to forge men who had a certain resilience, a toughness of character which made them more prone to fighting even than the peasants who lived on the fringes of the wasteland. And those bastards were hard enough, Simon reminded himself.

Hal chewed at his inner lip for a moment, then said slowly,

'Poor old Wally. You know, Sir Bailiff – Walwynus. You must have met him? Used to have his own small claim over there, beyond Misery Tor, down at the Skir Gut. Worked a stream. Had a good year some summers ago, but bugger all since, by all account. Wally tried to keep a smallholding going, and you know how difficult that's been since the famine. What with the dreadful weather, it's a miracle anyone can live by farming.'

Simon grunted in acknowledgement, staring at Wally's remains. The body was curled, foetus-like, into a ball, hands and arms over his head in a posture of defence. Two fingers were missing, which wasn't out of the ordinary: most miners lost fingers as a matter of course, just as timber workers and carpenters did. It was a natural risk of working with exceptionally sharp, heavy tools. Except in this man's case, the fingers had gone recently, from the look of the fleshy mess where they had been. There was a balled piece of cloth nearby, clotted with blood, as though it had fallen from his fist as he died.

Simon reluctantly passed the wineskin to Hugh and let himself down from his horse. He had no wish to approach the corpse and inspect its death wounds, but he knew he must do a formal identification if possible. It was a Bailiff's duty. Personally, Simon was happy to leave all the actual handling of the corpse to the Coroner and his jury. They were welcome to it, he thought queasily, standing over the body, waving under his nose an apple which he had wisely taken from the Abbey's kitchen and stuffed with cloves before setting off on this journey. It helped to neutralise a little of the hideous stench.

The body was lying between two furze bushes. One in particular was almost as tall as a tree. From here, south and east of Nun's Cross, near Childe's Tomb, not far from the marked track of the Abbot's Way, Simon could see more furze westwards, and grass, with the view extending all the way to the trees that stood on the hill above Tavistock. Before him, the path dropped down into the thickly wooded valley. Beyond, on the other side of the cleft in the ground, he could see glimpses of the moorland. Tors stood like oddly-carved statues left by the giants who had once inhabited this land. It was a harsh, bleak landscape, covered with tufts of grasses and occasional lumps of stone. The sort of land to break a man's ankle if he wasn't careful; or break his head.

Except this man hadn't fallen and knocked himself out. His head was a blackened mass, his hair matted and thickened with great gouts of blood which had spattered and marked the grass all about. There was a broad slick of it on a nearby furze bush, and Simon noted it. He would have to look at that later: it didn't look natural.

The victim had been severely beaten, from the look of him. The back of his skull was opened, with a three-inch-long gash that must have come from a heavy weapon. From what Simon could see Walwynus had tried to protect himself, for his forearms and left hand were broken, one whitened bone thrust through the skin of his right arm, and maggots had already begun to squirm in the flesh.

It was that which made Simon move away; the sight made his stomach churn. Truth be told, he'd have preferred to remain in the Abbey and leave this job to another official, but he was the Bailiff; under the Abbot he was responsible for keeping the King's Peace out on the moors, and if there was a possibility he might learn something about this man's murder by visiting the place, he had to make the effort.

The Coroner had already been sent for. Simon knew that Sir Roger de Gidleigh, the Coroner based in Exeter, would come as soon as he could, but that might mean a couple of days. There was never any shortage of suspicious deaths in the Shire and this one would have to take its place in the queue. In the meantime, the body had to be protected. That was the responsibility of the people who lived near the corpse, to see that no dogs or rats got to it and damaged it. It was illegal to move the body or bury it; either was a serious offence that could only result in fines being imposed, so

Simon knew that he would have to arrange for guards to look after the corpse until the Coroner could arrive.

He walked away from the body, towards the splash of vivid colour on the furze bush. It looked as if someone had taken a brush and painted it a dull red in a broad swipe. Peering down beneath the bush, Simon saw something, and he reached inside, wincing as the sharp thorns deep in among old growth stabbed at his hand and wrist.

He withdrew a heavy baulk of timber, maybe a foot and a half long and three inches square. One end was darker, and there was one little greyish lump stuck to it that Simon felt unhappily sure was a piece of bone. When he studied it more closely, he could see the small round-headed nails embedded within the hardwood, turning it into a more effective weapon, a 'morning star'. Obviously the killer had thrown this weapon aside after killing Walwynus. He would have had no use for it after that.

'Look at this, Hal.'

The miner peered at the piece of timber. There was a curious stillness about him, but Simon noticed it only in passing. It was no surprise, he thought. Old Hal must be feeling in a state of shock, maybe close to throwing up. He left Hal there while he took another look under the bush.

Hal said, 'It's just an old piece of wood.'

Simon could see nothing else at the bush. He took the timber back and studied it again. There were some scratches at the base, three lines with a fourth connecting them, like a set of vertical stones topped by another one.

'What's this?'

Hal glanced at it. 'Just some marks, nothing more. Could be a child did it. Let's see whether there's anything nearer him. Come on!'

Simon scrutinised it a short while longer, but there was nothing more to be learned. He dropped the club beside the bush and rejoined Hal, who was poking hopefully around another bush.

Simon asked, 'Where was his smallholding?'

'Over towards Skir Ford. There was a deserted farm there and he took the house and began working the land. Not that he did very well. Too much rain. Nothing grows well here in the moors.'

'That's no more than a mile from here,' Simon considered, gazing north as though he might be able to see the place. 'What was he doing here?' He snatched the wineskin back from Hugh as he saw it being upended again.

'Coming back from the coining, probably,' Hal said, gratefully accepting a drink.

'Was he there?'

'Yes. I saw him at the market.'

'I see. You're sure he had no money?'

The miner shook his head and spat, glancing back at the corpse for a moment. 'No. He had nothing – nothing saved, nothing to spend, nothing worth stealing.'

'He had something,' Simon said shortly as he thrust his foot into his stirrup and sprang up. 'Otherwise, why should someone kill him?'

Chapter Four

What was the motive for Wally's death. That was the thought which nagged at Simon as he and Hugh rode over to the dead man's home. A squat thatched cottage with small windows, the place was tatty and unkempt, like most of the miners he knew; like Wally himself. The wood was rotten at the door and shutters; the thatch was green and sprouted weeds. Moss covered the smoother stretches, and birds had dug holes in among the straws. It looked scarcely waterproof. A small shower would pass through it as though through fine linen.

Behind the dwelling was a small, weed-infested patch of unhealthy plants: alexanders, cabbages, carrots and onions. The latter had fungus rotting their stems, and the carrots all looked brown and decaying.

Hugh drew up his nose. 'As a gardener he made a good miner.'

'Remember he's dead,' Simon said sharply.

'Can't forget, can I? Not after seeing him. Still, truth is truth, and this is a midden.'

Simon couldn't help but agree with him, and it was no better inside. The cottage had a damp odour that the Bailiff was sure came from mushrooms in the walls or timbers. It was as though the house itself was dying, like a faithful hound that expires on seeing its master's dead body.

Dank and foul it was, but there was no sign of a disturbance of any kind, nor of a theft. If Simon had to guess, he would have said that the place was as Wally had left it. On a rough table constructed of three long planks nailed together lay a jug, a cup and a purse, which was empty. Two stools sat nearby, while there was a barrel

of ale standing in a corner. A palliasse leaking straw lay in a pool
of brown water, and a small box was propped against a wall.
Inside were Wally's pathetic possessions: a small sack of flour, a
thick coat, some gloves – all the accoutrements of a peasant with
little or no money.

So why should someone kill him if there was nothing to steal?

All the way back, that was the thought that circled round and
round in Simon's aching head. When the two reached the steep
hill on the way back to Tavistock, he had come no nearer to a
conclusion. Walwynus was only a poor miner, after all, if Hal was
right. A miner who had lost much of his livelihood since the
famine years, and whose miserable plot of land wasn't enough to
sustain body and soul.

He could recall the man. Walwynus had been out on the moors
when Simon first came here to take on his new job as Warden,
although he had stopped mining soon afterwards. Wally had been
a pleasant enough fellow, the sort of man who laboured daily
whatever the weather, enduring steady, repetitive toil that would
break most men's muscles and spirit in hours, stolidly digging his
pits and turning soil near rivers, always looking for new signs of
tin.

Yet as Hugh said, he could not be called a gardener. His
vegetables wouldn't have served to support him through the winter,
let alone given him excess produce to sell. So how had he
survived?

Halting his horse, Simon leaned forward and frowned at the
view. Through the trees he could see the Abbey deep in the valley
between the hills, enclosed neatly within its walls, safe from the
intrusive borough that crouched beneath the parish church. It was
a scene of quiet progress, the little town of Tavistock. Busy,
attracting men from all over the country to come and generate
wealth, it was a model for other towns to follow.

It was so tranquil-looking, it was hard to believe that a
man could have been bludgeoned to death so close. Perhaps he

was trying to reach the town, Simon mused, and was captured by someone who beat him to death from sheer evil spirit; or was he attacked by a gang of trailbastons or other felons? Simon had seen such things before, certainly, but usually there was a good reason for an outlaw to attack, especially armed with a club.

The club. It was odd, Simon realised, and his brows darkened.

A man who was poor might choose a morning star as a weapon because anyone, however destitute, could lay his hands on a lump of wood and hammer some nails into it, and while most would prefer to set out on a career of murder and theft with a sword or at least an axe or dagger, a very poor man might be glad to make do with a home-made club. Of course, a man that hard up would surely not then toss his weapon away. He'd keep it, unless he had managed to steal a better one from his victim. And yet Walwynus had had nothing other than an eating knife on him, the last time Simon saw him.

However, a man who was wealthy enough to afford a decent long-bladed knife or sword wouldn't have minded abandoning the murder weapon, especially if he intended pointing the finger of suspicion away from himself and allowing another man to dance a jig on the Abbot's gibbet.

Simon was thoughtful as he spurred his mount on, and he didn't like his thoughts very much.

When the Almoner, Brother Peter, entered the Abbot's chamber, he was aware of a faster beat to his heart, as though it had shrunk and he now possessed the tiny heart of a dormouse in his breast. It felt as if it was preparing to burst from its exertions.

'My Lord Abbot? You wished to see me?'

Afterwards he remembered it. Aye, at the time he saw Abbot Robert flinch, but it was so commonplace a reaction to the sight of him that Peter hardly noticed it just then. Only later would he recall it, and realise that the Abbot suspected him.

Different people reacted in a variety of ways. Some, especially the young, would first recoil with every expression of revulsion on their faces – although later, once over their initial shock, they would often speak to him about his wound and ask how he received it, how it felt, and even, could they touch it, please?

Quite often, Peter told untruths. God would forgive his dishonesty, he felt sure, for the stories he told invariably had a moral purpose. He would tell a child that he had received his scar when he was a little boy, caught stealing apples from a neighbour's orchard, or that he was found with money taken from his master's purse and fell into a fire while hurrying away from his crime, and every time he would solemnly declare that any child who was so naughty as he had been, would also be marked for life.

Aye, the children were easy, as he often told himself. It was the adults whose reactions were more difficult for him to cope with. The women, who once might have smiled and glanced back at him from the corner of their eyes, measuring his strong body against their private erotic gauges, now grimaced at the sight of him, as though he had some disease that could contaminate them. All knew that God infected some because of their sins, like lepers. Perhaps that was the reason behind the women's reaction: they assumed that he had been so foul in his youth that he had been branded in this way.

Well, so he had thought himself, once upon a time, he recalled, and yes, it was quite possible that this wound was payment for his earlier offences against God.

Men were prone to stare. God forgive him, but that hurt more than anything. Even if it was God's means of humbling him, it was a sorry trial, for never beforehand had he been looked at in such a foul manner. He was like a midget or a dancing bear, a curious sight, something to be watched with interest. Once he'd only have been looked at for a moment, and then he'd have made sure that the man staring would have to look away, but not now.

Now he must accept, aye, and forgive those who gawped at him so rudely, so unchivalrously. The fit and well, the unscarred.

'Yes, I wished to speak with you, Brother,' the Abbot said, beckoning vaguely with all the fingers of his left hand. 'How long is it since you first came here, Almoner?'

'Six summers, my Lord.'

'You know the men of the Abbey as well as most, do you not? Better than most, I'll wager.'

'I think I can claim to know many of the novices better than most, aye. And my Brothers are a gentle, goodly family. I feel very much at home here.'

'I am glad to hear it. I have been given some terrible news today, so anything that gladdens my heart is welcome.'

'My Lord Abbot?'

'We have a pewterer staying with us. A Master Godley from London. This morning he has come to me and told me that two pewter plates he had stored securely beneath his bed have gone. Stolen in the night.'

Peter sat back and stared. He had feared that something of this nature might happen, but had hoped that after talking to Gerard the lad would be sensible enough to desist.

'You know something of this, don't you, Brother?' Abbot Robert observed. 'I do not demand that you answer me with the culprit's name immediately, but I urge you to speak to the fellow and tell him that I can be understanding, but that I want those plates back right speedily. I will not allow the reputation of this Abbey to be harmed because of one felon in Benedictine habit!'

'I . . . I shall do what I can, my Lord,' Peter stammered.

'Have you heard that a man has been found dead?' His words shot out like a blade from a scabbard, making Peter still more uncomfortable.

'I had not heard, my Lord.'

'Up on the moors. Your friend Walwynus.' The Abbot's face was pulled into a frown of concern. 'I would not wish this Abbey to become a laughing stock. We are a small community, and any suggestion that we might be harbouring a killer – worse, a devil – would harm us severely, Brother.'

Now Peter understood. He felt his mouth fall open. 'I have had nothing to do with this, my Lord Abbot,' he protested.

Abbot Robert's voice was harsh with distrust. 'I took you in, Brother Peter, to help you and give you a place of peace. Your corrody, your retirement, was to serve as Almoner here. If you killed this man, tell me now. I can comprehend your crime, if I cannot forgive it.'

'I and he have lived in this town for a long time, Abbot. I forgave him in my heart many years ago,' Peter said, fingering his scar. 'I have had nothing to do with death since I moved here. Whoever killed Wally, it was not me.'

'The rumours will harm us,' Abbot Robert repeated. 'The Abbot's Way. My God in heaven, why did he have to be found on *that* trail, the Abbot's Way?'

The Almoner nodded slowly, his eyes hooded. Now the Abbot was making sense. According to legend, first the Abbot's wine had been stolen, then the Jew had been murdered. Aye, and then the thieving monks had been gathered up, so the legend had it, and taken away by the devil himself. 'It is a coincidence, my Lord,' he agreed slowly. 'But there is nothing to suggest that this man out on the moors had anything to do with the Abbey, is there?'

'You know how the people will talk. There doesn't need to be a connection, Brother.'

The Abbot's eyes were fixed on him with that intensity which Peter knew so well. Abbot Robert was no man's fool. No, and he could see a man's soul and judge it, Peter sometimes thought. Abbot Robert Champeaux had been elected to lead the Abbey after years of incompetence, and he had rebuilt it with a single-minded dedication. No man would be permitted to destroy what he had created.

'You were on the moors a few days ago, Brother,' the Abbot said.

Peter could feel the full force of his eyes upon him. 'I know nothing about the man's death, my Lord Abbot, I assure you,' he said as strongly as he could.

'You were up there?'

'After the coining. Aye, on the fast day, Friday.'

'You are Almoner and may pass beyond our doors, but why did you need to go up to the moors that day?'

'My Lord Abbot, I had to take alms to John, your shepherd with the hurt leg.'

'Oh! Young John? And then you came back?'

'Aye, but slowly. I was born in the wilds of the northern March, and the open spaces are in my nature.'

'You should have your humours tested then, Brother. You should be content with God's company here in the Abbey.'

'I try to be content,' he said, his tongue clicking in his mouth, it had become so dry.

'Do so. Did you see any man up there?'

'Only Walwynus. He was returning to his little hovel.'

The Abbot gazed at him. 'I see. Did you speak to him?'

'I called out to him, but he didn't seem to want to chat. He was crapulous, I fear.'

'Did you follow along behind him?'

'I went up to the moors, aye. And I came back. But I saw no dead man up there, my Lord Abbot.'

'No. Because if you had, of course you would have come back here and told me, wouldn't you? So that we could try to save the man's soul.'

'Aye, my Lord Abbot.'

The Abbot stared at him for a moment. 'And this was the same Walwynus whom you knew, wasn't it, Peter?'

'He was in the group who did this to me,' Peter said harshly, touching the scar again. 'I'd not be likely to forget him, Abbot. Yet

I had forgiven him, and I wouldn't have harmed him. In fact, I spoke to him and told him that he was forgiven, on the day of the coining.'

'How so?'

'I met him before the coining began, and told him. It was the first time I'd spoken to him since the attack on me,' Peter added thoughtfully. 'It was most curious, speaking to him again like that. I fear he was terrified. Probably thought I'd beat his head in.'

'For wounding you like that?'

'Aye. That and other things,' Peter said, but he didn't elaborate.

Gerard was relieved to be out of the church, as always, but he felt no great comfort. His predicament weighed too heavily on his mind.

He had been out in the courtyard when the tall, grim-faced Bailiff had returned, bellowing for messengers, for grooms and for the Abbey's man of law. Moments after he had stalked off to the Abbot's lodging, his discovery had been bruited all about the community. The dead man up on the moors was definitely Walwynus.

The news that Wally was dead – that was really scary. All the novices and Brothers were talking about it, especially the odd one or two who had a superstitious bent. The parallels between the story of Milbrosa and this dead man were too tempting: the thefts of the Abbot's wine followed by the murder of a tinner on the moors. Of course the miner hadn't been dumped in a bog, nor was he hugely rich, and there was no indication that a monk had anything to do with it, but that didn't stop them talking. There was little else of excitement ever happened in a monastery, after all.

Later, walking from the Abbey church out to the *dorter*, he felt the skin of his back crawling. He anticipated the thunderbolt of God's wrath at any time. At the very least he thought he deserved to be stabbed, to have his life expunged.

He'd seen the Bailiff before, and knew who Simon was, what his duties were. The man was bound to sense what Gerard had done. In fact, Gerard thought he could see the recognition in Simon's face. When the Bailiff looked at him, there was that expression of confused suspicion on his features, like a hound which has seen his quarry, but is doubtful because the beast doesn't run. Gerard had seen that sort of expression on a dog's face once when he was out hunting. A buck hare was there, sitting up on his haunches, but as soon as he caught sight of Gerard and his dog, he had fallen flat down on his belly, ears low, and fixed as stationary as a small clod of earth.

His dog was all for running at the thing, but Gerard knew it could easily outrun his old hound, and anyway, there was no need to set the dog after it: Gerard knew hares. He made the dog sit, and then walked away, up and around the hedge. The hound stared at him as though he was mad, and then returned to gaze suspiciously at the hare, which simply gazed back at him.

Gerard had no idea why hares would do it, but a hare would watch moving things rather than a man. He'd been shown the trick by an old countryman years before: the man had seen a hare, and rather than set the dogs free, he'd walked closer, then hurled his coat away. The hare stared at it as it flew past, and meanwhile the man circled around it until he could grab it by the neck and quickly wring it.

The same thing almost happened with Gerard's hare that day. He left his hound there, sitting, while he took off his jacket and screwed it up into a ball, throwing it as far as he could. He tried to circle around behind the hare, but it didn't work. Something alarmed the animal, and it bolted before Gerard had managed to get halfway. He turned to his dog to order him on.

The hound needed no second urging. He hurled himself forward, muscles cording under his glossy coat, and pelted off, but the hare had too much of an advantage. It had escaped beneath a tree-root, through a tiny gap in the hedge, and was gone, while

Gerard's hound sniffed and whined and paced up and down, trying to find a gap broad enough to wriggle through or a spot low enough to leap over.

Simon's expression reminded him of that day, because as he ordered his hound to stay put, and the hare sat still, he saw the quizzical doubt on the dog's face, as though it knew that the hare was a prey, and expected the animal to bolt. Only when the hare leaped up and ran did the dog feel comfortable that it was behaving true to form. Simon was the dog, Gerard his prey. Dogs chased when smaller creatures ran, that was the way of things, and Bailiff Puttock was waiting for him to bolt.

Gerard shivered as he came to the *reredorter* and walked to the wooden plank with the holes cut out. His bowels had felt loose ever since news of Walwynus' death had reached his ears. He had never thought, when he succumbed to the temptation of stealing a little bread, that it would come to this. He knew he should confess to Abbot Robert, but his master was such an intimidating man. Someone like the Bailiff who knew the Abbot only as a businessman or friend wouldn't see him in the same light, but to Gerard he was the strict interpreter of God's will, the man who translated His will for the poor fools like Gerard himself who couldn't comprehend it. Abbot Robert was the supreme master in this, his Abbey, and Gerard could no more face standing before him and confessing his crimes than he could before the King.

If only it had been the wine alone. Gradually, step by step, he had been drawn ever further into crime. Not because he wanted to, but because that evil bastard had forced him to. He could weep now, to think of the coins, the baubles, the little strings of beads, the wine and dried meats . . . All stolen by his nimble fingers, all gone. He was to blame, and the Abbot would exact a severe penalty for his crimes. At the least he would be humiliated, but he might receive a worse punishment. Perhaps he could even be sent to the Scillies, to the islands of St Nicholas, St Sampson, St Eludius, St Theona the Virgin and Nutho. Gerard had never been to the islands, and didn't want to. To be sent there was the punishment for only the most hardened of conventual criminals. The islands were tiny, with small communities of weather-beaten, uncommunicative men to whom piracy was a way of life whenever fish were scarce.

He hadn't wanted to get involved. Life as an acolyte was hard, in a regime like this, and he had occasionally stolen spare food or a little wine, but then he was spotted. Suddenly he had a master, a wheedling fellow who persuaded him to take 'Just one little loaf from the kitchen. Such a little thing.' And so it was, something which the two could share, and all for a small wager. If he had been discovered, it was no matter. He could have borne the strap on his bared arse. That was nothing – the sort of thing that all boys were used to. After all, a beating was easy, three or four rubs and the pain was gone. Far better to have the strap than to be detained indoors on a warm, summer's afternoon when the birds were tempting a shot with a sling, or when the dogs were baiting a bull in the shambles.

Although that was the beginning, it wasn't the end. If only it *had* been. The suggestions went from a loaf to loaves. There was nothing to it. Gerard was small, slender-waisted and narrow-shouldered, and could wriggle through the smallest of windows. He found it easy, and it was fun. There was never anything serious about it. Not for him there wasn't, but soon he was to realise that his exploits were not viewed in the same light by his confederates.

His enjoyment dimmed when his wheedling master neatly trapped him. He had been stealing to the order of his master, who now insisted that he continue. If he didn't, at the least he would be exposed; at worst, tortured. But if he complied, he would be safe.

Gerard had been tempted to go to the Abbot and confess everything, but then he realised how weak his position was. Gradually he had taken more and more and his easy manner had begun to fail him. Whenever he saw the Abbot's eye resting upon him, he was convinced he was about to be accused. It seemed so obvious. He became a nervous wreck. And then he had been told to steal the wine.

It made no sense to him. What was the point? They had no need to steal the better part of a pipe of the Abbot's best wine. It could only bring attention to them. To *him*. If only he had not succumbed to stealing the bread in the first place, then he would be safe. Perhaps he still could be.

He would never again steal from the Abbey, he promised himself. There was no cure for his soul for the damage he had already done, but at least he could try to atone by not stealing again, and try to make amends for the things he had already taken. That would be best.

Filled with this resolve, he rose and washed his hands in the trough before making his way out to the *frater*. This massive block was opposite the Abbey church, at the other side of the cloister, and he must walk down the steep stone stairs outside the *reredorter* and cross a narrow passage between the buildings to reach it.

At the bottom of the stairs he licked his lips nervously. A fresh thought had occurred to him. If Walwynus was dead, then the man who had killed him might have been motivated by the simple urge to steal whatever Walwynus had, as the majority of the monks suspected. Someone might have seen Wally walking about with a sack on his back on the day of the coining and decided to kill him and take whatever was inside. There were plenty of outlaws even in Devon who would be prepared to murder on the off-chance. And any man who did that would have found themselves in luck, from the quantity of pewter that was in Wally's sack.

Then another thought struck him, and Gerard felt his belly gurgling.

What if Joce had seen them taking the stuff from his house? Maybe he didn't even need to see them. For all Joce knew, only Wally had any idea where the metal was stored. He could have killed Wally and taken back his stolen metal. Unless Wally had already got rid of it, as he said he would. Then Joce would be discomfited, Gerard thought with a sudden grin.

But then his expression hardened. If Joce *had* caught Wally and then learned that his metal was gone, he would be enraged. Perhaps he had tortured Wally before killing him, demanding to know where the metal was, or to learn whether he had a confederate . . . What if Joce had learned that Gerard himself was involved, that Gerard had aided Wally's theft of Joce's stock?

All of a sudden, the acolyte felt the need to return to the *reredorter*.

Chapter Five

Simon sat at the table comfortably replete. The meal, as usual at Abbot Robert's board, had been excellent, the wine even better, and the Bailiff was aware of a gentle drowsiness stealing over him. Fortunately only one barrel of the special wine had been stolen, as the Abbot said, and this, as Simon was happy to agree, was a very good wine indeed.

As was usual when there was Stannary business to discuss, the Abbot was entertaining Simon alone. Other guests of the Abbey had to make do with the hospitality at the gate-house, but Simon merited rather better treatment. He and the Abbot had enjoyed a good working relationship for many years.

It was that fact which had annoyed Simon so grievously about the affair with the coining hammer, because he had never knowingly let the Abbot down before. He had always made sure that the Abbot's work was done, no matter what, and up until this year, he had been efficient and capable. The mines worked well, the law was generally observed, and Abbot Robert had little cause for complaint. Simon was sure of it.

While the Abbot spoke to one of his servants at the end of the meal, Simon's mind wandered.

This year, things had gone wrong: he couldn't deny it. First there was the fiasco of the tournament at Oakhampton, which was a terrible embarrassment to Simon personally; then the hideous murders at Sticklepath. Somehow they had laid a gloom over the Bailiff's usually cheerful demeanour. Or perhaps it had nothing to do with the problems he had encountered, and was more to do with the way things were at home.

Edith, his daughter, had been his most prized companion, maybe even above his wife herself, and now he was losing her. Just as Meg had said so often, she was growing, and with her slim good looks, she was attracting all the boys like bees about a honeypot. The difficulty was, Simon wasn't ready to let her go. He adored her, and seeing the unchivalrous, oversexed local youths pawing at her or doting upon her every word brought out the heavy father in him. Simon wanted to demand who their fathers were, how much land did they own, how much was it worth annually, and what were the lads' prospects . . . He had actually tried to do that once, but Meg had skilfully distracted him and led him from the room. As she later said to him, it was bad enough for Edith trying to mix with boys of her own age and class with her father scowling in the corner of the room like an ogre from the moors, without him interrogating them like the Bailiff he was.

They still had little Peterkin, of course. Their son was a continual source of pride and pleasure to him, but somehow Simon already knew that his son would be the favourite of his wife. It was his daughter who had been his own especial friend. Astonishing, he thought now, how good wine could make a man see his troubles so clearly.

Glancing up, he saw that the last of the food was gone from the table, and only the dishes remained to be cleared. Thinking that their meeting was over, he thanked the Abbot and prepared to stand and make his way to the guest's lodgings over the Court Gate, but the Abbot motioned to Simon to remain in his seat a while longer. He said nothing while the trenchers and plate were being collected by his two servants, but when they were gone, he leaned forward and beckoned to his Steward to pour them more wine.

'Bailiff, you appear less than comfortable. Have you received bad news? Is that why you forgot the hammer?'

Simon smiled thinly. 'It is nothing so important as to merit the title of news, my Lord. No, it is merely the ordinary trials of a father. I apologise for having allowed my domestic affairs to affect the coining.'

'I trust it will not last a great while.'

Simon gave a rueful shrug. 'I trust not,' he said, thinking that no matter what he wished, his daughter must soon find herself a lover and husband.

'I am glad. I almost mentioned this to you before, but I admit that I was annoyed after that hammer nonsense. No, not because of you alone,' the Abbot added, holding up a hand to stem Simon's expostulations. 'I had an inkling of something being wrong here in the Abbey, and then there was the stolen wine . . . You can imagine my feelings to then hear that my most respected Bailiff had made such a foolish error.'

'I can understand,' Simon said. He felt deflated. The meal and wine had persuaded him that the affair was over and done with, but the Abbot's words indicated that it was not yet forgotten.

Abbot Robert was toying with his goblet now. 'And now there is this poor fellow on the moors: Walwynus. His corpse is guarded?'

'I left the miner Hal Raddych up there. When the Coroner arrives, we can investigate more fully.'

'Of course. Who could wish to kill a poor fellow like him? It seems insane.'

'There are madmen about,' Simon said.

'Yes, but one hardly expects to meet them here. Do you think that this was a random attack from an outlaw? Someone who knocked him down just to filch his purse?'

'It is very hard to say, my Lord Abbot. But I shall enquire as I may, see if I can dig up something for the Coroner to use. When should he arrive?'

'Your guess is as good as mine. Tomorrow or the day after, I hope.'

Tuesday or Wednesday, Simon noted. He sighed. 'I only wish Baldwin were here.'

'Yes. He is a man of excellent judgement.'

Simon nodded, burped gently, and sipped at his wine. 'Baldwin is a good man to have at your side in an enquiry. He's so used to running his own courts as Keeper of the King's Peace that questioning people is second nature to him.'

'He has many duties,' the Abbot murmured. 'The duties and responsibilities of an Abbot are equally onerous: varied and always increasing. We are now to be asked to help the King again. His Host is marching to Scotland, I hear.'

'I had thought that they would have crossed the border by now.'

'Perhaps they have. The King is up in the north, I understand.' The Abbot smiled humourlessly. 'He wishes money for his bastard, Adam. The lad is to be blooded in Scotland, so we must all pay the King taxes so that he can afford to buy a horse and new armour for his whelp, I suppose.'

His tone was bitter. Simon knew that Abbot Robert resented having to send more of his hard-earned money to support the King in one of his campaigns.

'Every time he calls on his Host he expects us to pay our fee,' the Abbot continued. 'This Abbey once had to support fifteen knights, but now we commute that service with *scutage*, we have to pay for sixteen. Not only that: his sister is to marry, and he wants a subsidy from *me* to help pay for her wedding! When the King decided to march against Thomas of Lancaster earlier this year, he demanded that I should act as his recruitment officer. Now a man has arrived telling me I must do so again, and find men for him at the same time as paying a fine because I, as an Abbot, tend not to maintain knights here in the cloister. Pah! He wanted me to provide him with money to hire mere mercenaries, knaves and churls who will fight for any man if the money is right, against every element of Christ's teaching, and at the same time he demands my best, healthiest, strongest peasants to fill his army: no matter that he denudes my fields of the men I need during the harvest. My God! Save me from bellicose monarchs!'

Simon nodded understandingly, but he failed to see where this conversation was heading. Outside, the light had faded, and he wondered how much longer the Abbot was going to talk. For his part, the ride to Tavistock, the quick return to Lydford and back, followed by the trip to Wally's body, had made his entire body ache; the Abbot's good red wine hadn't helped. Simon longed to sprawl back in his seat, to close his eyes and dream of his wife, but he wasn't fooled by his host's affable manner. Abbot Robert was Simon's master, when all was said and done, and if he wished to talk on, Simon must listen. He felt his eyelids grow heavy.

'Bailiff, you seem tired.'

'No, my Lord. I am fine. You were talking about the King?'

'Yes. He wants more men, but he also wants money. I have no recruiting officers, and finding one in whom I can place any trust . . .'

Simon's heart sank. 'Of course, my Lord Abbot. If you command me.'

'No, I do not command you to take total responsibility, Simon,' the Abbot said with a faint smile. 'But I would ask that you assist the man sent to raise a force from the local men. I have no time for this nonsense, but if I don't have someone there . . . well, you know how it is. I cannot lose *all* my men.'

'This man is staying in the town?'

'No, as soon as he got here this afternoon, I had him sent to join the other guests and fed. He is there now, I expect. If you could spend a little time with him, I should be most grateful.'

'I shall help as best I may.'

'I am glad to hear it,' the Abbot said, and toyed with his knife for a moment.

Simon thought he looked distrait. 'Is there another matter, my Lord Abbot?'

'There *is* one other little affair.' The Abbot coughed. 'This morning, a man sleeping in the guest room with you came to me and alleged that there had been a theft from his belongings. I am investigating his accusations myself.'

'You do not wish me to help?'

'I think not. Not yet. If I am right, the villain should soon come to me and confess. There is little point in setting you after him. No. If someone asks you about the matter, please tell people that the pewterer has not lost anything.'

'My Lord?'

'You will not be lying. I have myself reimbursed him,' Abbot Robert said quietly. 'I will not allow one felon to drag the name of this Abbey through the midden. Whoever is responsible, I shall soon know, but there is no reason to have it bruited abroad that the Abbey is a hotbed of thieves and rascals. However, that is not the same as this affair of the dead miner. Surely that is much more important. You have set matters in train, you say?'

'Yes.'

'Good. Now, if you learn of any reason why someone should wish to have had Wally killed, you will of course let me know.'

'Walwynus?' It sounded peculiar to hear the Abbot using the diminutive. 'Yes, certainly, my Lord Abbot. But I don't know that I shall ever learn why he died. Probably it was a lone felon whom he met and who decided to kill him in case he had some money.'

'Very likely. I fear that if I were personally to waste time on every stabbing or throttling that happened out in the wilds, I should never have time to go to church.'

It was a thought which resonated with Simon as he walked to the gate-house to seek out his bed. He spent much of his life trying to soothe angry miners and prevent bloodshed, but all too often others were found stabbed or bludgeoned to death. Wally wasn't alone.

The night sky seemed huge, and in it Simon could see the stars, so clear and bright that he found his feet slowing as if of their own accord. Entranced by their beauty, he gazed up at them, sniffing the clean air. It was so calm, he felt his tiredness fading, and he leaned against a wall near the chapter-house, his arms folded. A dog was barking out in the town itself, the only sound he could hear. From the corner of his eye he glimpsed a dark shadow creeping along the wall of the monks' cemetery to his left, and he heard a plaintive miaow.

It was then, as the cat sprang down, that he heard a short gasp. Looking around, he saw a slight figure in the dark robes of a Benedictine. A monk who had been startled, no doubt, he thought to himself. Monks were known to be gullible, innocent and superstitious at the best of times. It was one thing to believe in ghosts and spirits, like Simon himself, and quite another to fear a cat in the dark, he told himself with a distinct feeling of superiority. Odd, though. He'd have thought that all the monks would have been abed by now. It was rare for them to be up so late, for they all had to rise for the Mass at midnight, and not many men could survive, like the good Abbot, on only three hours of sleep each night. Most needed at least six.

He watched the monk hurry away, over the Great Court towards the Water Gate, and only when he heard a door quietly close did he carry on his way.

The gate-house was a large, two-storey building with good accommodation over the gateway itself. Here, in the large chamber, slept all the guests. As Simon knew, the low timber beds were comfortable, with ropes supporting the thick palliasses, and he was looking forward to climbing back between the blankets. It felt like too many hours since he had been raised by that blasted acolyte, with the news of Wally's murder.

Only a few of the others, Simon noted with grateful relief, snored. Walking carefully and quietly between the beds and bodies, he went to the bed in which he had slept the night before, hoping that it might be empty, but even in the dim darkness, he could sense that someone else was there. At least this was the first time so far since the coining. On other occasions when he had come to visit the Abbot, he had been forced to share almost every night. However, there were no rumbling snores or grunts from his companion, and for that he was very grateful. As he untied his hose, pulled off his shoes, and doffed his shirt and undershirt, he sniggered to himself. He had wondered whether his sleeping partner might break wind during the night, but now he realised that if either of them were likely to, it would be Simon himself after so much rich food and wine.

With that reflection, he climbed under the blankets and lay with his arms behind his head. The other man in the bed grumbled a little in his sleep and rolled over, but Simon paid him no heed. He was wondering again about poor Wally. The dead man's face and body sprang into his mind, and with a shiver of revulsion, he too turned over, as though he could so easily hide himself from the gaze of Wally's ravaged eyes.

Gerard scampered across the court. Something told him that there had been someone out there who had seen him. He was sure of it. It was probably that blasted nuisance Peter. He was there, waiting for Gerard, just like he had been the other time. God! There was no escape, not in such an enclosed place as this. It was terrible; he felt as though his every waking moment was spent in planning to get away, to become apostate. He would have to, somehow.

Peter had caught him once before. Gerard had been about to enter the bakery, when the Almoner appeared. It was just before he'd given that talk about Milbrosa, a day or two after he warned Gerard to stop stealing, and he had stood staring at the acolyte, saying nothing, until Gerard scampered away, feeling as though everyone knew his crimes. Maybe several of them did know his crimes. Gerard knew that Reginald, an older novice, had been watching him, and Brother Mark was on to him, too; he'd threatened to tell the Abbot.

But it was all over and done with now. Gerard had spoken to Augerus. He'd told him that he wouldn't steal any more. Augerus could do whatever he wanted – tell the Abbot, tell the other

Brothers, Gerard didn't care. There was nothing the Steward could do which would make him feel worse. As far as Gerard was concerned, he would never steal again.

It had been a cleverly worked out scheme, though. He could admire Augerus' cleverness while detesting the way the older man had entrapped him in it.

An Abbey like Tavistock always had a certain number of people taking advantage of the Abbot's hospitality. Because of the location, near to some of the best tin mines in Europe, it was normal for several of the guests to be wealthy traders, pewterers or merchants, and often these men would carry plates or goblets instead of large sums of cash. They would know that they could hawk their metalwork for cash, and if need be, they could redeem their pieces later. It was easier and safer than carrying money.

Except, of course, when Augerus learned who the wealthiest visitors were, he could easily advise Gerard, and the boy would climb in to take the choicest bits and pieces. Never too much, and never too regularly. That might lead to questions. But once in a while, whenever Wally was due to be in town, then Gerard would go on his visits and bring whatever he could find to Augerus. Augerus in his turn would pass them items on to Wally, who would take them straight to Joce. That way, even if there were a complaint, there would be no evidence in the Abbey. A simple, but effective scheme.

Or so it had seemed until Wally died.

The court *looked* empty, but the shadows thrown by the trees lining the cemetery were so dark compared with the brightness of the area lighted by the stars, that he couldn't truly be certain. Mark, Peter, or another novice, like Reginald – the Abbot himself even – could be there, watching him now.

Nowhere was safe.

That thought ate its way through his brain like a worm eating through an apple. He had to gulp to prevent himself sobbing. It was too late now. His life's course had been defined, and he must accept the consequences. At least he had now made sure of his position, he thought, as he silently sat outside the door to the church, waiting for the monks to wake so that he could file in with them as soon as Mass was called.

Perhaps he was being foolish. It was possible that Wally had been killed by accident, or that he had been struck down by a common footpad. There wasn't anything to suggest that it was something to do with *him*. Surely nobody would connect Gerard with Wally. No, it was rubbish. Anyway, no monk would be able to kill. That was just madness. Although no monk was supposed to steal, either, and Gerard had been forced to do just that – by a fellow monk. And wasn't it said that a man who incites another to commit a criminal act is a felon, just as plainly as the man who actually carries it out?

Gerard sniffed miserably. At first it was fun taking the loaves, but he hadn't realised how things would escalate. And when Augerus gripped his shoulder as he dropped down from the high windowsill with the things in his hand, he had thought all was well; it was only later he realised his error. By then it was too late.

Augerus had greater plans for him. He had no intention of telling the Abbot and losing so useful a thief.

Brother Mark the *salsarius* closed his shutter and walked back to the low bed, but he wasn't ready to sleep, having seen Gerard scuttle across the court. Instead he sat on the edge of his bed, staring at the candle guttering in the gentle night breeze.

The thought of telling the Abbot about Gerard's thefts was unpleasant, but probably necessary. The acolyte had been stealing too many things just recently, and he could not stop because, as Mark well knew, Augerus was driving him to steal, and Augerus wanted the money to continue to flow into his coffers. It went against the grain to speak of another's crime, and up until now Mark had not been overly bothered, but matters were getting out of control. The reputation of the Abbey could be at stake.

Augerus was a greedy soul. Mark valued him, because the Steward was the source of a lot of useful information about the Abbot and the Abbot's thoughts, but Mark had no doubt that, should he report Augerus and Gerard to Abbot Robert, he would soon get to know Augerus' replacement and find him in every way as reliable as the Steward had been.

Mark didn't dislike Augerus. He didn't really dislike Gerard either. The ones he *did* dislike were the others, men like the pewterer who had lost his plates. The fool deserved to lose them. Mark wandered to his jug and poured a good portion of wine while he considered. The pewterer had enough money to live on, but still tried to make more. It was against God's rules, just as Mark's life had been before he came to the Abbey.

Just as Walwynus broke God's rules. Mark had known about him for a while. One night he saw Augerus dangling his rope with a small sack attached and later saw Wally walking from the garden carrying what looked like the same sack. An easy transfer. Mark wondered what Augerus would do now, with no confederate to collect his stolen goods.

Then, of course, Mark hadn't realised it was stolen property. None of the Abbey's guests had complained. It was only because that avaricious pewterer had gone whining to the Abbot this morning that Mark had realised what he had seen. He had found Gerard skulking about, it was true, but he hadn't realised *why* the lad was there. Now it made sense. Gerard took people's things, Augerus passed them to Wally, and he sold them on. A simple and effective chain.

Wally had deserved punishment. Surely he had tempted Augerus and Gerard into crime. Wally deserved his fate. No doubt with Wally dead the thieving would stop. Perhaps Augerus and Gerard would see the error of their ways and beg forgiveness.

Mark drained his wine and sat back. Yes. There was no point in running to the Abbot with stories. Better to wait and see what happened.

*   *   *

Still not asleep, Simon rolled on to his back once more and lay staring at the ceiling. A lamp outside in the yard threw a pale, flickering yellow light that caught the dusty cobwebs, making them look like small wraiths against the whitewashed ceiling; he tried to lose consciousness by watching their dance, but knew it wouldn't work. Instead he turned to face the small altar, placed there for the convenience of guests, and muttered a prayer, but that failed to bring on sleep as well.

The room felt close, hot and humid, and his bladder was full. Swearing to himself, he got up and walked to the window, which gave on to the court. He quietly slid down the shutter and was about to relieve himself when he saw a dark figure passing over the yard. It was a monk, but even at this distance he could see that it was a different one from the man he had seen earlier. This monk was tall, if slightly stooped, just like Brother Peter the Almoner.

Simon watched him pass from the Water Gate around the pig sties and across the court, moving silently like a great cat, slow and precise. Only when the monk had disappeared from view did he at last urinate, grunting as he shook himself dry. It was a peculiar time for a monk to be up, he thought, but then perhaps the Almoner had some special duty that he didn't know of.

Satisfied with his conclusion, he yawned, slid the shutter closed and plodded back to his bed.

Chapter Six

The rain woke Joce Blakemoor. The thatch on his roof was silent, and even in the heaviest downpour he could sleep through it, but his neighbour, a cobbler, had put a set of boxes filled with broken pots beneath his window on the day of the coining, and now the rain falling on them set up such a din that Joce could get no rest. Some people might have thought it a musical sound, but to Joce it was a cacophony; no more attractive than a chorus of tom cats.

He rolled over and over in his bed, hauling the blankets up to his chin, pulling his pillow over his head, but nothing could drown out that incessant row. Eventually he lay with his bleared eyes open, staring at the shuttered window, waiting for the dawn.

It was no good. He rose angrily, pulling his shirt and hose on, and selecting his third-best tunic and an old coat, for now the coining was all done and he had other work to be getting on with. First, though, he would deal with the neighbour.

Climbing down the stairs, he saw Art, his servant, asleep on his bench by the fire, and kicked him awake. When the lad didn't rise immediately, but lay back rubbing at his eyes, Joce tipped the bench over and the boy with it. Art's belt lay by his clothes on the floor and Joce picked it up, lashing at the child's back and flanks while he howled, hurrying on all fours to the wall, where he crouched, hands over his head, crying for Joce to stop.

That at least made the Receiver feel a little better. He threw the belt at the boy and stalked from the room. There was no excuse for a servant to remain sleeping when his master was awake.

In the hall, he selected a blackthorn club, then opened his door. Outside, he stood under the deep eaves and glared at the boxes standing against his wall. Geoffrey Cobbler shouldn't have had them left there. He'd dumped them on the day of the coining. Anger welled. His neighbour was a selfish, thoughtless bastard! But what more could you expect from a fool like Geoffrey, a newcomer from Exeter or somewhere, a blasted *foreigner*.

That was why he could only afford a *moiety*. When Tavistock had been made into a Burgh by the then Abbot, hundreds of years ago, the land here had been split into 106 equal divisions called *messuages*. Half had their own gardens, and it was one of these which Joce owned; others had no garden and were divided into two *moieties*, one of which held the civil rights of exemption from tolls and other benefits, while the other half was 'without liberty'. Although both paid the same rents to the Abbey, the one without liberty was naturally cheaper to buy, which was why the cobbler could afford his mean little property. He couldn't have afforded a place like Joce's.

The man's door was still barred. Joce hammered on it, waiting for an answer, and when there was nothing stirring, he beat upon the timbers with his club.

'Who is it? What do you want?' came Geoffrey's sleepy voice.

'Open this door, you shit!' Joce roared.

'I'm not opening it to someone who shouts like that at this time of the morning.'

'Ye'll open this door, or I'll break it in!' Joce's temper, always short, was fanned by the recalcitrance of his neighbour. Weak, feeble-minded tarse! 'You want to leave your garbage out here where it'll wake your neighbours, do you? I'll teach you to put it under my eaves, you great swollen tub of lard, you pig's turd, you bladder of fart!'

There was a crowd of people near him now, all trying to watch while avoiding the worst of the rain, and he gestured with his club at the door. 'This bastard son of a half-witted Winchester sow has no consideration. Listen to that! How could anyone sleep with a racket like that? This cretin should clear up his junk. Let him take it down to the midden, rather than leaving it here to irritate his neighbours.'

'It's not my fault.' Geoffrey's voice came as though disembodied. 'I never put it there. Someone else did.'

'You say it's not your rubbish, you lying son of a fox?' Joce roared.

'It's my stuff, but I never put it there. I left it by my door, but I'll get it cleared up as soon as I have time.'

'Come out here and do it now, you . . .'

Others in the crowd had heard enough. Two men exchanged a glance, and then went to Joce's side. Under the terms of the *Frankpledge*, every man had a responsibility to keep the peace, both by their own behaviour, but also in preventing others from breaking the peace. If they didn't, the whole community could be fined.

'Come on, Master Blakemoor. Put up your club and return to your house.'

'Keep your hands off me! I want that bastard out here, and I'll beat his head in.'

'I'm not coming out. I'm not!'

Joce gave a harsh snarl of rage. Exhausted, his eyes felt raw, his head light and dizzy, his belly queasy, and it was all because of this bastard. Leaping forward, brandishing his blackthorn, he swung it with all his strength at the door, and the wood cracked with an ominous splintering. Before he could swing a second time, the club was grabbed and wrenched from his fist, and he turned to find himself confronted by five men, all of whom watched him with stern expressions.

'Leave him alone, Blakemoor. You may not like him, but he's not doing any harm. What's got into you?'

'Hark at that racket! Could you sleep through that?' Joce snarled.

'It didn't wake *me*,' said Andrew, who lived opposite Joce. '*You* did, by all this shouting.'

'Oh, well, I *am* sorry!' the Receiver sneered.

'If Geoffrey moves all this stuff today, will you be content?' asked Andrew.

'I want him out here now!'

'You'll only fight him and break the peace. We won't have that, Joce.'

'Get him out here!'

Andrew studied him. He was a big man, the sort who looked as though he would move only slowly, but although his mind tended not to race too speedily, his body was capable of surprising bursts of energy. His dark eyes were calm, rather than stupid, and now he nodded towards a man at Joce's side. 'We can ask him out, and you and he can make it up. I won't have you fighting.'

'I'll do as I want,' Joce said.

'You'll do as you're told, unless you want to appear in the Abbot's court, you fool,' Andrew said firmly.

After promises of his safety, Geoffrey's nervous features appeared around the side of the door. He was profusely apologetic, insisting that he'd had no idea that the mess outside the building would upset his neighbour, swearing that he would have it all moved later than day, and with all the folks about him, Joce allowed his hand to be taken while both agreed, Joce grudgingly, to keep the peace.

That done, Joce spat at the ground and jerked his arms free of the neighbours who had held him back, biting his thumb at Geoffrey's door, and stomping back to his own house. His servant, Art, stood in the doorway, watching nervously. When Joce walked through to his hall and sat in his chair, Art scurried in and shed tinder and twigs on the fire, then began to blow, teasing a spark into flame.

Joce knew it wasn't like him to fly off the handle like that. Usually he could keep his temper under control, at least while he was in public, but today he felt as though there was a band about his forehead, tightening. The pressure was building in him, and it demanded release.

He tapped his foot on the floor. There was the trouble with Sara to begin with. That useless blubbering bitch couldn't accept that their thing was over. She'd believed his declaration of love.

The poor slut had thought she'd be able to talk him into marrying her in exchange for sex – well, she'd learned her mistake there, aye. What did she take him for – some starry-eyed youth with his brain in his tarse? Well, he wasn't. He was Joce Blakemoor, and he took what *he* wanted *when* he wanted. She'd tried to blackmail him, saying that she was pregnant, that she'd tell the whole town he was the father, and he had laughed. That was at the coining. The stupid wench. As if her threats could harm *him*!

And then that cretin Wally had tried to scare him off as well, the fool, on the morning after the coining. Joce had seen him first thing, in the street near Joce's house, and had nodded to him as he would any other fellow. Wally had looked away, as though ashamed to be acknowledged by him, but then he looked like he took his courage in both hands, and beckoned Joce into an alley. Joce had thought he had some more pewter or something, but no, the son of a donkey just wanted to persuade Joce to leave Sara alone. Wally said he was playing with her affections.

It took that long for Joce's anger to rise. He took Wally by the throat and pounded him. Ah, but it had felt *good*! He slammed Wally's head against the stones of the wall, then thumped him about the face and breast.

'Don't tell me whom I may see, you bastard! I was your master once, and if you are disloyal to me, I'll kill you. Remember that!'

There were other matters to concern him now, though. The whole town was buzzing with stories about Wally's death. He was gone, and no bad thing. Joce had noticed his glances at the coining. He suspected. Fine, but that meant Joce must find a new courier from the Abbey. He daren't stop his trade with Augerus, because he had a large shortfall in the Burgh's accounts to make up. The money he had taken, he had also spent, and now he must acquire more in order to refill the Burgh's coffers. Somehow he would have to contact Augerus. Perhaps he could go and collect the stuff himself, rather than employing someone else again.

Art had persuaded the fire to catch, and the pieces of wood crackled merrily. Over them he set one or two charred logs from the previous night and hurried off to fetch the griddle.

Joce watched him go with a sour expression twisting his features. He wanted a reason to be able to explode, but Art was giving him no excuse. In fact, Joce was more angry with himself than Art. His rush over to shout at Geoffrey's door was insane; what's more, it was unnecessary. He could see that now. Stupid. Much more sensible to wait until later, when Geoffrey was already up and about, and waylay him, beat the little shit half to death without his ever realising who it was, or why. Getting so enraged for no reason was ridiculous. He should never have allowed his neighbours to see him lose control. It was the lack of sleep, surely.

Art came back with more wood then set the griddle over the flames. While he worked, Joce watched him silently. And he saw Art's eyes go to his cupboard.

'Fetch my food, boy!'

Instantly Art rose and darted out to the pantry, returning with a tray on which he had set out a loaf, a jug with a drinking bowl, and some pieces of meat. Joce waited until the lad had put them all on the table, and then clenched his fist and slammed it into Art's belly. He could hear the breath woosh from his lungs, saw the lad's eyes pop wide, his mouth gape, his back curve over. Dispassionately, Joce observed his servant collapse to the floor, one arm reaching out to the table's edge, clinging on, while he retched and coughed, desperately trying to suck in some air while his face reddened and his whole body shivered.

'I am going out to get some real food, you useless cat's turd. When I come back, I want this place clean.' Joce kicked hard, once, and the lad crashed down, a hand clenching and releasing among the reeds and dirt that lay scattered all over. As he vomited, Joce smiled to himself. 'And don't stare at my sideboard like that, boy. If I ever find you've been inside it, I'll cut your tongue out and feed it to the cats. Understand me?'

Leaving his house, the smile remained fixed to his face. It was still there as he entered the little pie-shop at the top of his road. He felt much better for having punched someone. Violence was great for soothing the soul, he always found.

As Joce had begun thundering on his neighbour's door, Gerard was leaving the church with the other members of the choir. While the monks went to the great octagonal chapter-house to discuss Abbey business, he walked to the bakery to collect the bread. As a mere acolyte, Gerard wasn't permitted to witness the deliberations of the monks.

All the monks supported the poor of the Burgh. The lepers at the Maudlin were given tuppence each as their weekly pension, and there were generous donations of all the Abbey's used clothes and shoes, as well as the excess food which was doled out to the poor at the gate, but also the Abbey distributed fresh bread, generally to the families of the monks and novices, and today it was Gerard's turn to collect the food.

The bakery was a little building at the wall by the river, not far from the Water Gate, and Gerard scuffed his feet in the yard's dirt, thinking over his problem as he walked towards it.

Peter the Almoner was at the bakery, and called to Gerard. His voice startled the acolyte and he glanced behind him, considering flight, but then realised that there were far too many people around for Peter to think of hurting him.

The monk gave him a twisted smile. 'You don't want to talk to an older man like me? Aye, and I suppose I wouldn't either when

I was your age, lad. No, there are too many other things to interest a young fellow like you, aren't there?'

'I am here to collect the bread, Brother.'

'Then you can help me to take the loaves around to the needy, can't you?'

'I thought Brother . . .'

'Aye, well, Brother Edward and I have agreed to change our duties. He wasn't feeling very well, so he has gone to sit and pray and I shall take the bread with you. Why, you don't mind me helping, do you?'

Giving an ungracious grunt of assent, Gerard picked up the basket full of loaves which the baker's assistant had set before him, and followed the Almoner out through the main gate to where the beggars waited.

It was odd to watch the old man, Gerard thought. All the beggars could see him, apart from Blind Ban, of course, and they all flinched whenever he turned to them, avoiding his hideously wrecked features with that terrible scar. In fact, Gerard thought Peter looked as though he should be out here, living among the beggars, rather than being a monk inside. Somehow he looked too damaged to be one of God's own Chosen.

As the motley flock of poor folk dispersed with their bounty gripped tightly in their filthy fists, Peter glanced at him. 'Better get the rest of the loaves to the Maudlin, then, lad.'

'Yes.'

Peter shot the acolyte a look as they bent their way towards the Hospital of St Mary Magdalene which lay out at the westernmost point of the borough; the leper hospital. The Almoner was Rector of the hospital, just another of the duties which fell to Peter.

'It must be terrible to be a leper, to be declared legally dead,' he said after a few moments, considering their plight. The poor souls had little enough to occupy their minds other than the slow disintegration and death which awaited them.

'Yes, Brother,' Gerard said.

'They lose all family, all property. Their wills are enforced as though they were dead. I suppose an outlaw loses all as well, but at least a felon can run to another land and create a new life. A leper is unwelcome anywhere else. He must stay in his parish, where he knows he should receive a pension and food.'

Gerard grunted. The Almoner's words seemed a little too close for comfort. He had spent much of the previous night worrying, considering what he might do – what he *could* do – to get himself out of this mess, and flight had been one option which had appealed to him.

'Strange about that miner found dead up on the moor,' Peter continued.

'Yes. God bless his soul.'

'Aye. I doubt many will want to do that. Not when they hear about his trade, eh?' Peter suddenly fixed him with an eye at once bright and knowing and sad.

Gerard stammered, 'His trade? He was a tinner, wasn't he?'

'Aye, I suppose,' Peter said imperturbably. 'Odd, though. He spent a lot of time in the gardens here, not far from the walls.'

'What's that got to do with me?'

'Oh, nothing. Nothing,' Peter said. 'I just wondered why he went there so often at night. You know I don't sleep for long? I often have to rise in the middle of the night and walk about the Great Court or along the walls. You'd be surprised what you see late at night.'

Gerard felt his heart begin pounding. He was sure that Peter was warning him obliquely, but he couldn't speak. He knew Augerus would always tie the stolen goods in a small sack and dangle it by rope from a small window in the Abbot's own lodging, and Wally would come and collect it. Wally had told him so.

Their friendship had been short, but in some ways Gerard felt closer to Wally than to anyone else. Augerus had taken Gerard to a tavern one day, and Wally was there. While Gerard watched, the Steward passed a small purse to Wally, and Wally filled it with coins. Later, when Augerus left to piss outside, Wally and Gerard spoke briefly, and found in each other a kindred feeling. Gerard missed his family and felt forced into the thefts, and somehow he got the impression that Wally felt the same.

'You knew he hadn't found tin for over a year?'

Peter's words drew him back to the present. 'Why should I know that?'

'Common chatter, no more. Still, I thought you might have heard. It must be hard to keep body and soul together with no money. A man could turn to thieving.'

Gerard said nothing, but rebelliously averted his gaze.

'Odd that he's dead, up there so far from anyone, and on the Abbot's Way, too. Just like Milbrosa. You'll remember that story I told? About how the Abbot's Way was created?'

'Yes, but I don't see what any of it's got to do with me,' Gerard blurted.

'Ach, what could it have to do with a young laddie like you? You aren't allowed out, are you? No, you couldn't have killed that fellow, could you? I reckon,' Peter said, glancing up at the sun to gauge the time, 'it must have been those travellers.'

'Travellers?' Gerard stammered. 'What . . . travellers?'

'Didn't you hear?' Peter said as he led the way westwards to the Maudlin. 'There were a gang of them up there. Probably came here for the coining, and killed Walwynus on their way – or on their way back. You can't trust strangers on the moor, can you?'

'Who would know about these folks? I don't believe you. No one was up there, it was just an accident that Wally got killed. Someone thought he was a rich miner, that's all.'

'On his way to the coining, perhaps?' Peter asked.

'Where else would he have been going?'

'Oh, I just wondered whether he could have been on his way back.'

'Perhaps.'

'Maybe someone saw him here in town. Talked to him. And then he went home, and on his way, he was murdered,' Peter said ruminatively.

Gerard asked quickly, 'And who are these travellers? Has anyone seen them? I haven't heard about them.'

'I saw them. I was up on the moors that day,' Peter said.

Gerard felt his heart stop within him on hearing the monk's mild tone, and when he glanced at Peter's face he saw a flash of keenness in the old man's eyes which was soon followed by a knowing leer. He had spoken to provoke, and he had succeeded.

'So *you* murdered Wally?' was what Gerard wanted to say, but just now, looking into those bright, astute eyes, he found his throat drying.

He was terrified.

Chapter Seven

The pie-shop which Joce entered was a little single-storey build-ing, with no upper chamber like so many of the other places in the street, but that didn't affect Nob Kyng, also known as Nob Bakere and Long Nob, ironically, on account of his short and rotund shape. He didn't care. People could call him anything they wished, he reckoned, so long as they left him alone to do what he was best at, which was cooking.

He and Cissy his wife had come here many years before, making the arduous journey from far in the north when they were both in their mid-twenties, intending to create a new life, and so far they had been very successful. Nob had found a little place in which to set up shop, and with his meagre store of pennies, had leased it from the Abbot. At the time there were only two other pie-shops in the town, and although Nob had to work hard, he soon built up a good clientèle and felt as though he had never lived anywhere but here in Tavistock.

Cissy was a jolly, constantly smiling woman who originally came from Devonshire, so returning to the county felt quite natural for her. Although people had looked askance at the pair of them when they first arrived, Tavistock was a friendly enough town, and in a short space of time the two felt entirely at home. Nob would remain in the back of his shop, sweating over his great cauldron, braziers and oven, while Cissy transferred the cooked pies from her trestle table to the hands of her customers. It was easy and lucrative. Never more so than during the five coinings each year. They had done well for themselves here, and their son and two daughters were testament to their happiness.

'Come on, wench! I need to get these off the fire,' Nob called.

A merry fellow with gleaming blue eyes and a ginger beard, he was dressed carelessly, in a short tunic that was marked by a thousand fatty explosions, while his arms were protected by his torn and frayed shirt. Through the rope that encircled his belly had been thrust a cloth to serve as an apron, 'and to protect me cods!' as he often happily declared.

Cissy called, 'All right, all right, you old fool. I won't be long,' and returned to chatting with Sara.

Nob could see her talking, but he let her continue. Cissy attracted women who needed advice like a candle-flame attracted moths. Yesterday it had been Emma, and now apparently Sara wanted help.

Sara was always seeking the friendship of one man or another now she was widowed, and Nob had no doubt that his wife was offering some friendly and probably long overdue advice on how to disentangle herself from her latest admirers. There was always more than one, which was no surprise when a man considered her long, lithe body, slim haunches, tiny waist and swelling breasts. And all that, as Nob told himself, under a fair halo of strawberry-golden hair, slanted, humorous green eyes and those succulent lips, bright and red and soft as rose petals. Bloody good-looking, she was.

Cissy was going to be with her for a while, from the look of things, so Nob pulled the pies from the heat himself and set them on a large wooden tray to cool, taking them to the trestle.

'Now then, lass,' he called out. 'Is it more talk about men or not?'

'Shut up, Nob. If you want to be useful, fetch us a jug of water,' Cissy snapped curtly.

Nothing loath, for at the side of the water barrel was a second one filled with ale, Nob hitched up his rope, sniffed, and walked out.

'*Nob!*'

He poked his head around the doorway. 'Yes, my little turtle dove?'

'Enough of your smatter. And don't empty the ale barrel while you're there.'

Grunting, he tugged at his rope belt again. Since Cissy had already turned her back to him, the effect was somewhat lost, but he cocked an eye at Sara. 'Eh, Sara? How comes you always have all these fellows drooling over you, eh? Tell 'em you're mine, girl, and they'll leave you alone. None of 'em would mix wi' me, lass.'

Sara gave him a weak smile, and he winked and grinned before walking out to his barrel, reflecting that she appeared more upset than she usually did when she was suffering from man trouble.

Sitting with his large pottery drinking horn in his hand, he wiped the sweat from his brow and upper lip, then the back of his hair, using his cloth. Draping it over his shoulders, he sat back.

It was a long day's work, cooking. Up before dawn to light the first of the fires, then mix the flour and water to make the paste, and leaving it to rest a while before rolling out the little pastry coffins and filling them. Some liked plain meats – beef, pork, chicken, lark or thrush; others liked thick gravies or jellies. He always had half a calf's head and offal boiling in one pot ready to make gravy, while the animal's hooves were simmering in another for the jelly. No matter, Nob liked his work, and with the profit of the coining last week, he and Cissy had made enough money to be able to survive through to the big coining in the late autumn. That would be the last for a while, and the money he saved from now, together with the profit from the next, would have to keep them going through the winter.

Not, he thought with a contented belch, that he had much to worry about. The wood for the winter was stored. Their last pair of pigs were ready to be slaughtered and salted down, and the chickens which had stopped producing enough eggs had already been marked off in his mind. There was enough for them this winter. Thank God, he thought, virtuously crossing himself and glancing upwards, the harvest was better this year. The last few summers had not been good. No one had starved, but the cost of food was still too high.

Finishing his ale, he filled a cup with water and, as an after-thought, picked up a second cup and pitcher of cheap wine. Poor Sara looked as though she could do with a drink.

But Sara was already gone when he re-entered his hall.

'Trouble again, with that girl?' he asked.

'When isn't she in trouble?' Cissy said gloomily.

Nob nodded, waiting.

There were no customers in the shop to listen at the moment, so Cissy continued, 'She thinks she's got a babby on the way.'

'How many will that be?'

'You know. There's Rannulf, Kate, Will, and now she reckons she's going to have another. Missed her time this month and last. She's beside herself, poor maid, because her man's been dead two years and more, so people will know, and then what will happen?'

'Who's the father?'

'Wouldn't say. Someone who isn't married, she said, but that's no matter, is it? She thought he was going to offer to marry her, she said, but after he bedded her one last time, he turfed her out and laughed at the idea. His promise was nothing and there were no witnesses. Three kids already, and now this one,' Cissy sighed. 'She's one of those who takes a compliment like it's got to be paid for. Tell her that her hair looks nice, and she'll ask whether you want her bed or your own.'

'Never asked me,' Nob said innocently.

'Nob, the day you notice someone's hair is the day I'll become a nun,' she said scathingly as she walked to wipe crumbs from the table in front of her.

Nob returned to his oven, taking a shovel and throwing fresh charcoal inside. He reached in with a long rake to pull the remaining old coals to join the fresh pile, and used his bellows to heat the lot to a healthy red glow. Once it had been in the oven's centre for a while, he would rake the coals aside again and thrust fresh pies on to the hot oven floor.

Sara was a pretty girl, but she had her brain firmly planted between her legs, in Nob's opinion. She'd been married to a young poulterer, but he'd died, falling into a well after a few too many ales one night, and she'd had nothing left, other than two of his children and a growing belly. With no money, she'd been forced to sell up and depend on the charitable instincts of her brother Ellis, her neighbours, and the parish. That was when she first started talking to Cissy.

Cissy was known by all the young women in the town to be possessed of a friendly and unjudgemental ear. Girls could, and did, walk miles to tell Cissy their woes, knowing that she wouldn't usually offer advice, but would listen understandingly and give them a hug if they needed it.

Nob knew that Sara had received many of Cissy's hugs. The trouble was, although she knew she was foolish to keep allowing men into her bed, she couldn't stop herself.

'She's being called harlot,' Cissy said thoughtfully, shaking her head and, a rare occurrence this, poured a goodly measure of wine into her cup, ignoring the water.

'She'll be all right, love,' Nob said.

'Don't be so foolish. Haven't you got pies to make?'

Nob grinned to himself. Cissy was on her usual fettle. He sauntered back to the ovens and began making fresh coffins, rolling out a little pastry, spooning his meats onto the middle, and putting the coffin's lid atop. A few minutes passed, and then he saw her hand deposit another hornful of ale at his side. He smiled his thanks. After last night, he didn't feel that he needed much ale; water would have been more to his taste, but he wouldn't turn down anything today, not after keeping her awake all night. That was the trouble with going out and drinking. The bladder couldn't cope as well as once it had, and then he farted and snored too, making Cissy sharp with him in the morning just when he needed a little comfort. And if he sought a little comfort when he got home from the tavern, he would soon learn that she wasn't in the mood.

The thought made him feel a little better, and he was just grabbing her experimentally about the waist when a man called out from the shop.

'I want a meat pie. You know my sort.'

Nob glanced over his shoulder. 'Morning, Master Joce.'

'Cook,' Joce said, nodding. It was the nearest the town's Receiver would come to acknowledging the baker.

Pulling his apron from his shoulder, Nob hooked it back under his rope belt and turned to see to his fire. He must pump with his bellows to make the coals glow again, and then he scraped them all away, to the left-hand side of the oven's opening, near the entrance, where their heat would rise and sear the top of the pies. Grabbing his long-handled peel, he loaded it with uncooked pies and thrust them far inside, reloading the peel again and again until he had all but filled the oven. Only then did he set the peel down and rub his hands.

'Thirsty work, that,' he observed.

'Will it be long?' Joce asked sharply.

'Sorry it's not ready yet, Master. It'll not be very long. Do you want an ale while you wait?'

'No, I shall sit outside. Call me when it is ready.'

Cissy was watching Joce Blakemoor as he stalked from the room.

'What's the matter with him today?' Nob said. 'He's usually more polite than that.'

'Anyone would think he had something on his mind,' Cissy said.

'Hah! I think he probably does.'

'Like what?'

'Oh, nothing.'

'Come on! You know something. What?'

'There was talk in the alehouse last night, that's all.'

'Oh! You men are worse gossips than all the women in the town. What did they say?'

'Joce is the town's Receiver, isn't he?'

'You know he is. So what?'

Nob scratched at a blister on his wrist. A globule of fat had hit him there two days ago and it itched like the devil. 'So he's the Receiver, and he has to take in all the fines and so on, keep the accounts and pay over what is owed to the Abbey at the end of his term. Well, what if his hand got a bit close to the purses, and a little dribbled into his fingers? And once a little dribbled into his greasy mitts, he chose to take a bit more. What then, eh?'

'Rubbish! Joce Blakemoor a thief? You've been drinking too much ale for breakfast.'

'You can sneer if you like, but I know what I've heard,' Nob said smugly.

'And what have you heard, Husband?'

'Joce hasn't submitted the accounts for the last couple of years. Why should he do that, unless he's fiddled them?'

'Just because he's bad with paperwork doesn't mean he's stolen from the Stannary, does it? Christ's Balls, you've got nothing better than moorstone between your ears, you!'

'Oh, really? Then why doesn't he just ask the Abbot for the loan of a decent clerk, then?'

'Nob, you great dollop, the man probably didn't want his friends and other burgesses thinking he was as stupid as you! What if the gossip starts? Soon he couldn't get credit with the traders in the town. He'd never be able to get food, would he?'

Nob was silent, staring at her with wide eyes. She returned his gaze with sudden sharpness, and both glanced at the door.

'I'll ask him for cash,' Cissy promised, folding her arms over her immense breasts like an alewife blocking her door after throwing an alcoholically rebellious customer into the street. Yet while she stood there, she wondered. There was one thing that Sara hadn't told her, and that was the name of the man who had got her pregnant. Usually if a woman was in her position, she would tell all if the man refused to support her, and Cissy had expected to have the man's identity shared with her, but Sara had remained coy. Perhaps she still hoped he would look after her and the child; not that he was likely to, Cissy told herself. These men never did. They gave their lovers as much soft soap as they thought the girls needed, and then they ran like the devil.

Next time she saw Sara she'd ask his name. Not from nosiness; she wanted to know if he was preparing to try it on with another girl. Cissy wouldn't have him doing that if she could stop him.

Simon had been woken a little after dawn by a small and nervous-looking servant. He hated waking in a strange bed, and he much preferred to come to life with the gentle insistence of his wife Meg than with his shoulder being prodded by a pimple-faced youth whose fore-teeth had fallen in or been punched out. Probably the latter, he thought uncharitably as the boy hurriedly withdrew.

There was no sweet wakening here. No gentle kisses or soft, teasing caresses from his wife. Instead, as he yawned and stretched, he was reminded that he was in a room filled with strangers. There was the reek of armpits, of unclean teeth and rotten gums, of feet that craved cleaning with a sandstone rather than with water, and the foul odour of sulphurous bowel gas.

'Someone needs a physician. He's got a dead rat up his arse,' he muttered as he climbed from his bed and searched for his clothes on the floor, scratching at an itch on his lower belly and wondering whether it was a flea. If so, it could have come from the bed – or from the man with whom he had shared it last night. Hugh would still be asleep in the stables, where he could keep an eye on the horses. Simon had sent him there before going to the Abbot when he saw how many were making use of the Abbot's hospitality, for there were never any guarantees that a mount was safe when there was a thief about, but it was an irritation that Simon must seek his own clothing rather than have it presented to him as usual.

He glanced down at the man who had been his bedmate. The fellow still slept easily, lying on his back, a calm smile on his roundish face, his mouth slightly open to display one chipped incisor. On his chin was a dark stubble, while his brown hair had an odd reddish tinge at his temples that gave him a slightly distinguished look. He didn't look or smell like the sort of man who would harbour fleas, Simon acknowledged. At his side of the bed was a richly-scabbarded but well-used riding sword of the sort that knights would wear on a journey, light enough not to be uncomfortable over a distance, but still strongly built and balanced as a good weapon.

The others in the room were a less distinguished group. Those who had visited for the coining were gone, and they had been replaced by men who, from the look of them, were of a lower general order: traders of all types, one young friar who had craved a bed for a night, two pewterers who had come for the coining and were enjoying a break before returning, and a man who had a rascally dark head of hair and a scar on his breast, together with the swarthy features of one who has spent many days in the sun and rain.

If any of them were a recruiting officer, Simon thought, it was surely him. He would take money from one man to avoid putting his name on a list, and would replace it with another fellow's name, no matter that the second was broken-winded, half-blind, a drunkard and had only one arm. Money mattered, nothing else, and an Arrayer, a recruiting officer, would be paid a bounty for all the men he took on irrespective of quality.

With this sombre thought, Simon walked out and sought the services of the barber. The rain had stopped only a short while before, and the air was scented with fresh, earthy odours. It smelled as if the whole town had been washed. As Simon avoided the puddles, the sun came out, with enough strength to give him the hope that the day would remain dry.

The gatekeeper told him that the barber whom the Abbey used was called Ellis; he could be found two streets away. Simon located him in a small room near a cookshop, just behind a brewery. A brazier of glowing coals made the room unpleasantly hot, and a pot of water was boiling on top, with towels dangling. A pair of long-handled wooden tongs stood in it, jumping as the water bubbled below the cloth, threatening to push the tongs out every few minutes, as though a wild animal was trapped beneath.

Ellis the barber was a wiry man with green eyes and almost black hair. His oval face, which lit up with an easy smile as he saw Simon, instilled a measure of confidence, but more crucial than that, to the Bailiff's mind, was the fact that monks were keen on their own comfort. A barber who nicked the abbatial chins was likely to find himself unemployed right speedily.

'Aha! My Lord, how can I help you?'

'I was told that you serve the needs of the Abbey?'

'That is right, my Lord. I usually get there a little later in the day, though.'

'Good. I need my beard shaved. Have you razors?'

'Master, I have everything,' the man declared, arms held wide. 'Whatever you need, I, Ellis of Dartmouth, have it. Please sit here on my stool.'

So saying, he pulled the three-legged seat out to the doorway where the light was better, and darted about gathering his tools. A long strip of leather he hung from a hook set into the doorway at his chest height, and he picked up a razor, testing the edge on his thumbnail. Satisfied, he whipped it up and down the strop while chattering.

'Yes, I am known as one of the fastest shavers in the whole of Wessex, my Lord. Anyone wants a clean chin, they ask for Ellis. No one else will do, not once they've been done by me.'

'Do you ever shut up long enough to shave a man, or perhaps you just keep wittering on until your victim passes out through boredom?' Simon growled.

'No one falls asleep on me, Master. Well, not unless I intend them to so I can pull out a hard tooth, anyway,' Ellis chuckled.

Simon grunted. Fortunately he hadn't needed the services of a tooth-puller for many a long year. The memory of the last time was unpleasant enough for him to wish to avoid it in future. Just the thought made him reach into the crevice with his tongue.

'Don't pull your face about like that, Master. I might cut off your nose!' Behind the banter there was a genuine note of caution and Simon quickly set his jaw again.

'Good, Master. Now just a little warm water . . .'

He pulled a towel from the pot of water set over his fire, and waved it, steaming, in the air until he frowningly judged it to be ready, and draped it over Simon's entire face.

Simon leaned back so that his shoulders were against the doorframe, inhaling the sweet scent of lavender which had been left infusing in the water with the towels. The heat was wonderful, making his beard tingle, and just when he thought he couldn't bear it any longer, Ellis whipped it away and threw it over his shoulder. While Simon had been covered, Ellis had shaved slices from a cake of soap and beaten them with more hot water and a brush of badger fur, and now he daubed Simon's face with the light, hot foam. Satisfied, he stood back, swept his razor up and down the strop once more, 'For luck,' he smiled encouragingly, and held it up vertically. 'You haven't any enemies, Master, who'd pay me to slip, have you?' Seeing Simon's expression, he laughed aloud, and before the Bailiff could stand, he leaned forward, a thumb pulling Simon's cheek taut, and drew the blade in one long, slow sweep from his ear to his jaw.

Simon was glad that the man was steady while he performed his duty. So often a barber could be found with a morning's shake after too many ales the night before, but this one had an easy confidence.

'So, Master Bailiff, are you to be leaving us soon now the coining is done?'

'I have other duties,' Simon said as Ellis stropped the blade again. 'Like finding the murderer of the miner.'

'That bastard Walwynus?' Ellis stopped and stared, then shrugged as he returned to Simon's face. 'He won't be missed.'

'Why?' Simon asked, grasping Ellis's hand to halt him.

'He got my sister pregnant, that's why. Probably told her she'd be his wife or something. You know how it is. And you know how often a man will renege on his word when he learns there's a child to support.'

'She told you this?'

'No one has told me. I saw them, and when I spoke to him later, he denied it. Lying git! I saw them, the day of the coining. She reached up to kiss him. Won't be long before people see she's carrying his bastard. And then,' Ellis continued, gently withdrawing his hand from Simon's, 'her shame will be complete.'

'You realise that might have been the day he died?' Simon said.

'Well, not only I saw him that day.'

'What does that mean? Did you see someone else with him?'

'No – he had been battered. Someone had blacked his eye and split his lip. He'd been in a fight that morning.'

Simon was quiet as Ellis finished. Once the first shave was complete, the barber stood back and surveyed his work, then drew another towel from the fire and draped this too over Simon's face while he restropped his razor. Before long Simon had been shaved a second time, and a third hot towel was used to clean away the excess soap. Where there were spots of blood from irregularities in his flesh, the barber used ice-cold water to pat them clean, and the chill stopped the bleeding in moments. Any shave would always cause a little bleeding as the blade cut off occasional pimples and bumps, but Simon had felt none, the blade was so sharp.

'An excellent shave,' he said, passing the man a few coins.

'Master, I look forward to shaving you again,' Ellis said, glancing into his hand.

'That is fine, but one thing: did you hear that this miner had ravished other women?'

'No. I wouldn't have thought he was the sort. Well,' Ellis gave a harsh bark of laughter, 'not being such an ugly shit!'

'You said you spoke to him after you saw him with your sister. Where was that?'

'I saw him on the way to his house, the following morning. He denied anything to do with her, the lying bastard!'

'You sound like a man who would be prepared to see him suffer for what he'd done.'

'Whoever killed him, I'd shake his hand,' Ellis said.

'There was a morning star at his side. That was what killed him,' Simon said.

Ellis winced. 'A bad way to die.'

'You sometimes have to keep your patients still, don't you?' Simon said.

Ellis laughed drily. 'You think this killed him?' he asked, taking up his lead-filled sleep maker. 'I don't think so.'

Simon took it and weighed it. It was heavy enough to kill, but it was more practical as a means of knocking a man down before finishing him off. Yet at Ellis's belt was a knife. If he struck a man down, surely he'd stab his victim, not break open his head?

'Would you have killed him if he refused to support your sister?'

Ellis gazed at him levelly. He could have lied, but he saw no point. 'There was no way he could afford to support my sister. She's widowed, and I have to support her and the children. Another child means more for me to pay, not him. But if you mean, did I kill him, well, no, I didn't. But if I'd had an opportunity, I'd have paid someone else to do so.' He looked at the coins in his hand again, and thrust them into his purse.

Simon left the barber's room in a thoughtful mood. 'If I were you, Master Ellis, I would keep my mouth shut,' he murmured to himself. 'You are the most vocal suspect I have ever spoken to.'

He would have to see what others thought, but Ellis was certainly a convincing enemy of the dead miner.

Chapter Eight

It was only a short while after dawn and Sir Baldwin de Furnshill was relaxing before his fire when the clattering of hooves outside announced that he had visitors. He listened attentively as he strode across the floor to where his sword hung on the wall.

This was not peace. War had threatened for years now, for with a feeble King and over-powerful and ambitious advisers, the realm was like a keg of dried tinder standing under a brazier. It was only a matter of time before a stray spark must fall and ignite the whole kingdom. That was how Baldwin felt, and although he knew that his little manor near to Cadbury was safer than many parts of the country, it didn't make him feel any more secure. When armies began to march, there was no safety for anyone, great or small, city-dweller or countryman.

As he threw his sword belt over his shoulder, gripping the hilt, Jeanne, his wife, appeared in the doorway which led up to the solar. He shook his head once, firmly, and jerked it upwards. She was anxious, but she could see his concern. Quietly she pulled the door closed behind her and slipped the bar across.

It wasn't easy, but she knew that her man needed to be sure that she was safe in her rooms before he could concentrate on fighting, and she had no wish to be a distraction. She was only glad that he had insisted upon installing this sturdy metal bar earlier in the year. It made her feel more secure, knowing that no trail-bastons could simply push it open. She walked back upstairs to the bedchamber, where her maid sat rocking her baby.

Petronilla looked up with a smile, but Jeanne didn't notice. She was listening intently.

Downstairs, Baldwin walked through the screens passage and out to the back door. He was already confident that there was no threat out here. Experience told him that if felons had arrived and intended to plunder his home, he would have heard more shouting by now. Once outside, he saw his servant Edgar holding the reins of a shortish man's horse. He bellowed a greeting and climbed down as he saw Baldwin.

Coroner Roger de Gidleigh was a shorter man than Baldwin, but he had a barrel chest and shoulders that spoke of immense strength. He also had a large and growing belly from the quantity of ale he drank, which often put people off their guard, making them take him for a happy-go-lucky soul, the sort of man who would always welcome a stranger with a cheerful demand that they might share a jug of ale – but then the stranger might notice the shrewd, glittering eyes and realise that the only reason for the Coroner to be so interested and conversational was because he held a suspicion against his flattered babbler.

'Coroner! Thanks to God!' Baldwin cried with real delight.

'Sir Baldwin! Greetings and Godspeed, my friend. How are you? And Lady Jeanne?'

'Well, I thank you.'

'So you thought it might be outlaws?' Coroner Roger de Gidleigh said, nodding towards Baldwin's sword as the two entered the hall.

'It is best never to take risks. The rumours of war are as vigorous here as anywhere in the kingdom.'

'True enough,' the big man said, walking to a bench at the table on Baldwin's dais. 'We live in dangerous times.'

Baldwin rehanged his sword, then rapped sharply on the door to his solar, calling to his wife. 'I hear that anyone who wishes to talk to the King must pay the Despenser whelp.'

'You should be careful to whom you speak like that, Sir Baldwin. Some could report your words and accuse you of treachery to the Crown.'

Baldwin smiled. The Coroner was a friend, and he took the warning in the way it was intended. 'I know that, Roger. But while Hugh Despenser the Younger is Chamberlain of the Household, no man can speak to the King without his approval, nor without paying. It is not enough that Hugh Despenser the Elder has been made an Earl, nor that his son has acquired the Clare inheritance – they will seek ever more money and lands to enrich their lives.'

Coroner Roger took the jug of wine which Baldwin proffered. 'I dare say that may be true enough, but there is nothing we can do about it. It is human nature to enrich oneself, and that means depriving someone else.'

'The priests would argue that case, my friend,' Baldwin chuckled, but with little humour. 'They tell us that God's bounty should be shared, that no man should suffer or starve from want of money when his neighbour has enough to support both.'

'True. But the Church isn't exempt from making money. And although they talk about men sharing their wealth, I don't notice the Bishop in Exeter selling his house in order to give the money to the needy.'

'Coroner!' Baldwin exclaimed in mock horror. 'My friend, you have become infected with my own prejudices!'

At that moment Jeanne re-entered the room, and graciously welcomed their guest. Baldwin smiled and took his seat in his chair as his wife spoke gently and courteously, putting the traveller at his ease, soothing his tired muscles and bones with her cheerful chatter. Before long Sir Roger was smiling, and soon after he was laughing, and Baldwin allowed himself to relax.

It was not easy. Baldwin had been a Poor Fellow Soldier of Christ and the Temple of Solomon, a Knight Templar, the Order of warrior monks which had been respected and revered by all those who were most religious. Pilgrims sought out Templars for protection wherever they travelled in the Christian world, and Kings were proud to call them friends.

Yet the greed of the French King and the Pope were sufficient to destroy the noble Order. They had hatched a plot between them, Baldwin believed, in order to share the fabulous wealth of the Order. The fact that their greed must result in the death of thousands of God's most loyal warriors, that the future reconquest of the Kingdom of Jerusalem must be jeopardised, was nothing to them. They destroyed for their own benefit, and the Knights were tortured and burned to death.

It had given Baldwin an abiding hatred of political power and, most crucial, of any form of bigotry or injustice, and it was a mix of all of these that made him detest the Despenser family. Others hated them for their greed, while some loathed Hugh the Younger because of the rumours of his homosexual relations with the King. That was why, the stories said, the Queen was kept away from the King. Because he had no interest in her.

That was one aspect of the King's life which did not concern Baldwin. He had lived for a while in the East, and there he had learned tolerance for the sexual activities of others. No, although his wife might despise such unmanly behaviour, he was unbothered. Much more worrying to him was the sheer greed of the Despensers. The family was pillaging the realm every bit as rapaciously as the appalling Piers Gaveston had done only a few years before. Gaveston's acquisitions had only been halted when he was captured and beheaded, Baldwin recalled. He wondered whether a similar fate might await the Despensers. Somehow he doubted it. They had effectively destroyed all the powerful factions which sought to harm them. There were few left in the country who could challenge them now.

'So what do you think, Sir Baldwin?' Coroner Roger asked.

Baldwin realised that his mind had wandered so far from his guest as to be in a different county – or even country. He fitted a serious, intent expression to his face and turned to Jeanne, who was now sitting next to the Coroner. 'What do *you* think, my love?'

'I am sure I would not stop you,' she said sweetly, recognising his dilemma from his demeanour. 'I leave it up to you, Husband.'

'Thank you,' he said with a fixed smile.

'It would please me to have your company,' the Coroner said. 'And of course, the Abbot was very insistent. He has some regard for your skills, I think.'

'It is good that someone does,' Jeanne said.

Baldwin cast her a glance. She was shaking with suppressed laughter. 'Very well,' he said.

'Good, then we can ride for the moors this afternoon,' Coroner Roger said. 'For now, may I rest my limbs and head on a bench somewhere? I had to rise early to get here, and a short doze would do me wonderful good.'

'Of course,' said Jeanne. 'And where is this body you need to investigate, Coroner?'

'Out in the middle of Dartmoor! I am growing heartily sick of the wet, miserable, bog-filled place. It seems as though I must travel there every couple of months to view a corpse.'

At his words, Baldwin felt his stomach lurch, and when he looked to his wife, he saw her face had paled too.

He had paid well for a mere barber, but Simon was pleased. He felt clean and refreshed by the shave, and had learned a little more about Walwynus, or so he thought. No one else had mentioned that Wally was a man for the girls. It certainly sounded odd, though. Just as Ellis had somewhat cruelly said, most men wouldn't think a man like Wally could have struck a chord with women.

Still, for the first time since he had arrived at the Abbey and realised that he had left the hammer behind, Simon felt clean and content. The removal of the stubble at his chin had given him a new confidence, and he actually felt capable of finding Walwynus' murderer.

Walking along the lane towards the Abbey, Simon increased his stride. There was much to do today. He would tell Hugh to remain in the Abbey for the forseeable future, exercise their horses and see to their saddles. It was time they were both oiled and serviced. There were plenty of jobs for him to be getting on with, and there was no point in his joining Simon to watch a Commission of Array. Hugh might as well be doing something useful.

He was considering the idea of sitting all day with an Arrayer, a prospect which didn't appeal, when he almost walked into a man who erupted from a cookshop.

'Mind your step, you arse!'

Simon smiled grimly at the harsh greeting. 'Receiver. How very pleasant to see you. I note you are in a hurry, as usual.'

'Oh, it's you, Bailiff,' Joce said with no relaxation of his glower. 'You should be careful where you walk.'

'Have you heard of the murdered man?' Simon said, ignoring his rudeness.

'Who? I know nothing of this.'

'Walwynus, a miner. He's been beaten to death. Do you know of anyone who could have done that?'

Joce chewed steadily on his pie. This needed thought. It would be good to point the Bailiff in the direction of someone else, but Joce wasn't aware of any credible enemy. 'Could he have died in a drunken attack? That's what happened to his friend, I believe. Two years or so ago, Wally had a fight with his companion – a fellow called Martyn – and the other died. Maybe this Martyn had another friend or relative who was horrified to learn that Wally was not hanged?'

Simon nodded. Joce's voice, even when he spoke rather than blustering, had a grating quality. It was not like those who had lived in Devon all their lives. Joce had left the shire for some years to earn money as a merchant, and he had been successful, by all accounts. 'Did you know this Wally?'

'I saw him occasionally. No more than that. He was always at the coinings, but I doubt I exchanged more than three words with him in the last two years. He was not of my standing in the world, Bailiff.'

'You were at the coining all day last Thursday, weren't you?'

'Yes, of course – you saw me yourself, I am sure. And then I went to the inn, before returning home. Why, do you suspect me?'

'What were you doing on Friday?'

'I was here most of the day, in town. I had the accounts to write up and check on Friday morning, and then I walked about the streets.'

'Did you see anyone hurrying back from the moors, or acting oddly?'

'Not really. I was closeted indoors most of the time. Sorry, Bailiff. I can't help you much,' Joce said with a leering grin. 'You'll just have to go and interrogate some other poor bastard!'

Simon watched him go with a shrug and sense of failing to meet Baldwin's level of razor-sharp questioning. There was nothing more to be learned by standing in the street staring after him, though, and he bent his steps to the Abbey again.

By the time he had finished his meagre breakfast of bread and thin ale, he had come to the conclusion that he didn't like the duty imposed upon him by the Abbot. The thought that he should support and assist some fool of a recruiter did not appeal to him at all.

The arrival of other guests to enjoy the Abbot's hospitality reminded Simon that someone among them was an Arrayer, and he rose hastily and left the room. Outside in the cool air, he breathed in the freshness that comes only after a good downpour. It must have rained heavily overnight, he thought. He searched about for a place to sit, and finally picked upon the wall of the cemetery.

It was while he remained sitting there that he saw the Abbot's Steward and groaned to himself when he realised that the man was making his way towards him.

'Bailiff? I am Augerus, the Abbot's . . .'

'I know. What are you after?'

Augerus smiled thinly. Simon's irritability early in the morning was known in the Abbey, for he had stayed here often enough on his Stannary duties, but Augerus was a proud man who was well aware of his own importance. 'My Lord Abbot has asked me to introduce you to the Arrayer, Bailiff. But perhaps you are feeling a little tired still?'

Simon eyed the man. Augerus' expression told Simon that confessing to tiredness would be pointless. 'I apologise for being short, friend. It was just that my mind was on the murdered tin-miner.'

'Walwynus? I suppose you have heard the rumours about the travellers? Everyone remembers the tale of Milbrosa.'

Simon listened as Augerus led the way to the Abbot's lodgings. 'Some of the monks here believe in that sort of story?'

'Oh yes. Some are quite superstitious. Not me, I have to say. I believe that if God truly wanted to give mankind a message, He would pick a means which would be more easily understood. Surely He appreciates how often His creation manages to mis-understand Him, don't you think?'

'I haven't really thought about it,' Simon admitted. 'I find it's hard enough trying to understand what all the men on the moors are doing without worrying myself about His plans.'

The Steward tilted his head as though acknowledging that Simon was probably better suited to the world of men than to interpreting the will of God. He opened a door on the right of the passageway and stood back to let Simon inside.

'Master Bailiff, this is Sir Tristram de Cokkesmoor.'

Simon held out his hand and forced a smile to his face as he recognised the man with whom he had last night shared his bed.

Hal Raddych heaved himself to his feet, rubbing at his eyes and hawking loudly. Another miner should arrive today, to take his place guarding the corpse, and he squinted in the direction of the camp, searching for a figure that could be heading towards him, but there was nothing.

He swung his arms and yawned. Holding a finger first to one nostril, then to the other, he blew his nose clean, and wiped it on his sleeve. Thirsty, he smacked his lips. A stream lay a few yards away and he glanced briefly at the corpse before strolling around the hillside to the water.

A miner all his life, Hal was impervious to the cold. His hands and face might have been carved from an ancient oaken beam, for all the effect that the elements had upon them, and he kneeled at the side of the stream and scooped handfuls of icy moor water over his head and rubbed it into his face. It was his routine, summer or winter.

His ablutions complete, he sucked up a mouthful from his cupped hands, rolling it around his tongue like a spiced wine. Not as brackish as the water nearer his own workings, he decided. A fresher, cleaner taste.

Once, when he was younger, he had asserted in an alehouse that he could tell where he was in moments, purely by drinking the water. It was a proud boast, and a foolish one, which earned him a swift pasting from an older miner who resented his cockiness, but he still believed it to be true. All the streams and pools about the moor had their own distinct flavours. This, now, this was more like a pure stream with a hint of meat in it. His own was peatier and darker; any clothes put into that would invariably come out brown, no matter what their original colour. The water was filled with the stain of peat.

Rising, he pulled his hat back over his brow and stared about him. He was tired, after standing awake much of the night at Wally's side, and the bright morning sun made him wince, peering with his good eye like a sailor searching for a ship.

He walked back to the body, noting the smell of decay and the way the belly had expanded. If he knew anything, and he had seen plenty of dead men, this body would soon be ready to explode.

He left Wally's remains and went to the bush with the blood-stain, picking up the timber and looking at the scratches once more. They were his mark; the timber was from his mine. Any miner would recognise it as his. Some bastard had stolen it from him, hammered the nails into it, and used it to kill Wally. Who could it be, though? Hamelin? Christ's Cods! The man was a *friend*. But someone else could have wanted to frame Hal or Hamelin. Who? Tapping the timber against the palm of his hand, he let his eyes move to the mire ahead, to the smoke beyond that showed where another group of miners worked.

They were probably getting their cooking fires ready to heat a flat pancake of oats with maybe a little meat from a bird or a rabbit, whatever they could catch out here. And one of them, perhaps, had stolen a piece of his wood, knowing that he marked every balk against theft, and used it to murder Wally so that he, Hal, would be implicated. That thought was not a comfortable one.

Hal was one of the more successful miners. He had found tin in places where others saw nothing, and some said he possessed a magic, that a witch or demon had granted him the ability to find ore where others couldn't, but he asserted it was simply his organised way of looking. Others were slapdash, digging one hole, deciding there was nothing there, and moving on to a fresh site. Hal wouldn't do that. He dug one pit, then a line of others, running across the base of a hill where he thought a seam might lie. Sometimes he was right; often he was wrong – but the men who created malicious rumours about him ignored his failures.

Some men had grown to hate him, he knew. They were either scared of him, thinking that he was touched by the devil, or they were jealous, envying his success. He didn't care which type of man had used his wood to kill Wally. Whoever it was, Hal had other things to concern him, like what to do now?

His eyes dropped from the smoke and a small smile touched

his lips. He walked down the hillside to the green, shimmering land beneath. There was a pile of stones, as there were in so many parts of Dartmoor; this one was named Childe's Tomb. He walked past it and on, careful now, stepping cautiously over the soft grasses and rushes. When he found a boot sinking deep into a patch of mud, he stopped. He prodded the grass in front of him with the timber, and saw the gentle rippling that spread across it.

It was a mire. One of those evil spots where the water built up beneath a thin layer of soil and plants. A man or beast who put his foot on to that would sink through the grasses and drown in the thick, peaty waters beneath. There was no possibility of rescue, so far away from civilisation.

Hal studied his timber once more, and then pushed the end of it into the ground before him. It sank quickly, and when it had disappeared, the grasses and reeds floated back over the hole as though nothing had ever disturbed the smooth grassy surface.

Chapter Nine

There was no obvious justification in posting a sentry to watch Hal, but Rudolf was a practical man, and when he saw strangers about, he wanted to know that they weren't the precursors of an attack.

Rudolf was in his little tent when Welf, his son, returned. He was a sturdy young fellow, with broad shoulders and thick dark hair. He was trying to grow a beard, and the other men ribbed him about the fine fluff that was all he could manage, but never Rudolf. He believed that a man was no less a man just for the lack of hair on his face. A man was measured by other things, like physical strength and courage.

'*So? Was macht er*? What is he doing?'

Welf sat by the brazier that glowed with coals and held his hand to the warmth before answering in German. 'He stayed there all day with the body. Last night he settled down and remained near it. I went closer and watched until almost dawn. He was asleep by then, and that was when I returned to the cross and waited to see what happened when he awoke. He washed, then went down to the bog and threw in the morning star.'

'And now someone else is up there on the hill?'

'Yes. Brother Peter the Almoner from the Abbey.'

'Good. You have done well. Eat and sleep.' Rudolf sat a while longer, frowning at the fire.

They had travelled all the way here from an urge to see what the world was like. Rudolf was a pewterer by trade, and in his home lands in the mountains his work was prized, even among the nobles. Glancing about him, he couldn't help but curl his lip. This land was ever wet and depressing. There were bogs all over the moors, and the mountains were mere bumps in the soil, not at all like the crags among which his home nestled. There, men had to avoid the high passes, because they were populated by dragons and other monsters. No, people lived in the broad valleys and farmed peacefully.

Or they had. Rudolf's life had suddenly changed for ever at Morgarten. Until then, he had lived comfortably in his native Canton of Schwyz, but the Swiss lands were growing more important. When the Saint-Gotthard Pass opened, there was an easier, shorter road between parts of the Holy Roman Empire, from Italy to the Rhine, and the murderous Leopold of Habsburg decided to enforce his authority among the peasants who lived there.

It was a farce. Rudolf was no coward; he wanted peace, for men don't buy plate and pewter in wartime, they hoard their money and seek to store foods, but Rudolf felt he had a simple choice, make pewter or fight: sit back like a coward or resist and hope for freedom for his sons. It was an easy decision. If Leopold's armies won through to the towns, they would slaughter everyone. He chose to fight, to protect his lands and his people, and he was there at Morgarten when Leopold's army was crushed.

But Rudolf was not convinced that the free Cantons could survive. The Habsburgs were wealthy nobles, they could afford to buy up armies and crush resistance from tiny states like Schwyz, and Rudolf was not prepared to risk the life of his son and his wife. Instead he brought them out of the country, and worked his way from one town to another until they crossed over from France to England. He went to London, where he heard of the tin mines of Devon, and he decided to come here and see for himself where the English stocks of tin came from.

His household was small. Himself, his wife Anna, Welf, and a few others. Ten men all told, and seven women. Together they had crossed Europe, and here, Rudolf felt, they had hit the bottom. In his home, the sun always shone in the summer, while here it was always raining, or about to begin. Homesick, he longed for the meadows and pastures of his own land, high in the free mountains.

But he was here and while he was here, he had a duty to protect his household. He stood and pulled a strong leather jack over his shirt, then made his way along the path Welf had used.

From here all was fine grassland. A few rocks were dotted here and there, but it was still good land for sheep or cattle, with scarcely a stunted tree showing itself. However, Rudolf knew that there was one advantage to land like this, and that was that an enemy would find it very difficult to conceal himself. In the same way, it was not easy to move without being seen. That was why, as he reached the first of the crosses, he began to bend his back, his eyes staring ahead, making sure he couldn't see the man waiting at the side of the corpse.

There was another cross at the summit of the hill, to which he walked bent almost double, but when he reached it, he couldn't help but stare at it once more. The bloody imprint was still there, a foul mark that almost seemed to tempt the devil. Not that the devil would need tempting to come to a place like this, Rudolf thought. It was his own hell, this land. With a shudder that was more a convulsion of his entire body than a shiver down his back, Rudolf averted his gaze and continued. At Morgarten, he had hurled rocks and tree-trunks with his comrades at the Duke's knights below them, pitching the screaming, petrified men and horses into the waters of the Ägerisee, and he had not flinched. Yet that smudge of a dead man's blood made him feel sickened. Perhaps because the fool of a miner hadn't stood a chance. Rudolf had been angry, and now the man was dead.

The pewterer had work to do. He was past the stone cross, and crawled the few yards over the other side, peering ahead with a frown. 'Where is he, Henry?'

'There. He's sitting on that rock.'

Rudolf gave a short chuckle. 'I think your young eyes are better than my old ones. I can see nothing.'

'Can you see the other man?'

'Which other?' Rudolf demanded, his fears about an ambush reawakened.

'There. A man coming from the north. He looks short and heavy. Like a miner.'

Rudolf breathed a quiet sigh. 'Then he must be coming to relieve the first man, just as you relieved Welf. Has he done nothing else?'

'Not since I got here.'

Rudolf stared in the direction of the man, towards the body. 'Well, wait here for now, but I shall send someone to fetch you soon.'

'We are leaving?'

'You think we would do best to stay here?' Rudolf asked.

'It was him who tried to attack you, Rudolf. Self-defence is no crime.'

Rudolf spat, turning to stare back at the cross. 'The cretin tried to stab me and I put a stop to it. Yes, but the first time, in the alley, when I took his pewter – how many people saw us? Be ready to pack. I won't wait for them to come with a posse.'

Unbidden, the memory of a tall, cowled man in a habit sprang into his mind. 'When they want to find the murderer, they can seek another, not me!'

After giving pensions to the lepers, Peter the Almoner and Gerard made their way back through the streets of Tavistock to the Abbey. Once there, Peter ushered Gerard inside, but he himself walked back along the main street towards the town's shops.

His jaw hurt. It often did when the weather looked like changing. The day before yesterday it had been a constant ache, as though all the teeth which should have been there were simultaneously erupting with rottenness. He had to set his hand at his jaw and hold it. The action provided little relief, but it was comforting in the same way that a woman's caress could give some solace from the worst of a wound's pain.

The pain was not the sharp, stabbing agony that he had once known, in the weeks after the attack. No, it was just a constant part of him, a never-failing anguish, or at best a dull ache. It was worst at night, of course. When he wanted to turn his mind to pleasing, soporific thoughts, when he wanted to drift away, that was when the wound seemed to strike at him with renewed force. That was when he wept silently, so as not to waken his neighbour in the *dorter* – when he felt the hideous emptiness that was his life now. No love, only horror or curiosity.

It was that which made him turn his mind and abilities to other things. Such as the dead man, Walwynus. Still, Wally had enjoyed his last few hours. Peter had seen him in the town, somehow throwing his money about, although everyone had thought that he hadn't more than a few pennies altogether. Ale, wine and women. That was always the way of miners when they had a bit of luck, and Wally had obviously found some cash from somewhere, because Peter had seen him indulging in the drinking, even if he hadn't managed to find a woman to help him.

Peter entered the tavern and took his seat near the fireplace. A thin smoke rose from the logs on the hearth, and he sat behind it, waiting patiently, his head turned a little, which kept his wound to the wall.

'Brother? You want wine or ale?'

'Friend, I think I need a good pot of cider.'

The host left to fetch a jug and Peter watched as he went to one of the barrels and opened the tap. As soon as the greenish golden liquid was poured, he returned to Peter and passed the jug to him.

Sniffing it, Peter could discern the odour of sourness and sweetness that he found so addictive. He slurped as he drank, because of the failed muscles on the right side of his mouth, but when the publican made as though to move away, Peter held up his hand and pulled the pot from his mouth. 'Do you remember Wally being in here on the coining?'

'Yes, poor old git. Dead, i'n't he? Some thieving bugger killed him up there.'

'I saw him in here on that day, and he had plenty of pennies to throw about. Did he say where he got so much money?'

'Di'n't tell me anything. Might have told Sue, though,' the host said. He glanced about the room, calling over a girl with a loosened tunic. She walked across to them, eyeing Peter doubtfully, her hands going to her tunic's laces automatically, and Mine Host stopped her hurriedly. 'No, the Brother here just wants to ask you a bunch of questions, Susan.'

She joined Peter, sitting at his side and gently pulling the jug towards her. 'Well?'

'Did you know Walwynus – the miner?' he asked, allowing her to tilt the jug to her mouth.

She drank, nodded, and drank again. 'Yes,' she said at last. 'He was often up here and trying it on. Always said he had plenty of cash, that he'd buy me for a night. Never did, of course. Bastard just wanted to bury his tarse and didn't give a shit about paying. He used to stop me and the other girls in the roadway. Didn't even wait to get us in here. We get fondled often enough in here while we're serving, but it's different out in the street. We could get in trouble with the Port Reeve if he thought we were doing business outside. Not that he'd mind usually. He likes us, the Port Reeve does. Nice man.' She licked her mouth slowly, a faint smile pulling at her mouth. 'He likes me. Do you like me, Brother?'

'Very much, my daughter,' he said. And in truth he did. He often considered that the failed people were those among whom he was better suited to live. This girl was pretty, with her oval face and striking dark hair. Her slanted brown eyes were strangely bright in the firelight, her lips tempting, her breasts were small and high, as he liked them, while beneath her thin tunic he could see that she had long, fine legs.

She leaned against him softly, so that he could feel her thin figure. 'Would you like me, then?'

He felt the old stirring in his loins. It was many years since he had known a woman's comfort. That was before he had entered the Priory at Tynemouth, before he had been butchered, before *she* had been killed. This girl was much like her.

'Not now, Daughter,' he said, but without conviction.

She grinned and sat up straight, her hands going to her long hair, teasing him now. 'Then what do you want?'

'You say Wally never had any money?'

'That's right. Only pennies until the coining. He had some then, last Thursday.' She shook her head. 'If I'd known, I'd have made him more welcome, but I just thought he was lying again. And then I saw him throwing money around like a merchant. Too late by then,' she added regretfully.

Peter frowned to himself. When he had spoken to Wally on the morning of the coining, Wally had nothing on him, or so he had said. Yet after the coining he had money, if this girl was to be believed. So he had received it *after* seeing Peter, but before coming to this tavern. Perhaps during the coining itself.

'Do you know where Wally got his money from?' he asked.

'He took one of the other girls, and told her he'd found a new source of tin. Somewhere out on the moors, I suppose.'

Peter nodded. He patted her thigh, feeling the tingling in his palm at the firm flesh. 'Thank you, child. You have helped me. Now you must remember this. The Coroner will hold his inquest, and you must tell him what you have told me. It might be very important.'

'All right, Brother. What now?'

He stared at her blankly, and then he gave a weak smile when he realised her meaning. She winked cheekily at him as he left the room, but for his part, all he felt was an all-encompassing despair.

Leaving the tavern, he stood outside breathing heavily. It would have been all too easy to accept her offer. She was a cheeky, bright, pretty little thing – just the sort of girl he had so often longed for and, every so often, the sort of girl whom he had bedded.

He was lonely, sad, and had that curious emptiness, almost a hunger for companionship, that afflicted him occasionally. It was a desire, almost a lust, for simple pleasures and the conversation of generous-hearted, ordinary people.

There was a man he knew who could help him. Looking up the way, he could see Nob and Cissy's cookshop, and he turned up the lane towards it.

'Hello, Nob,' he said, but then he stopped with a slight frown on his face. 'Ah, Gerard. What are you doing here?'

Hearing his voice, Gerard dropped his pie with a startled cry.

'Master Bailiff, I understand the good Abbot has spoken to you already?'

Simon nodded. 'Yes, Sir Tristram. He tells me you are to collect men for the Host?'

'Quite so. There is a need for many fighting men now that the King has chosen to attack Scotland again and punish the Scots for their constant attacks over the borders and into English territory. They cannot get away with it.'

'Oh. So we won't see all our men die, like at Bannockburn.'

Sir Tristram's face hardened a moment. His eyes were like chips of diamond, Simon thought. They reflected light in the same way that a cut stone will shine from its facets under a light. Hard and uncompromising, but that did not necessarily make him an unpleasant man. Simon decided he would give Sir Tristram the benefit of the doubt.

'I think you should be careful who hears you making comments like that, Master Bailiff.'

He sat very neatly, a trim man with narrow shoulders and a slim waist. His robes were well fitted and richly embroidered, with plenty of fur at his neck and wrists. He had his belt on, with his sword, but at his right hip was a dagger with a magnificent enamelled pommel that looked expensive, like a gewgaw that was meant for show. That it was a working weapon was shown to Simon's quick eye by the roughened leather of the grip. It had been worn smooth and dark in places, where the knight had gripped it, presumably in battle.

'My friend, it was merely a pleasantry,' Simon said.

'Some comments like that could be thought dangerous. An uncharitable man might think they were seditious, even: tending to incite rebellion. Never a good idea.'

'I would never seek to spread sedition,' Simon protested. His chest felt constrained, as though he was already being shown the gibbet on which his body would hang. The charitable thoughts he had harboured burst into tiny flames and disappeared. This was one of those stuffy, self-important fools, he decided.

'I am glad to hear it,' said the knight. 'Come, shall we begin again? I am sorry if I sound harsh, but I have a lot of work to get through. There are so many vills down in this area, and as Arrayer I have to try to get to all of them. Tell me, are all the roads down this way as bad as the one on the way here?'

'Which way did you come?'

'From the north. I passed through Oakhampton, then came southwards. The men at Exeter strongly advised me to avoid the moors without a guide. There are mires there?'

'Many.' And I hope you fall into one, Simon added silently. 'They move each year. You need a man who knows his way there, it's true.'

'But the roads! It took me twice as long as I had expected.'

Simon shrugged. 'The weather has been inclement, and the roads aren't paved. At least you took one of the better ones on the way here. It follows the river in the valley. That is much better than others, like the roads between Oakhampton and Crediton. They are considerably worse.'

'My God!' Sir Tristram muttered, then gave Simon a wan smile. 'Well, at least I understand you are a good guide to much of the country about here. And the moors, of course.'

'I know the moors well enough,' Simon agreed, taking a goblet of wine from the Steward, who returned at this moment with a tray on which stood a heavy jug and two goblets. 'But that won't help you.'

'There are men there, aren't there? Strong, hardy fellows who dig and mine?'

'Oh yes, hundreds. But you can't have any of them. They are all exempt, by the King's own command. While they mine his tin, they are secure.'

'Ah. I see.'

'But there are many others about here. Strong enough, I'd guess, for your Host.'

'Good. Then perhaps we can begin today. I should like to see the good Abbot's vills about this town with a view to winning the strongest and fittest men for the King's service.'

'How many do you need?'

'As many as possible. You know how the Host is organised? I take twenty men and inspect and list them and put them under a *vintenar*; for every hundred, there is a *centenar* in charge, usually a cavalry man of some sort. When they are collected, they will march off to the King's army.' He paused and stared down at his hands. 'It will be a long, weary walk up to Scotland.'

'I thought that the King recruited his men from nearer to the border?'

'Yes, but the trouble is, there are so few. Since the famine and the murrains, the Scottish borders are denuded of men, and the ones remaining are scurvy-ridden and feeble. We need hale, competent fellows, like the farmers you have down here. It looks as though the famine didn't affect people this far west and south.'

'We lost many people,' Simon said shortly, thinking of those dreadful times. 'God forbid that we should have another famine of that ferocity.'

'Very good. So, are you ready to leave now?'

'Yes, of course,' Simon said. 'I shall ask for my horse to be prepared.'

'Ask for mine as well, would you? I shall just fetch my bag.'

Simon nodded ungraciously as he walked from the room. Outside he stood and took a deep breath. Arrayers were generally corrupt as hell, in his opinion. Maybe this one wasn't so bad as some, but after the knight's harsh introduction, Simon had taken a dislike to the suave Sir Tristram, and the thought that the vills about Tavistock were to be told to produce their finest men for this Sir Knight to take them away to war suddenly struck Simon. As he marched to the stables, he found his lips twitching into a grin.

He had a suspicion that Sir Tristram was not going to find recruiting men to be very easy.

Chapter Ten

By the middle of the morning the earlier groups of men had left the shop and Ellis could close the shutters, pack his scissors and razors, strops and soaps into his little satchel, and head for the tavern for a quick ale before going over to the Abbey and seeing to the chins and pates of the monks there.

Although not vain, Abbot Robert hated having a beard. He often told Ellis that he disliked the roughness, but Ellis also knew that the Abbot was keen to make sure that he and his monks all dressed in a manner which reflected their serious duties. They should look sober and professional, not slovenly like the mendicants so often did. It wasn't simply pride; Ellis knew that the Abbot thought it important that their pastoral flock should see in the monks men whom they could respect. Few felt, like Augerus, that they could flout his will about facial hair.

As far as Ellis was concerned, his job was merely to shave. He had taken up his profession because there would always be men with hair, beards, teeth and veins, and while there were, he could count on being paid to trim, shave, pull or slash.

An essential part of his business was the cheery patter that he had developed over the years. With some it was bantering conversation, often making mild jokes at his client's expense, sometimes simply being crude, but after seeing Wally, both at the coining and on Friday, he still felt little urge to be amusing. It was enough that he should keep his scissors away from his clients' ears, his razors from nicking their throats.

Sara must have been mad. She had flaunted herself at the miner, no doubt, and he had taken advantage. Ellis couldn't in all fairness blame the man. When he had seen her with Wally, he had felt his rage growing within him like a canker, but now he was able to be more sanguine. And since Wally's death, Sara had certainly been mortified. She had been wailing and weeping almost all the time. No surprise, Ellis thought, with Wally's bastard inside her.

He grunted sadly. A loyal man to his family, he had paid a lot of money towards his niece and nephews' upbringing. This would simply be another one for him to help feed.

Augerus waited until Simon and the Arrayer had both left the room, then he went in and collected the goblets and jugs, setting them on his tray and carrying them back to his little buttery. He rinsed one goblet, glanced over his shoulder, emptied the remains of the jug into it, and drank it off in a long draught before washing the goblet and jug, and drying them with a long piece of linen.

He had nothing to do at the moment, for Abbot Robert was gone. Whenever he could, he'd take his hounds out and see what he could catch with a few of the burgesses in the town. Canny devil, the Abbot, in Augerus' mind. He knew how to get his neighbours and tenants talking: he'd take them out for a good race through his park and afterwards, over wine and ale, he'd ask them what they thought about many of the issues of the day. That way he'd be the first to hear of dissatisfaction before any of his officials, and often he'd soothe disgruntled townspeople before their complaints could grow into full-blown feuds. It also gave him an opportunity to catch out his Bailiffs.

Augerus had heard him once, talking to a Gather-Reeve, the rent collector. The poor fellow was bowing nervously in the presence of his master, trying to show the Abbot a confidence he didn't feel.

Abbot Robert had stopped at his side and peered down at him. 'Aha! Reeve, and how is your lady this fine morning?'

'Oh, she is well, Master, well.'

'And your . . . let me see, you have two sons, don't you?'

'Yes, Master. They are well, very well.'

'I am sure they are. And you, you are well?'

'Yes, my Lord. I am very well indeed,' the poor fellow had answered effusively, visibly relaxing. If the Abbot was so kindly, it was hard to remain scared.

'Really? And yet my rents from Werrington have not been collected yet. I thought it was because you were unwell.'

'No, Master.'

'Or your children were.'

'Um. No, Master.'

'Or maybe even that your wife was ill.'

There was a disconsolate mumble.

'Well, in God's name get over there and do your job, man! You aren't employed by me to sit about swapping tall stories and drinking ale all day!'

The memory of the man's face as the Abbot rode off imperiously on his great mount would stay with Augerus for ever. He smiled as he worked, and when his jobs were done, he glanced out of the window at the shadows in the court. In an hour or two he would have to prepare the Abbot's table so that he could entertain whoever was with him today, but until then Augerus was free. He walked out of the Abbot's lodgings to the Great Court.

The *salsarius*, Brother Mark, who provided the salted beef and fish, also served the Abbey as *medarius*, holding the stocks of wine and ale. The Abbot himself had once drily commented that the arrangement made sense – the *salsarius* could, by serving ale as *medarius*, assuage the thirst that his salted meat provoked.

Seeing Augerus, Mark smiled broadly and waved him over.

'Aha! The Lord Abbot's Steward is in need of a little refreshment, is he?' he chuckled richly, and led the way into his domain. 'Try some of this,' he said, turning the tap on a barrel and filling a little jug. 'It only came in yesterday.'

'It's good.' Augerus smiled, smacking his lips appreciatively, pulling a stool from beneath the table and sitting.

This was an irregular morning routine for both. They tried to meet up each day, but only occasionally could they manage it. Mark was always having to rush off to supervise the salting of slabs of beef and pork at this time of year, ordering younger monks and novices about as the slaughtermen did their work, and often Augerus was held up as the Abbot demanded more paper, or reeds, or inks.

The two were friends, each respecting the other's value in the currency that really mattered in the monastery: information.

That was the hook which had formed their relationship early on, and although Augerus knew that Mark thought himself more religious, he also knew that Mark respected him as a source of prime information about the Abbot's thinking. That mutual trust was important to both. That was why they were wont to drink together when they had a chance. The last time had been only a few days before the coining.

Ha! Augerus could vaguely recall their meandering route back to the Abbey after so much wine; they had drunk enough to sink a ship. In fact, it was a miracle that they had managed to find their way back. For Augerus' part, he had collapsed straight onto his bed after a few more jugs of wine with Mark.

It was the odd thing about Mark. He had the ability to consume vast quantities of wine without any apparent ill-effects. Now Augerus, next morning, felt as if someone had battered his body with a club, and his insides were all in a turmoil. He couldn't eat anything; when he looked at a cup of wine he threw up, and the only thing which began to stay down towards the end of the day was a little water. Mark, on the other hand, had drunk more than Augerus, yet only suffered a mild headache. There was no justice in the world, Augerus reckoned.

Mind, Mark had had more practice. His red features and swollen nose bore testament to his regular consumption, testing to make sure all was well with his wines. He took his job seriously.

Now he was fixing Augerus with a serious glance. 'I don't like the look of Gerard,' he said abruptly. 'He looks like a boy with troubles on his mind.'

There was no need to say more. Both men knew that the only troubles which mattered in the Abbey were the thefts of the Abbot's wine and the disappearance of the pewterer's plates.

'I shouldn't think he would dare to steal from guests,' Augerus said.

Mark sniffed. 'Talk of the devil.' He waved a hand to attract the Steward's attention.

Leaning forward to peer through the door, Augerus saw Gerard himself re-entering the court. The novice glanced about him, throwing an anxious look towards the Abbey church.

'Did you see that?' Mark said excitedly. 'Did you? That lad is guilty, I'll bet you a barrel of Gascon wine. Look at him! He's definitely done something wrong. I have seen guilty novices before now, but never one who looked as depressed as him.'

'I am more intrigued by the stories about the others.'

'Which others?'

'Come, Mark! You must have heard the tale about the travellers on the moor? There is a party of foreigners out there, apparently.'

'Oh, yes. But even if they did kill that miner . . .'

'Wally.'

'. . . Walwynus, yes – even if they did murder him, what on earth could they have had to do with the theft from the Abbey's guests?'

Augerus smiled at the comment. In a way, it perfectly summed up Mark's view on the world. A murder out on the moors might as well have been committed in Scotland, for all the relevance it had to him. No, much more important was the embarrassment of thefts from those enjoying the Abbot's hospitality. 'You recall Milbrosa?'

'That old nonsense? Who doesn't remember it. But you can't honestly believe that there's any parallel?'

'I don't know,' Augerus said. His attention had returned to the boy crossing the yard. 'But the similarity seems curious, doesn't it?'

'Only superficially,' Mark said definitely. 'Nothing more than that. I don't believe half of the story of the mad monks and the devil. No, I think that the good Abbot of Buckfast was correct when he said that the monks fell into a mire and drowned.'

'Don't you believe in the devil?'

'Of course I do,' said Mark and crossed himself. 'But the devil doesn't have a monopoly. Accidents do sometimes occur. And I think that's what happened to the monk Milbrosa and his companions. They fell into a bog.'

'After they had sold stolen church silver from the Abbey to the travellers.'

'*If* the legend is true. Anyway,' Mark said, leaning back on his stool as Gerard disappeared into the cloisters, 'I'd be surprised if that young fool could have found his way to the guest house without a guide, so surely *he* didn't steal from the pewterer, guilty looks or no, I suppose. But I do wonder whether those travellers have something to do with the rosaries and plate which have gone missing. If someone in the Abbey were to steal, it would be easy to sell the stuff to the travellers, wouldn't it?' and he shot a look at Augerus.

'You knew, didn't you?' Jeanne hissed after they had left the Coroner sprawled on a low bed in their solar.

'My love, I had no idea what he was talking about. You saw that on my face,' Baldwin protested. 'In truth I have little desire to return to the moors.'

'The moors are evil. The more I see of them, the less I like them.' Jeanne was truly upset.

'It is only land,' her husband said gently. 'And yet I admit this year has been oddly unsettling. What with the tournament, and then the vampires.' He felt his ribs gingerly. The great wound, which had felt like his death blow, which he had received during the Oakhampton tournament, had almost healed. The black and purple bruising had faded to a violent yellowish discolouration.

'We have seen so many deaths there this year,' she said and shuddered.

Baldwin walked over to her and placed both arms about her body. Although she resisted momentarily, soon he was able to pull her to him, and rest his head upon hers while she nestled into his shoulder.

'My love,' he said tenderly, 'don't fear for me. I am not afraid of the moors.'

'You don't understand!' she declared, pushing him away with both hands on his chest. 'I fear that because you don't believe in the spirit of the moors, you will leave yourself open to danger.'

'We have talked about this before,' he sighed, and indeed they had. His wife had been fearful before he went to investigate the murders in Sticklepath, and had tried unsuccessfully to stop him going then.

She followed him now as he walked from the room and returned to his hall, picking up his jug and sipping at the wine. 'The Bailiff feels the same way as you do,' Baldwin mused, 'and I confess that I cannot laugh at Simon's reactions any more, since witnessing how disorientated I became when the mist surrounded us at Sticklepath. I can sympathise with other people when they give respect to the moors – but they *are* only moors, not wild animals. I cannot pretend to be afraid when I am not.'

'Baldwin, I—'

'My Lady, I have spoken. I shall go with the good Coroner, and I shall help, so far as I am able, to solve whatever little riddle he puts before me. What is the reason for this visit, anyway?'

'He said it was a murdered miner.'

'There you are, then. It is likely a man killed in a knife-fight

near the Abbey. There is no need for you to worry. It is probably
nothing more than a quarrel over a woman in the middle of
Tavistock, and no need to go near the moors. After all, that far
south, in Tavistock, the moors don't start until you travel half a
morning eastwards.'

Her face was a little easier on hearing his words, but she still
opened her mouth to speak again.

He held up his hand. 'I shall be very careful, and I shall not
take foolish risks, my love. But if the Coroner says that our good
friend Abbot Robert wishes me to help, I can hardly turn him
down, can I?' He gambled a final comment, watching her carefully.
'After all, if it weren't for the good Abbot, you and I might
never have met, might we? He has given me my most treasured
possession – *you*. If I can ever help him, I must.'

Peter walked back to the Abbey, scarcely noticing the urchins
begging at the street corners, the boys and girls who pointed at
him and called out names. He had grown all too used to the
condemnation of others since that dread attack.

Those days felt so far-off now. An evil time, it was as though
after the ruination of the Holy Kingdom of Jerusalem, God had
decided to punish the impious. Hexham had been destroyed in
1296, and the Scots grew braver at this demonstration of their
might. They were always raiding, riding ever further into England.
Nor was it only the Scots. The man who tried so hard to destroy
Tynemouth was the foul murderer Sir Gilbert Middleton and his
ally Sir Walter Sęlby, two notorious English men. They and their
followers, the *shavaldours*, were nothing more than marauders,
killers who robbed and kidnapped, fearless of punishment from
men or God.

It was five years ago now, in 1317 when they had committed
their most barbarous, daring act. The two Cardinals, John de
Offa and Luca de Fieschi, had been sent to England by the Pope
himself in order to negotiate a settlement between the English

King and the Scottish warrior, Bruce, the man whom the Pope himself referred to as 'him who pretended to be King of Scotland'.

Except Sir Gilbert was furious still about the way that the English King was doing nothing about the devastation being wreaked upon his lands and upon those of the barons north of York. King Edward seemed to care nothing for the north country. He merely enjoyed himself with his singing and dancing, acting like a peasant with his hedging and ditching, and bulling his favourites at night. Pathetic, puny man that he was. He was no King of a realm such as England.

When Sir Gilbert's cousin, Hamelin de Swinburn, was arrested for speaking sharply to the King about the abysmal state of the Northern Marches, it was no surprise that the furious Sir Gilbert chose to take the law into his own hands. He met with the Cardinals and their party riding northwards from York, near to Darlington, and robbed them of their money, their goods and their horses, and although he quickly released the two Cardinals to continue, more slowly, upon their way, he took Louis de Beaumont, Bishop of Durham, and his brother Henry hostage and ransomed them.

That act was their last. Sir Gilbert was entrapped by neighbours shocked by his sacrilegious behaviour; they had him fettered and sent to London in his chains. There he was condemned, and in January of 1318 he was hanged, drawn and quartered.

No one would have missed him. Certainly not Peter. After all, it was Sir Gilbert who had caused Peter's wound a little while before he captured the Cardinals; unwittingly, it was true, but if Sir Gilbert had not distracted the Priory by attacking, Peter wouldn't have been hurt.

It was because of Tynemouth. Sir Gilbert wanted to sack the castle there, to ransack the stores and take provisions, which during the famine years were more valuable to him than gold and jewels, although he probably wanted to see what plate and gold he could steal as well. Fortunately Sir Robert de Laval realised what was happening, and the castle and Priory were put on their guard. The Prior, a wise old fellow, commanded the monks to help Sir Robert's men to demolish the houses which ran up near to the monastery and the castle, and Peter had been one of the first to volunteer to help. With the others, he had taken axe and bar to the old timber buildings, flattening them and clearing the space about the castle and Priory so that defenders could see for a good bowshot. There could be no unseen attack.

Praise be to God, the castle and Priory were saved and Sir Gilbert's men were driven off in search of easier pickings. Peter and his friends and Brothers began to think that they were safe. That was when the Scots came.

The Armstrong clan had first arrived there six months before, but Sir Tristram de Cokkesmoor had all but destroyed them. They were feared all about the Marches. Brave they were, certainly, but Peter knew that their courage was only the outward manifestation of their pagan attitude to life and God. He had heard that border men, not only the Armstrongs, routinely demanded that their boy-children at their christenings were blessed with the exception of their right hands, that they might use them freely to kill.

There were many of them. Too many, when they arrived in the area. It was only the brutal raid against them, driven home with callous disregard for the understood rules of humanity, that shattered the clan before they could devastate the whole area, and yet some men escaped the slaughter. Even as Sir Tristram rode back with the heads of his enemies dancing at his saddle, some few remained and gathered together.

Wally had been terribly cut about and left for dead, probably because he managed to crawl away from the general bloodshed. Peter's lovely Agnes found him, and the Scots lass bathed and cleaned his wounds, sitting up with him for hours while he slowly recovered.

And the reward for Peter? He lived to see Wally again, but the next time, Wally was with two others. Martyn and another.

If it hadn't been for Sir Gilbert, the Priory might have had a chance. Usually, refugees from the raids bolted into the castle, fleeing from the blood-maddened Scots, but because of Sir Gilbert's attack, there was no warning.

While Sir Gilbert's men retreated southwards, pulling back towards their inevitable fate and Sir Gilbert's own hanging, the small party of Scots who were all that remained of the Armstrong clan approached from the north, seeking plunder of any sort.

The few men left had banded together under one leader, who was known only as 'Red Hand', a name that terrified all the peasants because it meant death to any who crossed his path. He killed, it seemed, for pleasure. And beneath him were others who had grown to the nomadic, warrior culture of the March.

When they arrived, Peter himself was outside the Priory's walls, searching for herbs with the infirmarer, and it was only when the pair tried to return that they were spotted.

Screeching their unnatural war-cries, the Scots spurred their sturdy little ponies towards the monks, who turned and fled as best they could, but it was an unequal race. The Scots soon ran down the infirmarer and felled him with a single blow from a war-axe that split his head in two, the halves falling to his shoulders while his body kept on running. It was a scene from hell, a sight which Peter would never forget.

The rider who dealt this blow was delayed while he retrieved his axe, but his companions chased after Peter, laughing like young girls, high and weird. Peter's own terrified screams seemed only to egg them on.

He almost made it. Not far away was a tiny vill with a stone house in the middle which would have given him ample protection, but even as he leaped a low wall, one of the men sprang over it on his pony and cut him off. Smiling, he trotted on, facing Peter. God! But he could never forget that smiling face. It was the face of a demon; the face of the devil himself: Martyn Armstrong. Behind Armstrong, he saw another pony, and caught a glimpse of Wally's horrified expression; Wally whose life Peter had saved.

The monk was no coward, and he squared up to Martyn with his fists, but the third man was already behind Peter. He had jumped from his horse, and Peter turned in time to see the axe swinging at him.

There was no time to deflect the blade, not even a moment to duck. He had instinctively swayed his body backwards, away from that grey steel, which perhaps saved his life, but it left him with this mark. The blow, aimed for his throat, instead caught the angle of his jaw, shearing through bone, smashing his teeth together and knocking all into shards, jolting his head back so sharply he thought he must be dead. He felt himself falling, as though in a dream. It didn't seem real, somehow. The wound, the death of his friend, all had a sort of hideous unreality.

When he lay on the ground, his body was lifeless, like a machine that had been shattered. There was no ability to move. His arms and legs were no longer a part of him. Not even the sensation of jerking as his attacker attempted to free his blade from Peter's jaw could bring life to his limbs. He was quite sure that he was dead. His eyes registered only a cloaked figure, a curious voice. Nothing more. His eyes would not focus.

At last the weapon was retrieved: the man planted his foot on Peter's chin and yanked it free. Hands wandered over his body, stealing his little leather scrip, taking his rosary, pulling him this way and that, before grabbing a handful of his robe and using it to clean the blade of the axe which had done this to him. None of the men appeared to think Peter could survive, and he himself had no doubt that he was dead. In his mind, he said his prayers, begging forgiveness for his sins – and he could vaguely recall beginning the service of the dead, first for his friend and then again for himself.

The three had gone. It was dark, and he found himself shivering awake, shaking with the cold, or perhaps not just the cold. He had seen men who were wounded after battles – my God in heaven, there were always so many up on the Scottish Marches – and some were like him, shaking uncontrollably. Perhaps that was what had affected him. The fear of death – or of life. It was with a certain thankfulness that he felt himself slipping away into oblivion again. One moment he had a hint of a thought, and then he felt himself falling away, as though the ground itself was gently accepting him, letting him sink softly into its arms, and all became black.

He never met the peasant who found him. The man had realised he was not dead and had dragged the monk into his room, setting him before the fire before hurtling off to the monastery to call for help. Soon gentle hands had come to rescue Peter, picking him up and carrying him back to the monastery's infirmary, and it was there that he awoke again, more than a week later, coming to life once more to find himself staring at the altar. The vision of the cross acted like a stimulant on his fevered and pain-racked body, and he burst out into sobs of gratitude, and of sadness, for he had partly hoped to have died and reached heaven. But it was not to be. Not yet.

Even the memory of that rebirth, which was what it had felt like, was enough to bring tears to his eyes, and he had to wipe his blurred eyes in the street, sniffing and muttering a quick prayer of thanks, crossing himself as he cast his eyes upwards. Feeling calmer, he carried on. He was thankful, of course he was, that God had given him this second chance at life. It meant he had a purpose. There must be a reason, surely, for his continued existence on the earth.

Perhaps He was right, but Peter couldn't remain in Tynemouth. The terror of his attack, the constant pain in his jaw, were enough to persuade him to beg his Prior that he might be permitted to move to a different monastery, somewhere further away from the

Marches. His Prior, ever a generous-hearted man, understood perfectly and not only gave his permission, he also wrote to friends in other Priories and Abbeys asking whether they could find space for his wounded monk. Soon he was told that there was an Abbey far away, down almost as far from Scotland as it was possible to go, where the kindly Abbot had agreed to take him on, and shortly afterwards he had made the long journey southwards to this quiet, peaceful backwater of Tavistock.

Abbot Robert was a good man and had taken Peter to his heart as soon as they had met. There were few who could see the monk's face without flinching, but when Abbot Robert saw him, he welcomed him with open arms and made a point of giving him the kiss of peace as though he was unharmed. That single act made Peter break down and weep. It was the first time that a man or woman hadn't retreated before him, but Abbot Robert had made it clear that he cared only for the man himself, not at all for the damage done to him; more, that he accepted Peter unreservedly into his Abbey.

Peter's heart glowed at the memory. He loved Abbot Robert. The Abbot had proved himself to be a great master, and Peter would serve him until death.

Not that he could forget the attack. It was always there, every time he shaved, every time he caught sight of himself in a glass or in a pool. As was the face of the Scottish rider who had blocked his escape. The grinning, fearsome features of Martyn Armstrong, and behind him, the appalled, deathly pale face of *Walwynus*.

He was only glad that he had not seen the face of the third man, the man with the axe. That man Peter could never forgive.

Chapter Eleven

Simon sat on a bench next to the Arrayer and surveyed the men before him without enthusiasm. This lot came from one of the Abbot's outlying manors; others would arrive over the next day. As Simon looked at this, the first batch, he wondered how the Arrayer would react. It was obvious that these were not all the men between sixteen and sixty demanded by the Commission of Array.

They were in the shelter of a tavern out at the western edge of the Burgh, staring at the scruffy and mostly, from the look of them, pox-ridden peasants. Simon had no wish to get too close to most of them, and not only because of their diseased appearance. The Commission of Array offered inducements to tempt men into serving the King, for not only would they be offered money, they would also be given a chance to win pardons for any past offences. Simon privately thought that those men who looked fit enough for service also tended to have fast-moving eyes which were filled with a grim suspicion – the expression felons so often wore when in the presence of a King's official.

All had brought weapons with them – a selection of bills, swords, axes, bows and arrows – while on their heads some wore cheap helmets or soft woollen caps. To Simon's eye, the healthiest men seemed to have the best-used weapons, another fact that spoke of misbehaviour. Still, the King wouldn't want soft-hearted boys for his army. He would be after strong, capable killers.

Looking about him, Simon was content with his first impression: these were the very dregs of the Abbot's manor. Whether or not they would seriously alarm the vicious warriors of the Scottish March, he had no idea, but he would be happier the sooner they were off and away from Devonshire.

'Three and forty,' Sir Tristram said. 'Is this the best the Abbot can do for the King from his manor of Werrington?'

'I'm sure you'll find that the Abbot has not had anything to do with selecting the men here,' Simon said. The Abbot would have made quite sure he had no direct involvement with picking this lot. And yet a man like Abbot Robert could make his wishes plain enough without putting them in writing, and the manor had obeyed the unspoken message in his summons. While men, women and children were still out with the harvest, no vill or hamlet was going to spare its strongest and fittest young men for service with the King. Instead they had picked all those who could be sent without imperilling their crops.

Ignoring the obvious felons, Simon considered that, of the young and simple there were three, while of the old and stupid, seven; of the rest, all were undernourished and weak. One had a massive goitre growing on his neck, making his throat look as though it had been taken from an ox and placed beneath his head in some cruel joke. Others had the thick lips and heavy, drooping eyelids of the mentally subnormal. The few fit and healthy men looked hopelessly out of place.

'This won't do at all,' Sir Tristram muttered. With him was a tough-looking, sandy-haired Sergeant called Jack of the Wood. This fellow stood grimly, staring at the recruits, and then, when Sir Tristram began to call men forward, he shook his head as though in horror at the quality of them. Sir Tristram waved the more obviously dim or ill away and began to take the details of the few he could use, discussing each with Jack, while a clerk sent by the Abbot scribbled his records down. He must note the name and weapons of each recruit.

There was little for Simon to do. He sat back, scratching at his head while Sir Tristram questioned the different men, telling each doubtful-looking villein that they had a duty to serve their King, describing with a sort of enthusiastic boastfulness the rewards they could expect from their King: money, plunder, and many women, because women liked strong, virile soldiers. They always did.

Simon had heard enough. He caught the eye of the innkeeper and nodded meaningfully, then rose and went in. Soon he was standing at a broad plank of wood which the keeper used as a bar counter, and drinking deeply from a quart pot of strong ale. It tasted very good compared with sitting outside listening to Sir Tristram's lies.

'Do you think all those poor devils are going to be sent up north?' the innkeeper asked, pouring himself a jug.

'Could be. Let's hope it's all over before they're needed.'

'It is always the same, isn't it, Master? The poor folk who are tied to the land are pulled away, while those who can afford to avoid it pay to stay safe.'

'I don't know that Sir Tristram there will be taking anybody's money to avoid danger. I get the feeling he is serious about providing troops for the King.'

'Do you think so?' The innkeeper sank a quarter of his pot and sighed happily. 'One of my best brews. Wonderful. I'll never be able to duplicate it. No, Master Bailiff, I reckon that fellow out there is going to make a good profit on this recruiting. Not that it's unfair. If the King wants him to help, he ought to be paid, that's what I'd say. Why should a man do something for nothing? But what I meant was, what about all those bastards up on the moors? They should go as well.'

'The miners are safe, you know that. They're the King's own.'

'And a more murderous bunch of cut-throats you couldn't hope to find,' the innkeeper said. 'Look at that poor devil killed up there.'

'Wally? Did you know him?'

'Of course. He was often here. I tend to get to know all the miners while they have money.'

'Did he stay here with you?'

'Oh, no. He had a comfortable lodging with friends of his – Nob and Cissy, up at the pie-shop. They were cheaper.'

'Do you think he was murdered by a miner?'

The innkeeper gave a low snigger. 'Think it? Who else but a miner? Wally came into town for the coining. He was in here on Thursday, and stayed behind to drink for some while.'

'I thought he had no money.'

'He didn't make much from his mining, no, but he never missed a coining. It was the one chance he had of meeting friends and having them buy him ale with the money they made from selling their tin to the pewterers. He always came in for a few drinks.'

'With his friends, you mean?'

'Usually, yes. He turned up last week during the coining with some new friend of his.'

'Who was that?' Simon asked keenly.

'Foreigner. A pewterer, I think. He was here with all his family, and I think I heard someone talking about pewter and how good the man's stuff was.'

'And they were talking to Wally?'

'Yes. Very matey they were, too. Came in, Wally and him, and sat in a corner. Wally had a sack with him, and they sat talking for ages. Never seen the man before, myself. Later Wally came back, and then he started throwing his weight around and buying drinks.'

'So he had money?'

'Yes. And not just that, he was in a happy mood. He was really content, not just cheerful from the ale. I've never seen him like that.'

'No?'

'He always had a small cloud all of his own hanging over his head, you know? Nothing was ever right. Like he had a ghost at his shoulder.'

'But why should you think that a miner killed him?'

'Who else would have been up there on the moors?'

'I don't know. But it's near the Abbot's Path, the track from here to Buckfast. Maybe it was a traveller.'

'What, like that foreigner?' the host mused. 'Odd accent, he had.'

'What, he came from London? The north?'

'No!' the man said scathingly. 'When I say foreign, I bloody mean it. He wasn't French. I've met some of them. Could have been from Lettow, I suppose. I knew a Teutonic Knight once. He spoke a bit like this one.'

'You think he could have killed Wally?'

'Doubt it. Why should he? If a foreigner wanted to rob a man, he'd pick a more likely-looking fellow. No, Bailiff, like I said, it was the miners. Who knows, perhaps Wally had actually found himself a working piece of land at last? Maybe he had sold some tin and had money in his pocket from that. It would explain why he was murdered.'

Simon nodded. 'Maybe.' He would ask the Receiver whether Wally had sold any tin.

'Who else could it have been – the monk?' the publican demanded.

'What monk?'

'Dunno – I wasn't there. If you want to know, speak to Emma, Hamelin's wife. She said she saw a monk running back to the town. Why, do you reckon it could have been a Brother? Wouldn't surprise me. The bastards are capable of anything, I reckon.'

'You honestly think that a monk could be a murderer?' Simon asked with a cynical smile.

'They are men, just like any other! The only difference is, they think they have a direct call to God when they've misbehaved, and get special treatment from Him. Me, I see them here all the time. Even the Abbot's own Steward. He was here a few days ago with their fat wine-keeper whatever he's called. Drunk as Bishops, the pair of 'em. I was surprised they could get out into the road, let alone get home. I sent one of my lads with them to make sure that they were all right in the end. If they'd come to grief, I'd never have heard the last of it!'

'Do the monks often come down here?'

'When the Abbot's away, yes. Not usually.'

Simon swallowed the remains of his ale. It was likely a miner who had killed Wally, but he supposed that it would be just as easy for another man to manufacture a club.

Even a monk.

It was quiet in the *dorter* when Gerard poked his head around the door, but as he walked inside, one of the other novices, a tall, well-made boy called Reginald, came pattering up the stairs and walked in after him, a determined expression on his face.

Gerard made a point of paying no heed, but instead walked through to the *reredorter* behind, and sat on the plank over the drop. Down below was a stone vault which was washed by a stream, removing the odours while leaving the valuable faeces behind so that they could be collected and spread over the fields. They were essential for the crops, but the stench was appalling in the summer, when the faeces gathered and the stream shrank.

Not that the smell affected him today. No, it was the realisation that the others knew it was him.

They knew he had stolen. He was sure of it. That was why Reginald was in the *dorter*: they'd guessed that Gerard was the thief and had set a boy to watch him. They wouldn't leave him alone in their rooms. None of them was supposed to possess anything, for they were committed to poverty and must give up all their possessions on entering the Abbey, but that didn't prevent a few from keeping trinkets and other oddments. Gerard knew that one of the boys had a small jewel with a chain which his mother had given him, and another had something hidden in a box, but he'd never been able to see what was inside it. The last time he had seen the boy looking inside the box, he had carefully moved it so that his back hid the contents from Gerard.

But he hadn't troubled his fellow acolytes. Only strangers! And no one had actually seen him. He was sure of that much. Maybe it was just that Reginald alone suspected him. Or more likely Reginald doubted all of them and thought it worthwhile to watch over his own little store – whatever might be there.

He stood and cleaned himself, washed his hands and slowly made his way back to the *dorter*. Reginald was sitting on his bed, and met his casual glance with a blank expression. There was no friendship in his look, only utter indifference. The complete lack of any emotion in his face was enough to convince Gerard that there could be no safety or peace for him in the Abbey now. He and Reginald had never been friends, but the other boy's attitude proved, if proof were needed, that Gerard's secret was known.

Walking past him with his head held high, Gerard averted his gaze, but before he could get to the door, he felt Reginald grab his habit. The larger boy tugged him backwards by the shoulder, kicked his legs away and hauled him over to fall on his back.

Gerard felt his head strike the corner of the nearest bed, and the jolt snapped his teeth together with a crunch that made him feel sick and faint. There was a rushing in his ears that sounded like the River Tavy in spate, and it was only with difficulty that he could hear Reginald speaking quietly.

When he was done, an angry Sir Tristram dismissed the men, giving them a penny each and telling them to return the next day. Once he had viewed the remainder of the Abbot's men, he would take the whole force and they would begin the march northwards. As the peasants filed from the yard, he turned and bellowed to the innkeeper for ale, before turning hard, cold eyes on to Simon.

'You are sure that the Abbot didn't intend this to happen?'

'What?' Simon asked innocently.

'Don't take me for a fool, Bailiff,' Sir Tristram grated. 'I have seen how men avoid losing their serfs before now. They leave the strong and hale men in the fields and send only the broken-winded, lame and stupid to the Arrayer.'

'I am sure that the good Abbot would be shocked to think that you could suspect such a thing. He would not break the law or try to hamper the King's plans.'

'Really? Then he must be unique amongst Abbots. He's like every other landlord. So long as his harvest is in, he doesn't care what happens in the north of the realm. It is men like him who conspire to see the Scottish destroy the whole land.'

'You surely don't suggest Abbot Robert is guilty of—'

'Don't look so shocked, Bailiff. I can say what I want, and I say here and now that I do not believe the Abbot's healthiest men were sent to me from that vill. My commission gives me the duty to select the best and fittest from all the men of sixteen to sixty, and take them to the King.'

'Are you from the north yourself?'

'I wasn't born in Scotland, if that's what you mean, no. But I have lands near Berwick which the last King, bless his memory, gave to my father for his efforts in pacifying the land during the old King's wars. My father helped bring the Stone of Scone to King Edward I, and it was for that service that the King gave him his own manors up there and the duty to protect the border, not that he could. The Scottish raided while my father was away and razed our house to the ground. Bastards! All they know is robbery and murder. They sweep over that border with impunity and devastate all the north, even down to York sometimes, and there is nothing we can do. They avoid our armies because they know they would lose in a fair fight. They are rebels and cowards.'

'So now our King will invade again?'

'We have to punish their crimes. Their whole life is based upon theft. They come into England to steal our cattle and horses, and then return, burning and slaughtering unnecessarily. They destroy the livelihoods of peaceful English farmers to their own profit. They are a cursed race, forever warring.'

'And you will lead men from here in Devonshire to make war on them,' Simon said, once more considering what the innkeeper had said. The Almoner Peter was from the north, he remembered. From interest, he asked, 'Is it true that the Scots make war upon monasteries and nunneries?'

'Aye, true enough. Those sacrilegious sons of the devil rape nuns, slaughter monks and rob any churches they come across. I tell you, they are the devil's own spawn.'

'Well, there are felons aplenty even here in Devonshire who would dare to steal the plate from a church at need,' Simon said calmly.

'Christ Jesus! Even here?'

'There is a monk here who was attacked and left for dead up in the north.' It was some months since Simon had last spoken to Brother Peter, and now he had to rack his brain to recall where he came from. 'Up near the border, I recall. Or was he near the coast? Ah, yes, Tynemouth. He was of the Priory there.'

'I know the area,' Sir Tristram said and spat. 'You know the worst problem with them? Those sodomites were the friends of the Scots! They cosseted wounded Scottish and parleyed with the Scottish King! Cowards and traitors the lot of them! If there's one of that immoral congregation here, keep the arse away from me, or I may throttle the life from the shit!'

Chapter Twelve

The rest of the day was quiet for Simon. He preferred to avoid the Arrayer, finding peace in solitude. After taking a little lunch, he rode up to the site of the body with his servant, but when he and Hugh arrived, they found that Hal had gone and in his place was a new watchman. Still, it was with relief that Simon saw that the corpse was not being further destroyed by rats or dogs.

However, he and Hugh were glad to get away from the place. The stench of putrefaction seemed to reach into Simon's nostrils and lie there, as though it had made his own sinus rot by contact. As he inhaled, he knew that the odour would remain with him for days. It was like pork that had been left out too long: sweet, but unbearably repellent.

Hugh clearly agreed. His face registered his disgust, and he refused to approach the corpse, remaining on his horse, glaring about him as though daring a felon to try to attack him in the same way that Wally had been.

Simon could fully understand Hugh's reluctance. He dropped from his horse, trying to breathe through his mouth and not his nose, but it didn't help. He stood a few yards away from the body, eyes narrowed, mouth drawn down, and as soon as he was satisfied that nothing had been stolen or altered, he turned away.

By chance his glance fell on the place where the club had fallen, and he walked to the spot with a frown growing on his features. 'Where's the club that was here?' he said, pointing.

'Don't know. Weren't nothing there when I came 'ere.' The miner was a burly, short, grizzled man with an immense curling beard. He stood with his thumbs in his belt and stared blankly at Simon's pointing finger. 'Don't know what you mean.'

'There was a morning star there. Home-made, just a lump of timber with a load of nails hammered into it. It's what killed Wally. Wasn't it here when you arrived?'

'No. Nothing there what I saw. And I haven't slept, Bailiff.'

'Shit!' Simon turned away and walked to his horse, his mind whirling. If this man hadn't taken it . . . He span on his heel. 'Who was here when you arrived?'

'Hal. No one else.'

'Good. Come, Hugh,' Simon said, mounting his horse. He considered riding out to see Hal now, but a quick look up at the sky persuaded him against it. Hal was only a short distance away, but Simon didn't know the safe route. To get to him would mean walking around the great bog, going far out of his way, and then it would soon be dusk. No, he must see Hal later, and demand to know what he had done with the club – and why.

The thin grey dusk had already given way to a clear, cloudless night, with stars shining bright in a purple sky. Having partaken of a loaf of bread and some pottage, he and Hugh sat back in the little chamber that stood at the ground floor of the Great Court's gate and drank from their jugs of ale.

From there, Simon could peer through the doorway to the court itself, and see when Sir Tristram was likely to appear. As soon as the knight did so, Simon planned to leave. He would say that he had to go and talk to a man who had been seen up on the moor when Wally died, or perhaps that the Abbot needed to talk to him – or just that he felt sick and was going to spew. Anything to keep away from Sir Tristram.

If only Hal was here, he thought. He would have liked a chance to talk to him about the disappearance of that morning star. It made no sense for Hal to have taken the thing, unless he thought that somehow it was incriminating and wanted to protect the real killer. Perhaps even protect himself.

Except Simon knew it made no sense. The nails could have been made by any one of a number of smiths in Dartmoor. Simon had seen them making their nails, setting a red-hot bolt of iron into the spike-shaped metal formers and beating it until it was pushed into the mould, the head gradually rounding over. It was easy work, if dull and repetitive. Similarly the wood of the club itself would give no sign where it had come from. There was no point, no point at all, in taking the thing away. All it could do was indicate that a miner was involved, but the fact that Wally had died up on the moors tended to suggest that anyway.

He was considering this for the thousandth time when he glanced through the door and observed a monk walking slowly, with bent head, along from the main gate and across the court. When the figure turned, Simon saw the flash of the scar shining in the torchlight. He left Hugh and walked outside.

'Brother Peter, may I speak to you for a while?' he called.

'To me, Bailiff? Aye, if ye're sure ye can cope with the ranting and ravening of a mad northerner,' Peter said in his thickest dialect.

'Do you often find people saying they can't understand you?' Simon smiled.

'Aye. And usually it's the most uncommunicative and intract- able shepherds or farmers who accuse *me* of being hard to listen to,' Peter snorted. 'Well, never mind.'

'No. Don't fear, though. I've lived in Devonshire all my life, and if I go and listen to moormen talking, I still can't understand a word they say. It's too broad for me.'

'Aye, but you're a foreigner like me, aren't ye? You come from at least two miles outside the moors.'

'True enough,' Simon said with a chuckle.

The monk was in an apparently contemplative mood. He walked slowly, and although he gave his lopsided smile in response to Simon's comments, he said no more. The Bailiff had the impression that he was waiting for him to speak.

Now that he was here, Simon wasn't sure how to continue. He wanted to warn the older man to beware of Sir Tristram, that the knight might lose his temper if he knew about Peter, but Simon's diplomatic skills were not up to telling a man whose face proved how terrible his time up in the north had been, that someone else wanted to hit him, especially since Sir Tristram's reason was in order to punish Peter for collaborating with the very men who had given him such a grievous wound.

'You appear ill-at-ease, my friend,' Peter said softly.

'It's Sir Tristram,' Simon blurted out.

'Aye. He's a hard man, Sir Tristram,' Peter said mildly.

'You know him?'

'I wouldn't say I know him well, but I've seen him a few times. He's a tough warrior, always out on the warpath. As soon as there was ever a hint that the Scots were at the border, Sir Tristram would take up his sword and lance and ride with his men. I don't think I could count the number of lives that man has ended.'

'He was telling me that the Scots raid over the border, though,' Simon frowned.

'It's always the way, isn't it? Somebody did commit the first raid. I wonder who it was? Perhaps it was the Scottish, for all we know, and then the English border folk decided to take revenge, and then the Scottish strong men took *their* revenge. It's easy to see how the border reivers could cross the border from both sides. And what happens? A few cattle are stolen and taken back to the other side of the border, or a house is found locked up and is fired, with the screams and pleadings of the women and children inside falling on deaf or uncaring ears, or perhaps they ride into a group of other men in the dales, and Armstrongs fight Elliots until all are dead, for none would give quarter.'

'And Sir Tristram was one of these?'

'Sir Tristram!' Peter said, and there was a chuckle in his voice, although his eyes didn't reflect any humour. 'I saw him once, you know. He had lost a pair of oxen, and he decided that reivers from the other side of the March were responsible, so he rode off with his men, great, fierce warriors, they were. I saw them come back. Sir Tristram was proud. He'd lost one man, but he'd killed three himself. Personally. Do you know how I know that?'

Simon shook his head.

'Because that honourable knight had their heads dangling from his saddle, Bailiff. Tell me, how do you order the law here? Do you slaughter and bring the heads back?'

'It is possible. If an outlaw is found, his head is forfeit.'

'Come, Bailiff, how often does a man sweep off the head of an outlaw? The man is taken prisoner and brought back to the Justices if possible, and if not, why then the fellow is fought, and his corpse brought to the Justices. If not, the Coroner would ask questions. Even if a felon's head is needed for the city's spikes in York or Exeter, so that all can see that the King's justice and his laws are still functioning, it is carried in a sack. Not much of a distinction, I know, but at least that demonstrates a certain respect for the dead man's soul. Not Sir Tristram, though. He kills, and enjoys the killing.'

He stopped and glanced up at the sky, which was darkening.'Perhaps I am just too old, Bailiff. I spent so many years trying to find peace where none existed, and then I received this, when the Scottish rebels came over the dale and attacked us in revenge for a raid that English reivers had launched on them. Where is the sense? Will the feuds never cease?'

'I am sure they will,' Simon said seriously.'Once the Scottish stop rebelling against the King's rule, and we become one nation again as we should be, the border region must be pacified.'

'Bailiff,' Peter said, smiling now as he faced Simon. 'You cannot pacify those men, only kill them. They won't stop fighting until they are dead, or all their enemies are, and there is nothing more for them to steal.'

'Then perhaps it is natural for Sir Tristram to want to fight them and protect his own,' Simon said hesitantly.

'Him? He is one of the worst of them,' Peter said, and his voice was suddenly terribly cold, as though he had seen the ghosts of all his friends who had died on the Marches passing before him. 'Few on either side of the border don't know of Bloody Tristram.' The old monk stopped and looked past Simon to the Abbey's church tower. 'He doesn't only attack the Scottish, our Sir Tristram. He is like the shavaldours – happy to rob *any* man for profit. No one may cross his lands without being attacked.'

'Are you sure?' Simon asked doubtfully. 'The King has sent him here as an Arrayer. Surely he wouldn't send a man who was untrustworthy?'

Peter looked at him; there was deep sadness in his eye. 'You think the King would object to a man like him? Sir Tristram gives King Edward all he wants: a constant fight to irritate the Scottish, and a boundless zeal for killing Scots and terrorising the whole of the March. Whenever the King wants men-at-arms or archers, he can go straight to Sir Tristram and find a ready source.'

'Yet he needs to send Sir Tristram here to fetch them?' Simon queried.

'At times the King needs more men. When he plans to slaughter even more Scottish than usual, or when the Scottish decide to raid more deeply into England, like a sword thrust, instead of their usual short stabs at the border, like daggers, then he needs more men. But whatever happens, Sir Tristram will not lose by it.'

Simon could say nothing. The pain in Brother Peter's face was all too evident, and the Bailiff wanted to distract him. 'You have heard about the dead man on the moors?'

'Poor Walwynus? Yes. Terrible to think of his being clubbed to death so far from friends, out on that bleak moorland. He lived out in the middle of the moors, didn't he?'

'Yes.'

'In among the tin-miners, then. Do you think one of them could have killed him?'

'It's possible, although I can't understand why.'

'You know how it is. Feuds.'

Simon shot him a glance. The old monk was facing the ground now, but Simon was sure that he was watching him keenly from the corner of his eye.

'Well,' he said at last, 'that will be for the Coroner to discover.'

'Who is the Coroner?'

'Sir Roger de Gidleigh,' Simon said, adding, 'He's a very astute man. The killer should beware. If there is any sign of who was guilty, Sir Roger will find it.'

'Well, shall I save you some trouble learning things, then, Bailiff?' Peter muttered.

'What do you mean?'

'Wally, the dead man – he was one of the group that did this to me. My woman had saved *his* life only a short while before, nursing him. Then, when he was hale and hearty again, aye, and could ride, he and his friends found me. His companion, Martyn Armstrong, headed me off from my escape, and Wally came up. I think, perhaps, he was going to try to save me, but before he could, a third man caught me and did this with an axe.'

Simon winced. 'You saw him swinging his axe at you? That must have been . . .'

'No, I didn't. He swung, but all I saw was a blur. And then I was down. But you know the worst, Bailiff? Aye, that was when I came to, and I was told that my girl was dead. Raped and murdered on the very same day. It was that which ruined me, more than this wound even, for in losing her, I lost my life.'

'So you came down here.'

'Aye, I came here, every day cursing Wally for leading his men to my woman and letting them rape her after her kindness to him. It was only last week that I learned he hadn't. He had stayed with the men and tried to lead them around her house, but they met a party with Sir Tristram and got separated. By the time Wally met them again, she was dead. They tried to escape by coming south, and Wally dared not confront his companions, for he knew he needed them to survive, the coward, but once they were settled here, he killed Martyn for her murder. They were drunk and Wally couldn't help but taunt him. When he accused Martyn, the mad Scot went for him, but Wally won the advantage.'

'He was happy to live with the man out on the moors until then?' Simon asked doubtfully. 'Even though he thought the man had murdered the girl?'

'By then the man Martyn was his only comrade in a terrifying world. Imagine if you were forced to flee to Scotland, Bailiff. Would you question a companion closely, if he was your sole contact with your old world? I think not.'

'Perhaps. I hope I never suffer such an existence. What of the third man?' Simon wondered. 'Did he come here too? Or did he die on the way?'

Peter shrugged. 'I care not. I hope he is dead and broiling in hell, but if I met him on the street, I would think it my duty to try to save his soul. I might even shake his hand. Repellent thought.'

Shortly afterwards the bell began to toll, and Peter sighed and gave his farewell, making his way to the church and the last service of the day.

Simon was strangely happy to see him go. He had never heard a bad word about Brother Peter; the Almoner was known among the townspeople to be a gentle, intelligent and mild-mannered man, but something about him today made Simon feel cautious. The monk had been interested to hear about the dead man, and if Simon was right and Peter *had* attempted to distract him, maybe drawing him away from the real killer and instead focusing his attention on the miners, that could indicate some form of complicity or guilt.

It was something that he should ask about, he decided. Turning, he was about to make his way back to the welcoming room and ask for a fresh pot of ale, when he caught sight of a figure standing at the top of the stairs leading to the guest rooms: Sir Tristram.

The knight was staring after the disappearing monk. As though feeling Simon's eyes upon him, he glanced down, his face empty of any emotion. Without even acknowledging the Bailiff, he suddenly turned away, into the guest room, leaving Simon aware of a sense of grim foreboding.

Cissy pushed the last of her customers from the pie-shop and shut up the door, dropping the peg into place on the latch so it couldn't be lifted, then shooting the bolt.

She was tired. After the coining the previous week, they hadn't stopped. Sunday, supposedly the day of rest, had been hectic: Emma, Hamelin's wife, who was always struggling to feed her children, while her man lived out on the moors for seven weeks in every eight trying to make enough money to keep them all, had burst into tears in the street, Joel in her arms and three of her brood hanging on her skirts, and Cissy had pulled her into the parlour, sitting her in one of Nob's chairs and warming a little spiced wine for her. She had always kept the toys her own son had played with, and now they were a boon. She brought them down from the shelf in their box and the three children fell upon them with squeals of delight. When Nob poked his head about the door, Cissy glared at him until he shamefacedly disappeared, returning to the alehouse he had just left.

'You sit there, maid. You'll soon feel better.'

Emma sobbed into her skirts, unable to speak while Cissy clattered about the place, cutting up one of the pies Nob hadn't sold the previous day and setting the pieces on the box for the boys, then slicing another in two for Emma. She had a bread trencher, and she put the pie on it, filled a large cup with the wine, and held it near Emma until she could smell it.

The girl looked at it, her brown eyes watery. She was not particularly attractive, with her large, rather flat nose, and the almost circular shape of her face, but her heart was good, and Cissy had sympathy for any woman who must raise six children, five of them boys, on her own. Many other women were in the same situation, of course, but that didn't make it any less tiring. What's more, poor Emma had lost both her parents and her husband's during the famine, so there was no family to help her. She had to rely on neighbours and friends with young families, and sometimes such people couldn't do much.

'What is it, maid? Things got on top of you?'

'It's my little Joel. He's fading away.'

The mite was only a year old, but scrawny, and hadn't ever had much of an appetite. Prone to crying, he was probably more than half the reason Emma was always so tired, because his whining wail could be heard all through the night, and Cissy knew that he kept Emma from her sleep.

'He's not eating?' she asked.

'Oh, he's eating a bit, but not enough. I don't know what to do!'

Cissy listened to the girl with a sense of futility. Emma was on the brink of despair. Her husband's venture was petering out and he was scurrying about trying to find a fresh deposit, but so far there had been no luck. It was maddening, but there was no guaranteed reward for hard work, and then the tin ran out, and it was beginning to look like her family would soon have nothing. No income at the next coining meant no food for the children.

'And my Joel, he won't eat now. He looks up at me like he's starving, but he won't eat anything when I try to get him to feed, and he's wasting away, the poor sweetheart. It's been three days, and he's not had hardly anything, not even when I've chewed it up and given it to him in a paste.'

'He won't suckle?'

'No. He refuses my breast, just turns his head away when I get it near him.'

Cissy pursed her lips. It was more usual for children to be breast-fed until they were two or three years old, and hearing that the lad refused his mother's pap was alarming. She had seen Joel only the other day and had thought then that he looked weakly and unhappy, although his belly was large enough. Asleep now in Emma's arms, he looked restless and irritable.

She was no midwife. Her own boy had been an easy child, although he had become more difficult to feed later in life, growing fussy with his food. For some reason he disliked his father's meat pies; but no, Cissy told herself sternly as her mind wandered, that was unimportant compared to Emma's present and very real problems.

'I have taken him to the Abbey, and they have said prayers for him, but what else can I do?'

Cissy sighed. She had remained with Emma for ages, calming her as best she could. If it was God's will to take the child to His arms, He would, and there was nothing that the people of Tavistock could do about it. All Cissy could do, in all truth, was try to soothe her friend.

'There is one thing you could do,' she said suddenly. 'You could mix some honey with milk, and give that to him. It sometimes works. Can you afford some honey?'

Emma sniffed and wiped at her eyes. 'Yes. Hamelin gave me his purse.'

Cissy's eyes grew round as she saw the money in Emma's hand. 'Whee! He gave you all that? He must have sold a lot of tin!'

Emma became a little reserved. 'No, he sold a debt to Wally before he died.'

'Some debt, girl. When did Wally ever have so much money?'

Emma concealed the money in the purse again. 'I don't know. Perhaps he grew lucky? There was no report of a man being robbed, was there? If so, perhaps I'd think evil of Wally – but no one has, so it must have been his money somehow.'

Cissy opened her mouth to argue, but then glanced at Joel and her expression softened. 'Right, well you have enough to do him some good, anyway. Buy honey and some milk from the first morning milking, when it's rich and creamy. Give him that, and then try him with soft bread dipped in honey too. Once he's eating again, you can change his diet.'

By the time she had hustled the girl from her door, Emma's tears were at least a little abated, although while her child refused to eat, she would remain petrified with fear that she was going to lose him. Also, now that her husband's mine appeared to be failing, she knew that the rest of her children might suffer the pangs of starvation before too long.

It was a terrible thing to lose a child. Cissy hated the very idea. A devoted mother, she adored her children. One boy and two girls, and all fine, healthy, strapping creatures who had given her, so far, seven grandchildren. Her only regret was that all had moved from the shop as soon as they had married. Of course it was usual for a girl to do that, moving in with her in-laws, but it was sad to lose a son. And such a son Reg was! Tall, hair as dark as a crow's wing, his eyes deep brown; she thought he was perfect. But he had been convinced of his calling, and he had needed to follow it. That was all there was to it. Perhaps in years to come he would marry and give her the extra grandchildren she wanted.

The thought of more children turned a little sour when she saw the state her Nob was in. As she said to him, he made her wonder whether she had married a child and not a man.

After such a long exile from his hearth, Nob was more liquid than solid when he eventually returned to the shop. Not that being overbloated with ale had been the worst of it, of course. She had known what he would be like, and he had more than fulfilled her expectations.

As soon as his head hit the pillow, he snored fit to shake the daub from the walls, and he wouldn't roll over and shut up even when she prodded him with an ungentle finger. No, he merely lay back with his mouth agape, the fool! And then, just when she was thinking that she was so tired she might fall asleep, he snorted, grunted, and rose to go to the pot. Except, of course, he was fearful of wakening her, so he had lighted a candle that he might see without stumbling. The rasp, rasp, rasp of his tinder had been like a blade scraping on her skull, and the knowledge that there was no point in arguing with him because he was still drunk did not soften her temper. At last, after making as much noise as the Lydford waterfall, he had returned to bed, but now the second evil of drink had made itself felt. He had broken wind, and soon she was reeling from the foul odour.

Next morning he had woken with a pained expression. It did not succeed in arousing any sympathy from her.

'I don't know why you do it to yourself so often. Can't you get it into your head that you're not a young boy any more? Look at you! A grown man, but you behave like a child, guzzling at ale like a baby at pap as soon as I turn my back!'

'It was just nice to have a chance to talk to some of our neighbours, woman – and stop shouting. You'd wake the dead, you would!'

'If you hadn't drunk so much, you wouldn't be so upset with a normal, quiet voice.'

'I didn't drink that much. I just got chatting, that's all. Like you were chatting in here with Emma. And anyway, it was you told *me* to bugger off. I didn't want to go there – I was coming home, remember?'

'You didn't have to go straight to the alehouse, did you? You could have gone and waited at our door, or visited Humphrey or someone.'

The mention of that name had made Nob give a fleeting wince, but not so fleeting that Cissy missed it. 'You didn't see him in there?'

'Look, I couldn't help it, all right? He just asked me to join him in a game of knuckles, and I didn't see the harm. When his friend challenged me, I had to accept.'

'Oh? And which friend was this?'

'Just some foreigner. He's Sergeant to the Arrayer who's in town. You must have heard about him,' Nob said, attempting a confidence he didn't feel while his belly bucked at the memory.

Humphrey had worn a serious expression, winking to Nob as he asked him over, and Nob soon saw what he meant. The Arrayer was here to take every able-bodied man from sixteen to sixty, and that meant Nob was well within the age range. If the Arrayer saw him, he could be taken – but if this Sergeant gained an affection for him, he might be safe. Nob and Humphrey set to with a will, gambling wildly so as to lose, and buying the stranger plenty of ale. It would be dangerous to openly bribe him in public, but the Sergeant must surely know what they were doing. It had been expensive.

'You haven't the brain you were born with, have you? Well, I hope you didn't gamble too much.'

Nob remained strangely quiet on that score, and Cissy had pressed him. Finally he had been forced to admit that his investments hadn't been blessed with profit.

Not only had he suffered the losses, but plying the Sergeant with good ale had proved ruinous. The man had an astonishing capacity for drink and hardly seemed to feel the effects. Then, when Nob went out for a piss, and the Sergeant followed him, grunting and farting as he did so, the Sergeant blandly thanked him for the gambling, accepting the money as his due from the run of the dice, no more. He had no idea, or so he said, that Nob had been playing to lose.

Nob was dumbstruck. As the Sergeant made to return indoors, Nob gave up, and with a bad grace he offered the money remaining in his purse. With an equally ill grace, the Sergeant accepted it – but somehow Nob didn't feel confident that he was entirely secure in the cold light of the following dawn.

'You're an oaf and a fool! You go in there and drink yourself to blind stupidity, and then you come back and want sympathy!' Cissy snapped, but then fetched him a morning ale to whet his appetite. 'I suppose you want me to give you some breakfast now.'

'No, I'll be all right with a pie,' he said with stiff pride. 'I wouldn't want to put you out.' He turned away and tripped over a stool, barking his shin on the seat. 'Oh, bugger, bugger, bugger!'

It was enough. Laughing, she took his arm and settled him in his chair by the hearth, and bent to cook him some bacon and an egg. She had some bread she had thrown into the oven the night before when he had finished cooking, and now she broke off a crust and gave it to him while his meal spat and sizzled on the griddle over the fire.

'You daft old sod,' she had said fondly.

No, Cissy thought now, it was no wonder that she was tired. No rest Sunday night, and Monday had been busy, too, what with all her work and Nob being unable to do more than grunt all morning. Monday night she had been so tired she'd only slept shallowly, waking at the slightest groan or squeak amongst the timbers of the house. And today, Tuesday, she had had to listen to poor little Sara as well. Sometimes it felt as though she was mother to all the foolish chits in the town.

Sara was a silly mare! She was always hoping to find a man who would help her, and she was so desperate that she would give herself to anyone, and now she must suffer the inevitable result of a fertile woman and be scorned as a whore. The parish had to keep her and her children, just as it would any child, but Sara would be fined the *layrwyta* by the Abbot's court. Her child would be known as a bastard, and while a King or nobleman could sire bastards all over the country without concern – why, even King Edward himself was taking his bastard son, Adam, with him to wars, if the stories were to be believed – a woman like Sara got off less lightly. Adam would be provided for by the King his father, but Sara's child would be despised by everyone, as an extra burden on the parish. No one would blame the incontinent man who had promised to wed her; no, they'd all blame the gullible woman.

Idly, Cissy wondered again who the father might be, but then she shook herself and told herself off for daydreaming. There were some crusts and scraps of pie in a pot, and she reopened the door and threw them out, and it was then, as she saw the bits and pieces fly through the air, that she saw a man recoil.

He looked familiar, she thought, a young fellow with broad enough shoulders, but then he was gone. Disappeared along an alley. Cissy closed the door thoughtfully. He was familiar . . . and then she realised who it was. 'Gerard, you poor soul!'

Simon was about to make his way to the guest room when, yawning, he heard a chuckle and turned to see Augerus and Mark sitting in the doorway to the *salsarius'* room.

'So, Bailiff, the strain is showing, is it?' Augerus asked, not unkindly.

Simon smiled and accepted a cup of Mark's wine. 'You fellows are never likely to suffer from thirst, are you?' Mark looked like a man who had already tasted more than a gallon of wine, Simon thought.

'We have a resonable supply, it is true,' he agreed. 'Why, any monk should be allocated five gallons of good quality ale and another five of weaker each week. Even a pensioner gets that. And Augerus and I have strenuous work to conduct for the Abbey. We need to keep our strength up – and what better for that than strong wine?'

'Shouldn't you both be abed, ready for the midnight services?'

'I rarely go to bed until later. I need little sleep,' Mark said with a partly boastful, faintly defensive air. 'I am like Brother Peter, the Almoner. He only ever has three hours a night. Never needs more than that. Most of the night he wanders about the place, along the walls and about the court. And look at him!' He belched quietly. 'He doesn't look too bad on it, does he?'

Simon noted that. So, Peter was always up and wandering about, was he? Well, it was hardly surprising. After his wound, maybe he found it hard to sleep. He was ever looking out for another band of attackers, perhaps?

'Have you found out any more about the murderer?' Augerus asked.

'Nothing.'

'Am I right, that the miner was killed by a club?'

'Yes. The sort of weapon that anyone could make,' Simon said. He saw no reason to mention that it had gone missing. Augerus or Peter was responsible for gossip, according to the Abbot, and Mark had already admitted his own interest in it.

Augerus glanced at Mark, then back to Simon. The Bailiff's tone was curious, he thought, and he wondered whether Simon harboured a suspicion against Mark. It was quite possible. After all, Augerus knew that Mark had been up on the moors, the day that Wally died. *And* he had argued with him. Perhaps the Bailiff knew that, too.

'I only asked, because I have heard that some mining men will scratch marks into wood they have purchased to stop others from stealing it. Perhaps there might be something on the timber that killed Walwynus?'

Simon was still a moment. 'Are you sure?'

'Take a closer look at the weapon. If it came from a miner, marks will be visible.'

Mark sniffed. 'I think Brother Augerus here has been drinking too much of my wine, Bailiff. Ignore his words. You will only find yourself wasting time. Have you learned any more about the thefts?'

Simon was suddenly aware that Mark's eyes were brighter and more shrewd than his voice would have indicated possible. Mark was perhaps inebriated, but that was his usual condition, and he was still perfectly capable of reasoning.

'What should I have learned? The Abbot did not ask me to investigate the theft,' he said, purposefully leaving the word in the singular.

'Aha! So you weren't piqued with interest? But perhaps other things have been taken from here, which could lead to the reputation of the Abbey being damaged – badly so. Don't you have a duty to seek out the truth?'

'Not if the Abbot told him not to,' Augerus said, and hiccuped. 'Isn't that right, Bailiff?'

'Yes,' Simon said. 'After all, I have no jurisdiction here, do I?'

'If a man is threatening to trample the Abbey's good name in the mud, he should be punished,' Mark said, but now his eyes were turned away, and Simon felt he was almost talking to himself. 'He deserves punishment.' Then he turned to face Simon again. 'Any man who dares harm this Abbey will suffer the consequences,' he declared. 'God won't allow blasphemous behaviour.'

Chapter Thirteen

After a long and strenuous ride, Baldwin and the Coroner had slept the Tuesday night in a pleasant inn at South Zeal. The weather had been kind to them, and they had made good time, riding fast on the swift road that led through Yeoford and then Hittisleigh, finally arriving in the village only a short time after dark.

Sore from their ride, Baldwin rose with a grunt as the innkeeper arrived and started opening the windows. This, Baldwin thought, was the worst aspect of travelling. Small inns so often had nowhere to put guests, and all they could do was make space for a man to sleep on a bench, or perhaps allow him to sleep on the hay in the stables. Perhaps he should be glad that at least there was space near the fire, because the weather was turning unseasonably cold. The landlord and some local men asserted that it was normal for the time of year, but Baldwin found it hard to believe that the weather so near to his own home could be quite so different. And the midges were foul, too. When he went out during the night to piss against a nearby tree, he found himself crawling with them in the space of a few minutes.

It was a great relief to be up and ahorse after a rushed breakfast of cold meat and some coarse bread. While he chewed, Baldwin saw the Coroner putting half his own loaf in a cloth and tying it into a neat bundle.

'What's that for?'

'I thought it would be as well to take something for our lunch.'

'There are plenty of good inns on the way to Tavistock, Coroner. We have eaten in some of them.' Baldwin eyed his own loaf. 'I certainly do not think that this would be comparable with some of the food at inns there.'

'No. If we were to ride around the north side of the moor, you'd be right,' the Coroner agreed. 'But I didn't intend that.'

'Which way do you want to go, then, Sir Roger?'

'Over the middle.'

Baldwin considered this. 'You do realise how quickly the mist can come down?'

'I have been on the moors and lived to tell the tale when that happened to me,' Coroner Roger said lightly. 'No, I merely wish to see the place where this death happened *before* we go to Tavistock and hear what people think we wish to hear.'

Baldwin nodded, but he was not content. Even when they had mounted their horses and he could see that the sky was almost devoid of clouds, that the top of the nearby hill was smooth and an apparently easy ride, and that the ground underfoot was dry and not at all boggy, he still felt a nagging anxiety.

'Come on, Sir Baldwin. Courage!'

They had left the inn, and were riding down the main street, past all the houses in their burgage plots on either side, and then turned right at the bottom of the road, heading for the great hill Baldwin had seen before.

'I am not fearful,' he said stiffly. 'Yet I swore to my wife that I would avoid spending too much time on the moors. Every time I visit, there is death and murder.'

'Well, that's why we're here, isn't it?'

Baldwin grunted. He could not put his feelings into words. He was aware of a curious awe about the moors which bordered on the superstitious; probably, he told himself, because his wife's attitude had coloured his own. Earlier this year, before the double disasters of the tournament at Oakhampton and then the murders at Sticklepath, he would have scoffed at the idea that the moors could themselves be unlucky or fated, but now he was growing to feel if not a fear, certainly a degree of apprehension.

'How do you know where we are to go?' he asked. 'I thought you only knew that the body was over towards Tavistock.'

'It is. It's down near Fox Tor. I know that way a little – there was a knife-fight there some years ago and a man died, and I had to go there to hold the inquest. It was one of my first cases, so of course I recall it well.' Cheerfully, he related the tale of a man who had come to the area with a friend, both seeking to become miners, but then one day they argued, and one stabbed the other.

Baldwin listened with only half an ear. They had followed the narrow lane for some hundreds of yards, with the land rising steeply on their left, while on their right there was an area of pasture with a small stream beyond, chuckling merrily. Their track took them right, down a dip and up the other side, and here Baldwin realised that they were climbing the hill.

From a distance it had looked immense, like a great bowl which God Himself had inverted on the horizon, and Baldwin was glad that the daunting sight of it was concealed by the thick woods that grew here at its base. In among some of them pastures had been cut, and the woods were receding as the men from the borough cut their winter logs and coppiced and cleared, but there were enough trees to hide the vast bulk.

They wound upwards, and then took a left fork. 'No point climbing to the top,' the Coroner muttered as he led the way. 'This is the peat-cutters' track.'

The track led between two walls, both of which had bushes and trees growing in them and reaching high overhead, creating a tunnel of verdure. At their feet, it was metalled with rocks of moorstone which had sunk to an even level, so that packhorses could pass up here even in the worst of the winter weather, and Baldwin was glad of it because at the side of the trail was a trickle of water. If there were no stones, this would soon become another quagmire.

The way climbed, but more shallowly, and at last they were out into the open, leaving the trees behind.

Baldwin took a deep breath. The last time he had been up on the moors he had seen another death, and it had touched his soul with sadness. That was partly why he was growing to detest the moors, because he could only ever associate them with death and murder. Not that this visit would make him feel any more content, with another murdered man at the end of the journey.

Here, though, it was hard to view the surrounding landscape with anything but awe and delight. The ground dropped away to their left, while on their right was the steeper rise to the summit, the side of the hill scattered with a thick clitter of stones. A tough climb on foot.

Coroner Roger took him on, past a strange little triple row of standing stones. 'God knows what they're doing here!' and on to a lower hill. From here, he pointed south. 'All this land is the King's. He must have magnificent hunts over here, eh?'

Baldwin could not help but agree. As they trotted on, he marvelled at the odd, soft beauty of the place. It was as though the only people alive were he and the Coroner. No noise of axe or pick reached their ears, and no house could be seen. There was only the endlessly rolling little hills, mostly smothered in a bright mantle of purple heather.

'Beautiful, isn't it?' the Coroner said, smiling at the sight of Baldwin's face.

'Very!' Baldwin twisted in his saddle to take it all in. Some hills were surmounted by great hunks of stone, while others were smooth, shallow ripples in the grass and heather. Here and there a stream cut through a hillside, casting a sharper shadow like a gash in the grass, but mostly it was all soft-looking undulations.

They stopped at the side of a stream, freeing the horses to drink their fill and crop the grass while the two men idled on the banks, and then remounted and rode on unhurriedly. The weather remained clear, and Baldwin could feel his trepidation falling away: as he had believed, it was superstitious in the extreme to blame the land itself for the evil actions of the men who trod upon it.

He hoped his attitude would not change again.

They followed well-trodden tracks for some more miles, but then Sir Roger began searching about, peering at the horizon.

'What is it?'

'Miners. There should be some near here. Aha! Over there!'

The Coroner pointed and Baldwin saw in the distance a thin plume of smoke rising. They rode towards it and found themselves in a small miners' camp. Having asked for directions, they were soon on their way again, and this time they reached a larger camp where a well-built miner pointed over to a hill. 'See where that stream is? You'll find poor old Wally there. But don't go straight. Head up that hillside west of here, then go south until you come to the cross. Then turn east again. Not until you reach the cross, though. The mire's deadly down there.'

Hearing his words, both agreed that his advice was sound. Soon the two were walking their horses up a hill. The cross was not difficult to see – a tall, somewhat rough-hewn shape. There they turned east and crossed a pleasant ford.

'If it's true that he was beaten to death, surely another miner was responsible,' Roger grumbled. 'Those bastards are always quarrelling. And they've got so many potential weapons to hand.'

'Quite so,' Baldwin said.

'Except you don't mean it. What's on your mind?'

'I trust the judgement of my Lord Abbot. He would only call us both out if there was good cause. Otherwise he would surely only ask for you to be here.'

'You mean he doesn't trust *my* judgement?'

Baldwin smiled innocently. 'I mean he probably has more than one concern. He knows how busy you are, Coroner. If there were another matter, he would hardly dare take up more of your time than he need, would he?'

'Oh. You *do* mean he doesn't trust my judgement!'

* * *

'The little devil,' Augerus said. 'If he couldn't be bothered to come and help me, the least he could have done was let me know.'

It was early afternoon, and the two were seated in the *salsarius'* room amidst the odours of gently curing hams and sausages, and the sharp tang of sea and fresh wind from the open steeping barrels in which the salt fish had soaked yesterday. It could take many hours for the salt to be washed out, and Mark had other duties, so he tended to leave the fish to soak for as long as possible, sliding the slippery fillets into a wooden trough to wash off most of the salt, then dropping them into the barrels of fresh water as early as possible on the Tuesday, ready for cooking today, Wednesday, the fast day. The barrels were still full of the fishy water, waiting to be emptied.

'Novices are not as respectful as they once were,' Mark said.

'I had thought Gerard wasn't so bad,' Augerus said. 'He is the best-behaved acolyte I have had dealings with for many a year. Quiet, unassuming, quick to learn. He has been candle-bearer for months now, and never late for the Mass, always well-mannered. But this proves he's just the same as the others. No doubt he thinks he can get away with sloping off back to his bed. He was kind enough to leave it for Nocturns, but as soon as Matins were finished, off he went.'

'Maybe he was told to help another Brother and didn't realise the time,' Mark said charitably. He wasn't really very interested, and he could afford to be generous: Gerard wasn't *his* acolyte.

'Well, he's not turned up for me,' Augerus said irritably. He had caught Mark's tone and felt miffed: whenever Mark had a problem with his own charges, Augerus always listened to *his* complaints. 'He was supposed to be in my undercroft to help me check the stores. I can't do it on my own.'

Mark sipped at his wine and cast a glance at his friend. Augerus sounded quite het up; it seemed as though there was something else on his mind. 'Don't worry. Maybe you'll find him waiting for you when you get back to the undercroft.'

'I should hope he arrives before that – I've sent a servant to fetch him from his bed.'

Mark peered through his doorway. 'Did you send *him*?' he asked, pointing.

As Augerus joined Mark in the doorway, the tall figure of Reginald hurried across the court to them.

'Where *is* that boy?' Augerus grated. 'If he's pretending to be ill . . .'

Mark threw him another look. Augerus was always so calm and unflappable, but now there was a tone of real anxiety in his voice. It was most unlike him. Mark almost wanted to reach out and pat his shoulder.

'Brother Augerus, Brother Mark, he's not there.'

Mark gazed at the lad with patient good-humour. 'Did you check in the *reredorter*?'

'I did, Master, and he isn't there either. I checked the *calefactory*, the *dorter*, the refectory, the church . . . I don't know where else to look.'

'Are you sure he wasn't in his bed?' Augerus demanded.

'No, he wasn't there, sir. I did look there for him.'

Mark touched Augerus' shoulder. 'He probably went out to the orchard and sat on a bench and fell asleep, or perhaps he went to the stable and dozed off in there. The Good Lord knows how often I have done that, although I couldn't count the number of times myself.'

'I must tell the Abbot he is missing!'

'There is no point – not yet. Wait awhile. He will turn up. You know what boys are.'

'But what if the poor fellow has fallen under the mill-wheel, or into the well?'

'If so, there is little you can do to help him now. Leave it until noon. I'm sure he'll reappear with a hangover, and you can give him a thrashing. He'll wish he'd never seen a barrel of ale or wine!'

Augerus turned to him and smiled, but there was in his face such a terrible sickly fear that Mark was hard put to return it.

The land was a natural bowl, Baldwin thought as they approached. It was a great depression surrounded by low hills. One miner trailed after them on a pony; ostensibly, as he said, because he was heading into Tavistock himself, but more likely, Baldwin considered, in order to see what the two travellers were doing here.

He was a swarthy fellow dressed in cheap fustian and leather, with grizzled hair, a thin wispy beard, and sharp eyes.

'That there,' he said, pointing a grimy finger at a great rounded mass directly ahead of them, 'that's Mount Misery, that is. Lots of men have died around the foot of it.'

'Why is that?' Baldwin asked. 'The mire?'

They were following the side of a stream, but now they left it and climbed an incline. The hill to their right was a mass of tumbled rock, the ground to their left a grassy plain with small silvery gleams where water lay or ran.

'The mire's further north,' the miner said, shooting him a look. He stared ahead and said nothing more for some minutes, then, as they breasted a small rise, he squinted ahead. Pointing again, he called, 'Do you see that cross?'

Baldwin ambled his horse to the man's side. A short way from their path was a small mass of tumbled rocks, with what looked like a well-made cross standing propped in the middle. 'What is it?'

'Childe's Tomb. 'Tis said Childe was a hunting man, and he was out hunting here in the winter, when the snow began to fall. He knew he had to get home, but all was white. He couldn't see anything. No sign of the trail, no hills, nothing. That's what the weather can be like out here.'

Baldwin remembered Belstone in the snow. He nodded slowly. 'When the snow falls, you had best find yourself beside a fire.'

'Ah. True enough, Master,' the miner said emphatically. 'Childe, he had no fire. Only him and his horse. He couldn't ride forrard because he didn't know which way *was* forrard. He might ride straight into the mire, see? So he went over to a hill and got off his horse, and he killed the horse and disembowelled it, thinking, see, that he'd got shelter and heat all in one, and he climbed inside, away from the bitter wind.'

The Coroner lifted his brows enquiringly. 'And that worked?'

Baldwin motioned towards the cross. 'Our friend called that a tomb, Coroner.'

'Aye,' the miner agreed, seemingly pleased that Baldwin had spotted the weakness of Coroner Roger's suggestion. 'Childe was found there days later, still inside his horse, as cold as the snow all about him.'

'Wouldn't he have been covered in snow?' the Coroner asked.

'Maybe the snow had all gone. That was why they could see him.'

'Oh. So he wasn't that cold, then. If it was warm enough to drive off the snow, he must surely have . . .'

Seeing the glower sweeping over the miner's face, Baldwin interrupted smoothly. 'And why should the folk have seen fit to bury him here and with such a magnificent tomb? Was he much loved?'

' 'Tis said that he was a rich man, and he left a paper . . .' He stole a glance at the Coroner. 'I think it was written on a piece of the horse's hide, written in blood.'

The Coroner gave a loud sniff of derision.

' 'Tis what's said! Anyhow, this paper said that whosoever found and buried his body could have his lands. So the folks, when they heard, all came to get him. The monks of Tavvie, they got to him first, and they were all set to carry him home, when the people of Plymstock appeared. Childe's lands were all Plymstock manor, and the folk there didn't want them to be given to Tavvie, so they stood on the riverbank and threatened to steal the body back.

Except the monks, they builded a little bridge and got over further up. And got him home to Tavvie and buried him.'

'So we can find his tomb in Tavistock?' the Coroner asked.

'Aye. You'll find it there.'

'So why was this tomb erected?'

Baldwin quickly said, 'They buried him here, obviously, until they realised that the monks of Tavistock could benefit from his testament. Then the monks came and disinterred him and took him back with them as this good miner has said.'

'He didn't say . . .'

'Perhaps we should simply continue?' Baldwin said, and as they rode on, he mused, 'There are so many ways for a man to die out here, so far from family and friends. It is a hard land.'

'Not hard, Master,' the miner corrected him. 'Just unforgiving. You have to be hard yourself to survive out here.'

'Do you think this dead miner Walwynus was hard enough?' Baldwin asked curiously.

'I did think so when he first came here.'

'How long ago would that have been?' Baldwin said.

'Several years ago. He arrived with a friend, but they argued and one attacked the other. Wally lived, Martyn didn't. Martyn was an arguing, vexatious man, while Wally was no harm to anyone, so it was easy to see that Wally had been innocent. He never fought, normally. Here on the moors you have to fight sometimes, even if you don't want to. Wally wasn't that hard. So he's dead.'

The Coroner nodded. 'I told you I remembered this area, Baldwin, that I'd held an inquest here? It must have been Wally who killed the other fellow. What was the victim's name?'

'Martyn Armstrong. He was a vicious bastard, he was. An evil tongue in his mouth, too. There were plenty were glad that Wally got rid of him.'

'That's the bugger!' the Coroner cried with satisfaction. 'Yes, Martyn the Scot, I remember now. The two men had been drinking, and Martyn was seen to pull a knife and thrust at his friend, but Walwynus managed to grapple. He got his own knife out and killed Martyn, although he was wounded at the same time. Still, he was released by the jury. They all agreed with him that Martyn had it coming.'

'But they had been friends?' Baldwin enquired, looking back at their guide.

'Yeah.' He spat a long dribble of phlegm at the ground and eyed the horizon thoughtfully. 'I was on the jury, and I reckoned with the rest that it was almost certainly Armstrong's fault. Wally was always pacifying him when he lost his temper. Not that he ever did with Wally. I thought that they had some sort of bond, like warriors. You know? You see two men who have served in the King's Host, and they'll be companions for life. These two seemed that way. But one day they flared into an argument. Hal was nearer – he reckoned he heard them shouting about some girl. It's often about a woman, isn't it?'

'Local girl?' Baldwin asked.

The Coroner answered first. 'No, it was a girl from their home, up in Scotland. I recall now: Walwynus said that some wench had been raped and killed, and Martyn made some comment about her.'

'That's right,' the miner said. 'Hal heard them and he asked Wally about it later. Wally told him this girl, she'd saved his life when he'd been at death's door. She'd nursed him and protected him, and Martyn took her memory and insulted her. He was in his cups, of course, but he said something about her being a brave, eager slut, and that got Wally so angry, he was about to jump on Martyn, but Martyn saw he'd gone too far and pulled his knife first. And that was that.'

'Did you ever learn where these two came from?' Baldwin asked.

'Christ! Miles away. Up northwards somewhere. They always spoke like foreigners. Scotland somewhere.'

'Would anyone else know more accurately? A friend or some-one?'

'That monk, the scarred one. He knew them up north, I heard tell. Hal said so. Said Wally told him. They weren't friends, though. Wally was terrified of the monk.'

'You think he thought the monk posed a danger to him?'

'Don't know about that so much,' the miner grunted. 'But he was scared, right enough. Scared shitless.'

'Did Walwynus have many enemies?' Baldwin asked.

'No. Most liked him.'

'Then was he killed for money?'

'Doubt it. He had little enough.'

'Can you think of any other reason why someone might choose to kill him?'

The miner gave a sly grin. 'There is a man might know.'

'Who?' Coroner Roger demanded. 'Come on, fellow, this is like drawing teeth!'

'True enough!' the miner cackled. 'You should ask Ellis the tooth-butcher. See what *he* has to say.'

They had arrived at a flat space, and Baldwin could see a body lying on the ground almost at the same time as he smelled it. A scruffy man in worn clothing stood blearily by, a long polearm in his hand as he wiped the sleep from his eyes. At his side was a small barrel which showed the cause of his lethargy.

The Coroner dropped from his horse and began to study the corpse without touching it.

While he was thus occupied, Baldwin leaned to the miner again. 'Who is this Ellis? Why should he wish to see the man dead?'

'Because Ellis reckoned Wally here was giving his sister one! You ask Ellis about his sister Sara.'

'How do you know this?'

'Because Ellis was here last Friday morning. I saw him, heard him shouting and threating Wally. Go on – you ask Ellis!'

Chapter Fourteen

After the previous day's rainy beginning, it had been a relief to wake to bright sunlight. Simon hadn't needed the prodding finger of the novice to wake him, for he could feel the warmth of the sun reaching out to him even through his closed eyes. Lazily, he had opened them to find himself gazing at Sir Tristram's bare body. The knight had swung open the rough board shutter and was staring down into the yard. Seeing him thus naked in the morning light, Simon was surprised at the number of wounds on his body.

There were two star-shaped scars, both on his upper left shoulder, which looked as though they must have been made by arrows. The great barbed arrows of old would have done far more damage, but the modern 'prickers', designed to penetrate mail, were little more than square-sectioned steel needles. Simon had seen other men wounded by these arrows, and they always had this characteristic star-shape. On his flank there was a great gouge lined with sore-looking red flesh that probably resulted from a sword or axe blow; his left upper arm bore a long, raking slash; both legs were mottled with scars, some fine, thin ones like cobwebs, others deep-looking stab wounds or slashes, as though he had been in a hundred different fights with all different types of weapon.

Simon couldn't help but let a low whistle pass from his lips, and Sir Tristram whirled round.

There were many knights whom Simon had met who had been suave and silky in movement as well as tone, men who would turn elegantly upon hearing someone behind them. Others, like his old friend Baldwin himself, were strangely precise in their movements. These were the masters of defence, men who had trained all their childhood and youth, men who could pick up any weapon and use it effectively, men who could fight as though dancing, while holding a seven-pound sword in one hand as if it was as light as a willow-wand.

This was not one such. Sir Tristram spun around like a man expecting death and the devil. His face was pulled into a snarl, his teeth bared, his whole being transfigured. From a tall man at a window he became a crouching, bestial creature, one hand forward, the other held back, ready to punch. But there was something missing. It was as though Sir Tristram had seen knights fight and knew how to emulate them, but lacked their skill; a man might, after all, pick up a hammer and beat at a piece of metal, but it took a smith's experience to bend that metal to his will.

Then, in an instant, Sir Tristram had reverted to a tall man at a window. He stood again with a faintly sneering smile. 'Aha, Bailiff. I didn't realise you were awake.'

'I'm sorry if I startled you,' Simon said carefully. 'But I noticed your scars, and I was surprised to see so many.'

Sir Tristram's face relaxed. He almost seemed to be listening to voices Simon couldn't hear. 'Perhaps you were just as surprised to hear how I spoke of the Scottish. This should explain why,' he said, motioning at his flank and legs. 'The Scots did all this. These fine scratches were from a razor. A Scot caught me on my own lands and sought to punish me. He intended to kill me, after torturing me, but I managed to get the better of him. A man of mine arrived and knocked him out, rescuing me, and I myself cut off his head, the bastard!'

'What of the arrows? When were you hit by them?'

'In the service of the King. One at Bannockburn, one at Boroughbridge. As you can see, places beginning with the letter "B" are not lucky for me!'

'I have never seen so many scars as those which lie on your arms and legs.'

'These are all from Scottish scum! They stole my inheritance from me, and whenever I have fought them to win back my lands, they have wounded me, but never have they conquered! Every encounter you see marked here upon my body, every one has been avenged. Not one man who marked me yet lives.'

'And now the King wants more men to end the border fighting once and for all. That will be a good thing for you, I suppose. You can enjoy peace once the fighting is all done.'

'Peace? Yes, I suppose so,' Sir Tristram said, but without conviction. Simon had the impression that he was less interested in peace, more in the potential that his returned lands would give him for exacting punishment on those who had thwarted him over the last years.

He didn't speak again while he and Simon dressed, but walked from the room as though sunk deep in thought. Simon was glad when he had gone. There was little pleasure to be gained from so morose a companion, and he groaned inwardly to think that he must remain with this man all day, surveying a crowd of grimy peasants all reeking of sweat, garlic and old ale.

When he found himself sitting at the table in the marketplace, inspecting all the men, the reality was even worse than his fears. The stench of unwashed bodies was almost overpowering in the still, hot air, and as each man stepped up to the table to be viewed and considered while his weapon was surveyed with greater or lesser contempt, the foul wafts from rotten teeth turned Simon's stomach. It would be almost preferable, he thought, to be up on the moors at the side of the putrefying corpse.

He was here in a semi-official capacity, mainly to see that the Arrayer didn't take too many of the Abbot's men, and he found the task tedious, but knew that he couldn't slip away. He must sit here and look intent, concentrating hard on serving the Abbot while also not appearing to help anyone obstruct the Arrayer. Waving at the innkeeper, he ordered a jug of ale and drank deeply as soon as it arrived.

By late afternoon, he had had enough. Rather the stinking remains of poor Walwynus than this slow repetition of the same old questions, followed by the same dull responses.

Simon was surprised at his reaction, for he disliked anything to do with corpses. However, in the last six years he had become increasingly involved in cases of murder than in the more usual aspects of his job – catching thieves, punishing miners or the peasants and farmers who lived near to Dartmoor and broke the Stannary laws. He was fortunate that his master, the Abbot, was keen to see that justice was impersonal, and that every murdered man still had access to justice.

If a man was murdered, he deserved to have his case looked into, and of course the Abbot couldn't ignore the fact that his courts were also highly profitable: trying a man for murder was always lucrative. The felon's chattels became forfeit, then there were the fines imposed upon him and any accomplices, plus the murder weapon became *deodand*, its value payable to the Crown . . .

With that idle thought, Simon wondered again what had happened to the murder weapon in Wally's case, but at that moment he became aware of shouts from the back of the crowd. Even the peasants before him were growing restless at the noise, with some shifting from foot to foot, muttering amongst themselves. One, an older man, looked suspicious, as though a watchman was chasing him for some previous misdemeanour; another fellow, who was quite bald, looked equally alarmed. Simon vaguely recognised him, quite a young fellow, he thought, but he knew thousands of men by their faces on the moors. There was nothing too familiar about him. The guilty expressions made Simon want to laugh. The men must have come here knowing that the King had offered pardons for all those who enlisted, and hoped to have taken his money before they could be caught.

Glancing across at Sir Tristram, he exchanged a knowing look, then rose and made his way through the crowd. Sir Tristram should be able to take whomsoever he wished. The local Bailiffs and constables must leave their prey today, because the King's need came first.

He arrived at the back to find a hot and flustered young monk. 'Oh, thank goodness, Bailiff. The Coroner is here and is asking for you.'

Rudolf was pleased to be on the move. After so many years of travelling, he and his family had the matter of striking and breaking camp down to a fine art. In no time at all the fires were doused, his pack-horses laden, and the carts filled ready to travel. With luck they should reach Ashburton before dark, although Rudolf hoped they would find a better path before long, for his two-wheeled cart was lumbering unevenly behind the horse, making the beast roll his eyes with alarm.

They had barely managed a mile when disaster struck. Rudolf was in front, leading his own sumpter, a gentle mare who could carry a vast quantity on her broad back, when he heard a warning shout, a terrific splintering crunch, and then a series of curses as a horse whinnied high with panic.

It was all because of a great lump of stone. The wheel had caught the rock, which had moved suddenly, letting the wheel fall into a deep rut. It jammed, and the horse had slipped. The beast was maddened with fear, and sprang up again, jerking sideways, but the wheel was firmly fixed, and wrenching it like that, the timbers snapped, even the metal tyre shearing. The cart had broken its wheel and axle as well. They would need not only a wheel-wright, but a capable carpenter as well, and in the meantime they were stuck here.

There was no point in trying to redistribute the load – Rudolf had seen that instantly. They wouldn't be able to transfer enough to the other mounts, and the petrified horse pulling the cart had been so frighted that one hoof slipped into a small hole, and with a sound like a tree cracking under the weight of an avalanche, the leg snapped.

His wife now stirred the stew which that horse had contributed. They would have a good meal today, but that was little consolation, knowing that they would not reach safety until his son had returned from his urgent journey to Buckfastleigh to ask for help. He must find another pony or horse to carry as much of the load as was possible on its back, because there could be no doubt that a cart was little use here.

'Rudi? You want some wine?' his wife called.

'No, Anna. I am not thirsty yet. I shall wait a while,' he responded. There was no point in anger or bitterness. All he could do was try to ensure that he and his little team were safe. His son had left soon after dawn. It was only a few miles to the town, from what he had heard, so with a little good fortune, Welf should be back with a horse before nightfall. Then all they would have to do would be to wait for the morning, break camp, and be off. He hoped there would be no more hold-ups.

'Don't worry, Rudi,' she said, walking to him. In her hand she held a large wineskin made from a goat, and she held it out to him. 'Drink. There is nothing more to be done tonight.'

'I hope Welf is all right. I had prayed that he would be back already.'

'You are fearful about that pewter, aren't you?'

'It was a very good price,' he said obliquely.

She laughed. 'You mean, it was too cheap to be legal! Well, we bought it in good faith. If it was stolen, it is not our concern, is it?'

'It may grow into our concern. A man's dead back there, and we were too close for comfort. It is all too easy for a foreigner to be blamed.'

'All we need do is tell them the truth. That we bought the metal from a merchant, and then wanted to be on our way.'

'Yes. One day after I fought with the man who is dead. The fool! Why didn't he leave us alone?'

* * *

When he entered the guest room, Simon instantly recognised the stocky figure standing in front of the window with his back to him.

'Coroner! Godspeed!'

Whirling, the Coroner studied him with a grin. 'It seems as though wherever you go, someone is soon murdered, Bailiff!'

'It's good to see you, Coroner,' Simon said with genuine relief. 'I was beginning to wonder whether the body would have completely dissolved before anyone got here, what with the strong sunshine.'

'I shouldn't worry. I'm not like some – no need for money.'

Simon smiled. Many of the Coroner's colleagues would haggle over money, demanding payment for going and doing their duty, but Simon knew that his friend was not formed from such a corrupt mould.

'Now, you have a body for us,' Coroner Roger said. 'A good thing, too. It was growing tedious being at home with my wife all the time. You have never heard a woman nag until you've witnessed my Lady in full flow.' The Coroner spent all his time, when out of her earshot, complaining about his wife, but it was plain as a turd on a leaf that he adored her.

'Us?' Simon queried. 'You want me to help you?'

The big man blinked with surprise. 'Hadn't you heard? Baldwin is with me. The Abbot specifically asked that he should accompany me. That was why we took a while to arrive.'

'No, the Abbot didn't tell me,' Simon said, and as he told the Coroner all about Wally's death and the discovery of his body, he felt his heart sinking.

It wasn't that Baldwin was here. That was a cause for delight so far as Simon was concerned. The knight was astute, swift to spot problems with evidence, an acute questioner, and a good companion. No, it was the inference that the Abbot had decided that Simon wasn't capable of dealing with the matter on his own.

If it were only that, Simon wouldn't have been concerned, for he was happy to confess that Baldwin was the better investigator of them both, but it wasn't only that. Suddenly there sprang in upon his mind the attitude of the Abbot on the day when he had been told of the robbery of the Abbot's wine.

At the time, the Abbot had said that he was worried about Simon's ability to cope, hadn't he? If not then, soon afterwards. Damn that hammer! It had reduced Simon in the Abbot's eyes, that much was clear. And it could cost him his position. There were always other men who were thrusting hard at his heels. Many would be glad of the post of Bailiff and the money it brought.

If the Abbot had lost faith in him, and he was to lose his post as Bailiff, he wasn't sure what he would do. It would be hard enough to work under another man, if the Abbot decided that he was competent enough to remain but only in some lower, more subservient Stannary position, but it would be impossible for him to maintain his lifestyle. He depended upon the money to support his family.

When he reviewed the last few months in his mind, he could see why the Abbot would have lost all trust in him. It wasn't only the most recent problem with the hammer. Earlier in the summer he had been steward in charge of the tournament at Oakhampton which had turned out to be pretty much of a disaster. Several men had died, and although the killer was found and his guilt proved to the satisfaction of Lord Hugh de Courtenay, something about the resolution of the case continued to niggle at him.

Perhaps the Abbot was right to doubt Simon's abilities. After all, the Bailiff so rarely had any idea why people committed their crimes, and without that insight, what was the point of employing him? Far better to ask Baldwin to come and seek the guilty. Baldwin always succeeded, he told himself bitterly.

'Are you well, Simon?'

The Coroner's voice broke in upon his gloomy thoughts. 'Oh yes, I am fine,' he replied hastily. 'Where is Baldwin?'

'The Abbot asked to see him as soon as he arrived here. I don't know why.'

'Oh.'

That response served only to increase Simon's fretfulness. So now the Abbot wanted to speak to Baldwin alone. Simon knew that the Abbot had always had a lot of respect for Baldwin, but surely this meant that Abbot Robert was asking Baldwin for particular advice about matters while his mere servant, Simon, entertained the Abbot's other guest, the Coroner.

Simon tried to put a brave face on it, but it was very hard. He no longer knew where he stood, and his confidence was leaking away.

Had he known his Bailiff's gloomy thoughts, the Abbot would have been horrified, but at the moment he had more pressing matters to concern him.

'Sir Baldwin, I am sorry to have to ask you to come here and see me after such a long journey, but I felt it was essential.'

'I should have liked to speak to our good friend Simon and then begin to help Coroner Roger as soon as possible,' Baldwin admitted, taking his seat near the Abbot when his host motioned to it. 'Yet you are clearly very concerned about something, Abbot Robert. You know I will help in any way I might.'

'I am very glad to hear it, Sir Baldwin. Very glad. But I am distracted! Where is my sense of hospitality? Did it take you long to get here?'

'We travelled to the outskirts of the moor yesterday, and continued today, coming over the moors past the body of the dead man.'

'Oh, do please excuse me! I forget my manners. Please, take some refreshment. Wine? Some stew or a pie?' When Baldwin refused any food, he ordered a jug of wine for them both. Once

Augerus was gone, he continued, 'The fact is, I fear that the murder of this miner out on the moors could soon get out of control. Let me explain. Have you heard the story of Milbrosa and the Abbot's Way?'

'Oh, I recall it vaguely.'

'You are quite right to be dismissive, of course. It's a piece of dull-witted nonsense! How anyone could believe that a monk could steal the Abbot's wine, then remove monastery plate and hawk it, and later choose to murder a man to conceal his crime – well, it is ridiculous, to my mind. And then they say that the devil took him.'

Baldwin smiled gently. 'Perhaps you should tell me the whole story again, Abbot? I think that perhaps I am starting from a position of not enough knowledge.'

He listened intently as his host related the tale of the Abbot's Way and explained how Milbrosa was supposed to have sunk so low, eventually dying when the devil himself took him and his companions away. Then the Abbot went on to tell of the death of the miner.

Baldwin shrugged. 'This is mere idle gossip and speculation, nothing more. A miner has been murdered out on the moors. Almost certainly a felon struck him hoping to win a good purse, and found he had knocked down the wrong man. There is probably no more to it than that. Chitter-chatter can dream up as many daft explanations as people want,' he added, thinking of the miner's words about 'Ellis the Tooth-Butcher', 'but it won't change anything.'

'There's more, Sir Baldwin,' said the Abbot heavily. 'Only last week I told our friend Bailiff Puttock that someone has been stealing from my personal undercroft. Wine has gone missing. Lately I have heard of plates being stolen from a guest staying here with us. I refused to believe it could be one of my brethren, but now . . . perhaps someone is trying to repeat the story for some reason.'

'Surely not. Someone could have stolen from you for personal gain, certainly, but in order to copy a tale of hundreds of years ago? What would be the point?'

'Perhaps if the devil himself decided . . .'

'I scarcely think that the devil would bother to get himself involved in so petty a crime,' Baldwin smiled. 'No, this is certainly a man who wants to steal from you to benefit himself. And your drawn features suggest that you suspect one among your own brethren. Is that not so?'

'Alas! I wish it were not so, but yes, I am afraid I do have my suspicions. And it is most unpleasant, Sir Baldwin, to have to conclude that. The companionship of the religious life is very close. Very important. If one of your companions betrays that, there is nothing else left.'

'Do you find your suspicions leaning to any one man?' Baldwin asked.

The Abbot shook his head as though still debating with himself whether he should discuss so sensitive a matter with a man from outside the cloister. 'I spoke to Bishop Walter at Exeter recently. He told me of the service you did him regarding Belstone's convent.' He looked up and met Baldwin's gaze. 'I would be grateful if you could keep all this to yourself, Sir Baldwin. Repeat it to no one.'

'Even Simon? If I need to talk about my theories, I shall have to let him know all that I know myself.'

'Then when that becomes necessary, you may tell him, but until then, please keep it secret that I suspect one of my own Brothers. It is too grave a burden for the ears of the gossips in the town. I trust Simon entirely, but as soon as a secret is shared, it is no longer a secret.'

'I confess I see no point in concealing matters. Is Simon aware of the stolen wine?'

'Yes. And the dead man, of course, but I . . . I pray it might not be so. If there is a connection, Sir Baldwin, then the only possible conclusion is that not only is one of my brethren guilty of stealing from my undercroft, but also he is guilty of . . .'

'Of murder. Yes. But surely there are other possibilities?'

'I find it hard to believe that a man from outside the Abbey could have broken into my stores and taken out a barrel-load of wine as well as escaping,' the Abbot said with some acerbity.

'True. Yet there are always possibilities. I should prefer to be able to confide in Simon. I have utter faith in him.'

'So do I, usually,' the Abbot said. He stared down at his table. 'I told him to ignore the theft from my stores. I had only mentioned it in his presence in order to raise gossip and possibly bring the thief to his senses. I had thought that the guilty man might confess to me – but my hope has been dashed. What if the thief *is* the murderer?' he muttered distractedly.

'If there is no connection between the two crimes, there can be no harm in telling Simon, and if there *is* a connection, I will be able to find the man with more speed if I have Simon's assistance.'

The Abbot said nothing, but frowned, and Baldwin continued: 'Surely others will already have heard about the wine? They will be thinking that there are parallels between this and the story of the Abbot's Way.'

'Yes, you may be right.' The Abbot stared hard at him. 'But Simon, as you know, has a moorman's concerns, a tin-miner's superstition. I have one fear, and that is that his own partiality to ghosts and pixies could influence his investigation of the dead man. Does that make sense? If I ask him to concentrate only on the dead miner, he can enquire into that without being swayed by stories of the devil.'

'I suppose that is sensible,' Baldwin allowed cautiously. He too knew how superstitious Simon was.

'As regards the matter of the wine, already one other of my monks has raised the name of a fellow with me, suggesting that he suspects him. You know Brother Peter, the Almoner?'

'Of course. The man with the terrible scar.'

'That is he.' Abbot Robert paused a moment before going on.

Sir Baldwin waited patiently. He thought the Abbot looked very tired. No doubt it was partly the weight of carrying suspicion in his heart, suspicion that was aimed at one of his colleagues, but then Baldwin knew that the Abbot had been elected to the abbacy in 1285, thirty-seven years ago. That was a long time for one man to run a complex administration. Baldwin had seen how strenuous the work was during his past, when he was a Knight Templar.

If the men with whom Baldwin had served had suffered because of the destruction of their Order, then Abbot Robert had suffered from the sheer length of his service. It was not a thought which had occurred to Baldwin before, but now as he looked at Robert Champeaux, he saw that the lines about his face were deeper, the laughter lines at his eyes less obvious, and the general impression he gained was one of exhaustion. Baldwin's heart went out to him. If he could help the man, he would.

'It is not only myself, you see,' the Abbot went on. 'I know that one other monk has seen the same signs. He too suspects. And he has come to speak to me, and I have to decide what I should now do. And I have decided. I shall let you know the suspect's identity so that you can look for evidence. If you find it, I shall call upon the fellow to confess to me, and then I can act as his confessor. But if he refuses . . . Why then, I must be sure that I am correct and that he is guilty.'

After this speech, Abbot Robert was silent again for a long time. He fiddled with his papers, stood and walked to the open window, staring out along the rows of apple trees and beyond before he could work up the courage to name one of his brethren.

'I have to wonder how long this thieving has been going on for,' he said eventually. 'Perhaps all my guests in the last few years have had small items disappear while they were here under my roof, and all were too polite to mention it to me. How could someone believe that a felon could infest an Abbey, after all? They must have blamed themselves for mislaying their property, perhaps thinking that they left it behind in the last inn where they passed a night, or that a light-fingered servant took it. But I believe that it was the same thief who stole my wine. He has grown bolder and feels secure enough to confront me personally!'

'What do you fear, Abbot?'

'Me? I fear many things, Sir Knight: the devil himself, bogs on the moors, a clumsy horse, and most of all my own over-confidence and stupidity! But more than all of these, I fear accusing a young man unjustly and later realising that I have blighted his life without reason.'

'I trust God wouldn't lead you astray,' Baldwin said fervently, but then his expression sharpened. 'A youngster? You mean . . .'

'I am advised to watch a young novice. An acolyte named Gerard.'

Chapter Fifteen

Almoner Peter had finished his duties early and was heading for the *calefactory* with the intention of finding a pint of wine and following that with a short snooze, if possible. He felt as though he deserved it.

But then he saw the arrival of the Coroner and the knight from Furnshill, and loitered shamelessly as he watched them unloading their packhorse and taking their belongings up to the rooms which had been allocated to them. A short while later he saw Augerus running over and hurrying up the stairs himself, then he reappeared with the knight and the two men walked quickly over to the Abbot's lodging.

The Coroner's face was familiar enough, aye, to fellows in Western Devonshire where he tended to ply his trade, so for Peter, his presence must mean that Wally's body on the moor was to receive its inquest at last. That was a matter of interest to Peter – as was the identity of this second man who was of such importance that the Abbot would ask him to visit before even thinking of seeing the Coroner.

It was not fear for himself that motivated him, but concern for the Abbey itself. If stories should spread about the wine, perhaps about other things which had been taken from the Abbey, that could only harm the great monastery's reputation, even the reputation of the Abbot himself. The Abbot must already be worried, to have asked this man to visit him, for having seen the urgency displayed by the messenger and Baldwin in responding to the Abbot, Peter doubted that it was merely a social call.

He watched a little longer and saw the Bailiff striding in through the gate and entering the guest rooms. Good, he thought: so the Bailiff and the Coroner were to talk about the body, presumably, while the Abbot was to talk to the stranger knight about . . . what? If the good Abbot wished to discuss Walwynus' murder he'd surely ask the Coroner and the Bailiff to join them, wouldn't he?

Aye, but it was odd. The Abbot was not the sort of man to demand that visitors should dance attendance on him as soon as they reached Tavistock after a strenuous journey, and the man's appearance told of a long ride and stiff joints.

Coming to a decision, Peter changed his mind and the direction of his steps. Instead of the *calefactory*, he walked to the brewery and out to the racks of barrels behind. He filled a jug and took a cup, blowing into it to remove the dust and a spider. Peering into the Great Court once more, he decided that he might as well go to his own room; he could see what was happening from there. He was sitting at his rough plank table, when he saw Sir Baldwin walking slowly and pensively out of the Abbot's lodging, crossing the yard to the Great Gate, and thence up the stairs to the guest rooms.

Leaving his cup in his room, Peter wandered outside. When he glanced about him, he saw grooms at their work with the visitors' horses. There was no fraternity closer, Peter always considered, than the brotherhood of horse-lovers, and among the grooms here, Ned the Horse was well-named.

He was there now, and Peter walked over to him, intending to learn all he could, but before he could do so, Brother Augerus strode up to the Ostler, a look of determination upon his features.

Peter just had time to retreat to an alcove, where he leaned against a wall and overheard the entire conversation.

Augerus spoke as though holding back his irritation. That was quite fascinating in its own right, Peter thought, for it meant that not only had the Abbot *not* taken him into his confidence, he had also sent Augie away on some menial task, presumably because the canny old bugger knew that Augie would listen at his door if he wasn't sent off.

'Ned – that's a good-looking mount. Whose is it?'

'This'n? B'longs that C'roner.'

'Oh, so the good Coroner from Exeter has arrived at last? That is good news. He will be able to tell us who killed the miner.'

'Reck'n us know. Can't bugger wi' the devil.'

'You know what the Abbot says about rumours of that kind. It's nonsense to think that the devil has had a hand in the death of Walwynus. It was someone else up on the moors.'

His only response was a grunt.

'What about that other horse? Whose is that?'

But Ned appeared to have taken Augerus's snapped comment as an insult. Ned himself was a professional, and although he was not the social equal of Augerus, whose post as Steward to the Abbot gave him an elevated status, Ned was easily the best horseman in the town, and knew it.

'Man with your master now,' he said, after some thought spent gently brushing the horse. A large scab of dried mud took his attention and he ignored the furious Augerus.

'Come now, man. I know his name is Sir Baldwin de Furnshill, for that is the name the messenger gave the Abbot. I was merely wondering what he was here for. Do you think he's here to help the Coroner?'

'P'raps. Dunno.'

'He arrived here with Sir Roger, didn't he?'

'Reck'n.'

'Ned, what do you know about him?' Augerus demanded. In his exasperation his voice had risen, and now Peter could imagine the long, steady stare that the horseman gave him over the back of the great mount.

'None of my bus'ness. Ask Abbot.'

Augerus spun on his heel and stormed away, passing Peter with a face as twisted as that of a man who has bitten into a blackberry, only to find that it was a sloe. The Almoner chuckled to himself, his hand up at his mouth and touching his old wound like a man reaching for a talisman. Once Augerus had disappeared, he sniffed, eased his shoulders, and walked around the wall.

'Hello, Ned.'

'Almoner.'

'That looks a fine animal.'

' 'Tis that.'

'Has the Abbot bought it? It's another of his own, is it?'

'No. Guests.'

'I see. It's the Coroner's, is it? I saw that he had arrived.'

'No. It's a knight's. Friend of C'roner's.'

'Oh, someone who's here to help the Coroner, I suppose. Another dull-witted clod of a city-dweller who thinks he knows all about moors, livestock and horses. They see a few animals in their markets and think they know enough to tell farmers how to raise them; show them a good Arab horse and they'd use it in a plough.' He gave a dry laugh.

'Most of 'em are daft enough to put a mount like this to a cart,' Ned agreed, a gleam of amusement in his eyes at Peter's sally – but then Peter had often brought him wine when the weather was cold over winter and had never commanded him to do anything. By comparison, Augerus had always been keen to let the servants know his own importance.

'Let's hope this daft fellow won't cause too much trouble, then, eh?'

'This 'un's not here just for the murder. Abbot asked 'un 'bout the theft.'

Peter feigned astonishment. 'The theft? Which?'

'Which do you think? The wine, of course. You want to know how I know?' The Ostler lowered his voice. 'That overblown bag of wind Augerus was told to clear out of the Abbot's room, right? So he couldn't stand and eavesdrop like he's wont. That means it must affect *him*. So, Brother – what's happened that affects him? The stealing of the wine, that's what! I reckon the Abbot thinks his Steward has a taste for strong red wine.' Ned guffawed.

'My friend, I think you have a most perspicacious mind,' Peter said with genuine respect. Ned's argument did indeed make sense, and the Almoner wondered whether the Abbot had heard evidence against Augerus. It was possible. For his own part, Peter was convinced that Augerus was a malign influence on the boy. It was for that reason that he had spoken to Gerard, trying to warn him to stop thieving.

'Not just that,' the groom said. He sniffed loudly, hawked and spat. 'Reckon Augerus has his hose in a tangle.'

'Why?'

'That Gerard. He's disappeared.'

'Oh?' said Peter. 'Really?' Although he tried to feign surprise, he gave Gerard the thief little thought. There were more important matters for him to consider. After all, he knew what had happened to Gerard.

Cissy was relieved to close up that night. Nob had kept away from her, sensing her mood, and had remained behind the trestle, cooking with an urgency she had never seen before. Now that all the customers had gone, he could avoid her no longer.

'Well? Come on, Nob, you great lump!'

'It wasn't my fault.'

'That'll make a nice change for you.'

Nob scowled. 'What would you have done? Left him to his fate?'

'It's none of our business, that's all.'

'Oh, wonderful! So we just leave him to get killed because it's nothing to do with us?'

'He wouldn't have been killed.'

'How do you know, Cissy? He certainly thought he would, and that's what matters.'

Cissy sniffed. 'If only that fool Walwynus hadn't gone and died.'

'Well, I doubt he wanted to.'

'Don't you snap at me, Nob Bakere! I won't have that in my own shop.'

'It's *our* shop, woman. And I'll talk how I bloody want in it.'

'All I meant was, if only he hadn't been so stupid. Bloody Wally. Well, he lived up to his name, didn't he? He was a right Wallydingle.'

'Was he the man Sara said had got her with pup?'

'No, she said nothing about the man. Wouldn't talk.'

Nob nodded morosely. He walked out to the back of the shop and fetched a jug of wine. Taking a good swig, he passed it to Cissy and sat at her side.

'Poor old Wally,' Cissy sighed.

'Not so poor, though, was he?' Nob tapped the side of his nose.

'What's that supposed to mean?'

'Well, he had the money after all, didn't he?'

'He had some, but maybe that was just from selling some veg.'

'Cissy, he was drinking all day and much of the night. That's more than the price of a bunch of carrots and a turnip, and then he gave all that to Hamelin. You saw how much.'

'What are we going to do?' she said quietly after a pause.

'Where could he have got that money from?'

'Who cares about the money?'

Nob looked at her. 'Probably the man who killed him.'

'But if Ellis killed him because of Sara, then he wouldn't have been interested in stealing from him, would he?'

'I don't reckon Ellis had anything to do with it. Wally had money, Cissy. Think! How would anyone know that he had cash on him? If someone bought something from him, then just maybe that same someone decided he'd prefer to keep the thing *and* the money both.'

'Any idea who that could be?'

Nob shrugged. 'Not a single one.'

'So we're back where we started. All we know is that we've committed a mortal sin.'

He sighed along with her. 'Yes. Still, if that young lad wasn't suited to the convent, surely God will forgive us?'

Cissy sniffed. All at once the tears were close again. 'We've been happy here, haven't we? And now we're going against the Abbot's own wishes. He'll not look kindly on us, not when he learns we've helped one of his novices to commit apostasy.'

Nob shook his head gloomily, taking a long swallow of wine. 'No. Well, that's just something we'll have to get used to, I think.'

'Perhaps. But I don't feel guilty. I feel that I may have saved a life,' Cissy said. And it was true. She could see the acolyte's face so clearly as they helped him climb into normal clothes and bundled up his habit.

'Poor boy,' she said. Gerard had looked so lost, so scared.

Surely it was their duty to save him.

Baldwin and the Coroner had travelled a good many miles in two days, and Sir Roger spoke for both when he said, 'My arse feels like it's been beaten with hazel for hours. I want a good, solid chair that won't move and a jug or two of strong ale. Then I need a haunch of beef or pork, hot, and dripping with fat and juice. After that I might feel half human again.'

'I see. Half human is as close as you feel you can ever hope to achieve?' Baldwin enquired.

'If I wasn't so bruised, Sir Knight, I'd force you to regret your words,' Coroner Roger said, grimly rubbing his behind. 'But under the circumstances, I'll forgive you if you only find a means of shoving a quart of ale in my hands.'

'Come with me,' Simon said. 'I know a small tavern which keeps a good brew.' He led the way from the gate and into the town itself. 'Ah, I'd thought he'd have finished,' he breathed.

Before them was the tavern outside which Sir Tristram had

been gauging his recruits. He was still there, speaking seriously to the clerk who had been scribbling the names of the men he had recruited and which weapons they had brought with them.

Seeing Simon, Sir Tristram straightened. 'You decided to come back, then?' he said rudely. 'This town has a poor number of men, Bailiff. Very poor quality. It must be the wet weather down here. The damp settles on the brain, I understand. Maybe that's why these clods are so gormless.'

As he spoke his eyes passed over Baldwin and Roger, appraising them. His attention rested for a moment on their swords: Coroner Roger's a heavy-bladed, rather long and slightly outdated lump of metal with a worn grip; Baldwin's by comparison a very modern blade with a hilt of fine grey leather. Simon could almost hear the thoughts in Sir Tristram's mind: one looked heavily used and was familiar to the wearer's hand, while the other was new, which could mean that the knight was new to his status, or that his last sword was broken and he had chosen to replace it with the very latest model.

Simon hurriedly introduced his friends to Sir Tristram. 'The King's Arrayer,' he added. 'Sir Tristram is here to recruit for the King's war in Scotland.'

'I wish you Godspeed, then,' Coroner Roger said. His eyes were moving beyond the knight already, to the bar in the tavern, and, joy! to the serving girl who caught his eye even as he lifted his brows hopefully. She smiled and held up four fingers. The Coroner hesitated, then gave a faint shake of his head and held up three.

Sir Tristram didn't see his glance or movement. 'I thank you. With some of these oafs, I'll need it.'

'Will you see more tomorrow?' Simon asked.

'There would seem to be little point. I have found forty men and two who could function as *vintenars*, so I am ready enough to fulfil the King's requirements. I shall leave tomorrow or the next day, when I have provisions, and hope their feet will survive the journey. God knows but that I am doubtful. In the meantime, I shall stay at the inn, rather than abusing the Abbot's generosity,' he added with a harsher tone. 'I can collect my horse tomorrow.'

He left them, graciously taking his leave and bowing, and the three men watched him in silence as he passed off along the street.

'What an arrogant . . .'

'Master Coroner, there is no need to use language which could embarrass the serving maid,' Baldwin said with mock severity.

'Embarrass you? Could I?' Coroner Roger asked archly as the girl appeared.

She giggled as his hand quested the length of her thigh. 'If you worked hard at it, Master.'

'I may just do that, my dear,' he drawled as she walked away. Then his face fell and he took a long draught of his wine. 'Trouble is, she's the right age to be my daughter.'

'Grand-daughter,' Simon corrected.

'Don't rub it in. My wife does that often enough.'

'How is the lovely Lady de Gidleigh?' Baldwin asked.

'The same as usual,' Roger said glumly. 'I think if I were to give her poison, it'd only make her stronger. She's built like a mule, there's nothing can knock her down. Even a simple disease gives up at the sight of her. She never loses her balance. Her humours seem as steady as a lump of moorstone. It's not fair. Hah! No, if I were to find some poison, I'd be better off drinking it meself. It would,' he added with a slow shake of his head as though in deep gloom, 'at least end my suffering,'

'My heart bleeds for you. You'd be terrified if the girl agreed to bed you,' Simon said with a smile. He and Baldwin knew that for all his harsh words, the Coroner was devoted to his wife.

'You think so? I tell you, I'd take her tonight, except it's hardly respectful to the Abbot to take a wench back to his own guest room and use it for a bulling shop, and it would be a rude rejection of his hospitality to stay here the night with her.'

'You are so thoughtful,' Baldwin said with a straight face.

'Some of us are. It is a hard cross to bear, though, old friend,' Roger sighed.

Simon was desperate to find out what the Abbot had wanted to see Baldwin about, but Baldwin avoided the subject. There was something about his manner which sent a tingle down Simon's back. Baldwin would not hold his gaze. His eyes seemed to touch on Simon fleetingly, then move on as though he was ashamed or nervous about something, and his fingers drummed on the table-top like a man waiting to be interrogated, rather than a man who was used to questioning others.

'Tell us what you know about this murdered man,' Baldwin said, apparently considering the barrels racked at the far end of the room.

Simon told them all he knew about Walwynus, and then spoke about the weapon, and how it had disappeared when he visited the second time.

'Interesting,' Baldwin murmured, his eyes narrowed.

'Could the guard have fallen asleep?' Roger said. 'I've heard of animals getting up really close to a man to steal a lump of meat. Look at rats. They'll take food from your hand while you sleep. Maybe a wildcat or wolf took this thing because it smelled of blood?'

'Roger, please!' Baldwin scoffed. 'A balk of timber? You honestly think a wolf would be stupid enough to carry that away when there was an easy meal within reach? No, that cudgel was removed by a human. The question is, was it taken away by the killer, which would be worrying, or was it grabbed by someone else?'

'That's what I thought,' Simon said quickly. If the Abbot had suggested that his mind was fogged or stupid, Simon wanted to prove to his two friends that the Abbot was wrong. 'If the killer went back to take it, then he might intend to kill again. A weapon like that is impossible to trace to a particular man.' He decided not to mention the marks, or Augerus' words. Perhaps he could raise that later, to impress the Abbot.

Coroner Roger stirred and snorted. 'What if it's not the murderer?'

'Why then,' Simon finished, 'it might well be someone who knows who the killer is and intends to avenge Wally with the very same weapon that was used to murder *him*.'

'There is another possibility, of course,' Baldwin said mildly.

'What?' asked Simon.

'That the club was taken purely in order to conceal it more effectively. Perhaps there *was* some way to identify it that you couldn't see, Simon, and someone took it in order to stop us finding the killer.'

'So he could himself kill the murderer,' Simon nodded.

Baldwin shot him a look from narrowed eyes. 'Perhaps . . . but perhaps the murderer was well thought of. Maybe this Walwynus was not liked and the miners about him were not distressed by his execution. It is a thought.'

'I don't see it would make much sense,' Simon protested.

'There is another thing, too,' Baldwin said. 'The killer need not have been a man. A woman could wield a morning star as easily as a man.'

'Surely few women could so devastatingly crush a man's skull?'

'No, I daresay you are right. I am merely speculating. But I shall look forward to seeing this corpse again and considering the wounds. I hope it hasn't disintegrated too badly before we get to it.'

Simon shrugged. Baldwin's smooth summary of the position had made him feel his own inadequacy compared with the knight's, reminding him of his incompetence before the Abbot. It was a terrible thing to recognise it in himself, this stupidity that could cost him his job.

Baldwin could see that Simon was upset, so he smiled and patted his friend's arm. It was always the case that Simon felt sick at the sight of a dead body. 'You do not have to come with us to the inquest if you do not want to,' he said kindly.

Simon's eyes hardened, and Baldwin withdrew his hand in surprise at the Bailiff's sharp tone. 'Why? Don't you think I can help you? Am I too stupid?'

Baldwin was too astonished to answer immediately. He could see that he had insulted or offended the man, but he had no idea how. When a scruffy messenger appeared, he was glad of the diversion.

'Sir Baldwin, the Abbot wants to see you again, sir. As soon as you can, please.'

'Yes, of course,' he said. 'No need for you two to leave your wine. I shall see you later.'

To his dismay, he saw that his words seemed only to increase Simon's gloom.

Chapter Sixteen

Hamelin approached the door of his house in Tavistock with dread curling in his belly like a worm. Again, there was no noise, no wailing or weeping, but he stood outside for a moment or two, listening, wondering how Joel, his infant son, fared.

He had been back at the mine since Friday, trying to concentrate on digging and keeping the flow of water at the right level, while Hal busied himself looking for a fresh source of metal. This area was all but mined out, but Hal had a nose for tin, and he said he thought that there was a new spot which others had missed – but if it was there, they had yet to find it. Still, it had taken Hamelin's mind off his sick son.

Hal had discovered the body of Wally first thing on Monday. He'd gone up there because he was beginning to wonder why there was no sign of a cooking fire or any other evidence of life at Wally's place; the corpse sent him running back to Hamelin to tell him, and then he took his pony and hurried off to town to inform the authorities, leaving Hamelin to protect the works. In all honesty Hamelin was incapable of concentrating. Hearing that Wally was dead had dulled his mind, and for much of Monday he merely sat and stared at the water running through the wooden leat.

Wally's death affected him profoundly. It felt as though there was a sign in this, as though Wally's life and his son Joel's were connected. One had died – perhaps the other would live? It was something to cling to.

It had been hard to get anything much done for all that long day. Hal, who had ridden back from Tavistock, stayed over at the corpse's side to protect it, but when he finally returned late on Tuesday morning, he was gruff and uncommunicative. He cast odd glances at Hamelin every now and again, but then looked away. It made for an uncomfortable atmosphere, and Hamelin was relieved when Hal went into the hut to sleep; next morning, he announced that he would return to the body and take over from the man waiting there.

Hamelin was nothing loath to see him tramp off towards Wally's corpse. They had hardly exchanged a word since Hal's return, and in any case, Hamelin had decided that he had to make the journey back to town to see his boy. Hal wouldn't know, because he would be at Wally's place all night.

Filled with trepidation, Hamelin pushed at the door and heard the leather hinges creaking, the bottom boards scraping along the dirt floor. When he could sidle around it, he entered, and had a glimpse of the room.

At the corner he could hear the thumping of a dog's tail; there was the snuffling of a child with a cold; an irregular crackling from a good fire, and then a metallic tapping. As he walked in, he saw his wife Emma standing at a good-sized cooking pot that rested on a trivet over the fire, and she was stirring a thick pottage. Hamelin felt saliva spurt from beneath his tongue at the smell of meat and vegetables.

She turned, startled, and stood gazing at him for a moment, white-faced in the dingy gloom of the room, and then ran to him, throwing her arms about him. Silently, she pulled him away from the door and down to their bed. There, lying well wrapped in an old woollen shawl, was their son. He looked so pale that Hamelin knew he was dead, and he felt a terrible emptiness open in his breast, as though God had reached in and pulled out his heart.

And then Joel muttered, and rolled over in his sleep, and Hamelin felt the tears flowing down his cheeks with pure joy.

* * *

It was very peculiar, Baldwin thought as he strode back towards the Abbey, the youthful messenger skipping at his heels.

Baldwin had known Simon Puttock for six years or so, and in all that time the Bailiff had been easygoing and cheerful, except during that terrible black period when Simon's first son had died. That had affected Simon and his wife Meg, as it would any loving parent, but even through all that pain and anguish, Simon had tried to maintain his sense of humour, and to see him so snappish about this killing was strange. Perhaps Simon had simply seen too many bodies?

No, it most surely wasn't that! Simon wasn't a weakling, he just had a weakness of belly when he found decaying human flesh; most of the population felt the same way. It was Baldwin who was different, for he had no fear of dead bodies. To him they were mere husks, the worn-out and discarded shells of men who no longer had a need for them. But when those husks were the remains of murdered men and women, Baldwin knew that they could still speak, and sometimes tell who had murdered them, and why. All it needed was an eye to look and a mind to notice – and an absence of bigotry or hatred. Too often people jumped to conclusions based upon their own prejudices; after his experience as a Knight Templar, Baldwin had no intention of committing the same sin.

The Abbot was standing beside his table when Baldwin entered, his face troubled. 'Thank you for returning so promptly, Sir Baldwin. I wanted to tell you as soon as I knew. After speaking to you, I decided to approach the novice to ask him point blank about the thefts, but I couldn't.' For a moment his composure evaporated and his face showed his anger and concern. 'The acolyte Gerard has disappeared.'

Baldwin's eyebrows shot up. 'Disappeared? Do you mean he has simply vanished?'

'As good as, I fear. There is no sign of him. I understand he hasn't been seen all day, but my brethren didn't tell me, thinking that he was misbehaving and would be back soon.'

Baldwin was already moving towards the door. 'Would you come with me? It would be easier to speak to your brethren if they know that I am acting on your behalf.'

'Of course.'

'Who was the last man to see him?'

'I fear I don't know,' Abbot Robert admitted, his sandals pattering on the flags as they went along the short passage out to the yard beyond.

'Do you know when he was last seen?'

'No, I only heard about this myself a short while ago.'

Baldwin said nothing, but his mind was whirling as he took in the symbolic impact of this boy's sudden disappearance. It would play into the hands of those who wanted to believe that the theft of the Abbot's wine was tied to the travellers on the moor, and to the murder of Walwynus. The lad's going would make everyone assume that the novice had been involved in the thefts and that the devil had taken him away, just as 150 years ago, Milbrosa had been spirited away. Baldwin didn't believe that story, but he knew that others did, and he also knew that an unscrupulous man would be keen to divert attention from his crime by blaming others. And who better to blame than the devil himself?

The Abbot walked hurriedly out through his door and down the staircase, leading Baldwin to the monks' cloister. He entered and walked quickly up the steps which led to the *dorter*.

In the great long room with the low screens which separated each little chamber, ensuring that no Brother ever had total privacy, Baldwin could see that each little cot was made up carefully, the blankets drawn up to the head of the bed. There were no Brothers here, for they would be talking and laughing in the *calefactory* or the brewery, preparing for an early night, ready to rise at midnight for the first service of the new day.

'Which was his cot?'

The Abbot beckoned to a young novice who was sweeping the floor while trying to appear uninterested in their conversation. 'Reginald, come here.'

'My Lord Abbot?'

'Which is Gerard's bed?'

The lad carefully set his besom against a wall and took the two to a cot that sat fifth along the wall on the right.

Baldwin studied it with a frowning gaze, silent except for a bark directed at Reginald to stand still, when the boy was about to return to his sweeping. Reginald froze, eyes downcast. He was petrified with fear, convinced that they knew what he had done, too scared to confess. God! All he'd tried to do was frighten Gerard. The silly bugger had been filching too much, and he couldn't be allowed to go on. But when Reg pushed him, and he went over, that was that. All he could do was get rid of the mess. And get rid he had. But pushing Gerard in the first place was sinful, and the result was worse. Reg hadn't ever committed a mortal sin before, and now, knowing that the Abbot and the knight were here to investigate Gerard's disappearance, his marrow turned to jelly.

At length Baldwin spoke. 'The bed has been made, just like all the others in this room. Who makes the beds?'

'Each Brother makes his own.'

'When?'

'We rise very early, as you know, and go straight to church. When *Matins* is done, most will come to the cloister to read and study, and later they return to the *dorter* to change their shoes, and then they will also make their beds. There is not much to do, after all. Only shake out the blankets and straighten them.'

Baldwin nodded. Each bed had its own blanket smoothed down over the palliasse, some more smoothly than others. Although they were not made of horse hair, the coverings were certainly thick and rough-looking, hardly the material to provide a man with a good night's sleep.

'Reginald, did you see Gerard today?' he asked.

Although tall and firmly built, more like a young squire than a monk, Reginald suffered from an explosion of acne. Baldwin could recall the mountain of Sicily as he passed by on board ship, the glowing summit belching fumes, and somehow it looked less unpleasant than the eruption on Reginald's face.

The boy must have read something in his gaze, for he dropped his eyes as though in shame. 'I can't remember. I've been busy.'

'What of yesterday? Did you speak to him then?'

'I might have done. It's hard to bring it to mind.'

'Did he look upset?'

Reginald couldn't say anything immediately. The memory of the dull-sounding thud as Gerard's skull hit the corner of the bed would never leave his dreams. He should confess his sins to the Abbot or another confessor, but he couldn't. It was too dangerous now.

At last he mumbled, 'He seemed a bit upset about something, I reckon. Maybe that was it. He had something troubling him.'

'So you do recall seeing him,' Baldwin noted. His attention was moving about the room, covering first the wall, then the screens, and last the floor and ceiling. There was nothing to indicate that anything had been amiss. 'He was a tidy fellow?'

The Abbot nodded. 'It is baffling. He was a neat young man, well-mannered and quiet, the perfect acolyte.'

'Why did you ever suspect that—'

The Abbot stopped him with a raised hand, then ordered Reginald from the room. With the relief bursting in his breast, Reg took up his broom and bolted, shutting the door behind him as quietly as his urgency would allow. Staring at the door, he thought he might be able to catch what the two men were saying, but his conscience wouldn't allow him to eavesdrop. Instead, he left his broom and walked down the stairs to the chapel, and entered. Kneeling before the altar, he covered his face with his hands and suddenly, before he could stop himself, his entire body began to shake from sobbing.

He was still in there, weeping, when Peter walked in later. The Almoner stood quietly watching, then walked to his side.

'It wasn't only you, boy,' he said. 'I helped you do it, and Gerard will find himself in a better place. If either of us should carry the guilt, it is I, not you. So calm yourself. Let me carry the crime on my own soul.'

A step outside made one of the dogs growl softly, and Emma was startled awake in a moment. She silently sat up and motioned to the dog to be silent before he could wake her children or husband, but she knew it was already too late when she felt Hamelin stirring at her side.

She stroked his cheek, liking the roughness of his stubble. Her love towards her man and her children was never stronger than when she saw them at night, sleeping. Even a mature man like Hamelin had a childlike quality when he was asleep. Now his face twitched slightly, just like young Joel when he was dreaming. Emma smiled and cupped her open hand about his jaw, peering more closely in the dim, unlit room. The only illumination came from the few logs which had been left to glow undamped at the middle of the fire. In the summer, the fire would be put out overnight for safety, but at this time of year, with the cooler weather, she kept the room warm if she could, and now that they had the money, she was determined that the family wouldn't suffer from cold. A friend of hers had woken the last winter to find her boy-child frozen stiff and dead at her side, and it had unbalanced her mind. Emma wouldn't have that happen to one of her own.

She looked about her at the children lying with them on the bed. Joel was cuddled up with a tangle of legs and arms, and Emma couldn't see who it was, but it was no matter. Both were breathing easily, and that was all that counted.

'Can't sleep?'

His low voice made her jump, unsettling Joel, who whimpered and snuffled in his sleep, but then she chuckled softly. 'Not easily, no. Do you think we could afford a larger palliasse?'

Rather than talk among their children, they rose from the bed and moved to the fireside. Emma had made a mat of pieces of material, and they sat on it, wrapping Hamelin's great woollen cloak about them. Hamelin prodded the embers into flame and added more logs, before staring into it.

'Where *did* Wally get all that money?' Emma asked after some while.

'I just don't know. Nowhere he should have. I got the feeling that he was keen to get rid of it. He was pleased to have found an excuse, I think, like it was stained with another man's blood or something.'

She shivered at the thought. 'You don't think it's cursed?'

Hamelin was silent for a while. 'You know, I felt today as though Wally and Joel were somehow connected. Like it seemed unfair that Joel should die so young, so perhaps God had taken Wally instead, like there was some sort of balance of fairness. Wally had lived long enough, so he died. Especially since he'd been involved in something he shouldn't have.'

'But what?'

'Haven't a clue. He never had any money, that was certain, not from his farming and his attempts to grow vegetables, and yet he always managed to scrape together some pennies for drinks whenever he came into town.'

The dog started to growl again, a low, menacing rumbling, and Hamelin threw a stone at it.

'Husband, don't you think you could find work in the town, rather than having to go up to work on the moors?' Emma asked reluctantly. They had been through this many times before.

'No,' he said uncompromisingly. 'If Hal and me can only find another source of tin, we'll be laughing. It's just this early period that's hard. We'll soon be on our feet again. Don't you worry. And what else could I do here without money? That bastard Mark made it impossible for me to start a new business.'

The dog began again, and this time they could hear the steps outside. Soon there was a light tapping at their door.

Hamelin snatched up his knife. It was a good weapon with a foot-long blade, and he held it to the door as he went to it. 'Who is it?' he hissed.

'Watchman. Is that Hamelin? Don't open the door, there's no need. I've been asked to tell you, the Abbot wants to see you first thing tomorrow. Go to the Court Gate when it opens. That's all.'

Hamelin relaxed as he listened to the footsteps leaving. He thrust his knife back in its sheath and returned to his wife's side.

She was frowning. 'What could the Abbot want with you?'

He shrugged. 'I don't know. Who cares? Maybe I've infringed one of his Burgh laws, spending too much time in the town when I should be out on the moors working.'

'Not our revered Abbot, surely!' she chuckled, nestling into his shoulder.

'So long as he doesn't want to fine me.'

'That would be that overblown bag of pus Joce Blakemoor, wouldn't it? He's in charge of fining miners.'

Hamelin grunted. 'I heard that no one ever liked him. Not when he was growing up here, not when he grew to be an adult. Everyone was delighted when he went away to learn to be a merchant, and no one was pleased when he came back.'

'How did he get to be elected Receiver if no one liked him?'

'It's one of those jobs. You buy it, and then get to cream off all the profits for your own pocket. He had money when he came back.'

'It's easy to make money when you have some.'

Hamelin turned to kiss her, then he gently laid her down on her back. 'We'll have money too, my love. Trust me. Nothing can go wrong for us now our little Joel is all right.'

* * *

Up in the dorter, the Abbot lowered his voice. When he was young, he would have been sorely tempted to stop outside and listen, and he only hoped that Reginald wouldn't submit to the same temptation.

'The matter of theft is repellent in a place like this, Baldwin. In a close-knit community like this, where the Brothers all sleep, eat and pray together, supposedly in one large family, the family of Christ, it is uniquely abhorrent to think that one of your companions is prepared to flout the laws of God and steal from his own Brothers. I do not wish to spread such a rumour. Especially, I should say, among the novices like Reginald. They talk so much, and they believe all they hear. Something like this – well! To think that a lad like Gerard is capable of stealing is, is . . . It is *dreadful.*'

Abbot Robert looked so upset that Baldwin wanted to open his heart to the man, to explain that he *could* easily understand the revulsion – he had himself been a Knight Templar, a warrior monk, and had taken the same three vows of poverty, chastity and obedience as the monks in this Abbey – but he knew he could not. That would mean confessing to his membership of the Order, which would inevitably colour Abbot Robert's opinion of him, and might even lead to the Abbot insisting on his being evicted from the guest room. Hospitality was one thing: harbouring a man whom the Pope had branded a heretic was quite another. Whether the Abbot believed, as some few English prelates did, that the Templars could be guilty, was beside the point, as Baldwin knew. The main thing was, Abbot Robert would be exposing himself and his Abbey to danger.

'I think I understand,' Baldwin said kindly.

'In that case, you will understand, too, that accusing a Brother of theft is an equally serious matter. Especially one who is so young.'

'Yet one of your monks did accuse him,' Baldwin said.

'He is an older man, Sir Baldwin, neither a bigot, nor a fool, and when he came to me and told me that one of my novices could be responsible for the thefts, I could not ignore his words.'

'Did he not seek to talk to the youth himself?' It was more common, Baldwin knew, for those who suspected a comrade of an infraction of the rules to speak to that person and give them a chance to put matters right before setting the facts before someone of the Abbot's stature.

'I think he would have tried, but he didn't feel that the novice Gerard took note.'

'Who is this paragon of virtue?'

The Abbot licked his lips. 'I shouldn't tell you without letting him know first. It's a matter of courtesy, you understand . . .'

'Yes, naturally,' Baldwin said, and he did not mind. Other issues were more crucial at present, such as what had happened to the acolyte. Yet there was another point, surely. He looked at the Abbot. 'My Lord Abbot, this is hardly a matter for me. A youth has been accused of theft by someone, and has decided to run away. How can I help?' Apostasy was considered a vile crime, and those who committed it were liable to be sought out and dragged back, but that was no reason for a secular official to become involved.

'It's that story of Milbrosa.'

'Ah, I see. You want me to find the lad because otherwise people will say he *has* been carried away by the Prince of Darkness.'

'Yes. I know it is ridiculous, but it is precisely that kind of rumour which could ruin us. I have dedicated my life to this Abbey, Sir Baldwin – all my adult life. I have converted a bankrupt institution into a tool for God. We give regular pensions to the poor of Tavistock and the lepers in the Maudlin, we provide comfort and safety for travellers, we work day and night for the protection of the souls of those living and the dead, and all this work depends upon money. It is no use telling me that money is irrelevant and despised by God, it is an asset like any other, and we depend upon our patrons for it. If a rumour should escape from within these walls that there was a second monk whose behaviour was so corrupt that his soul was taken away by the devil, how would that chime with the men who support us? Who would want to give us their money, if they felt that our behaviour was so foul that the devil looked upon us as his natural prey?'

Baldwin screwed up his face as he considered the task ahead. 'You want me to concentrate on finding this lad, then?'

'Yes, Sir Baldwin. I want you to find him, but I also want you to make sure that the murderer of the tin-miner is found as well, for while no man confesses to that crime, people's tongues will wag. And if people gossip, which would they prefer to talk about, a chance encounter with an outlaw, or an evil monk who has a heart as black as his Benedictine habit, and who is the prey of the Evil One?'

Baldwin smiled, then reached down to Gerard's bed and pulled the covering aside. 'There's nothing to see here,' he said. He sat on the bed and looked about him, but while he sat there, he became aware that something was wrong. There was nowhere to hide anything. All the Brothers swore themselves to poverty, so there was nothing, not even a small casket, for private belongings.

'If he had stolen anything, where could he have hidden it?' he asked.

The Abbot gazed about him distractedly. 'I have no idea! There are so many places all over the Abbey where someone could store things. It would be impossible to find them all.'

Baldwin nodded. It was as he expected. Standing, he picked up the rough base of the bed and tipped it, so that the palliasse was turned over, before setting the base back on the ground.

'Dramatic, I know. But if there are so many places all over the Abbey to hide things, why ever should he have left these here?' Baldwin asked as two plates bounced across the floor.

The Abbot gasped. 'What sort of fool was he, that he would

conceal them in his bed?' he demanded, bending to pick up one of the plates.

'I should think the most innocent fool,' Baldwin said harshly. 'Someone was determined to make him take the blame for something. Pah! Plates under his palliasse?'

'You think that the lad could be innocent? In truth?'

Baldwin smiled at the hopeful tone. 'Yes, indeed, my Lord Abbot. But do not blind yourself to the fact that only one of your congregation could have got in here, I assume.'

'I fear so. Only the choir itself could enter here – and one or two of the lay brothers, of course.'

'Then it is among them that we must seek the thief.'

'Sir Baldwin . . .'

'What is it?' Baldwin asked, seeing his sudden stillness.

Abbot Robert went over and touched the bed in the opposite partition. When he stood up, his face was anxious. 'I am no expert in death like you, but this stain . . . could it be dried blood?'

The knight's face was serious. 'I think we may have to prepare to find another body, Abbot.'

He had no idea that his words would prove to be correct so soon – nor that they would also prove be so wrong.

Chapter Seventeen

The next morning Baldwin saw that there was another guard at the corpse when they all reached the scene of the murder.

A crowd of miners had gathered, a grim band of men with the uniform of peat-stained, ragged clothing and eyes bright from malnutrition and overwork. Some were staring at Wally's body, but for the most part they appeared content to stand as far from it as was possible. When Baldwin and the others drew nearer, it was easy to see – or, rather, to smell – why.

Simon had said nothing about his concerns to Baldwin. Indeed, the two men had scarcely spoken. When Baldwin had returned from his private meeting with the Abbot, Simon had hoped that he would say something – but Baldwin made no reference to the lengthy interview. This made Simon think the worst – that the Abbot must have wanted to talk about Simon, probably warning Baldwin that he wasn't capable of doing his job any more.

It was terrible, this certainty that his best friend was aware of his position; Simon felt as though he was marked out, like a felon waiting to be caught. Not that there was any guilt, as such; it was more a deep sense of failure. He wanted to shout, to punch someone, to take control of events which seemed to be conspiring against him, to show that he was the same man, unchanged, as able as any other. But he couldn't.

He rode silently to a gorse tree that stood a few yards from the body, thankful that it was upwind of Wally's remains. Dropping from his mount he gave Baldwin a pleading look, and the knight gave him a nod as he too dismounted.

In the past Baldwin would have smiled or winked at his old friend, but his sympathy was beginning to wear thin. It wasn't a bit like Simon to be so ... what, sulky? It was the best word Baldwin could find to describe his morose temper.

Occasionally, it was true, Simon could be pensive, such as when something occurred to him that might have a bearing on a matter that they were investigating, but more usually they enjoyed an open, easy relationship. When the Coroner was with them, all three relished telling jokes or stories about the fire. They were comfortable with each other, unworried about hurting feelings, but last night Simon had been gruff and all but silent. Soon after they had returned from the alehouse, he complained of being tired and went to his bed, but Baldwin knew it was not to sleep. There was no grunting and snoring, but a deathly silence.

It wasn't only he who felt the atmosphere. The Coroner himself had spoken in a hushed voice, with many a glance at Simon, as though wondering whether Baldwin and he had fallen out. It was almost as though Simon suspected Baldwin of molesting his wife – a ridiculous thought, but that was the only comparison Baldwin could think of that in any way reflected Simon's attitude.

Perhaps it was because he simply did not wish to be here, Baldwin thought. Although the knight could never quite understand why Simon was so squeamish about corpses, he could appreciate that for some people, the sight of a putrefied mess could be the last straw.

With that thought, he began to concentrate on Wally. Although the body's odour was not pleasant, it was as nothing compared to the stenches Baldwin had been forced to experience in Acre during that city's siege in 1291, when the fresh corpses would be bloated and fly-blown within a few hours of death. It was impossible to eradicate that odour from his memory. In comparison, this corpse smelled almost fresh.

While the clerk whom the Abbot had sent with them to take the Coroner's notes sharpened his reeds and prepared his papers and ink, his eyes enormous and fearful as he gazed at the figure, Baldwin and Coroner Roger squatted by the corpse.

'All consistent with a beating,' Baldwin observed. 'Extensive damage done to his skull, poor devil.'

'Yes. Nothing to give us an idea of who did it or why, just a ravaged skull. What of the rest of him?'

The two stood aside while two men stepped forward. One was a gravedigger and sniffed unconcernedly, grabbing the shoulder and hose to pull Wally on to a blanket brought for the purpose. 'Good clothes, these,' he said appraisingly. He would be wearing them in a few hours, Baldwin thought.

His companion was more reluctant, a younger lad who wrinkled his nose and narrowed his eyes, as though he was likely to be sick at any moment.

Baldwin and Roger moved to a more open space in front of the jury while the two men dragged the body on the blanket over to them, dropped the corners and waited for another order. The Coroner told them to remove the victim's clothes, and while the older man immediately bent to his task, the younger one vomited noisily into a gorse bush.

'Don't worry, boy. You'll get used to 'un,' the gravedigger said as he worked a puffy arm through a sleeve.

Baldwin and Coroner Roger were soon confronted by the body of a man in his early thirties, slender of build, like one who has worked long and hard with not enough food or drink. His face was terribly beaten, his jaw broken, one eye-socket smashed in and the temple crushed. Dark brown stains of his blood lay all over his body, yet, as the gravedigger turned him over and then over again, there were clearly no recent stab wounds nor any sign that the fellow had been throttled, although there were some appalling scars from previous wounds, well healed now, about his shoulder, his flanks and one leg.

'What do you think, Sir Baldwin?' the Coroner asked.

'You can see as much as I,' Baldwin responded thoughtfully. 'He was killed by a blunt weapon, and I am sure Simon was right when he suggested that the studded timber he found was responsible. Apart from that, his body has lain here unmoved, from the look of the grass beneath him. It's paler compared with the rest.'

'I agree.' Coroner Roger eyed the jury of miners and began to call out his findings for the clerk to record. Later, when the Sheriff came on his annual perambulation, these records could be presented by the Coroner so that the guilty man might be held. Still later, when the Justices came in their own turn, the Coroner would once more attend the court and his records would be used to confirm the guilt or innocence of the accused man and, some felt more importantly, to gauge the extent of the fines and taxes to be imposed on the populace.

'There are no obvious stab wounds,' he said, eyeing the clerk sternly. Hastily the man began scribbling.

'No, but there are many scars. All healed now, but he must have been severely treated at some point,' Baldwin noted.

'Who saw this man last week?' Coroner Roger called out. 'Does anyone know what led to this happening to him?'

'I saw him on the day before the coining.'

Baldwin leaned to his left, peering past a tall red-headed man with a fierce-looking, bristling beard. Behind him was a shorter man with sallow complexion and intensely bright blue eyes in a weather-beaten face.

Roger pointed to him. 'What's your name?'

'Ivo Cornisshe. I work at the bottom of Misery Tor, not far from Wally's old place, and I saw him setting off for Tavistock early on the Thursday morning.'

Simon scowled about at the men. 'Where is Hamelin? He lived nearest, up at Wally's old place. Why isn't he here?'

There was no answer from the men arrayed before them.

The Coroner nodded to Ivo to continue. 'How was Wally when you saw him?'

'Cheery. I asked him why and he said he was looking forward to a good quart of ale. He hadn't made much money recently, he said, and he was miserable as the Tor itself with the thought of drinking any more water off the moors.'

'His mining wasn't successful?'

'It wasn't too bad, I suppose,' Ivo said with transparent honesty. 'He did well at first, but then he could only just scrape together enough to live on. That was why he tried farming instead.'

'Near here?'

'Yes. A mile or so. His rabbits and vegetables kept him fed. At least he didn't have a family to keep. Trouble is, veg is tough to grow on the moors. Especially if the rabbits get to them,' he added as an afterthought.

Coroner Roger glared about him to quell the sudden ripple of laughter that spread about the gathering. 'And he had little money?'

'None of us have much of that. If a mine is working, then all is well, but it only lasts so long. You dig and dig, wash away the rubbish, dig again, and then you have enough ore to fill a few bags. Melt them, pay the owner of a furnace, carry the ingots to Tavistock and pay your tax, pay your feed bills, have some ale, and suddenly you've got nothing left again, and you have to come back to the moors to try to dig out a load more tin or find a new claim.'

Simon interrupted. 'I have been told that on the day of the coining, he had money aplenty. Where did he get it?'

Ivo shrugged. 'Maybe he found it?'

There was a quiet comment, a miner suggesting that he could have sold his remaining asset, his body, to one of the rich women who were always passing by here, and some coarse sniggers were silenced only when the Coroner barked, 'Shut up!'

Simon was still listening as the Coroner began asking about Wally's sudden wealth, but standing at the edge of the miners, his eyes ranged over the men. Ivo was known to Simon, but then most of the men here were, by sight if not by name. It was natural that he should recognise them all, for there weren't all that many miners, especially since the famine years when even places like Hound Tor had been deserted.

He stared fixedly at Hal. The man knew something. It was obvious in the way that he stood with his legs apart, as though preparing for a verbal sparring match. His arms were crossed over his chest, with a long staff hooked in one, and he was perfectly still, as though he was at his ease, but his good eye was sharp and moving swiftly from Baldwin, to the Coroner, to Simon, below his black brows.

Seeing the swift flash of Hal's eye, Simon lifted his eyebrow, and he saw that his guess was correct. Hal looked away so fast, his head actually moved, and immediately the Coroner was on him.

'You! What's your name?'

Hal's head dropped lower on his shoulders. He threw Simon a bitter look as though the Bailiff had betrayed him, then cleared his throat. 'Hal Raddych, sir.'

'You're a miner as well?'

'Yes, sir. I protected this body the first night and last as well.'

'Very good. And tell me, did anyone come here and move the body while you were here?'

'No, sir.'

'What of the club that was used to kill him, Hal?' Simon interjected.

'The club?'

'The blood is still there on the bush. It's obvious that there was something there.'

'Perhaps it was stolen away, sir.'

Simon stood and hooked his thumbs in his belt. 'You take me for a fool?'

Hal looked away. 'No, sir. But I don't have the club, and I don't know anyone who does.'

'You don't know anyone who does? You mean that your guard yesterday took it?'

'I don't know where it could have gone. Maybe a dog took it, or a fox, I don't know. It doesn't matter, anyway. It was only a lump of timber.'

'It matters how many nails there were in it,' Coroner Roger said. 'We have to know how much it was worth for the *deodand*.'

Simon smiled. 'It must have been worth at least two shillings, Coroner, for someone to bother to take it away.'

'I agree. Unless we find it, I shall value it at two shillings. Sheriff to come and collect and so on.' He looked at the clerk. 'You know the right words to use, don't you?'

'Yes, sir.'

'So it comes to this, then,' the Coroner said. 'We have a dead man, murdered by a man or men unknown, his head bashed in. He was a poor man, yet he somehow had collected money. We don't know where from, but he splashed it around liberally. We know he was at the coining from what the good Bailiff has learned. Did he sell something? When he left his home to go to Tavistock, did he have a lump of tin to sell? Did he have a packhorse or anything? Did he look as though he was suddenly wealthy?'

Ivo answered. 'No, he had nothing but a small wallet on his back. His purse didn't rattle, either.'

'Could he have had tin in his wallet?'

'I suppose, but that much would be worth little. That was why he was so dependent on his rabbits. He used to sell the meat to other miners, the pelts separately. They were good on a winter's day, those pelts. He knew how to cure them with salt. Took him time, but he was good at it.'

'And yet he had enough money to buy drink?' the Coroner asked.

Hal interrupted. 'He was probably just looking to get some credit with a tradesman in Tavvie.'

Simon watched him closely. Hal looked deeply uncomfortable, as though he was trying to move the conversation on, afraid that something might be discovered.

'Hmmph,' the Coroner grunted. He was staring at the clerk, and Simon saw that he was taking Hal's words at face value. He was surprised – then afraid that he really was losing his touch. If he thought that the man's evidence was so clearly dishonest, perhaps it was because his own judgement was at fault, because Coroner Roger obviously didn't share his misgivings.

Then he felt a shiver of resentment pass through him. He refused to believe that he was so incompetent that he didn't understand his own miners. Simon had spent six years getting to know these men, and he'd cut his own cods off if Hal didn't know more than he was letting on. Simon would speak to him separately. It would show that he still knew a trick or two. Maybe it would teach the Abbot that he was trustworthy still. It might even prove to Baldwin that Simon wasn't burned out and only good for the midden.

There and then Simon determined that he would learn all that Hal knew, and if he could, he would discover the murderer of Wally before anyone else.

Nob belched as he finished the last of his ale and glanced up the road. The kennel was filled with mud and filth, and even as he watched, he heard the familiar bellow of 'Gardy loo!' from Tan the cobbler's place up the road. There followed a minor eruption of green liquid from an upper window, narrowly missing a well-dressed merchant who stopped in the middle of the lane to roar and shake a fist upwards with fury.

This was such a small street, it was no surprise that pedestrians would often get spattered, but there was little choice for house-keepers. They had to empty their pots somewhere.

Ordering another ale, Nob wiped his mouth with the back of his hand and considered the place. It was only a little town,

Tavistock. Not like other places he'd been. Mind, some of them weren't so disorganised as this. The trouble was, Devonshire was so hard to get to. Most towns he'd been to, there was some sort of plan about them before the houses went up. Like Longtown in Herefordshire. Even newer towns in Devonshire had some thought invested in them; he remembered South Zeal as a pleasant place with a good broad road and pleasant plots set out regularly along it.

Tavistock was older, though. It had been a Burgh since the days of Abbot Walter, many folk said (although exactly how long that meant Nob didn't know), and the lanes and streets wound their way untidily about the town. But there were advantages to it. Such as this, the quiet little alehouse not far from his pie-shop, hidden from the main roads by a bend where the lane was forced to curve around the back of Joce Blakemoor's large house.

It was an imposing property, although Nob himself reckoned it gaudy. Joce was supposed to be a wealthy man, and this was one of the most impressive places in town. The front opened on to the main street, and there you could see that the owner was important. All Blakemoor's goods were stored in the undercroft, a massive, stone-vaulted chamber that lay under the level of the road. Between the undercroft and the roadway was a large channel, like a moat, which must be traversed by a set of wooden steps, like a drawbridge, which led up to Joce's shop, where he sold his bolts of cloth, everything from the coarse, cheap dozens to linens and fine wool materials. He even sold silks occasionally, the only cloth merchant to do that this side of Exeter.

Behind the shop itself was Joce's hall, a high-ceilinged room with doors at the back which gave out to the parlour and service rooms, while a ladder led to the bedchambers at front and rear.

Nob knew the place well. On several occasions he had been instructed to bring pies here and set them out for Joce's friends, and he and Cissy had been led through to the great hall, its fire roaring in the middle of the floor, then out to the parlour and storerooms beyond. While Cissy went though some final details in the arrangement of the pies, for she was never satisfied, Nob had taken the opportunity to go upstairs and have a look around.

Joce had made a lot of money, that was obvious. The tapestries hanging from the walls, the pewter and silver on his shelves, all spoke of enormous wealth. A merchant selling fine cloths to the men and women of a place like Tavistock could earn himself plenty. Yet the last time Nob had visited, there were fewer plates on the cupboard, less pewter. Joce was obviously selling or pawning his things for cash. He had made more money than Nob ever would from flogging pies, but then, as Nob told himself, he had enough for himself and his family, and that was all a man could ask for.

He was a fortunate soul, Nob told himself again. Good wife, good food, enough to buy himself ale whenever he wanted, and his children all doing well. What more could one want? Especially when the alternative was to live like Joce, always trying to keep up appearances, spending lavishly just to maintain his position in society.

Not that his position was that impressive, in Nob's view. Nor was he highly respected. Especially now, since his temper seemed to be growing shorter.

Tavistock was a quiet town, and violence was a matter for conversation, so when a man like Joce went to his neighbour's house and threatened him, that news was soon the subject of gossip up and down the place. And when a man beat his servant for no reason, especially a likeable young fellow like Art, that too caused much quiet speculation. After all, it only took one fool whose brain was in his fists, to lead to fines for all the people living nearby. It was every man's responsibility to keep the King's Peace.

'Drinking so early?' said a smooth voice, and Nob recognised the figure of Sir Tristram's Sergeant.

'Jack!' He smiled broadly, partly because he wanted this man to look on him in as friendly a light as possible, but also from the hope that since Sir Tristram was thought to be done in the town, Nob himself should be safe from being recruited. 'Fancy an ale?'

'Don't mind if I do,' Jack said, taking his seat with a grunt. 'I've been up half the night keeping an eye on the pitiful little company Sir Tristram's hired. A drink would be welcome.'

'Perhaps a game or two while we're here?'

Jack smiled hawkishly. 'Now wouldn't that be fun?'

'Oh, yes,' said Nob, gesturing to the host to fetch ale and dice. Soon they were throwing the cubes on the table-top, and before long a number of coins had transferred themselves from Nob's purse to Jack's.

Trying to distract him, Nob said, 'You lot all off now?'

'As soon as the men have been fed and have collected water, we'll set off. Sir Tristram has more men waiting for us at Oakhampton and further north. We'll have a long and weary march to get up to Scotland.'

'It sounds a miserable land. Cold and wet all the time,' Nob shivered. 'I knew a man from up there – Wally, his name was, but he's dead now.'

'Aye?'

Nob winced as he caught sight of Jack's throw. 'Yes, he was murdered. The inquest is today.'

'There's a monk who came from up there, too, I've heard.'

'That'll be Peter. The wounded monk.'

'Oh aye? How's he wounded?'

Nob took up the dice with a sinking feeling as he eyed his losses. He explained about Peter's jaw, and saw Jack nodding.

'That's what Sir Tristram told me. Peter, eh? Well, I'll be buggered. Never thought he'd survive that one. We killed most of the men, but some of those bastards got away. And that bloody Brother had helped one of them.'

Nob listened with his mouth open wide as Jack told how Wally's life had been saved and how he had then participated in hunting down Peter.

'So Wally and these others escaped?'

'Yes. I was with Sir Tristram even then, and we chased after the three as soon as Peter was found, but they split up. First we knew, we came across this hut where Peter's woman had lived.'

Nob thought Jack's face seemed to harden at the recollection. The Sergeant leaned both elbows on the table and grimaced. 'She'd been raped, poor lass, and then she'd been killed – slowly. She was such a beautiful girl, too. I tell you, I'd seen the Armstrongs' handiwork before that, but I'd never seen anything so ... so pointlessly cruel.'

'Did you never catch any of them?'

'They all escaped into England and we couldn't chase them. There were other clans rattling their swords. We sent to warn other towns and villages, but no one saw them again. I'd thought they'd died – maybe fallen into a bog or died from the cold. Not hard enough as a way to perish, but then nothing would be cruel enough for bastards like them.'

Ellis put his strop on the doorpost and began to stroke his razor up and down it. He was still standing there when his sister appeared at the doorway with her children. She sent them to play with some sticks in the alley, and walked to him.

He looked tired, she thought. Weary, like a man who's been working too hard without enough to eat. 'Ellis?'

'What is it?'

His tone was grumpy, and he didn't meet her eyes as she stepped behind him and leaned against the wall, watching her children. 'I'm sorry, that's all. I thought he loved me, and I thought he'd marry me, and that would be my life settled and secure. All I wanted was to look after the children. Was it so terrible that I slept with him? He had told me that he'd marry me. Ellis, *please*!'

'What?'

'Look at me! Put your razor down and listen to me. I didn't mean to upset you.'

'You did, though. What will men call you now, eh? Slut, slattern, draggle-arse . . . *whore!*'

'He swore he'd marry me,' she said obstinately.

'And you'd trust the word of a fucking miner?' he spat.

'Miner?' It felt as though she was losing her grip on reality. 'He's no miner.'

'No, but he was, wasn't he?'

'I don't think so. Wasn't he always a merchant?'

Ellis gazed at her. 'You mean Wally, don't you?'

'Wally? What's he got to do with anything?'

'Wasn't it him? The father?'

'What do you take me for?' she gasped. 'You think I'd lie with . . . Good God!'

Ellis weakly grabbed a chair and sat. 'But who, then?'

'Joce, of course.'

'But I went up to Wally and . . .'

Sara felt her heart stop in her breast. She put her hand to her throat as though to massage air into her lungs. 'What? Ellis, what did you do?'

'Nothing, Sara. Christ's Bones! But I could have,' he shuddered.

Sara was relieved to hear his denial. He had never, to her knowledge, lied to her. 'What happened?'

'The next morning – Friday morning – I went up to the moors first thing. I wanted to scare him away from you, and I shouted at him, threatened him.'

'Did you hit him?'

'No! I didn't need to. Someone else had already laid into him. But I told him to leave you alone. He looked confused, denied anything, but then just agreed. Said he'd agree to anything if I'd just go.'

'Did anyone see you?'

'Only a monk.'

Sara pulled her tunic closer about her against the chill which had filled her. 'You could be accused of killing him.'

'Perhaps. If it happens, it happens.'

'I'll protect you,' she whispered, and hugged him.

For the first time that day, he looked a little easier.

Nob grunted when Jack scooped up his coins – *Nob's* coins – into his purse, said goodbye and thanked Nob for their game.

'Bastard!' Nob muttered. It was bad enough that Jack had taken his money – but he had played while drinking at Nob's expense too. Never even offered to buy a round.

Jack had wandered up the alley, and shortly afterwards, Nob heard what sounded like shouting. Hoping that someone was beating up his opponent, probably, as Nob told himself, to avenge his cheating at dice and general tight-fistedness, he glanced that way. Immediately his eye was caught by a flash of metal up beyond Joce's house. Throwing down some coins, he headed in that direction.

A fight was always worth seeing!

Chapter Eighteen

It was the Arrayer. Nob had heard of him, and seeing Sir Tristram at the front of all the men, striding along with a clerk at his side, talking loudly and slapping his hand on a piece of paper, it was easy to guess that he was a military commander. He appeared, from the sound of it, to be arguing about the amount of food that the town was going to provide for him and his men. Looking about him, Nob saw Joce, white-faced and furious, standing at a shop's table at the edge of the men.

'I will have none of it,' Joce said, and although his voice was quiet, it carried marvellously. 'You have your men, and the King demands that they be fed on the way – that is fine, but I will not give you food to take with you. If your men want food, they should bring it themselves from their own larders, not expect us to provide for them here. The King's writ demands food for his Host while marching and when they have been marshalled at a battlefield, but this is no battlefield, and they haven't been marching. If you had collected them from Cornwall and brought them here, then maybe you would deserve to take something, but you haven't.'

Nob leaned against a wall with the contentment of a man who could recognise good entertainment when he saw it. A little way off, he could see Jack, who stood scowling at Joce with his hands thrust into his belt. He appeared to be shaking his head as though a little confused.

Sir Tristram continued.

'You are deliberately preventing me from setting off, man, and that means you are thwarting the King in his aim of protecting his realm.'

'No, I am not!' Joce spat with fury. 'Don't you try to tell me that I am a traitor, you pig's turd! I may not be a knight, but I am not stupid enough to hold up the King in his ambitions, so don't you dare suggest I am! I am only standing up for the rights of this town, and I will not allow you to steal from the shops here just because you want to protect your own profits. You are the Arrayer; you have your men. *You* feed them.'

'You have a responsibility, Receiver! I demand that you—'

'You can demand what you like – you'll get nothing here, Arrayer! Ach! I have nothing further to say to you.'

Sir Tristram's face was purple and Nob could see that the crowd was enjoying the sight of a King's official almost apoplectic with rage. It was always good to see a lying bastard being roasted over the coals, and in Nob's world any man who rose to the heights of political or administrative power was, by definition, corrupt.

Not that in his view Joce Blakemoor was any better. The sole difference was, the pool in which Joce swam was smaller. Both men were like pikes, vicious, always hungry, swallowing up any fish smaller than themselves. Sir Tristram moved in that huge pool the Royal Court, while Joce fed off the provincial town of Tavistock, but both were as willing to destroy anyone or anything that stood in their way.

Nob couldn't understand it. Such men were always struggling to accrue a little more power to themselves so that they could cradle it to their hearts like a woman, but like any incontinent lover, as soon as they consummated their lust with that trophy, their eye was roving for the next.

There were many men who were like that with women, he knew. Men who were good fathers generally, who were kind and attentive to their wives, and who yet sought others. To Nob it was incomprehensible. His wife was his lover, friend, and a cheap housemaid too. What would he want with another? It was a right mystery.

But when there were two officials like these, there was bound to be fun. Nob could see that neither was going to withdraw; to leave the field now would be to lose face for ever, and that was one outcome that neither could tolerate. Except one man had an edge: a small army.

Sir Tristram barked an order. While most of the men were milling unconcernedly listening to the argument raging, there was one who looked on with more concentration.

When Nob glanced at Jack, he saw that the Sergeant hadn't immediately heard Sir Tristram's command. He was standing stock still and staring at Joce. Then he acknowledged the order and strode forward, gripping his sword. Nob saw the blade sliding free.

A young, shaven-headed man turned and paled at the sight of the Sergeant heading his way. Nob opened his mouth to bellow a warning, but before he could do so, the fellow had melted away into the crowd. Nob breathed a sigh of relief. 'Good lad, Gerard,' he muttered. 'Don't get into trouble when you don't need to.'

His attention flitted back over the crowd, and now he saw that Jack was heading directly towards Joce.

'*Joce!*' Nob bellowed.

It was impossible. Joce couldn't hear, didn't want to be distracted while he stood watching the Arrayer, expecting the danger to come from that side. If he did nothing, Nob knew he'd die. He didn't want that. No foreign bastard man-at-arms had the right to come here and kill the Receiver for doing his duty. It wasn't right!

Almost without thinking, Nob reached down and pulled his knife from the scabbard. He didn't want to fight anyone, but he couldn't let Joce get himself killed, and he started to hurry around the crowds, trying to get to Joce before the other man could.

But the man was gone. One moment Nob was hurrying around, keeping an eye on him, the next he was nowhere to be seen. And where he had stood, now there was a tall and apologetic-looking monk holding a long staff.

'Brother Peter,' Nob breathed. He swallowed, shoved his dagger away before anyone could notice he had drawn it, and offered a quick prayer of thanks. And then, as he glanced about the crowd, he saw Gerard's frightened face, and whispered, '*Godspeed*!'

Sir Tristram hadn't seen the collapse of his man, but he was aware of a certain confusion; having given his order, he expected it to be carried out. And then he saw the grim-faced monk and his face paled with a kind of fury that was near to madness. He turned on Joce again. 'So you have the monks on your side as well, do you? Think you've got God with you?'

'I have right on my side, that is all,' Joce said, but a little uncertainly. He was convinced that he had missed something. There had been a shout, he was sure, from the crowd, as though he was in danger, but when he cast a quick look about him, all he saw was the stern-looking figure of the monk watching the Arrayer, and now the Arrayer seemed even more choleric than before.

He stood his ground, waiting for the Arrayer to make a move. It was impossible for a knight to back down even in front of a crowd like this without losing the respect of his men.

His blood tingled. His hand was near to his sword and he felt the thrill of the moment keenly, ready to sweep the weapon loose and defend himself. The knight may have some skill, but Joce was trained as well, and by one of the best masters of defence in the whole of Devonshire. Joce was confident that he could win a straight fight, and excitement surged through his body, leaving a heightened awareness in its wake. It was as though he could feel the whole of his life balanced on a razor's edge, teetering this way and that. If he were to lean to one side his entire future could be thrown away, and Sir Tristram would kill him, but if his fortunes swayed in the opposite direction, he would prevail. Either he would kill Sir Tristram, or there would be no fight, and it was time he fought Sir Tristram. This, Joce felt, was a fight that had already been too long delayed.

Yes: he wanted to fight. Joce was frustrated and that had always made him turn to violence. It had helped him in business, forcing other men to give him deals which they would not have considered had Joce not stood over them; his natural aggression had also prevented some from taking revenge on him when a smaller, weaker man would have been attacked. Sometimes men tried to – but when they did, each time Joce had defended himself.

It was a lesson he had learned early in life. He had been orphaned when he was but a lad, and it was the kindness of the Abbey which had saved him. The Abbot had generously taken him on and seen him educated in the school with other boys, but like so many children with an obvious weakness, they had picked on him. Initially he was an easy target because all they needed to do was call him names and he would burst into tears, or weep as older fellows bullied him, but then one day he had snapped.

Usually he had been a calm, self-contained lad, but that one day he had already been pushed about, tripped up by one fellow and kicked on the ankle by another, both boys bigger than him. He hadn't dared do anything to protect himself, and the sense of inability to defend himself added to his feelings of inadequacy.

That was in the morning. Afterwards, he had gone to the *frater* for his meal and sat at the table with all the other boys, under the stern and watchful eye of the novice-master. The older boys sat at one end of the table, one of his chief tormenters, Augerus Thatcher, among them, and doled out the food for each of the boys.

With a smile of contempt, Augerus served Joce's food while holding his eye. He slopped the weak pottage into Joce's bowl and passed it along the table. It was mere water, with scarcely any barley or greens to colour it. Joce stared at it disbelievingly. Augerus must have carefully held the ladle to the side of the pot to prevent any meat or vegetables falling into it, just to be mean. Then the bread was passed along the table, but when it arrived at Joce, all that remained was a thin, meagre loaf, one with hardly enough to fill a mouth, let alone a hungry belly. Joce looked at Augerus, but Augerus stared back as though daring him to complain.

Joce was silent. He had been beaten so often that one more insult was easy to swallow in public. He drank his soup, used his bread to soak up the last traces of liquid, and sat at his place gazing hungrily at his empty bowl while the voice from the pulpit droned on, reading some text about turning the other cheek.

Afterwards the older boys left first, walking out to the cloister; Augerus went into the yard, and Joce followed him. Augerus made his leisurely way to the Water Gate and went out beneath it to the bridge. As soon as he was through the gate, Joce leaped.

That Augerus had been unsuspecting was evident from his squeak of alarm. Joce caught his habit at the shoulder and pulled him towards him; unbalanced, Augerus toppled, and with a little effort Joce could haul him to the Abbey wall, shoving him hard against the unyielding rock. Augerus' head struck the stone audibly, and his eyes opened wide as Joce's fist thumped into his chest. His breath came in sobs, and his eyes clouded a little with pain and fear, then flinched as Joce drew his fist back a second time.

'You're not doing that again, you sod,' Joce cried.

'I didn't do anything.'

'You gave me small measure; you did it on purpose! You do that again and I'll really hammer you!'

'I didn't, I didn't!'

Joce wavered. There was a note of conviction in his victim's voice, but he didn't care. He had suffered from the boys here long enough. 'I didn't!' he whined mockingly, and drove his fist as hard as he could into Augerus' nose.

It was so satisfying. He could feel the bone breaking and there was a loud crack which he could feel and hear simultaneously, almost as though it was his own knuckle breaking. Augerus' eyes gleamed a moment, then dulled with shock and fear, and then, only a moment later, the dams broke. First Augerus' nose gushed with a crimson stream, then his eyes flooded and his wailing started.

From that moment on, no one had ever bullied him again. Not at the school and not afterwards. Joce was powerful; he was strong, but he also enjoyed inflicting pain on others. It was an almost sexual pleasure; once tasted, it led to a hunger that couldn't be assuaged.

Watching Sir Tristram, Joce saw the man's anger flee, to be replaced by a certain anxiety. He could read the thoughts running through his mind as clearly as if Sir Tristram was enunciating each one. Sir Tristram thought Joce a rough, uncultured bully, a fool who would be taught a lesson as soon as the King heard of this treatment; yet he couldn't be sure that Joce didn't have the law on his side. Perhaps it was Sir Tristram's own failing, not having told the men to bring their own provisions. But Joce needed to be punished nevertheless. He should be beaten, maybe killed. That would teach him to raise his voice to a knight and an Arrayer. Especially since the Arrayer had all his recruits with him, over forty of them. And yet all these men were from the Burgh of Tavistock, and they all knew Joce. He was the Receiver of the town, and they might feel that they owed more allegiance to him than to their new leader, Sir Tristram. The latter could have tested them, could have ordered one or more to arrest Joce, but would they obey him?

Then Joce saw the knight's eyes flicker to one face in the crowd, and he heard Sir Tristram say, 'Oh, so it's you again, Scot-lover!'

Peter shifted his staff from one hand to the other. Joce was some distance away, but Peter could sense him thrusting his way forward to stand belligerently in front of Sir Tristram. The whole place was held in the grip of powerful emotions, Peter thought. Men squaring up to each other like game-cocks, both determined not to strike the first blow, both keen to be seen to be acting in defence, neither willing to back down. It was the sort of behaviour that led to feuds.

'Lordings, calm yourselves,' he said loudly with an enthusiastic, cheery tone. 'This is a silly situation. What a fine kettle of oats! Look at you both. You're here, both of you, to do your duty, one to the King, the other to the town. But the town is the King's and the King loves the town, so why should his officials come to blows?'

'We do not have to give up our profits to the Arrayer. The men can fill their bellies once they are on their march, but they don't get free food here,' Joce grated uncompromisingly.

'No more should they,' Peter chuckled. 'But there is no reason why they shouldn't *buy* their own food, is there?'

'They are the King's men now,' Sir Tristram blustered. He was staring past Peter, wondering what had happened to his Sergeant. Jack had been there, Sir Tristram was sure he had seen him. Jack had moved as though about to draw his sword, and Sir Tristram had transferred his attention back to Joce, thinking all he need do was keep him talking and distracted so that Jack could stab him in the back for delaying the King's Arrayer, but he'd disappeared.

'Then why d'ye not give the Receiver here a piece of paper that confirms that you have bought food from him on behalf of the King, and that the King must pay the town later?'

Joce laughed. 'A paper like that, unauthorised by the King, isn't worth the cost of the ink.'

'Well now, if it was confirmed by the King's Arrayer, so that if the King wouldn't honour it, his Arrayer himself would, that would serve, wouldn't it, Receiver?'

'I'd consider taking that, I suppose,' Joce agreed cautiously.

'You may take it, but I wouldn't give it!' Sir Tristram spat, his anger rising again. 'What, give an assurance that I'd cover the debt myself? I might as well give you my purse and the key to my manor!'

'Come, now,' said Peter. 'You tell us that it's the King's service you're on, that these men are owed food from their service to the King. Surely since they're in his service, any food they crave must be bought at his expense.'

'It is the custom that towns feed the King's Host.'

'Then the King would seek to recover any money paid out, wouldn't he?' Peter said. 'So you need have no fear on either account. If you are right, of course.'

'You are threatening me?'

Joce smacked his hand against his sword-hilt. 'No, Arrayer, *I* am threatening you. This good monk is trying to save you injury.'

He watched as the knight gave in with a bad grace. It was a pity, because Joce had expected, had craved, an opportunity to stab someone in the belly. He yearned for that moment of release. Yes, Joce regretted not being able to test himself against this knight. Sir Tristram didn't look very competent. Not compared with some Joce had fought.

He nodded curtly to the Brother, and set off homewards. At the steps which led to the entrance to his shop, he paused and glanced back at Sir Tristram, and in his angry, flat stare, he felt sure that he would soon have an opportunity to test himself against the knight. As far as he was concerned, it couldn't come too soon.

Joce had only gone a few yards down the alley when a figure darted out from a doorway. He drew back, his hand falling on his dagger. Then he saw who it was.

'Sara, what do you want?' he sneered. 'Come to ask me to wed you again?'

'It's not for me, Joce. It's my brother. Won't you help us?'

'Piss off, wench! I've got business to see to.'

'Joce, just a favour – please! You can help us.'

'Why should I?'

'Because,' Sara swallowed hard, 'because I'll swear to deny you fathered this child. I won't cause you more expense.'

'It means nothing to me. You can charge me with whatever you wish, but I don't think your litigation would succeed,' he said coldly. He thrust the dagger home in the scabbard with a flourish. 'No, I don't care to help.'

'All I ask is that you use your influence, that's all,' Sara said hurriedly.

'For what?'

'Ellis! He went to see Wally the day that he died because Ellis thought Wally was the father of this child. I didn't tell him about you.'

'Does he still think that?'

'No. I've told him the truth now. But Ellis was there, on the moors, and he saw Wally. People saw him; they could believe him guilty of the murder.'

'Aye. I could myself, at that.'

'But Ellis couldn't do something like that – you know that full well! All I ask is that you speak for him if he goes to court. Tell the truth about him.'

Joce shook his head. 'No. He could well have killed Wally. If he is accused, then damn his eyes. I don't care whether he hangs or not.'

Sara felt her blood chill. She had thought that this man who, when he tempted her into his bed had been so suave and sophisticated in his flattery, would at least agree to help her with this. Although he denied that his oaths last Thursday had been made honestly, she had persuaded herself that he must hold some affection for her, but his face and demeanour denied it. He was as cold as a lizard.

He continued, 'It seems my whole life is taken up with you. The last time I saw Wally, I had to thrash him. You know why? Because the fool sought to warn me away from you. He told me not to play with your affections. And now you say your brother went to see him? Perhaps all Wally's bruises at my hand will be laid at your brother's door!'

She could take no more of his gloating.

Suddenly she felt rage explode within her. She took the hilt of her little dagger and pulled it free, then with a wild shriek she launched herself at him.

He scarcely bothered to exert himself. As she aimed the point at him, he sidestepped, wrapping the edge of his cloak about his forearm with a rapid whipping motion, and clubbed her knife down. His other hand rose to her shoulder and thrust her back, hard, against the wall, then he took hold of her knife hand and wrenched it severely until she gasped and dropped her blade.

'You pathetic little whore,' he hissed. 'Should I demand compensation for this? Maybe I should take you indoors now, get you to undress one last time for me. Or should I just kill you now?' He chuckled unpleasantly. 'Or leave you alone to think about what will happen to your brother? He's a hothead. Maybe he did murder Wally. So, perhaps he'll soon be in gaol, and when he is, and you have no money to support yourself, why maybe then I'll let you come to my house every so often. You can warm yourself by my fire, for as long as you behave. Wouldn't that be amusing?'

With a last effort, she snatched her arm from him and drew away. 'Ellis won't be hanged. Nobody could think he was guilty,' she said in a voice that shook.

'We'll see,' Joce jeered. He thrust her aside and entered his house, bellowing loudly for his servant.

But Art could not hear him.

As soon as Joce had left the house, the boy had put his plan into action. It wasn't fair, that bully thrashing him every time he was angry. It wasn't Art's fault if he couldn't read Joce's mind and know what his master expected from him, and he was determined that he wasn't going to suffer like this any longer. So when Joce was called away by the meat-seller, worried about whether he'd ever get paid if he supplied Sir Tristram's men, Art packed his meagre belongings into a large cloth, tied his bundle together, took a stick from the pile lying ready to feed the fire, and left.

He knew which way Joce had gone, and he consciously took the opposite direction, walking to the Abbey, then circling around it to the bridge and crossing over the Tavy. As soon as he did so, he knew he was committed. The river was his personal boundary. Now he had passed over it, he felt as though he was free, and it was with a joyful scampering gait that he set off on the steep roadway that led up to the moors.

At the top, he took deep breaths, surveying the view. This, he knew, was the last sight he would ever have of Tavistock. He was going to where the money was – Exeter, maybe, even London. Perhaps he'd take a ship and learn to be a mariner – that appealed. There were so many possibilities.

The lad was less fit than he had realised. Two years in Joce's service had weakened his frame, and he had to stop often before he had covered five miles. There were occasional travellers passing by this important path, taking the direct route from Tavistock to Buckfast, but he avoided all. He had a small loaf, and this he ate when he was hungry, and then he realised that he had nothing else. It should not matter, he decided. He would arrive at Buckfast and ask at the monastery for charity, food and a bed. That would be sufficient for him.

Yet as he travelled, he grew aware of a great noise of men, and suddenly realised that he was near to the inquest. He had heard that there was to be one, but he hadn't thought of it. Joce could be there! Without hesitation, he dropped into the path of a stream and followed it away from the noise, trusting to the water to keep him safe.

Cold, shivering and fearful, he continued miserably on his way. The early optimism which had fired him was gone, and now he was a bedraggled, weary and hungry soul.

When the strange man jumped up from behind a rock and drew his sword, Art felt only relief. A man meant fire and warmth.

Chapter Nineteen

Peter held on to his staff with that little, apologetic smile still on his face. He could see the raging anger in Sir Tristram's eye and wouldn't turn his back on the man, but he made no threatening gestures, simply stood peacefully, all the while gripping his staff, ready to defend himself should it become necessary.

Sir Tristram bit his thumb to Peter and turned away contemptuously, walking swiftly towards an alehouse.

Peter sighed in relief, but he knew that this wasn't the end of the matter. There would probably be a complaint to the Abbot; it might even be a good idea to remain in the Abbey until the raggle-taggle of the King's men had gone. That way he would save putting temptation in Sir Tristram's path.

That wasn't strictly true, though, he admitted to himself. There had been almost a hope in his heart that the man might indeed attack him. It would have been pleasing to strike down one of the most notorious of border reivers. It was against his religion to strike the first blow, but that wouldn't have affected the sense of gratification which he would have felt from knocking Sir Tristram over. Like Joce, he craved the opportunity of a fight.

He was offering up a prayer for better self-control when he heard a scream, a high, keening sound. His head snapped around in time to see a woman appear at the end of an alley, arms thrown out as though she was pleading for help, her clothing bespattered with blood.

'Murder! Murder! Murder!'

* * *

Simon listened to the drawn-out procedures of the Coroner's inquest with a new sense of purpose. He watched the men of the jury and the witnesses as they gave their evidence, but there was little more to be told.

Wally had left his home early on the Thursday morning with the small satchel but nothing else. He had been seen by plenty of men during the coining. Initially, people said, he had looked despondent, watching the tin being assayed, but by the time he arrived in the drinking houses, his mood had undergone a great change. He was laughing and joking with the other customers, chatting up the whores and offering them money to sleep with him. The last that was seen of him that night was him disappearing with two women into a back room.

'Died happy, then,' was the Coroner's sour comment.

The following morning, once most of the miners had spent the money they had earned from selling tin, on buying provisions and ale or wine, all began their slow, painful progress back to their workings.

'What of Wally?' Coroner Roger asked.

Ivo answered drily. 'Coroner, we were marching under a grey, miserable cloud. We all had sore heads, and many had sore guts too. We weren't looking out for one man who wasn't one of us, not really.'

'You must have noticed a companion like him.'

'Why? I wouldn't have known if my own brother stood at my side. We live out in the wilds, Coroner, and when we have a chance to get into town with money in our scrips, we don't dilly dally. We drink! I got through more than a gallon of strong ale myself that night. Woke up in the kennel in the middle of a lane. By the time we set off for home, my head was like an apple in a press. Looking up was hard enough, my head was that heavy.'

'Did any man see him?' The Coroner looked about the group. 'What of anyone else?'

In the ensuing silence, the Coroner declared that Walwynus

had been murdered and stated the value of the fines to be imposed. Soon the men began to move away, muttering amongst themselves, swearing and complaining about the expense. Simon kept his eye on Hal, and as the man walked off, Simon darted after him, catching him by the arm.

'Come on, Hal. What's this about?'

'What? I don't know what you mean.'

'Yes, you do. That club – what happened to it?'

'I don't know . . .'

'Don't lie to me,' Simon hissed. 'Look at me, Hal. You've known me five or six years now, since I first came out here to the moors. I've never treated you badly or given you any problem, have I?'

'I'd like to help, but . . .' His eyes slid over to the Coroner.

Following his glance, Simon saw that Baldwin was watching them with interest. 'Don't worry about them. Anything you tell me will be between us and only us. All right?'

Hal met his gaze.

'I swear on my oath before God,' Simon added. 'Now do you trust me?'

Hal gave a grudging nod. 'I suppose so. Although I don't know how much use it'll be. I was with a group of the lads coming back on the Friday morning. There wasn't much talk. Wally was ahead of us, and we gradually caught him up. When I saw his face, it made me feel a lot better. He was in a much worse way, poor sod and he'd been in a fight. I gave him a good day, but he only grunted. It didn't take long to pass him, and we soon left him behind.' Hal paused. 'When I reached the Nun's Cross, I stopped and took a look behind me, just to check if Wally was all right. I could see him coming over the brow of the hill, and this time he wasn't alone. There was a monk with him.'

'Which monk?'

'The tall one, the one with the wound – you know, the scar along his jaw.'

'Brother Peter!' Simon breathed.

'That's the one. I couldn't hear what they said. I was heading homewards, and I didn't want to dither so I left them to it.'

'Was there anybody else on the moors that day, Hal? Come on, man!' he expostulated as he saw the miner look away. 'Wally's been killed. While his killer is free, he might strike again.'

'There was a group of travellers out there. Just like the old story,' Hal said quietly, and there was a shiftiness in his face. 'Look, Bailiff, you may not believe the legend, eh? But when you live out here on the moors, you get to hear funny things at night, you see strange things you didn't ought to. Sometimes things happen. If Wally was killed by the devil or one of his black angels, I don't want to get in *his* way.'

'I know what the moors can be like,' Simon said. 'But it's rubbish to think that the devil killed Wally. Why should he? Wally couldn't have sold his soul to the devil, could he? If he did, he made a poor bargain. I thought the devil offered worldly wealth.'

'And Wally suddenly had all that money last Thursday.'

'Bull's cods!' Simon said. 'Why did you take the club away, Hal?'

'What makes you think I did?'

'Your friend who guarded the body after you had no interest in it, did he? He didn't even seem to know there'd ever been one. Where did you put it?'

Hal squinted up at him, then shrugged. 'I threw it in a bog.'

'Why?' Simon asked. 'What good would that do you?'

'It was a timber from my mine,' Hal said gruffly.

Simon caught at his sleeve. 'How can you be sure?'

'You saw the marks. They were mine. When I bought it, I scratched my own sign into it. I always do that so others don't try to steal from me. Someone must have tried to make me look like the murderer; me or my partner, Hamelin, who shares my workings and the timber.'

'Not necessarily. It could have been someone who merely passed by and took up the first bit of wood he saw. Who could have found this timber and used it?'

'I left for Tavvie early in the morning before the coining. The timbers were all there at my mine from that morning to the day after the coining, so for two or three days they were left unguarded. Anyone could have helped themselves.'

'We know that Wally was alive at Nun's Cross on the Friday – you saw him. Did you see him after that? Or see anyone else?'

'No. Last time I saw him was breasting that hill with the monk.'

'But you were heading towards your mine. Could the monk have run ahead, stolen the timber, run back, and stored it ready to kill Wally?' Simon mused.

'No, I doubt it. But someone else could have, and left it there for Brother Peter to pick up and use to kill Wally.'

'It's all a bit far-fetched. Why should someone try to implicate you?' Simon considered. 'Not that they did that very well. After all, I didn't recognise the marks myself. How many would have?'

'Any miner who looked during the inquest.'

'Maybe. In which case perhaps a devious mind thought fit to put the blame on you. But it's more likely that it was someone else entirely, someone who wanted to kill Wally and who knew that your mine was empty. He could go there, hammer some nails into the timber, bring it up here and do the deed. Perhaps it was someone who lives up here and merely stole timber from you because your works were close or convenient.'

'Yeah. Could have been. There are plenty of men up here, what with miners, travellers and others.'

'You saw Peter walking up with Wally. I think that means he can't have been the killer. Whoever did this must have got to your camp before you, stolen the wood and made a weapon out of it, then made his way back up here. He hid and watched until Brother Peter moved on, then he attacked Wally and killed him.'

'Maybe.' Hal shrugged. 'It's hard to tell exactly what happened.'

But Simon was content with his reasoning. It was not a comfortable thought that a man like Peter could be a murderer, even after the terrible provocation he had suffered. The idea that a monk in the Abbey could be involved in murder was unsettling. Members of the clergy were as prone to anger as any other man in the kingdom, but it was horrifying to think that a man in Holy Orders could stray so far from his Rule and the Commandments as to kill another man.

Yet Simon was also aware of a niggling doubt at the back of his mind: if a monk did wish to murder, he would scarcely leave Tavistock carrying a large club studded with nails! He would prefer to concoct a weapon out on the moors, where no one could see and comment.

The shouts of 'Murder! Murder!' brought Nob to his senses. He leaped forward, shoving through the crowds, and soon reached the side of the fallen Sergeant. He paused, looking down at the body. As he did so, he saw a grimy hand reach out to the man's purse and a dagger slice through the laces that held it on the belt. Then a pair of pale eyes glanced up and met his, before the lad suddenly turned and pelted through the crowds.

'Oh, bugger!' Nob swore, and set off in pursuit.

The boy was fleet, but there were too many people in his way. He tried to dodge and slip between legs, but as Nob came closer, he gave a squeak and dropped the purse, sprang through a narrow gap, and then hurtled off along an alleyway.

Nob stood catching his breath. The boy was unknown to him, and to be honest, he didn't want to see him get caught. There was little satisfaction in the hanging of a mere child. He took up the purse and weighed it. It was heavy with his own coins! With a discontented grunt, he took it back to Jack, and dropped it onto the Sergeant's breast.

The Sergeant coughed and tried to sit up. 'Eh? What? Who fucking hit me? I'll break his sodding neck, the—'

'It was a monk. He didn't want you to kill someone right in front of him. A cutpurse took your money. It's there.'

'Sod the money! I was going to knife that bastard when someone hit me,' Jack said, every word making him wince. 'It was "Red Hand" Armstrong, God rot him!'

'Who?'

'The murderer who attacked the monk, the man who murdered Peter's girl, the man who led the Armstrongs after they were slaughtered by my master and me!' Jack exclaimed, struggling to his feet, but as soon as he was up, he staggered as though his knees were turned to jelly.

Nob wasn't sure what he was talking about, but to him it sounded as though Jack's head injury was worse than he'd thought. When Jack bent and threw up, his opinion was confirmed. 'Wait here, I'll get you help,' he said kindly. Asking another man to keep an eye on him, he hurried off to find Ellis. It was obvious that Jack really needed a vein opened.

Ellis was finishing shaving a man's chin when Nob found him. He completed the job swiftly, threw some knives and a bowl into a bag and went back with Nob to find Jack.

'Bare your arm, fellow,' Ellis said. 'From your face, your humours are all unbalanced. I have to bleed you.'

'Oh, shit. I don't usually have to pay to lose my blood,' Jack said with a feeble attempt at humour. He held out his forearm, and the knife was applied, the blood caught in a bowl held beneath.

'Where has the bastard gone?' Jack asked, staring about him with a frown.

'Who?' Nob asked.

' "Red Hand!" He was here. I was going to kill him, but someone struck me down first.'

Nob shrugged and Jack went through the story again, of how he and Sir Tristram caught the Armstrongs and slaughtered them, but missed 'Red Hand' and two others.

'What did he look like?' Ellis asked sceptically as he studied the congealing blood in his bowl, stirring it with a finger, while Nob applied a styptic and bandage to the cut.

Jack told them, and then caught sight of their expressions. 'What name does he use here?'

Ellis shot a look at Nob. 'Joce Blakemoor. Could he be a felon?'

Baldwin listened to the Coroner with only half an ear while he contemplated the body.

This was an unpleasant little murder, a brutal killing with no evident motive, and there was also the second issue, that of the disappearance of the novice. The two could well be related in some way, but it was hard to see how. Surely such men as a tin-miner on the moors and a novice from Tavistock were so far divorced from each other that they could not have met?

The Coroner had soon dismissed the jury and witnesses, and when they were all leaving and Baldwin could talk to Sir Roger alone, he raised the matter although, conscious of the Abbot's stipulation, he did not mention the reason for his interest.

'Do you think that the miner would have any involvement with the Abbey?'

Coroner Roger raised an eyebrow. 'Why? What's the Abbey got to do with him?'

'I don't know. I was merely wondering whether there could be some connection with the Abbey rather than with the poor folk who work out here.'

'And that's all?' the Coroner asked. 'It seems to me you know something I don't.'

'I know nothing, but I have been asked to look into things,' Baldwin agreed. 'The problem is, there is an ancient superstition here, that a band of monks were so debauched and irreligious that they were taken away by the devil. People tend to keep that kind of story close to their hearts and lend more credence to it than they ever would to the truth. I merely wondered whether there could be any substance to that sort of tale.'

The Coroner rubbed his chin. 'Seems odd that people should get that feeling if there's nothing there. What's this story about?'

Grudgingly Baldwin told him of the legend of Milbrosa, while the Coroner eyed him keenly. When Baldwin was finished, he sighed and stared out over the moors.

'Look at this land. Desolate, wind-swept, cold and foggy even in summer, and during the winter, you have to avoid almost all of it because of the bogs and mires. It's no wonder people like to make up tales about the place. So there's a mad monk here too, is there? Folk in Tavvie would believe that easily enough.' He cast Baldwin a swift glance. 'I suppose you won't tell me any more. Well enough. But I think you have more information that you could give me, if you had a mind.'

'I assure you, I have told you all I can,' Baldwin said disingenuously.

'Hah! Is that the truth? Anyway, I won't put you under any more pressure. If you're keeping something back it's because you either can't trust me with the truth, which I'd find hard to believe after the cases we have investigated together, or that someone with more power has ordered you to keep it to yourself. And the Abbot is a powerful man, isn't he?' He held up his hand to stop Baldwin's quick denial. 'Enough! Your protestations prove my guess. Very well, so we need to consider whether this miner could have been tied to the Abbey in some way. Certainly he was at the coining, so he could have had some sort of contact with the Abbey. Perhaps he went to pray at the shrine? Or simply bumped into a monk he knew?'

Baldwin wasn't convinced. He glanced over his shoulder, and seeing Simon talking to the old miner Hal, he led the way to them.

'Simon, may we ask this miner some questions?' Baldwin asked.

There it was again, Baldwin thought to himself. The usually cheerful Bailiff gave a most ungracious nod without meeting Baldwin's eye. It made him look almost shifty, and Baldwin was convinced that there was a block between them, a wall of resentment. He couldn't understand it. Simon and he had never had a hard word. They had been friends for six years now, and Baldwin was sure he had not given his friend any reason to be angry with him. Perversely, he began to feel a reciprocal bitterness rather than a desire to offer sympathy and find out where the problem lay, and he turned a little from Simon to face Hal.

'You knew this man Walwynus?'

'I've told the Bailiff all I know.'

'And now you're going to tell us as well,' the Coroner said happily.

Hal glared at him, but said nothing.

Baldwin said, 'Did he go to the town often?'

'No. Hardly had a penny to spend. He only went for the coinings. Four, five times a year.'

'Was he friendly with any of the monks?'

Hal shrugged, glancing at Simon, who was standing a short way off, listening intently. 'Don't know.'

'Do you often see monks out here?' Coroner Roger asked.

Hal tilted his head and flung an arm out towards a tall cross at the top of a nearby hill. 'See that? That's a way-marker for the Abbot's path. There are always monks wandering from Buckfast to Buckland to Tavistock. We see them all the time. When they aren't walking about and being a nuisance, they're talking to folk and getting in the way, or sometimes preaching. They're a pain in the cods.'

'Are they always monks?'

'What do you mean?'

Baldwin smiled reassuringly. 'There are others who wear the habit, aren't there? Friars, for example. And novices.'

'Oh, yes. The Almoner, Peter, he sometimes has younger lads

up here. I think it's to teach them safety on the moors, in case they
are ever sent out to Buckfast.'

'This Almoner is a regular visitor up here?'

Asking the question, Baldwin heard Simon make a tiny sound,
like a grunt, as though he was suddenly listening so carefully that
he had all but forgotten to breathe.

'Peter's often up here, yes. There's a shepherd boy over toward
Ashburton – John, he's called. Orphaned, he's been looked after
by the Abbot for some years. Recently he was crushed by a falling
tree-limb and broke his leg. The Abbot's Almoner is often up that
way to see him and pay him.'

'Pay him?' Baldwin asked.

'Yes. He has a half-wage while he's ill. The Abbot takes his
charity seriously,' Hal said without irony.

'Are you aware of the Almoner or any of these novices talking
to Walwynus?'

'What would an Almoner have to do with a man like him?'

'He was a poor man; a poor man is often provided for by
alms.'

'What, you think Brother Peter would give out his money to a
miner who fell on hard times? Wally would have to have been
beggared in the town itself for Brother Peter to consider him;
Wally had land and the ability to work.'

'Perhaps one of the novices knew Walwynus before taking the
tonsure?'

'It's possible. But if you reckon to suggest Wally was father to
any of them, well, I'd guess you'd be wrong. He enjoyed the
whores when he could, but I doubt he'd have had a child without
me knowing. If he had, it'd be living in Tavistock still, not out
Ashburton way.'

There was no way to put that to the test, Baldwin noted, yet it
could be a useful line of enquiry for the future. He was worried
about the disappearance of the novice still; the idea of the lad
running away was attractive, if only because the other possibility,

that he had been killed, was so repellent. That would surely mean that another novice, or monk, was a murderer.

That thought led him to muse, 'This Peter . . . some monks have fathered their own children, and . . .'

'Brother Peter only came here a few years ago,' Simon said. 'If this boy was a shepherd, he must be more than eight years old.'

'He's fourteen,' Hal supplied.

'Not his own, then,' Baldwin said reluctantly. He glanced at Simon, acknowledging his help, and Simon tried to smile. He looked as though he was suffering from piles. What on earth was the matter with his friend? Baldwin wondered. He swore to himself that he would tackle Simon as soon as he could.

He turned back to the miner. 'Have you seen any monks or novices up here recently? Or just travellers generally who look out of place?'

Hal scowled up at him. 'There was one fellow earlier during the inquest. I saw him, running as if the devil and all his hounds were after him. Straight up along the Abbot's Way, past us and on eastwards.'

'Who was it?'

'I've seen him before.' Hal stuck out his jaw and scratched at his chin. 'Lad called Art, who works as servant to Joce Blakemoor, the Receiver.'

Baldwin's eyes followed his pointing finger. 'What lies that way?'

'Go far enough and you'll get to Buckfast.'

'Is there anything between us here and the town?'

'Only the travellers. Don't think there's anything else.'

Baldwin smiled. 'One last thing. These travellers. Where would we find them?'

Chapter Twenty

Joce stalked across his hall still bellowing for his servant, but Art was nowhere to be seen. Feeling thwarted, Joce stormed through to the buttery and drew off a quart of wine, himself carrying it back to the hall, where he sat down before his fire. The embers were smouldering pleasantly, and he threw some sticks onto it and sat back to wait until the flames should begin to lick upwards.

It was good that he had managed to see off that cretinous fool of an Arrayer. It would be better still if Sir Tristram failed to win the King's approval for his contract and had to pay for the food for all those peasants out of his own pocket. Not that Joce cared much now. He had enjoyed the altercation while it lasted, had done his duty as he saw it. He drank and sullenly gazed at the fire.

This had been a bad week, he thought. First there was the problem with the girl, then the neighbour, and finally the death of Walwynus. That was a problem, too.

With that thought, his eyes went to the cupboard. He hadn't looked at it since that night when Sara had come here, he thought. When she arrived he had been counting all the pieces. Next week he would ride off to Exeter with it all and sell it. That would settle his debts and turn him a handsome profit.

It was as he rose and was about to walk to the cupboard, that he heard the rapping on his door. In two minds whether to answer it or leave it, Joce stood a moment, but then swore and strode out to the front of his house.

'Thank God you're here! I came as soon as I heard . . .'

'Calm down, you fool! Jesus! What are you doing up here? You useless piece of donkey shit, what have you got between your ears – cloth?'

'Let me in. It's not me who's going to be hanged, is it?'

Joce grabbed a handful of the man's habit, hauled him inside and kicked the door shut. He thrust hard, and the man was forced against the wall, then up, with Joce's hands beneath his chin. He held his face close. 'Are you threatening me, Brother?'

'Let me down!'

'Why, Brother Augerus,' Joce said, leaning closer so that he could see the naked terror in the Steward's eyes, 'how nice of you to drop in. Would you like some warmed wine? Or mulled ale? Or would you prefer me to throw you into my fire and leave you there to burn?'

'Joce, let's talk, all right? I came here as soon as I heard.'

'Heard what?'

'That the boy has bolted! Gerard, the acolyte we used to steal for us, he's gone! Ran off last night, from the sound of it.'

'So what?'

'What will he live on, Joce?' Augerus allowed a little sarcasm to enter his voice. 'We monks are sworn to poverty, aren't we? What if he takes money or plate from someone else to pay for his escape?'

Joce wavered, drew his head back and eyed Augerus. 'What are you saying?'

'He'll be caught. He will have to steal to live, won't he? And he'll get caught. Felons always do. And when he is, he's bound to tell them everything, isn't he? He's committed apostasy already, so there's nothing to lose by telling the truth.'

'Shit!' Joce licked his lips. 'I'll clear it all tomorrow. It's earlier than I intended, but I'll have to. Once it's all in Exeter, sold, no one can appeal us.'

'Good. Be quick, then. All that plate came from the Abbot's

coffers or the church. Christ Jesus! If they find it on you, you realise you'll hang?'

'Get out, you craven cur. Leave it to me as usual. I'll get it sorted.'

Augerus nodded and slipped through the doorway like a wood-louse scuttling under a stone.

Joce locked the door and marched back to his hall. The cupboard was at the wall opposite, behind his table, and he went straight to it, fumbling with his keys. Then he pulled the doors open.

He was so astonished to find it bare that, although his mouth dropped open, he didn't have the wherewithal to swear.

The camp was set out in the bend of a little stream, one of those few whose course had not yet been changed. So many were being diverted to feed the miners' works, it sometimes seemed as though there was nowhere which was left alone. There were times, when he rode over the moors, when Simon felt as if the place was being systematically raped rather than farmed.

Here there were plentiful signs of mining. Small pits had been dug all along the plain before him, the smooth surface of the grass ruined, like a beautiful woman's face scarred by the pox. These were the results of prospecting. All miners were constantly searching for a new lode because either the existing workings were soon to be exhausted, or they already were. No miner could afford to be complacent.

This place had been worked extensively. There were what looked like thousands of pits, some of which had grown to become great trenches, while others had deepened into shafts. Small piles of rock showed where miners had stored their tools, and little turf-roofed sheds stood all about where the men had lived, but now all looked desolate. They had overtaken several miners on the way here, but this area wasn't empty because of the inquest, it was deserted because the area had been worked to extinction.

Simon could remember when the miners had been here, four or five years ago now. Wally had been here before that, six years ago, digging with his friend in a small claim. After the death of his companion, he had enjoyed some little success, Simon recalled.

But the place wasn't empty now. Smoke curled up from the fires of the small band of travellers.

They were a colourful group. Men and women alike wore bright reds and greens, oranges and purples. Some of the younger women had their hair braided and unconcealed by wimple or veil, while the men had their hair longer than was strictly fashionable. Simon grunted to himself, thinking that they looked like a band of actors or musicians on the move.

That they were not intending to remain here in one place for long seemed evident by the pony carts that created a defensive wall; one, with a badly broken wheel, sat in an ungainly manner, its shafts pointing to the sky. The folk rested inside this palisade, their rear defended by the stream and, from the look of the cotton-balls dancing in the wind, a bog of some sort.

As the trio rode slowly down through the thicker grass, watching carefully for stones or pits which might harm their mounts, Simon could see that the people were wary and alert. Three men stood and walked forward, all grabbing long staffs or axes; two youths stood behind them with crossbows strung, bolts held negligently, ready to be fitted in the slots. The women grouped near the stream, children protectively gripped by the shoulders.

Glancing across at his companions, Simon acknowledged that they had good reason to suspect any visitors. This was too out of the way for most travellers, and it was always alarming to find horsemen approaching, even when two of the three were clearly belted knights – or perhaps especially because two were knights: there were too many men of noble birth who were prepared to resort to robbery and murder. No one on the road could afford to take the risk that the smiling face of the man next to him didn't belong to the advance guard of a raiding party whose sole intention was slaughter and pillage.

'Godspeed!' Baldwin called as they approached within hailing distance, lifting his hand to show he meant no harm.

Simon kept his eye on the two bowmen. They were still standing without pointing their weapons at the three, but the bolts were fitted now, ready to be fired.

'God's blessings on you.'

The man who spoke was dark-faced, with raven-black hair and clear, unblinking brown eyes. His lips were bright, like those of a woman, but although they made him look young, Simon saw that he was older than he appeared at first sight. As he sat on his horse swatting the flies away, Simon could see that the man wore fine wrinkles at eyes and brow.

His accent was strong, but curious. Simon hadn't heard it before. It was strangely guttural, quite thick.

It was clear that Baldwin had heard his accent before. The knight smiled and bowed to the man. '*Grüss Gott*. It is pleasant to hear a man from your land again. You are from the mountains?'

The man bowed with a faint smile. 'Yes, we are from the Forest Cantons.'

'Then believe me when I say that you need have no fear of English knights,' Baldwin said, introducing himself and the others. 'We are here to ask your help.'

'You are welcome. I am called Rudolf – Rudolf von Grindelwald. Would you like a little wine?'

Soon the three were dismounted, and they took their seats outside the little encampment on a group of rocks. The two men with crossbows removed their bolts and carefully released the tension in the bows, while the others set their own weapons to rest on carts, although none of them let them far from their hands, Baldwin noticed. He would not have expected them to.

The woman who came to serve them as guests of the leader of the travellers was a buxom creature in her late thirties, with hair pulled back and tied in a bun. Her limbs were long and elegant, her hips broad and swaying, her waist narrow. Her face was long, somewhat oval, with prominent cheekbones and full lips. Not beautiful, she was nonetheless extremely attractive, with the slow, economic movements of a dancer, and Baldwin thought her great blue eyes calming. She wore a long tunic, but at the hem and on her apron there were a multitude of tiny embroidered flowers. When Baldwin looked up at her, she smiled with her eyes, although not her mouth; it gave her a soothing expression that could calm a man's nights for the whole of his life, he thought.

'What do you do?' Baldwin asked.

'We have been attending fairs. We sing and dance to amuse. Many men call us to their halls for entertainments,' Rudolf lied. It was untrue, but the sort of thing that these men would believe.

He could kick himself. If only they had ditched the rest of their things. Welf had only returned a short while ago, and the pony he had brought was scarcely able to carry half the load which they had on the cart, so they might as well have carried on the day before. By now they could be lost in the streets of Ashburton, far from an enquiry. Instead here they were, being questioned by three grim-faced officials.

Not least of his troubles was the youngster hidden away. The boy could prove to be more than a mere embarrassment.

'There are few halls about here,' Simon observed.

'*Ja*, but we are tired. We have sung our way across France and now England. We were about to travel to York, but then we heard of the King raising his army, and we thought we would be more comfortable away from a war.'

'Many would go with the armies,' Simon said. 'There is good money in entertaining men-at-arms.'

Rudolf smiled. 'There is better money in a lord's hall, and the food is better. Also the company.'

Baldwin gave a short nod of understanding. He motioned

towards the women. 'And a King's Host is not the place for women
– except those of a certain kind.'

'*Ja*! I would not place my wife and children in danger.'

Eyeing him, Baldwin doubted whether this Swiss was actually
worried. There was a hardness and competence about him, like
that of a trained fighter. 'We are trying to learn about a man's
murder.'

Rudolf appeared uninterested. 'What has this to do with me?'

'We wished to hear whether you had seen this man,' Baldwin
said, and described Walwynus, explaining about his final journey
and the discovery of his body. Watching the Swiss closely, he was
sure that Rudolf knew of Walwynus. His eyes had been fixed on
Baldwin with a curiously intense concentration, but as soon as he
realised that Baldwin was observing him closely, his gaze began
to wander, first to Simon and the Coroner, then to the men walking
about his camp, as though there was nothing in this to hold his
attention.

'No,' he said. 'I do not know of this man. I have seen so many
miners here. They seem to be everywhere, and they leave the land
like this.' He encompassed the ruined plain with a hand. 'You say
he was here before last Thursday. We were here then, but many
men came past here.'

'There was a coining at Tavistock. All the miners would have
gone,' Simon said.

'Are you sure you didn't see this man?' Baldwin pressed him.
'He carried a leather satchel with him.'

'I saw several men, but no one who was alone,' Rudolf said.

The woman approached with a large loaf broken into pieces on
a tray and a large metal pot of soup fresh from the fire. Placing
bowls near the men, she passed bread to them, and one of the
children brought a jug of good wine. The woman poured and gave
each of them a cup, listening to the men as she did so.

When she reached Simon, he looked up to thank her, and saw
that her attention was not on him. She was carefully absorbing the

conversation between Baldwin and Rudolf, as though making sure Rudolf didn't slip up. She reminded him of a woman he had once seen at a court, listening to her man tell his story at a trial of felony. Later Simon had learned that she and her lover had concocted a story between them, rehearsing it together, to give each other alibis. The jury didn't believe them and the man had been hanged.

That sudden insight made Simon wary. He glanced over at the other men in the camp, and was relieved to see that they didn't appear to be ready to launch themselves at the three, but he couldn't shake off the sense of impending danger. Shifting slightly on his rock, which had suddenly grown uncomfortable, he repositioned his sword, moving the scabbard so that he could grasp the hilt more easily.

She saw his movement, and for a moment he saw naked fear in her eyes. It was fleeting, but he hadn't missed it, and although he smiled up at her and questioningly held out his cup to be refilled, he saw that he hadn't eased her anxiety. Her eyes went back to Baldwin with a kind of nervous exhilaration, as though fearful of what she might hear.

The Swiss picked up his cup of wine and took a good drink, glancing at Anna as he did so. She was all but petrified, and he smiled at her reassuringly, pleased to see that she appeared to be soothed by his easy confidence.

Baldwin stared up at the hills. 'You know, I never visited the Forest Cantons. I hear that they are beautiful.'

Simon added, 'And I have heard that the metalwork is excellent.'

Rudolf felt his stomach lurch. Behind him he heard a slithering noise, and he turned to scowl at Henry. His son shamefacedly allowed the bow to uncock, setting it aside. Turning back to face Simon, Rudolf stared at him coolly. 'What of it?'

'Nothing. I was only passing a comment. You have many pewterers in your country?'

'Some.' Rudolf was watching his face closely, wondering whether this was the face of a man who sought to destroy him, or whether he was a man who could be trusted. It was so hard to gauge. Some men who looked honourable were devious, lying fools who would kill you just to see how long you took to die, and would cut your fingers off because it was easier than pulling rings from them.

The shorter knight he didn't like the look of. That man had dark features and black eyes like gleaming flint. The second knight had a face which had seen much misery, with lines of pain etched deeply into his forehead and at the side of his mouth. He and the Bailiff both looked like men who could be trusted, he thought.

Simon knew Baldwin was staring at him, but he refused to return the look. His eyes were fixed upon the Swiss, while his ears strained to pick up any signs of nervousness from the woman. 'I heard you were a pewterer yourself.'

Rudolf lifted a hand and glanced over his shoulder, but the bows were unstrung. There was no need to worry about the hotter-headed fellows. He kept his hand in the air, beckoning his wife, and she walked to him and took it, grasping it firmly, like a drowning woman grabbing at a spar. 'And what else have you heard of me, Master Bailiff?'

As soon as Peter had heard that dismal cry, the terrible anguished shriek of the widow, he felt his heart dissolve and a huge emptiness open up inside him.

'Woman, who is dead? Who is it?' he cried as he ran to her.

He was not the first to arrive at her side. Before him was a decrepit watchman, who stood helplessly wringing his hands. Peter grabbed her hands and kept them still, trying to impose his stolid calmness upon her. He stared into her maddened eyes and spoke soothingly. 'Come now, woman. You know me, don't you – hey? You know who I am. I'm Peter the Almoner. Now what's all this about a murder? Who's dead? Where is he?'

'Help us! He's in the alley! He only came home last night, and now he's dead! In the alley, outside our door!'

Men were gathering about her, fingering their weapons, wondering whether they should be chasing after a murderer, and if so, whom they should seek. Peter shoved his way through them all, hurrying back along the alley from which she had come.

It was a noisome little place. Not much more than a couple of yards wide at the entrance, but with extended buildings reaching out overhead, some all but touching, and shutting out the sun so effectively that he felt as though he was swimming through an almost impenetrable murk.

He knew which was Emma and Hamelin's house. If he didn't, he soon would have, from the sounds of wailing children.

It was a tatty building, with the plaster falling from the walls and the lathes exposed. In the winter there would be terrible draughts whistling through, Peter thought absently. It said little for the couple that they hadn't done the same as so many other peasants, and made a thick, sticky paste from the glutinous earth that lay all around to patch the wall to shut out the winds. But Hamelin was a miner, he remembered, so he probably rarely had time, while his wife was permanently exhausted from raising and feeding her brood.

Some of them were outside now, and as Peter approached, one young lad turned his head to him. With a shock of horror, Peter realised that the darkness about the fellow's face was not the darkness of the alley, but was blood, great red streaks down both cheeks. His hands and fingers were covered in it, and he had transferred the blood to his face as he wailed.

At his feet was a mess of broken shards of pottery. At first that was all Peter could see, but then he realised that there were feet protruding into the alley, and he felt his heart sink further. He approached, making the Sign of the Cross as he squatted beside the body.

'Who is it?'

Nob had followed the noise and now stood at his side, shaking his head.

'I think it is that poor girl's husband,' Peter said.

'Hamelin? Could be, I suppose. Christ Jesus, what a mess! He has been stabbed, hasn't he?'

Peter hardly heard him. He was considering the man's position. 'He was dragged here and thrown on top of this pile of rubbish. Why should a man pick up another and throw him atop a midden? It would seem a strange way to treat a body.'

'Hey, you looking for sense in a murderer? Come on, Brother. There's no point in that. Look for sense in a tavern full of drunks more like!'

Peter glanced at him, and his expression made Nob silent in a moment. 'This man has been murdered, Cook. Take those children away and see to them, and tell someone to advise the Abbot. And in the meantime, stop your idle chatter!'

Chapter Twenty-One

'I have heard much about you,' Simon said. He avoided the eyes of Baldwin and Coroner Roger, but instead leaned forward, holding Rudolf's gaze. 'I think you paid Wally money for a sack at an inn in Tavistock, but you have broken no laws. The trouble is, you are fearful of being accused of his murder because he died soon after you saw him – especially since you took his sack from him.'

Rudolf could feel Anna's fingers tighten about his own hand, but he didn't look up at her. She was reminding him that they had the two secrets to preserve now: there was the boy as well. Rudolf ignored her. He was measuring Simon, staring deeply into his eyes and gauging whether or not he could truly trust him. 'It is easy to arrest a foreigner and convict him of crimes he knows nothing about,' he said at last.

'It is as easy to accuse a man wrongly as it is to allow an evil man to go free,' Simon countered. 'All it takes is for the innocent to hide the truth, for the innocent to be accused and the guilty to walk free. What would you do, friend? See the innocent hang, or see the guilty caught and made to pay?'

'Make the bastards pay!'

Simon grinned. 'We have no wish to see the innocent suffer, but we are all King's men. We have to try to catch the guilty. Would you help us?'

'What is all this?' Coroner Roger asked silkily. 'I have heard what you've said, Bailiff, but I confess, I am confused. You talk of pewterers and money, but this man tells us he is a mere actor and entertainer. Which is true?'

Simon smiled, but maintained his eye contact with Rudolf. 'Friend, we do not want the wrong man, but to catch the right one we need to know the truth. How could we persuade a man to tell us the truth?'

Rudolf gave a deep sigh, then motioned to his wife to fetch more wine. 'I met the dead man in an alley in Tavistock,' he began, and Simon knew he was hearing the truth. 'He was jumping from a window in a big house with limed woodwork and a blue painted shield above the doorway. In his hand was a sack, filled with metal. I caught his accomplice, but he was a monk. In my surprise, he escaped. When I captured the other man, people saw us together, and I had my knife out. I made sure he couldn't run away, but he persuaded me to take him to a tavern and let him explain. It seemed a reasonable idea at the time. This man Walwynus told me that the plate had been stolen from others, and that if it were left in the house from which they'd taken it, it would be sold to the thief's profit. He and the monk thought it better that the metal should be 'rescued', and so they took it. That was when I came across them. Then he told me that I could have the metal if I wanted, and he named a price which seemed to me to be ridiculous. So! I bought it and gave him coin in exchange.

'I went back up to the moors with the sack. Next morning, Walwynus caught up with me and asked me to return the pewter. I refused, for a bargain is a bargain, but he swore at me and said that he would pay me more than the pewter was worth if I would only give it back. I refused again, for I wanted it. That was when he drew his dagger and made ready to attack me. I pulled my own knife out, and when he lunged at me, I stabbed at his knife hand. I caught him, and his hand lost some fingers. He stopped fighting, and started weeping. I left him. The pewter is in the back of my wagon. If you want it, you can buy it back.'

Baldwin had sat staring a while, and now he blinked in astonishment. He shot a glance at Simon, who sat nodding knowingly. 'This pewter . . . may we have a look at it?'

Simon said, 'I doubt whether that is necessary, Baldwin. No innocent burgher has reported the theft as yet. Any man who had all this plate stolen would notice immediately – unless it was already concealed. Concealed because it was stolen! This is all from the Abbey – that's the point. Maybe Walwynus thought he was stealing some pewter from a wealthy man's house, but he didn't realise that it was all originally taken from the church. And as soon as he learned that, he hurried here to persuade Rudolf to give it back. He failed, so he tried to take it by force, but Wally was undernourished and slow, while Rudolf here was quick and assured. So Rudolf won and Wally lost his fingers.'

'It was out by the cross just west of here,' Rudolf confirmed. 'The westernmost of the three. He fell when I had struck his fingers from his hand, and he collapsed beside the stone cross. I saw him stand, his hand resting on the cross itself to help himself up. I felt sorry for him.'

'He left his blood there,' Simon said.

'There were no fingers,' Baldwin observed.

The Coroner muttered, 'There are enough scavenging animals here to take them. Magpies, crows, buzzards . . .'

Simon nodded. 'Why did you fear to speak to us, Rudolf?'

'I had been seen drawing my knife against him in the town, and then again out by the rock. It seemed natural to me to think that I would be viewed as the man's murderer when I heard that he had died.'

'Who saw you out by the cross?' Simon asked.

'It was a monk. I don't know his name, he was just a man standing there with the cowl and habit. Oh, and he carried a stick.'

'So! I suppose you'd defend this man's murderer as well, would you?' Sir Tristram sneered.

Peter hadn't heard him walk up behind him, and now he turned, his lips still moving as he spoke the words of the *viaticum*. He refused to rise to the bait, and continued through the office until he had completed the prayers, and only then did he stand and confront Sir Tristram. 'Well? Are you so offended that I should serve another?'

'You! You serve your own ends at all times, don't you? Scotch-lover!'

Peter felt his scar pull as he smiled. 'You never understood how our faith demands that we should protect and serve even our enemies, did you?'

'The Bailiff told me that there was a monk here from Tynemouth. At the time it never occurred to me that it could be *you*! I thought you were dead long ago.'

'You would have preferred it. If you had swung this blow . . .'

'I would not have missed your scrawny neck, monk.'

'You have never forgiven me, have you? All I did was help a brother monk to save a man's life.'

'He was a Scots raider. You are lucky you weren't found with him. If I'd found you, you'd have died.'

'My woman found him,' Peter said. He could remember her racing towards him, her braids flying in the wind, panic in her face. His friend and he had hurried to the man's body. When he tried to turn his memory to her, he found himself seeing her broken body – although he had *not* seen it. She was buried while he lay near to death.

'More evil. You are supposed to be chaste, yet you lived with your concubine.'

'She was a good woman,' Peter said defensively.

'She was a Scottish whore.'

Peter's anger flickered, but there was little energy to fan the flames. Not after so many years. 'It was wrong. Yet it is also wrong to label her that way. She was an honourable girl.'

'Honourable? Perhaps the slatterns in the alehouses are honourable, then. And what did the man you saved do, hey? He took her for himself, didn't he? He took her and raped her and killed her. All because you saved him. You would deal with the enemy.'

'She was no man's enemy. She was a woman caught up in a stupid, irrational war of greed,' Peter flared.

'And she persuaded you to forswear your oath, Brother. You screwed her, didn't you? And that makes you an oathbreaker.'

Peter looked away, his anger dissipating, trying to call her face to memory again. Somehow her smile was what came to him, and he thought of the girl in the tavern who had reminded him of her. With a flash of insight, he realised why Wally would have gone to that tavern, why he had tried to secure her for himself before he had any money. It was surely because he remembered that girl, high up on the Scottish moors in among the heather, Peter's Agnes.

She had been a beautiful girl. Strong in the body, with long legs and powerful thighs, dark hair to her shoulders, a slim figure and small, high breasts. She was always laughing, although whether at herself or at him was difficult to tell. More often than not, Peter was sure her laughter was aimed at him. It was no surprise. Now he looked back on himself, he could see how stuffy he must have seemed. Agnes had lived for the moment, uncaring about what the next day might bring, while he was anxious every moment that he would behave as God would expect. His entire being was focused on the life after this – she was content that the present moment was pleasing, to her and to those whom she loved. It was that attitude, more than anything, which had made him adore her.

Walwynus loved her too, of course. Probably because she was such a good nurse to him. She had fed him with wine and bread while he suffered from his fever, and then helped him to take his first tottering steps when the wound was almost healed. It was only natural that Walwynus should love her. He had wanted her, but she refused him. Not that her refusal had stopped Wally. When he was well, he had left, but then the bastard repaid her kindness and Peter's by returning. While Peter was lying wounded and waiting for death, Walwynus had gone and raped her, or led his friends to her, so that they all had a share in her murder.

There was no law in the Marches. That was the first thing that a man realised as soon as he was old enough. No one lived there apart from the peasants and a number of poor devils who were tied to the place, like the monks. Everyone else left as soon as they could.

Peter shook his head sadly. She was long dead now. And Walwynus had died too.

'If she made me break my oath, so be it. It was many years ago.'

Sir Tristram spat into the dirt, sneering, 'You blaspheme now! You think you can swear to God and then discard the oaths you choose? Which other oaths have you broken, monk?' Then his eyes hardened and there was a cruel glitter in them. 'What now, eh? Have you another little goose here? I suppose a lusty man like you would find it hard to live without your piece of skirt, wouldn't you? I wonder which you have now. Perhaps the Abbot would like to know, too. Now there's a thought. I wonder if he knows of your woman in Scotland?'

There was no need for Peter to answer. Sir Tristram's smile showed that he could see Peter hadn't told the Abbot.

'So I wonder what the good Abbot would think of you, if he knew you had kept a whore, Brother?'

Nob had listened to their talk with increasing annoyance. Now he pushed the monk gently out of the way and stared up into the knight's face. 'Before that, what do you know about "Red Hand"? Was he an Armstrong?'

Peter glanced at him in surprise. 'Why? How did you hear of him?'

'He was the murdering bastard nearly killed this monk and then slaughtered his woman,' Sir Tristram said shortly. 'Why?'

'Your Sergeant there reckons he saw this man in the crowd today,' Nob said.

'Sweet Jesus! He can't be here!' Sir Tristram said, looking about him as though expecting one of the crowd to confess to being the outlaw.

'Did you ever see him?' Peter asked sharply.

'I don't think so, no. Jack did, but only once. No,' the knight said, 'he must have been wrong. The man couldn't have got so far down south.'

'Wally did, and so did Martyn Armstrong,' Peter reminded him. 'Whom did this Jack accuse, Nob?'

'I don't know,' Nob lied, glancing at Peter. He wasn't going to accuse a man for no reason. Especially before Sir Tristram. Nob didn't like the Arrayer. 'Someone in the crowd.'

'He must have been mistaken. Where is he?' Sir Tristram demanded, and when Nob told him, he hurried away.

'What do you think, Brother?'

'The Sergeant must have been mistaken. Perhaps I hit him too hard!' Peter was still gazing along the alley after the knight.

Nob nodded. 'Ah well, that's a relief.'

Something in his tone caught Peter's attention. 'Why?'

'The man that Sergeant accused: it was the Receiver, Jocè Blakemoor.'

'Joce!' Peter hissed. He stared at Nob a moment, then slowly turned and made his way back to the Abbey.

He felt his wound flashing with pain as though he had been struck again. All those years ago he had been hit by a man, and he hadn't caught more than a glimpse of a figure, no face. It could have been anyone who swung the axe.

Wally had come here with Armstrong. Peter had thought that there was a curious coincidence in their arriving here, but perhaps a companion of theirs had advised them to return with him to his old home? Perhaps Joce had told his comrades that if they wanted to be safe, all they need do was pass south with him and declare themselves miners. Thus they would become the King's men and be secure from capture.

Peter had reached the Abbey, and he turned to the Abbey Church, passing along the aisle in a daze, and then tumbling to his knees before the altar.

'God, please don't let this be so!' he whispered. 'Was it not enough that I had to live so near to Wally all this time? Didn't you test me enough? Do you now tell me that the man who tried to kill me is here as well? Perhaps the man who murdered my Agnes? And you had me save his life today?'

It was late in the afternoon when the three men arrived back at the Abbey, and Simon dropped from his horse feeling filthy, sweaty and tired. The weather felt thundery, with heavy clouds forming in the west, and the humidity was almost intolerable. While he stood in the middle of the court, waiting for a stableboy to collect his horse from him, he glanced up at the hills to east and west, rising high above the line of the Abbey's walls, and rubbing at his chin. It was rough and itchy, and he decided to have a bath and another shave with Ellis. That would take the worst of the dirt from his face.

The Coroner was hungry. Nothing would do but that he should be fed immediately, and he tried to persuade the others to join him, but to Simon's dismay, Baldwin refused him and instead said he would go with Simon for a wash. Seeing Hugh loitering near the guest rooms, Baldwin called to him to fetch clean clothes for them both, and then led the way to the barber's.

His companionship was not welcome, to Simon's mind. He had looked forward to a few moments of peace, during which he could forget his worries, especially Baldwin's apparent alliance with the Abbot and Simon's own misery at the thought of his losing his job. It was painful to admit it, but this man Baldwin, who had become Simon's closest friend in only a few years, had now become almost a rival, an enemy. Baldwin had the appearance of a friend, but his mannerisms seemed to show that he was edgy in Simon's presence.

The sack of pewter was still bound to Simon's saddle. The Swiss had appeared almost relieved to be shot of it, saying with a grimace that he had got nothing but bad luck since he had acquired it. Although he had paid good money for it, he was prepared to allow Simon to take it back to the Abbey if the Bailiff would swear to ask the Abbot to reimburse him, either by replacing it all with fresh tin, or if not, by giving him back the money he had spent with Wally to buy it. The Swiss party would head for Tavistock as soon as they might to claim their recompense.

Simon felt giddy with the heat. Perspiration was dripping from him, his hair was glued to his forehead, and his armpits were rank. He licked his dry lips, which were gritty from the dust kicked up by his horse's hooves. Where the sweat was gathering on his forearm, he noticed a grey-black smear of dirt, and it revolted him. Then he wondered where it could have come from. Thoughtfully he touched the sack. It left a black mark on his finger, like coal dust.

'Curious.'

It was a relief when Baldwin offered to take the pewter to the Abbot's lodgings. For Simon it meant at least a few moments of peace. It was only when Baldwin had gone that Simon suddenly thought that the knight could have been taking it to the Abbot to curry favour. He rejected that idea almost instantly as being dishonourable and certainly unfair on Baldwin, and yet it was insidiously attractive, coming so soon after his suspicions. Baldwin still appeared edgy in his presence.

The bath was in the barber's room near to the infirmary, close by the brewery. Water was boiled in the brewery fire, and taken by bucket to the great barrel that was the bath, a strong vessel cooped with strong copper bands. Simon called there for Ellis, and the barber soon appeared from a door that led to the brewery itself, wiping his mouth shamefacedly.

'Ah, my Lord Bailiff! You wish for another shave?'

'Yes, but first I need a bath. Have the thing filled.'

Simon felt considerably improved after soaking his body and washing away the filth of the moors. He sponged himself clean with water that was filled with fresh herbs, rubbing himself down with soap and rinsing it off with fresh, rose-scented water. He was almost finished when Baldwin arrived, his dark face drawn into a scowl.

Once Simon's hair was washed, he felt greatly refreshed. Sitting on Ellis's stool while the barber draped almost-scalding towels over his features, he felt renewed, and a curious sense of fatalism enveloped him.

This fear, this nervousness about Baldwin was ridiculous. If there was some suggestion from the Abbot that Simon was not to be trusted, that he was too incompetent to keep his job, that was not Baldwin's fault. In fact, if Simon was fair, it was the Abbot's alone. Baldwin was probably fidgety because he knew that Simon was to lose his position, and feared how the Puttock family would survive without the income that his post as Bailiff brought him. Perhaps that was all it was, Simon thought: Baldwin was consumed with compassion and sympathy for his old friend.

Anyway, Simon was no fool. He would soon find a new job even if the Abbot decided to dispense with him. There were always other masters. And if that didn't work out, Simon should be able to live on the proceeds of his farming. Other men managed to, and he had a good property in Sandford still, the place to which he had brought his wife when they married. She had always adored it, with the far-off views of Dartmoor and the rolling hills surrounding it. They had been very happy there. It would be closer to Baldwin, too, and easier to see him and Jeanne more often. The life of a free yeoman farmer was not so bad. Good food was plentiful, if the harvest was kind, while there should always be ale and wine to be drunk. Yes, Simon reckoned he could live happily as a farmer. It would be different, there would be economies that he and Meg would have to make, but they would survive. And what else mattered, than that he and Meg should be able to live together in peace? Meg was a farmer's daughter. She would be pleased to return to a farming life.

Although she was content where they lived now as well, he reminded himself, and it might not be easy to persuade her to move home once more. Still, when she saw it was necessary, she would no doubt agree.

Then his buoyant attitude underwent a change. He felt a cold emptiness in his belly at the thought of having to admit to his failure. It was no use telling himself that such things happened, that his position in life was owed entirely to the whim of the Abbot, that he had no more control over the direction of his life than a chicken in a yard: it was his duty to provide for his wife and family. Without achieving a stable, financially sound future for them all, his life was a failure. He knew that Meg would support him, of course, but that didn't help. There would be hurt in her eyes when he told her that without his money as Bailiff, they would have to leave their home at Lydford, that they must be more frugal in future. That he might not be able to afford the dowry he had intended for their daughter.

Baldwin had climbed into the bath, and he lay back with his eyes closed while all this passed through Simon's mind. There was silence in the room as the barber thumbed back Simon's skin and brought the shining blade of his razor down around Simon's cheek, along the line of his jaw, then under his chin and down to his neck. When he had relathered Simon's face and repeated his operations, Baldwin spoke.

'Simon, are you all right? You look anxious.'

Baldwin's gentle voice broke in on his thoughts. He opened an eye as Ellis held the blade away. 'Just tired, I think.'

'Good. I am glad.' Baldwin nodded, but he couldn't help telling himself that his friend had appeared to be tired ever since he had arrived in Tavistock with the Coroner. 'What do you think about the mystery of the dead miner?'

'Someone met him and killed him. There appears to be nothing else to learn.'

'Simon, please, forgive me for asking, but are you quite well?'

'Why shouldn't I be?'

Baldwin gazed at him with exasperation. 'Because you look away from me when I talk to you as though the sight of me pains you, you snap at me or don't respond at all, you walk away from me as soon as we arrive anywhere, you go and question people as though trying to exclude me from your enquiries, and you sit drumming your fingers there as though you are waiting to have a tooth pulled!'

His last words made Simon give a dry smile. They reminded him of his own feelings about Baldwin.

Seeing that Ellis had finished Simon's shave, Baldwin motioned the barber to leave the room. Nothing loath, Ellis left by the door and returned to the brewery. 'Please, Simon, my friend, you would tell me if I had offended you?'

'Of course. I would trust you with anything. Would you trust me the same?'

'Me?' Baldwin said with surprise.

'You went to the Abbot and told me nothing about the meeting. Is it that you don't trust me any more?'

Baldwin gave a low grunt. 'Now I believe I understand. The Abbot asked me to keep this from you.'

'Why should he do that?' Simon asked sarcastically. He thought he knew the answer.

'The Abbot didn't want to spread the tale about the town. You have heard of Milbrosa?'

'It's an old story. The maids of Tavistock use it to scare their children,' Simon said scathingly.

'Some say that there are too many similarities between that tale and the things which are happening here now.'

Simon squinted at him. Baldwin was staring contemplatively at the doorway. The room opened westwards, and the sun was already quite low, shining directly in and lighting Baldwin with a warm, orange glow. It made him look tired, emphasising the deep lines of pain and anguish that Simon had all but forgotten, and reminding him that this man had suffered more in his life than he would be able to appreciate. Baldwin had not told Simon every-thing about his time as a Templar, but Simon knew enough about the way that the Order had been destroyed to know that almost all its members had been tortured and then slaughtered on the pyres. Baldwin had escaped because he had been travelling on the day that the arrests were made, but evading the physical punishments seemed only to have created feelings of guilt in him.

Simon asked tentatively, 'There is nothing to tie the two stories, is there? Only the fact that Wally was found dead on the moors. In the tale of Milbrosa, the monks hid even that proof of their crime. The Abbot's wine has been taken – but that may only be a thoughtless prank. How can the two be connected?'

'The Abbot asked that I should keep this secret even from you,' Baldwin said. 'But I cannot maintain my silence. I cannot think of an explanation, not without your help.'

Simon listened with astonishment as Baldwin spoke about Gerard and his sudden disappearance.

'So just as in the tale of Milbrosa, the Abbot's wine was drunk and plate was stolen,' he muttered. 'And now the supposed perpetrator has been carried away? Was the Abbot sure that this boy Gerard was actually guilty? Perhaps someone else took the wine and things.'

'The Abbot seemed quite convinced,' Baldwin said. 'Another Brother had suspected him.'

'Did the Abbot say why the lad was suspected?'

'Not that I recall, no.'

'Then we should find out,' Simon said firmly. 'But before that, I had better reciprocate.' He related all he had learned, although he refused to tell Baldwin who it was who told him about the club. He had promised Hal he would keep that silent, and he would not break his oath.

Baldwin was drying himself and pulling on fresh clothes, and Simon wiped his face and did the same, shouting for Ellis. When the barber put his head around the door, he passed him some coins.

Just as Ellis was about to leave the room, Baldwin held up a hand to stop him. 'I am glad to have an opportunity to speak to you,' he said quietly. 'Barber, I have heard that you detested Wally because he had got your sister with child. Is that right?'

Ellis gave the knight a sickly grin. He had been expecting to be questioned ever since the two men appeared, and the anticipation had been terrible. When they had told him to leave them, he had thought he was safe, but they had only been lulling him.

'It was, but I was wrong,' he said in a choked voice.

'Oh? Who was this mystery lover of hers, then?'

Ellis's face hardened a moment, his jaw clenching and un-clenching. 'Master, I have got myself into trouble once by saying who I thought was her man. I won't say any more, since Sara herself asked me to keep her shame secret.'

Baldwin nodded. 'Back to Wally, then. At the time of his death, you still believed he was your sister's lover?'

'Yes. Look, I went up there on Friday morning to give him a warning, but I left him alive. He was in a state, because he had been drinking and whoring all night and he could hardly concentrate, his head was so bad, but he was alive. I just shouted at him to leave my sister alone, that was all.' Ellis hung his head.

'Did he deny an affair?'

'Yes. But then I expected him to. Look – I didn't lay a finger on him, all right?'

Baldwin eyed his razors and knives. 'I rather think you'd have picked a more simple means of despatch, had you intended murder,' he admitted.

'Did you see anyone else up there?' Simon asked.

'Two monks. One was Mark, that *salsarius*. The other one, I don't know.'

'Could it have been Peter?' Baldwin asked.

'Might have been,' Ellis agreed after a contemplative pause. 'Don't know, really.'

'Where was this Mark?'

'He was walking towards the middle of the moor. It was only a fleeting glimpse, but you don't forget a man like him. He's so big. You could practically see the glow from his red face!'

'Did you see him again?' Simon asked.

'When I got back, yes. A little while before I pulled Hamelin's tooth. Mark came back down from the moor alone, and I saw him hurrying off to the Abbey. He was there later when I went to shave some of the Brothers.'

'So he was up on the moors while Wally was alive,' Simon said. 'And came back *after* you, when you had left Wally in good health?'

'Yes.'

There was a sudden commotion outside, and Simon and Baldwin ceased their questioning. With Ellis trailing in their wake, they went outside to the court, to investigate.

Simon arrived there first, rubbing a hand over his smoothed cheeks and enjoying the sensation. At the Abbey entrance he saw a horse with the well-wrapped body of Wally thrown over its broad back. Some monks and lay brothers had wandered over to view this arrival, although several of them had retreated from the odour emanating from the blankets. A pair of stolid peasants cut the body free from the packhorse and allowed Wally to slump to the ground like a sack of grain, but the knife must have slashed the rope binding the blankets, for they opened and Wally's bloated, discoloured face was exposed. Worse, the horse was startled by his load falling, and set to bucking and struggling, making everyone in the yard bolt, all but Ned, who walked over grimly and took charge.

It was just as Ned grabbed the horse's reins and hauled his head down, gripping it with a finger in each nostril and a fist in its mane and swearing viciously into its ear, that Sir Tristram appeared in the entrance to the stable, looking about him to find the cause of the disturbance. Seeing the body, he peered at it a moment, and was about to walk away, when Simon saw him hesitate, turn, and stare at it more closely.

Simon was about to go to him, when a rotund fellow with an apron tied about his waist with a string came into the court. 'Is there a Coroner here?' he asked.

'Who wants him?' Baldwin called sharply.

'I am Nob Bakere, and I've been sent by Brother Peter of this Abbey to ask for the Coroner. Hamelin Tinner's dead.'

Baldwin immediately sent to find Coroner Roger, but Simon stood a moment. Sir Tristram had reached the body and now he stood over Wally, staring down with an expression of contempt twisting his features.

'What is it, Sir Tristram?' Simon asked, walking to his side. 'Do you know this man?'

Sir Tristram looked up but barely acknowledged the Bailiff. 'This man? Oh yes, I know *him*!'

'Where have you met him?' Simon asked with surprise.

'He was a Scotch raider up in the March. I fought with him once, but failed to kill him. He was taken in by . . .' His voice didn't alter, but Simon saw that his eyes focused more firmly on him. '. . . by the man who lives here as Brother Peter, the Almoner. This man was one of those who attacked Brother Peter, and raped and murdered his woman. What's he doing here?'

'His name was Walwynus. He was the miner found dead up on the moors,' Baldwin said. 'Are you sure you recognise him?' he added doubtfully. 'His face is badly beaten.'

'He was a Scotch raider, I tell you. A reiver. I would recognise him in the midst of the fires of hell – where his soul is burning even now,' Sir Tristram said, and spat into Wally's contorted face.

Chapter Twenty-Two

While they waited for the Coroner to arrive, Simon told Baldwin what Sir Tristram had said about Wally's real identity. When Sir Roger de Gidleigh arrived, still wiping his cheeks to rid them of pastry crumbs, Simon and Baldwin hastened with him and the flustered-looking Nob to the alley where Hamelin lay.

Nob was not only hot and bothered, he was also plagued by doubts. In the past he would never have considered divulging information to an official, not unless there was some money involved, but now he was reconsidering.

It was this sudden death of Hamelin. First Wally had found some money from somewhere, and then he'd given it to Hamelin and died. Now Hamelin was dead too. It was too much of a coincidence. As they reached the mouth of the alleyway, he stopped to face Coroner Roger.

'Sir, I don't know if this is important, but I feel I should tell you . . .'

The Coroner was panting a little, and rather than unnecessarily expend more breath, he motioned with his finger for Nob to continue.

'Sir, my wife knows this dead man's wife well, and she told my woman the other day that Hamelin had been given a purse of gold by the miner who's died.'

'You mean Wally?' Simon asked. 'Wally gave him money? Why?'

'Ah, that I don't know, but I do know that Hamelin said Wally had bought a loan from him – a debt owed by a monk. The monk wasn't in Holy Orders when he borrowed the money, but when he lost it all, he joined the monastery, so Hamelin couldn't get his cash back. That's why the poor soul was working out on the moors. He was desperate to make a bit of money.'

'But the debt would be worthless,' Baldwin said. 'Why would this Walwynus give good money for a debt he couldn't recover?'

'Must have been mad,' Coroner Roger said, moving into the alley.

'And shortly afterwards Wally dies,' Simon mused. 'It's almost as though the money was evil and Wally wanted to get rid of it. But why should he?'

'Know that and we'll know the full story,' Baldwin said as he set off after the Coroner.

Peter was standing at the body's side. With him were the nearest neighbours, all called to have their names noted so that they could be amerced for this infringement of the King's Peace. None looked happy, but that was no surprise. In Simon's experience, people rarely liked having to part with their money.

While the Coroner took charge of the men gathered, Simon addressed Peter. 'I have just been talking to Sir Tristram. He says he knew you in the north – that you were attacked by Walwynus when you got that wound. Is that true?'

Peter tilted his chin defiantly. 'Yes. Sir Tristram was a marauder, as I told you. He raided from the English side to the Scottish, while Wally came down the other way.'

'Was it Wally himself who gave you that wound?' Baldwin said.

'No, one of his companions. But the pain was the same. He rode me down when I was with a friend. They killed my friend outright, and then his companion attacked me. Then some of them went to my home and raped and murdered my girl.'

Baldwin's eyebrows shot up. He knew that many priests and monks failed in their vows, but to hear a Brother mention it so frankly and almost in passing, was oddly shocking to him. It would have been less so had Peter said that he himself had murdered. Baldwin had taken all the three vows very seriously, and the hardest to adhere to, without a doubt, was that of chastity.

'What girl was this?' Simon asked.

'Her name was Agnes. It was a lonely country up there, Bailiff. I was young, and she was beautiful. It was common enough for monks to seek . . . companionship. We found Walwynus when Sir Tristram's men had all but killed him, and saved him, carrying him to my home where Agnes nursed him back to health. He repaid us, so I thought, by raping her while I lay near to death.'

'He sounds the sort of man whom you could hate for ever,' Baldwin observed quietly. 'I suppose that your story explains some of the wounds we found on his body, though. Did you kill him?'

'Me? No – why should I? Would it bring back my Agnes? No. Would it take away this scar? No. Would it give me back my teeth? No. What, then, could it achieve? I had forgiven Walwynus, Sir Baldwin.'

'You knew he was here?'

'Yes. But he always avoided me. It was not until the coining a week ago that he somehow gathered together the courage to speak to me. I was out there in the square, and he walked to me and said he was sorry. That he had felt the guilt ever since. And I told him I forgave him, so far as it was in my power. Aye, and in any case, he denied harming my Agnes. He said he thought that his companions killed her. Martyn or the other.'

Baldwin nodded. 'Did he say who this third man was? This man who attacked you so viciously?'

'No,' Peter said with a shrug. 'What good would it have done me to know his name?'

'You did not ask?'

'I had no interest. After forgiving Wally, and seeing his delight, that was enough for me,' Peter said with transparent honesty. 'I felt as though his joy washed away my own pain. Aye, and the years of distress.'

He hesitated a moment as he thought of Joce, and the allegation that Joce was himself the third man, but chose to say nothing. God had given him some peace, and he reflected that the accusation was unsubstantiated. Too many men were convicted because of rumour. No, Peter would confront Joce personally if he could. If not, perhaps then he might repeat what Nob had told him, although by then others would probably already have heard.

'You are telling me that you forgave the man who caused that to be done to you even after you had saved his life before?' Simon said disbelievingly.

'I am a man of God, Bailiff,' Peter said imperturbably. 'What would you have me do? Grab a sword and sweep off his head? Jesus told us to love, not hate. He told us to turn the other cheek, didn't He? Well, I was prepared to try it. I told him I forgave him, and he burst into tears at first, but then his face shone and I confess, I felt a little like God myself, as though He had acted through me. Holy Mother, it was good. When I left him, he was happy and content.'

There was a clearness in his voice that brooked no argument. Simon was still doubtful, but Baldwin nodded understandingly. 'I believe you, Brother. Apart from anything else, it would be an unconscionable amount of time to sit back and wait for an opportunity to kill him.'

'If you knew him,' Simon said, 'did you know that man with whom he arrived down here? The man whom he later killed?'

'Aye. He was one of the party which killed my friend and tried to murder me too. An evil man. His name was Martyn Armstrong, or Martyn the Scot. It was the third man who actually swung the axe that did this,' he added, touching his scar.

'You must have hated Wally.'

'I did at one time, but it is hard to stay hating a man for ever. I had no part in killing him, if that is what you mean.'

'You were seen up on the moors on the day Walwynus died,' Simon stated. 'Why?'

'I had to go and visit one of the Abbot's shepherds who has hurt himself, taking him some money to help him through his illness.'

'Did you come across Walwynus?'

'Yes. I spoke to him on the way. He was hungover. I got the impression that he had drunk a great deal the night before, after I told him I forgave him.'

'You were seen with him.'

'Aye, well I walked with him a way, as soon as I saw how bad he was. He could easily have fallen off the trail and into a bog, he was that far gone. I stayed with him until he was home as an act of charity.'

'You went with him to his home? What was he doing back here, then?' Simon burst out.

'I have no idea. His cottage is on the route to Buckfast, so it wasn't out of my way.'

'And then?'

'I carried on to find the shepherd who was deserving of my Lord Abbot's kindness. An orphan.'

Simon sucked at his teeth. 'And Walwynus was fine when you left him?'

'Yes. I swear it. Although . . .' His face was suddenly troubled, a crease marking his brow.

Simon said sharply, 'Yes?'

'It is likely nothing, but while we were talking, he denied having raped or hurt Agnes. He confessed to being part of the raiding party which attacked me, but said that he wouldn't lead the men to my hovel, because he wouldn't have allowed anyone to harm Agnes, not after she'd nursed him back to life.'

'And that worried you?'

'It made me think that I had misjudged him, or that he wasn't prepared to confess with honesty, but . . . perhaps his memory was playing him false. It can do things like that to people. I don't know. Certainly he appeared greatly upset when I left him. He was sitting at his stool, weighing his purse in his hand unhappily.'

The next morning, when Augerus woke, he remembered the corpse and shuddered. He had seen Wally's body being brought in, but had hurried away before the poor devil's ruined remains could be uncovered. He had known Wally as a sort of business associate, a drinking companion, too, well enough to not want to see the wreck of his body out in the open like this. Reaching the Abbot's undercroft, he had unlocked the door and entered, pulling the door closed behind him and leaning on it, panting heavily. With the little cup he used for tasting the quality of the wines in the barrels, he had drawn off a good measure of the strongest, red spiced wine, and sank it at a gulp, grateful for the warmth that spread through his body, driving off the chill fear.

Now, in the first light of a chilly grey morning, he felt a queasiness in his belly at the thought of what had happened to Wally, although in his drowsy state he couldn't deny a stab of pleasure at the way he had treated Joce.

He had given the bastard a shock, a real good one. Standing there and grabbing Augerus like he was some menial who had misbehaved! The thought that Gerard might tell everyone about their little game hadn't occurred to him, not until Augerus had made him see sense. Now maybe he'd get rid of all the stuff quickly. *Before* it could be found! Augerus reflected for a moment on the enraged features of his accomplice as he'd held him by the throat up against his front door. Joce could fly off the handle at a moment's notice.

When he had attended the morning Mass and seen to the Abbot's breakfast, he pottered for a while in the undercroft, then went to visit Mark. The *salsarius* was welcoming enough, but he too appeared to have his mind on other things, and after only one bowl of wine and a few slices of dry-cured ham Augerus left him to it. He wanted to visit the parish church to see Wally and pray over him.

He entered the dark church with a feeling of sadness. After making the obeisances, he walked down the aisle to where Wally's body lay, lighted by the guttering candles. It was gloomy here today, with so little light. Clouds smothered the sun and the great windows with the coloured pictures depicting scenes from the Bible all seemed grim and accusing. As they should be, Augerus nodded to himself, bearing in mind how much this man had stolen from the Abbey.

The sight of a decomposed body was not so uncommon that it was a shock, but to see old Wally lying here was depressing. This was the man with whom he had so often enjoyed a drink, the pal with whom he had swapped jokes and stories around the fireside. Later on, Wally had become his partner in crime, the accomplice with whom he had robbed the Abbey's guests.

The loss of a partner was always sad, he thought to himself. Even if the thieving bastard had tried to gull him, taking a larger share of the proceeds than he should. And there was the wine, too. It was hard to forgive him that. Pinching the good Abbot's wine was a sick joke. Even now, Augerus wasn't sure how he'd managed it. Somehow he must have used Gerard. Jesu! But the lad was a marvel! So slim he could even wriggle through the metal bars at the Abbot's own undercroft, with a bit of squirming. And then he had the brains to take whatever he had been told, even when he must have been terrified of being discovered.

The acolyte was a natural, although, of course, he had needed to be broken in carefully. That Ned talked about breaking in horses gently, but he had no idea. Taking a dumb brute like a horse in hand was one thing; a boy was quite another. Augerus had been looking for a lad like him for an age.

It hadn't been easy to start with. The boy had been tough to persuade. In fact, the first thing Augerus had wheedled him into doing was to take a little rosary of Augerus' own, which he had loaned Brother Mark, with the promise that it would make Mark laugh. And it did, for Augerus played a little with Mark, making a wager that he had lost it. When Mark couldn't find it, Augerus made up a story about how Mark had dropped it from his habit, and Augerus had seen it fall and picked it up again. Easy. It allayed Mark's concerns when Augerus refused to allow him to honour the wager, thereby convincing the *salsarius* that all was well, while at the same time demonstrating to Gerard that taking things could be fun.

Next it had been a loaf of bread. That wasn't so difficult. There were plenty of them, and one thing that could be guaranteed about acolytes was that they were always hungry. Too much food, it was thought, made a lad drowsy and ruined his concentration. It had been easy to tell Gerard that the baker had bet no one would dare to take one of his loaves, and that no one could break in through the bars over his windows. As soon as Gerard heard that, he had willingly agreed to prove him wrong.

Then, Augerus said, the baker refused to believe that one had gone. He told the Steward that he was lying, and what could Augerus do? Obviously he must prove it beyond a doubt. So Gerard must, for a joke, steal three more loaves: one for himself, one for Augerus, and one for the baker. That would convince him. And if the baker still doubted, why, Gerard could climb in there right before his eyes!

Gerard had thought this a great lark. He laughed delightedly when Augerus explained the cunning plan. Gerard climbed up through the window again, with Augerus, and passed the loaves to him through the bars; afterwards, he had squeezed himself out again. Chuckling quietly, he scampered back to Augerus' chamber, giggling to himself at the thought of the baker's face when he saw the three loaves gone.

Except when they got back to Augerus' room, the Steward ate a half loaf and persuaded Gerard to eat another. The acolyte balked

at first, but then his hunger got the better of him and he set to.
And as he finished his meal, Augerus told him the truth.

'I think we'd better keep this secret between us, boy.'

'Between us and the baker, you mean.'

'No, between us alone. I wouldn't want to see you thrown out
of the Abbey, or dumped on the Scilly Isles, far from anyone and
with only pirates in your congregation.'

The poor dolt had stared at him as if he was mad. 'Why should
that happen to me? I've done nothing wrong!'

'You have stolen bread from the mouths of beggars.'

'But you told me to! It's for a joke!'

'Yes, I did, didn't I? But I forgot to let the baker in on the joke,
I am afraid, so you see, you are a thief. And that will mean you'll
be punished.'

That was the difficult moment. Augerus had done this before,
and he knew that as the bait was snapped up, the fish could slip
off the hook and run off. Some had done so before. They had
stood up to him and stared him down, threatening to go straight to
the Abbot and denounce him. To his credit, Gerard tried that, but
when he did, Augerus merely laughed.

'Fine, my cocky. You tell him anything you like. And *I* shall tell
him that I caught you stealing from the baker. *And* that I caught
you stealing my rosary from Brother Mark, but that I concealed
your crime because I thought I could help you come to a state of
grace. We'll see whom it is the Abbot trusts most. An acolyte, or
his favoured Steward.'

After that it had been easy. For a share of the rewards, the boy
had stolen any little trinkets he was told to. His nimble fingers
and sharp wits meant that there was a steady stream of goods
arriving at Augerus' door. And as soon as they arrived, they were
parcelled up and pushed out through the little window that gave
onto the orchard, where Wally would collect it and convey it to
Joce. Never too much, only small items, and only ever just after a
large service with many people, so that it would be impossible to

guess who might have been the thief. That was the way of it.

But the little devil was gone now. And Wally was dead. Well, Augerus sighed, Wally was unreliable, had been for a while. In a way, it was a good thing he was gone.

Augerus was out in the court now, and was about to make for Mark's room when he saw Joce standing red-faced outside, gesticulating with a kind of restrained fury.

He groaned inwardly. He could still feel the pressure of Joce's hand on his throat. It was only then that the realisation hit him: Joce was supposed to be on his way to Exeter with a sackload of pewter.

'God's Blood! What the hell are you doing here still?' he whispered as soon as they had slipped down an alley.

'You bastard! You set him up to do it, didn't you?' Joce grated, pulling the monk towards him by his habit.

'Get off me, you cretin! Who – and to do what?'

Suddenly Augerus heard a rasp of metal and felt a point at his belly. 'What the . . .'

'Where is it? Come on – tell me! Wally didn't have it. Gerard didn't run away with it, did he? Have *you* got it?'

Joce had spent an angry, bitter night. Tossing and turning, wondering where his plate was, where his servant was, he was wild-eyed and more than a little mad-looking. It was a miracle he hadn't exploded from anger. The *shits*, the devious, lying, thieving *bastards*, whoever they were, had taken all his money. That was what the metal meant to him: money! He needed it to conceal the amount he had stolen from the town's accounts over the last year, and it was gone. It made him want to spit with fury, or stab and slash and kill everyone who might have taken it.

'*Where is it*?' he demanded again through gritted teeth.

'How do you know Wally and Gerard haven't—'

'If Wally had it, it'd be back here in the Abbey by now, wouldn't it? And a boy running away carrying a large sack of pewter? He wouldn't get far, would he? No, I think someone else must have it. And if you don't squeak soon, you'll be squeaking all the louder!'

Augerus could feel that terrible point screwing one way and another, gradually grinding forwards through his habit. 'Stop! I don't even know what pewter you mean.'

'Everything from my cupboard. It's all gone.'

'But . . .' Augerus gaped. The sudden movement at his gut made him gabble quickly. 'Look, *I* don't have it. I couldn't break into your room if I wanted to! Only Gerard could have done that. Your hall is locked, isn't it? Who else could get in?'

'Where has he put it, then?'

'How should I know? Maybe he had an accomplice, who hid it himself?'

Joce gasped angrily. 'Bloody Art!'

'What?'

'My servant. He hasn't come home. It must have been him stole my stuff. Thieving shit! When I find him, I'll make him eat his own tarse! I'll hamstring him and make him crawl, the bastard! I'll cut out his liver and eat it! I'll—'

'Where is he?'

'What?'

'This Art – where is he? If he has the pewter, he can't have gone far, can he?'

Joce felt as though a cloud had passed and suddenly the sun was shining full on him. 'Of course – I know where the bastard will be! Come on!'

'I can't. I must be ready to serve the Abbot his midday meal.'

'He can wait.'

'You can kill me now, if you want. That will alert people to your guilt. Or you can force me to come with you, I suppose, but how would I explain my absence to the Abbot? If I am caught, I . . .' Augerus thought about threatening Joce, but the point of the knife was too noticeable. '. . . I cannot help you again, can I? It's better that I stay inside the Abbey and you go to find this fellow.'

Joce held his gaze for a moment. 'Very well, but don't forget: if I am caught, you will die too.' He suddenly pulled the knife away and thrust it into the wood of a beam at the side of Augerus' head, the edge nicking his ear.

'If they catch me, Augie, I'll get you first. So help me, you'll feel this blade in your guts.'

Peter was unhappy to have been summoned to the Abbot's room again, but he was more concerned when he saw that Sir Baldwin and Simon were both there, the Coroner too.

The Abbot waved the monk to a seat and began speaking before Peter was sitting.

'When I spoke to you on Monday, you hinted that you had a good idea who might have been behind the theft of the pewterer's plates.'

'That is true, my Lord Abbot,' Peter said, keeping his eyes firmly fixed upon the Abbot himself and refusing to glance sideways at the other men.

'How did you learn about the other small theft?'

'I have heard mutterings from other guests, my Lord. Sometimes they have mentioned the loss of items to Ned the Horse, other times I have simply overheard them talking.'

'In terms which would embarrass the Abbey?' the Abbot shot out.

'Never. If they had, I would have mentioned it to you, my Lord. I could do nothing that would harm you or the Abbey.'

'Then what did they say?'

'Simply that the innkeeper in the last town had managed to take their stuff, or that they must have been careless in packing and left something by mistake. Never that they thought the Abbey could be responsible. Until the pewterer.'

'He noticed.'

'Yes, because he had personally set the items beneath his bed the night before. He knew that they had been stolen from him.'

'Why should you think you knew who had been responsible?'

'Because, as you know, I can rarely sleep a full night. I waken, and cannot return to slumber. Rather than sit in my cot and listen to others snoring, I get up and walk about the court in prayer, or rest before the altar and pray.'

'So you are often up and about when all others are asleep?'

'Yes.'

'And you have seen the thief?'

'I did say that I wouldn't confirm it to you, Lord, until I was sure that the culprit wouldn't confess of his own volition.'

'True. But since then a boy has disappeared and two men are dead. I begin to feel that matters are more pressing than one man's decision to hold his tongue, no matter how moral was the basis of that decision,' the Abbot said sarcastically.

'Very well, my Lord. I have often seen the boy Gerard wandering about during the night. It seemed odd to me.'

'So he stole the items,' the Abbot said, shooting a look at Baldwin.

The knight smiled thinly. The Abbot believed that this was proof of the boy's theft of the two plates found in his bed. Baldwin still doubted that.

Peter continued. 'I also saw how the plates were disposed of. I once observed Gerard hurrying from the guest rooms to your own lodgings here, Abbot.'

'Here?' Abbot Robert said with surprise.

'Yes. And a few moments later, from the walkway at the top of the wall by the river, I saw a window open, and a small sack descend on a rope. It was collected.'

'By whom?'

'Walwynus. I saw him quite clearly.'

'And you did not see fit to tell me!' Abbot Robert said coldly. 'This is extraordinary! After all this Abbey has done for you, this is how you repay us? Fortunately another Brother saw fit to tell me!'

'My Lord,' Peter said calmly, 'if I had told you then, it is likely that Wally would have simply denied the charge and accused me of wanting revenge – nothing more. You yourself would have been sorely troubled about my mind. And you would have questioned whether I could have seen the man that clearly at – what? – perhaps some fifty yards in the dark.'

'You should have trusted me!'

'And tested your confidence in me. Perhaps so. I'm afraid I chose the harder route. I sought to speak to the men responsible. And in Wally I found a ready ear. I fully believe that he felt his guilt and was prepared to redeem himself. I think that he was going to try to return the value of the metal to the Abbey for you to do with as you saw fit. It is only sad that he died before he could do so.'

'So you think that this deplorable boy had access to my lodgings and could pass the things to Wally from my own window?'

'Unless he had help.'

'From whom?' Baldwin interjected. 'You saw someone else during your ramblings at night?'

'I did. Occasionally, recently, I have seen Brother Mark. I think he feared that I was observing him, for he hid a few times when I noticed him, but he was never quite swift enough.'

'Brother Mark,' Baldwin muttered, and looked at Simon.

The Bailiff said nothing. He was considering Peter with a slight frown on his face. Mark, he thought. Mark who had been seen up on the moors on the day Wally died, if Ellis could be believed. Mark, who had been ostentatiously putting away that syphon tube on the day that Simon had been taken to the empty wine barrel, as though showing that anyone could have taken the tube and had access to the wine. Mark, who hated the idea of stealing from the Abbey, if his protestations meant anything.

'At least we know that Wally did indeed try to bring back the pewter,' he said, and he saw Peter close his eyes in a short prayer.

When he opened them again, Peter turned them on Simon. 'I am sure he did, and for that his soul deserves peace,' he said calmly. Simon nodded, but his mind was already turned to another issue: the Abbot had said that another Brother had already told him about Gerard. Glancing at the Abbot, Simon almost asked who it was, but his master's expression did not invite such a question.

Chapter Twenty-Three

Nob had felt a great sympathy for the miner. As he raked the coals aside in his oven, he couldn't help shaking his head and sniffing a little. Poor Hamelin! So he'd got hold of a load of money, and come back here to share it with his wife and try to save his son, and all he'd won was a dagger in the guts.

It was a decent sum of money too, from what he'd heard Emma saying. Not that it could do him any good now.

The night before, when he had taken the Bailiff and others to Hamelin's corpse, he had decided to make himself scarce. There was no advantage in being around when a Coroner started doing his work, for that only led to fines and more expense. Instead he frowningly retreated while the three began their discussion and questioned the others in the area, until he arrived at the end of the alley, and there he turned and darted back to his own shop.

Cissy was at her place by the bar, serving a couple of drunken yeomen, both recently thrown out of the tavern across the way, and she had looked up with an expression of thunder on her face as the two tottered clumsily from the shop, clutching their pies. 'And where have you been all this time? Down at the alehouse again, I'll bet. When will you ever grow up? You don't need—'

'Quiet, woman! I've not been near the alehouse.' He took hold of her hand. 'Hamelin is dead. I was there when he was found, stabbed.'

Cissy went white. 'Oh, poor Emma! What will she do now? I hope she still has all his money.' Cissy pulled the table aside so that she could squeeze past. 'I'll have to go to her right away. You mind the shop, Nob. I'll stay with her overnight and make sure she's all right.'

'All right, love. Off you go.'

His wife had been as good as her word, and he had slept alone but for the companionship of his barrel. Now, this morning, his head felt a little furry, his mouth tasted sour, and he couldn't help but burp every so often.

Taking a drinking horn filled with ale through to the shop, he ensconced himself behind the table and pulled it back into place. Before long, Joce appeared at his door and demanded one of his meat-pies. Nothing loath, for Nob always liked to have someone to talk to, especially when he had a sore head, he served Joce with the juiciest and plumpest one on the table.

'Terrible days. First poor Wally, now Hamelin. Who'll be next, eh?'

'Where's Cissy?'

'She went off last night to help poor Emma.'

Joce finished his pie and wiped his mouth on his sleeve. Hamelin's life or death had no interest for him. He was a cretin of a miner. A poor man who could achieve nothing but dig, dig, dig for tin. He might as well have been a serf. The man could be consumed by hellfire for all he cared. He grunted, 'Have you seen my servant last night or today?'

'What, young Art? No, why? Has he disappeared?'

'Bastard's vanished. Not there when I got home last night. There's no food, nothing – and some little pieces of jewellery have gone missing, too. Small things, but enough.'

Nob whistled. 'You think he stole them? That's bad, that is. Where could he have gone?'

'Have you seen him?' Joce repeated through gritted teeth.

'No, but I'll tell you if I do. Have you told the Watch?'

'Oh, damn them and you!' Joce raged suddenly and stormed from the shop.

All the pie-cooking fool could think about was that sick cretin Hamelin, as if the death of a miner was a matter of any consequence. And Cissy had run off to 'help' the widow, as though she could do anything useful. Emma was widowed, and that was it. Unless Cissy was prepared to offer her money, she would probably have to fall back on the support of the parish. Another damned pauper for men like Joce to maintain. As if there weren't enough useless mouths to be fed.

Like his little *shit* of a servant. That bastard would regret the day he was born, when Joce caught up with him. Not that it should be too difficult to track him down. Joce had a good idea where the lad was. He strode along the roadway, out past the middens on the northern road, and over the bridge to the eastern riverbank. Turning left, he followed the water until he came into view of a large pair of barns. Seeing the flames flickering between the trees, he walked more cautiously now, until he could get a good view of the men.

It was Sir Tristram's little army; they lay, still asleep, or sat and stared at the campfires while a guard leaned against a door and kept a wary eye upon them all, making sure none of them tried to escape.

Joce cast his eyes about them, but there was no sign of Art. Some bodies were sprawled on the grass, wrapped in blankets or coats, and he studied them in case Art might be among them, but he saw no figure that looked like him. One man was familiar, but Joce wasn't sure why. The lad had a shaven head, like a penitent, and gripped a soft felt cap in his hands. He looked nervous, and every time that the sparks flew up, his eyes moved anxiously from side to side as if he was fearfully watching the men about him.

As well he might, Joce thought, his attention moving on again. Somewhere here, he was sure, was the thieving sod of a servant who had robbed him. That acolyte could have a hand in it, too. The bastard had enough balls to break into his house and steal all his pewter. Although what he would have done with it afterwards was another question. Like Augerus said, it would be difficult for him to carry away that much stuff. Perhaps he had hidden it in the town, and was planning to sneak back to collect it. That was the sort of thing that Joce would do. It would make sense – wait until the Hue and Cry had died down, and then sidle back and collect the lot. Only it suggested that this acolyte was brighter than he had thought. Brighter than Augerus had thought too, for that matter.

There was no sign of his servant, and he set his jaw. Art wasn't bright enough to come here – or perhaps he was *too* bright. Anyone must think of coming here and taking a squint at the poor buggers all lined up in a row ready to march. Joining Sir Tristram's group would be an easy means of escaping.

It was while he was leaving the camp that the bald lad's face came back to him, the pale features with the large bright eyes. Why should someone shave his pate? Monks did it as a sign of their devotion; others might do it to change their appearance. Damn it! Even a monk might want to change his appearance, and how easy it would be to conceal a tonsure by shaving all the hair about it.

Especially, he thought with a dawning realisation, if the hair were red. Like Gerard's.

That morning, Baldwin and Simon broke their fast with the Coroner, and then spoke to a servant and requested Peter to join them in the guest rooms.

Without preamble, Baldwin asked the Almoner, 'Sir Tristram was in the Northern Marches at the same time as you and Walwynus, wasn't he? He knew the dead man – we know that from the way he reacted to seeing Walwynus' body. Could he have ridden out to the moors and killed him?'

'I wouldn't know. It's possible. He knew of Wally in the north, and he hated all Scots. Aye, but didn't Sir Tristram arrive here only after the coining?'

'We have to verify that,' Coroner Roger said.

Simon mused, 'He wasn't in the Abbey, but that doesn't mean he wasn't near. Maybe he was staying in Tavistock.'

Peter gazed at him. 'Why so much interest in *him*?'

'From all that you've said, he is violent enough to kill,' said the Coroner.

Simon considered. Sir Tristram had been there in the Northern Marches at the same time as Wally. He had hated the man, that much was clear from his spitting into the corpse's bloated face. 'Peter, have you seen Sir Tristram down here before? Has he come here as Arrayer at any other time?'

'Not so far as I know, no.'

From the look Baldwin gave Simon, it was clear that he had reached the same conclusion. 'What of the man killed yesterday?' he asked.

'Hamelin? He was a tinner up on the moor not far from Wally. I think they knew each other a little, but not too well. They were not bosom companions,' Peter responded slowly. 'How was he killed? Was he stabbed? There was lots of blood.'

'Hamelin was stabbed, Brother Peter,' the Coroner pronounced. 'Yes, no one in the roadway admits to the faintest idea why he should have been killed. They all say he was but a likeable man.'

'Aye, well, that is often the way of it, isn't it? The poor man was found by his wife,' Peter added sadly. 'Poor Emma is half out of her mind. It is a terrible thing to have this happen!'

'A knight would be as able to stab a man as any other, wouldn't he?' Simon said. 'And Sir Tristram knew Wally. Perhaps the Arrayer chose to finish some of his business. He came here during the coining, saw Wally, recognised him, chose to kill him to settle some score from years ago, and presumably left Wally's purse unopened because he wouldn't need the money. But he counted without Hamelin. Hamelin saw him attack Wally and when he rushed down to the body, he found his friend dead and the purse there for the taking. It's no surprise if he took it, for he had great need of money, and he brought it here for his wife. But while in Tavistock he stumbled into Sir Tristram – and the knight executed him. It makes more sense than Wally buying Hamelin's debt!'

Peter had been listening carefully, but now he interrupted them. It was time to speak. 'Lordings, the answers may be closer to home than Sir Tristram. I heard yesterday that Sir Tristram's Sergeant recognised a man in the crowd. It was Joce Blakemoor. The Sergeant saw him in Scotland, where he was the leader of Wally and Martyn Armstrong. It was he, according to this Sergeant, who killed and raped my Agnes.'

'How could he know that?' Simon wondered. 'Was he witness to the rape and murder?'

'I do not know,' Peter admitted. 'I am confused. If Blakemoor killed my Agnes, perhaps he was also the man who did this to me,' he added, fingering his scar.

Simon gave a low whistle. 'It's possible, I suppose. Joce left Tavistock to trade, or so he told everyone. But he could have gone anywhere: all people here know is that he returned with a purse of gold.'

Baldwin said, 'Absence from here doesn't necessarily make him guilty.'

'No.' Simon was thinking quickly. 'And why should Joce want Wally dead? Because he was a threat to Joce's future, knowing too much of his past? What of Hamelin? Could he have seen Joce? But then, Sir Tristram might have recognised Wally and chosen to execute him. Hamelin again could have witnessed the attack.'

'I still wonder about this weapon, though,' Baldwin objected. 'I do not understand why he should have taken a club to kill. Surely either man would have preferred a dagger or sword?'

'Yes, but surely he's been trying to throw us off the scent. That was why he made his own morning star from timbers he found lying about in Hal's mine. He came across them and thought he might as well use them.'

'Perhaps,' Baldwin said. 'Let us go and ask them.'

Simon set his jaw grimly. He could not help but observe that Baldwin was tugging at his sword hilt, easing the blade in the sheath like a man expecting a fight.

'Who do you want to talk to first, Baldwin?' he asked.

Baldwin looked at Coroner Roger. 'My choice would be to see Sir Tristram, because as soon as we have talked to him, we can use his men to help us arrest Joce. If it is true that Joce was this . . .'

' "Red Hand",' Peter supplied helpfully.

'Thank you,' Baldwin said, ' "Red Hand", then we may need more than a few men to corner him. He sounds thoroughly unscrupulous and determined.'

Sir Tristram was awake when the three arrived at his camp, and he watched them with a sour expression as they rode into the clearing. They secured their mounts to the horse line, a rope stretched between two trees, and picked their way through the still-sleeping bodies to where he stood.

'Sir Tristram, we have some more questions for you,' Coroner Roger said gruffly. He never much liked to have to question his peers. He always had a sneaking suspicion that justice was something that should be imposed upon the poorer folk; it wasn't intended to control the richer and more important men like Sir Tristram.

'Well, you'll have to ask them while I eat, then. I haven't had anything yet today.'

'Certainly, Sir Tristram. So long as you don't mind us sitting with you,' Coroner Roger said politely.

'Where is your Sergeant?' Baldwin asked.

'He was hit on the head yesterday in Tavistock during a scuffle. I sent to tell him to rest overnight in the tavern and I'd collect him today. Why?'

'What were you doing yesterday?' Simon asked bluntly.

'Me? When? I am a busy man.'

'In the afternoon. I doubt Hamelin was dead before noon.'

'What? Do you propose to accuse me of some stranger's death?'

'Another miner found killed. Where were you?'

'Damn your impudence, man! I shall report this to the King himself, I assure you!' Sir Tristram's face was as red as his crimson tunic, and he felt almost apoplectic. He held the same views as the Coroner in some matters; it was unthinkable that a knight should be forced to answer questions like any serf, especially while eating. He almost stood, but then the expression on Baldwin's face persuaded him to remain where he was.

Simon leaned against a tree, his left hand resting on his hilt, his right thumb hooked into his belt. 'Well?'

'I was with my men, as I should have been. What business is it of yours?'

'And where were you on the morning after the coining?'

'What, last Friday?' Sir Tristram's temper, never cool, was warming rapidly. He was tempted to draw his sword and see how these impudent fools answered then. 'I was on my way to the Abbey with my Sergeant. What of it?'

'You knew Walwynus.'

'So?'

'And hated him, from the way you spat in his face last night.'

Slowly and menacingly, Sir Tristram brought himself upright, holding Simon's gaze with a fury that was unfeigned. 'You mean to accuse me of murder, Bailiff? If you dare, say the words, and I'll carve the word "innocent" on your forehead. Go on! Say it. Say you accuse me, and see what happens.'

'If you try to attack the Bailiff, you will have to fight two knights first,' the Coroner stated flatly.

'I would do so gladly,' Sir Tristram replied. 'Do you offer trial by combat?'

'Be silent!' Baldwin roared. 'Christ Jesus! Do you want us to accuse you? We are here to establish your innocence, but if you wish to prove guilt, continue! There are enough questions which suggest you might be a murderer, but there are others which suggest you could be innocent.'

'Which have you decided upon, Sir Knight?' Sir Tristram sneered. He watched the three men through narrowed eyes, expecting a bitter rejoinder, and was somewhat surprised when Simon set his head to one side and surveyed him pensively.

'I have almost convinced myself you must be innocent, but I do not know why. I find it hard to believe that you could have found your way to the miners' camp and selected a balk of timber and a handful of nails and constructed a morning star. Such premeditation seems unlike your character.'

'Should I be grateful for that?'

Simon ignored him. 'If you were angry with a man, I think you are bloodthirsty enough to take a sword or axe or mace and use it. Thinking about protecting your good name wouldn't occur to you. No, I think you would avenge an insult or remembered slight with a swift response. If you hated Walwynus enough to want to kill him, you would take a sword to him and damn the consequences. You are a fighter. You would scorn subterfuge. Also, you would not have known Wally was here, let alone where he lived. Perhaps you saw Wally and Peter, and followed them up to the moors, but then you'd have got to Hal's mine after Hal, and he'd have seen you steal his timber. If you came up *before* Wally, how would you know where to find him later? And how could you know where to go for wood and nails? No, I don't think you could have killed Wally.'

'A thousand thanks for that, dear Bailiff.'

'Of course, it all depends on what you say about where you were last night and on the day that Wally died.'

'Look – I hated Walwynus. I'll admit to that gladly. He was a Scotch reiver, a murderer. That fool Peter rescued him and saved him when I and my men nearly had him. He would have died, him and that evil shit Martyn Scot, Armstrong as he was called. If they had, Peter would never have received that wound, so I suppose there is some justice.'

'You tried to kill Wally; Peter saved him, and then Peter's woman was raped.'

'So?'

'Wally denied doing it.'

'Perhaps it was Armstrong, then.'

Simon closed his eyes a moment, then opened them again to stare at Sir Tristram. 'This woman had saved his life with her diligent nursing. And you suppose he would have taken two friends of his to see her so that they could rape her. Does that sound credible?'

'Have you ever fought in a war, Bailiff?' the knight asked scathingly. 'If you had, you would know that the worst actions are always possible. Sometimes they are inevitable. A man who is desperate for a woman will take her wherever he may, and if he has companions, he will offer them the same woman. It's a matter of courtesy.'

Baldwin took a deep, angry breath. 'I have fought in many wars, and I have *never* heard of a man who was saved by a woman and who then repaid her courage and kindness by raping her and offering her to his comrades, finally killing her. That, to me, does not sound true. If it were, it would be the act of a callous and unchivalrous coward.'

'You can say what you want. I merely offer one possibility.'

'I offer you another,' Simon said. 'You adored this woman Agnes. You craved her, and *that* was why you hated Peter! He had her; you didn't. So *you* raped her. You took her the only way you could, at the point of a dagger. And then you killed her, just so that she couldn't tell Peter and embarrass you.'

'That is a disgraceful lie!' Sir Tristram exploded. 'You pathetic little turd, you spawn of a poxed sow and a drunken Scotch reiver, you—'

'Swear it on the Bible.'

'What?'

'You heard me. If I am wrong, we can prove it. You may swear your denial on the Bible before the Abbot.'

'Never!'

'Why not?'

'Because it is nonsense!'

'Your own Sergeant might not realise you were guilty,' Simon speculated. 'If you were haring about the country searching for outlaws, you could have come across this woman and taken her, later laying the blame for her violation and death at the door of known felons.'

'This is rubbish!'

'If you knew her already and desired her, it would make a perfect crime, wouldn't it? And if you later mentioned to your Sergeant or others that the felons had taken another victim, who would argue?'

'I say I did not!'

'Perhaps,' Simon said. 'But I believe you are innocent of the murder of Walwynus and I can see no reason why you should have killed Hamelin, but by God Himself, I believe you could have murdered the girl Agnes – *and* instructed your Sergeant to accuse another to protect yourself!'

'Her death is nothing to do with you here, though, is it? She died in Scotland, not in England. Different country, different times,' Sir Tristram sneered.

Baldwin looked at him. 'Your smugness seems proof of your guilt. It may be true that we cannot pursue you here, but your soul will suffer if you don't seek penance. Remember that, man! You may have succeeded here, but God will seek you out when you die, and punish you.'

'Yes, well, if He wants, I'll take His punishment, but not for something I didn't do! In the meantime I won't sit listening to lectures from another knight. You declare me guilty. I say I am not. I leave it up to Him to decide.'

Simon nodded. 'If you weren't the murderer and rapist, then who was?'

'I still say it was Wally and his men.'

'Under their leader, "Red Hand"?' Simon asked.

'That was his name. Why?'

'Your Sergeant said yesterday that this man was Joce Blakemoor. That Blakemoor and Wally and Martyn Armstrong came down here together, all fleeing from you and your men.'

'Christ alive!' Sir Tristram said, stunned.

'So you see, if you are innocent, we'll need to catch Blakemoor to prove it,' the Coroner said. 'Could you lend us a few men to help catch him?'

'You can have as many men as you need. All I ask is that you get him,' Sir Tristram ground out. 'And that you kill him.'

Chapter Twenty-Four

Gerard stirred as he heard a crackle. All about him there were grunts and snores, the faint murmuring of the stupid or fearful young, the snuffling of the infirm, but the noises were comforting in some odd way; just the fact of the companionship of all these people made him feel a little safer.

It was odd to have had his head shaved. He hadn't expected to have to have this done, but when he spoke to Cissy, she was certain it would make enough of a difference to save him from being recognised, and he wasn't going to argue. Especially when he had been seen by Nob in the crowd. Far better that he should suffer from the cold for a while than be caught and made to pay the penalty for his thefts and apostasy. Mind, the shaving had hurt like hell. There was an almighty bruise on his head where that damn fool Reginald had caused him to fall and strike it in the dorter.

If only, he thought, there were a pie or a loaf here now. It would make such a difference. His belly felt so empty, and food would warm him. He had lain near enough to the fire to feel the warmth, but since then three men had rolled themselves up in their blankets between him and the embers, and now he was chilled to the marrow. Memories of piping hot pies and pasties came to mind, the rich gravy of beef, the heavenly scent of pepper. The mere thought made his mouth water.

He rolled over onto his back and stared up at the sky. It was deep grey, as Dartmoor mornings so often were, and he could see tiny orange sparks gleaming as they shot upwards from the fire, glowing for a moment before they expired. He sighed and put his arms behind his head. It was nasty, the thought that he was going north to war, but as Cissy had said, there was bound to be a way of earning a living once the battles were done. He grinned to himself. The trouble was, the only way he knew of earning a living was by thieving. And that wasn't a good idea once he was out of the Abbey. He could try to claim *benefit of clergy*, but that was no guarantee of safety.

There was always the possibility that he might become a decent man-at-arms or archer. Some lord might decide to retain him, and he could then give up his life of petty crime and become a professional man. Fighting always had a chivalrous aspect. The women loved men-at-arms, so it was said. Even lowly archers got their wenches, and that was an appealing idea. After the enforced celibacy of the Abbey, a warm, fleshy woman cradled in the crook of his arm was a very attractive concept indeed.

Certainly better than the short life he could expect if he had remained in the Abbey. Reginald had made that clear. He had said that the other acolytes knew Gerard was stealing their things, and that if he didn't stop, they were going to break his head. In fact, even if he did, Reginald said, they might decide to punish him anyway. Gerard's selfishness had made all their lives more difficult by taking away those little trinkets they valued most. They wanted him to suffer for his greed.

It had been little use trying to explain how it hadn't been *his* idea to rob them. The time when he could have confessed was long past. Nor could he accuse another monk, for all would simply assume he was passing the blame to others to protect himself. Peter and Reginald believed Gerard, but who else would?

A man rolled over, broke wind loudly, and Gerard turned his face away. There was another crackle of twigs, and he gave a faint 'tut' of annoyance. Someone must be tiptoeing around – but why? Perhaps they were searching for something to steal. Well, Gerard thought, they can take the whole of *my* bag, if they want. There's nothing of value at all in there.

He felt his belly with a tentative hand. His bladder was so full, he felt about ready to piss himself. He rose, stepping carefully over the bodies of the still-sleeping men, and in past a short line of bushes. There he recognised voices, and turning back, he saw the three men questioning Sir Tristram. A brief panic overtook him, and he thrust himself through the branches and into a small clearing.

Crouched over, he stared at the men, feeling certain that they were here to catch him. He mustn't be found! His heart was thudding painfully, and he had a hollow feeling in his throat. His attention was so strongly focused on the group that he didn't notice the snap of another twig until it was too late.

And then he felt the ice-cold touch of a sharp blade at his throat.

'Wake up, monk! We have business to attend to!' Joce hissed.

The three men left Sir Tristram still fuming. As they untethered their horses, Simon glanced back and saw the knight pick up his mazer and hurl it at a tree.

Baldwin saw it too, and murmured drily, 'I think we have seriously discommoded the good Sir Tristram.'

Soon four men on sturdy ponies had joined them, and the small party set off. They pulled their mounts' heads back towards Tavistock, and Coroner Roger glanced from one to the other. 'Well? What do you think? For my money, I somehow doubt he's the killer.'

Simon nodded. 'I agree. I think we have to look for another man.'

'But whom?' Baldwin said.

Simon was thinking furiously. 'Surely the disappearance of the acolyte, the murder of Walwynus, and the thefts from the Abbey must all be linked. And probably the death of Hamelin as well.'

'The body of the acolyte has not been found,' Baldwin said. 'And yet the Abbot and I discovered bloodstains near his bed.'

Simon felt almost dizzy with the thoughts that whirled in his mind. He pulled his horse to a halt. 'This Gerard would surely have been found by now if he had been killed. Wally and Hamelin weren't concealed, were they? There is no reason to suppose that Gerard would be either. He may simply have fled the place.'

'Because he felt himself to be under threat,' Baldwin supposed.

'A novice who ran away would find himself caught again in no time,' the Coroner said.

Simon gave a groan. 'I am a cretin. The Arrayer's hiring! I saw him, and I didn't recognise him!'

'Eh?' the Coroner asked, but Simon had already turned his horse and was spurring it back towards the camp. He rode through the midst of the men, halting before Sir Tristram. 'Sir, there was a recruit with no hair under his cap. You remember him?'

Sir Tristram gave a curt nod. 'Large, gangling lad. Clumsy, but capable. What of him?'

'You took him on?'

'Yes.'

'Where is he now?'

'Here somewhere with the rest. Why?'

'I think he could be a renegade,' Simon said, but would say no more. Sir Tristram jerked his head at a man, sending him strolling casually through the recruits. Soon he came back with a thin blanket in his hands, a scowl on his face. 'He must have scarpered when he saw you lot get here.'

'God's Cods!' Simon swore. 'Sir Tristram – this man is an apostate. The Abbot demands his return.'

Baldwin put his hand on Simon's arm. 'There's no need to search for him here. Sir Tristram can find him, and we'll be able to talk to him later. For now, let us try to see what might have caused the murderer of Walwynus to execute Hamelin as well.'

'I will find him, you can assure the Abbot of that,' Sir Tristram said.

'I suppose you are right,' Simon said unwillingly. He felt instinctively that it would be better to remain here with the Arrayer's men, searching for Gerard, but Baldwin was probably right. The lad could have gone in any direction. There was little to be gained by the three joining in the search. Sir Tristram had enough men at his disposal.

There were other people to see. 'Who do you want to speak to?'

'Joce first, but then somebody who knew Hamelin and Walwynus. I keep remembering what the Swiss said, that the pewter was sold to him by Walwynus in an alehouse. I see no reason to doubt Rudolf's word, and we know that later Walwynus was to spend a lot of money on women and wine, so that part of the story tallies.'

'We know Walwynus collected the stolen goods from the Abbey?' Coroner Roger said.

'Yes, and yet we do not know who passed him the sack from the window, as Peter saw. Someone inside the Abbey stole the stuff and passed it to Walwynus, and the miner hid it. Then, once he had a great enough stock, he sold it. Was it Gerard who entered the Abbot's lodging to let the sack down to Wally?'

Simon nodded. 'Gerard took the stuff and passed it to Wally – but why should Wally be there in the first place?'

'Surely he must have.' Coroner Roger said.

'It would be easy enough to pass them through a window or over a wall as Peter said,' Simon speculated. 'If hurled over a wall, the metal would have been dented, and the noise should have brought guards running. The things must have been passed out quietly.'

The Coroner grunted. 'So what? Does it matter?'

Simon said nothing, but when they arrived at the bridge and had clattered over its rough timbers, he led the way past the Water Gate and up around the Abbey. While the Coroner grumbled about guesswork, Simon carefully surveyed the perimeter of the main court, which was enclosed by the great wall. The northern, western and eastern walls were all high, and castellated, with no windows through which to pass stolen goods. With all the folk who wandered about and guards at night, Simon was sure no one would throw things over the wall or dangle them from a rope. There was too much risk of discovery. Only one wall was possible, the last they reached. From the road they could look over the low orchard wall at the final barrier.

'It was all passed from the Abbot's own lodging, according to Peter,' Simon breathed. 'He's right. It's the only way they could have got it out.'

Baldwin was frowning. 'It is certainly possible,' he conceded. 'But how on earth would the acolyte have reached the Abbot's rooms? Surely he could only hand Walwynus the metal during the dark, for else the miner would have been seen.'

'There was another accomplice inside the Abbot's lodging,' Simon said. 'But at least that explains how the things were taken from the Abbey. As Peter told us, they were passed from a window here, down to Wally, who carried them away with him.'

'All the way to the moors?' Coroner Roger shook his head. 'No. Too much risk of being seen. Carrying stuff like that would be an invitation to the Watch. He must have kept the things securely here in the town.'

'Yes,' Simon said. 'You are right, of course!'

'Let's go and see Joce, this "Red Hand" and find out what he has to say for himself.'

They rode to the Abbey's stables and left their mounts before hurrying out through the Court Gate towards the road where Joce's house lay. Sir Tristram's men eyed the trio as though doubting their sanity.

Simon didn't care. He was feeling the excitement of the chase now. All fears and insecurities were fading, leaving in their stead this thrilling in his blood. He felt as though they were near to understanding the whole story, that there were only a few small details which needed to be teased out and fitted into their relevant positions. In reality, of course, there were still some terrible blank spaces.

There was no hint of a motive for killing Wally, and the same went for Hamelin's murder too. Money had appeared as though from nowhere, murderers had run down to Tavistock from Scotland – and there was little sense to any of it. Why should Wally and Martyn have come here? And then light dawned. If Joce truly was 'Red Hand', Wally and Martyn, after fleeing from Sir Tristram and his men, would have gone where their leader told them they should be safe: the place he himself knew, his own birthplace. And when they arrived at Tavistock, what could be more natural than that they should take up spades to try their hand at tin mining?

But if their attempts met with little success, it would be easy to imagine small niggling annoyances growing into disputes or violent explosions. One such must have led to the argument during which Martyn died. One man couldn't mine successfully. What would Wally have done? Obviously he'd have gone to his master and asked for assistance.

They had reached Blakemoor's door. Baldwin pointed to one of the men with them, who drew his dagger and hammered on it with the hilt, but there was no reply.

While they waited, Simon caught his breath. 'Baldwin, do you remember what that Swiss said about the house he saw Wally and the lad jumping from?'

'Yes, he said it was built of limed wood, and that there was a blue shield painted over the doorway.' Baldwin followed Simon's pointing finger. 'So Wally and his accomplice were robbing Joce.'

'You lot stay here, two at this door, two at the back. Wait here until I send word you can go,' Coroner Roger said.

Simon looked about him. Seeing Nob's shop, he recalled his conversation with the innkeeper on the day when he was helping the Arrayer select his men. 'Baldwin, that pie-shop there. It's owned by Nob, the man who spoke to us last night and took us to Hamelin's corpse. Wally used to stay there. Let's go and have a look. We might learn something.'

When the three marched inside Nob's shop, they found it deserted. Simon strode to the table and thumped upon it with his fist, while the Coroner eyed the pies with an interest that was not in the least professional. He reached out with a finger and experimentally poked at one.

'Hoy! Don't bugger about wi' me pies'

The stertorian voice came from the open doorway at the back of the shop, and soon Nob came through, using his towel to wipe his head and face with one hand, while the other gripped a large drinking horn.

'That's meat. You want meat, fowl or fish? It's Friday, so you should be eating fish.'

Simon said, 'You spoke to us yesterday about Hamelin. Did Walwynus come here to sleep when he visited Tavistock for the coining?'

'Yes. He always came to stay here when he was in Tavistock.'

'Do you mean that he came here often?' Baldwin enquired.

'Yes. Every few weeks, whenever he needed supplies. We sort of took pity on him. Well, my Cissy did. She's always like that, looking after the waifs and strays. Daft cow. Why do you ask?'

'Did he stay in this room?' Simon asked.

'No, he'd be out in the back.'

'Show us.'

'Why? I don't see why I . . .' His protestations were ignored as the three barged past him and out into the room behind. 'Come on! What's all this about?'

It was a small room, with a second door that opened out to the garden space behind, sparsely furnished. There was only

one small table and a couple of stools. A barrel was standing
on the table-top. Apart from that, the room appeared to
be a storeroom for a small quantity of flour to make the baker's
paste for pies, and for the charcoal which he needed to fire his
oven.

'Where do you buy your coals?' Baldwin asked, picking up a
small sack.

'Up the way. Look, what is all this?'

Simon had found a balled lump of black material, and he
opened it out to find it was a man-sized tunic, but there was
nothing in it, so he let it fall back on the floor. Nob strode over to
him and kicked it aside angrily.

'I've had enough of this. I want an explanation.'

'We're investigating Walwynus' death,' the Coroner said curtly.
'So shut up and answer our questions.'

'Old Wally? What does this place have to do with him?'

Simon took the sack from Baldwin. Like the one which had
contained the pewter, this was impregnated with charcoal dust.
'Nob, I think you have been a very foolish man.'

'Me?' Nob squeaked. 'I've done nothing!'

'But you allowed a felon into your home. Someone stole pewter
from the Abbey and passed it out to Wally, and Wally hid it. Now
we have more stolen pewter, and it's in a sack – one of these ones
you keep your coals in.'

Nob dropped with a thump on to one of the stools. 'Oh God,
no, not Wally,' he said. 'Oh, my God! You mean things have been
stolen from the Abbey and stored here? My heavens! That is
terrible.'

'Did you know anything about this, Nob?' Simon asked keenly.
He moved to the cook's side and stood over him threateningly.

'No, of course not. What do you take me for, eh?

'Is there anywhere here Wally could have hidden a sack this
size?' Coroner Roger pressed him.

'Where else would he have taken stolen things?' Baldwin

demanded of the anxious Nob. 'There can't have been too many people whom he would have visited.'

'I never saw him carry a sack, sir. Never. Sometimes he had his small bag, but never one of those sacks.'

Simon gasped with understanding. 'Baldwin, the sack we got must have been a whole collection. Wally had an accomplice outside the Abbey, and when he had collected enough, he filled his sack and sold it.'

'But the Swiss told us that he found Wally jumping from Joce's window. Shit! I don't understand what this is all about! Wally knew Blakemoor,' Coroner Roger's belly grumbled; he wanted to reach into the cook's shop and take a pie.

'Suppose so. Blakemoor's the Receiver. We all know him,' Nob said.

Simon asked, 'What did Walwynus say about him? We've heard that they were close, that they might have been comrades.'

'I suppose it's possible,' Nob said thoughtfully, 'but something changed on the day of the coining.'

Simon peered at him. 'Why do you say that?'

'He came in here partway through the day, bought a pie, but he was very quiet. Not himself. Swore about Joce for some reason, but wouldn't explain why. Then he ran out as soon as he saw some young monk.'

'A novice?' Baldwin asked.

'That's right,' Nob said more slowly.

'Do you know his name?'

'Oh, er, he was just a lad, you know. The red-haired one.'

Simon shot Baldwin a look. 'Gerard has red hair.'

'So now we have a connection between Wally and Gerard, and between Wally and Joce,' Baldwin said. 'And we know that they robbed Joce. I'd think that was a good enough motive for him to murder Wally, if he learned Wally was involved.'

'*If* – yes.' Simon was frowning. 'But why should Wally go and steal that pewter from Joce?'

'Because as this estimable cook has told us, Joce and Wally fell out. Wally came here and took back all the pewter at a time when he knew the Receiver would be held up at the coining.'

'Why should they fall out?' Simon wondered. 'That's what I want to know.' Something was nagging at his mind, but he couldn't put his finger on it.

'Well, we'd best track down Joce, then,' said Coroner Roger impatiently. 'He's the man who needs to answer questions now.'

'In a moment,' Simon said. He was studying Nob with a certain intensity. 'What of Hamelin? You told us he had come into some money, which he brought here for his wife. Do you still believe he sold an old debt? It sounds odd, if Wally knew he couldn't recover that debt.'

'You need to ask Emma about that.'

'Where is she?'

'At Hamelin's place.'

Chapter Twenty-Five

Joce pushed Gerard along in front of him, the knife in his hand pricking the lad whenever he slowed. He shoved him through brambles and gorse, on and on, until Joce felt sure that they were safe from immediate discovery.

They were up the hill which led to the moors. From here, Joce could look back and see the smoke rising from the fires of Tavistock, and the Abbey itself. The road along the eastern riverbank was hidden by the lie of the hillside, but that was little concern, he thought, panting after the exertion.

Gerard's hands were bound with Joce's belt, and Joce had firm hold of it. Now he jerked on it viciously, and kicked Gerard's shin, knocking the boy to the ground.

'Don't kill me!'

Gerard sobbed, petrified with fear. It felt as though he had escaped one danger only to fall into a still worse one. When he had felt that awful knife at his throat, he had thought that he was going to die. It struck him as ironic that, having escaped the clutches of Reginald and the Abbot, he should have fallen among cut-throats and felons who wanted to kill him for the little money he had in his scrip. And then he had been startled as he recognised the voice: *Joce*!

He knew Joce, of course. Everyone did. The Receiver was recognised by everyone in the town because he was so powerful. He was responsible for all the money paid in tolls and fines, for justice and the smooth running of Tavistock. No one could live in the area without knowing Joce.

But Gerard knew more about him, because Gerard knew Art,

his servant. Art regularly cursed his master. All masters would beat their staff on occasion, of course, but according to Art, Joce took a profound pleasure in beating his charge that went beyond all the bounds of propriety. And even in the Abbey, there were whispers about the recent heated argument between Joce and his neighbour over the midden heap.

If he were free of Joce, he could have giggled to recall that. The pile which had so incensed Joce had in fact been carefully put there by Wally and himself, making a decent pile of rubbish on which Gerard could climb to gain entry. Once he was inside, he went downstairs and let Wally in as well, and then the two searched out the pewter which had been stolen.

When Wally had seen Joce standing in the market for the coining, he had realised that the man's house would be empty. And that led to his idea that he and Gerard could break in and steal back the pewter. They could share the profits, he said, although Gerard had refused his allotted portion. He had pointed out that he had no need of money. His reward was to ensure that the man who had ultimately led him to a life of felony would not benefit by it.

Wally had gone to Nob's place and seized a sack, and then the two were inside. As soon as they found the locked cupboard, they forced it open and filled the sack with pewter. Then they heard the sound of a door. Fearing discovery, they swiftly shut the cupboard and bolted, and all but brained that foreigner out in the alley. Still, it had been good in a way. Wally had sold the stuff easily enough. Apparently the foreigner was looking for tin to mix with lead to make his own pewter, but he was soon persuaded to take the metal he was offered. He was not so scrupulous as to turn down an offer like that.

Scrambling to his feet as Joce lashed out again with his boot, Gerard gasped, 'No, don't hurt me, please!'

'Where is it, you bastard?' Joce grabbed Gerard's shoulder, pulling him towards the knife.

'I don't know what you . . .'

'Oh, you think I won't dare to hurt a man of the cloth?' Joce asked mildly, and then he slashed once, a long cut with the sharp blade.

There was no pain. That was the first thought in Gerard's mind as he saw the blade, now bloody, dancing in front of his face. There was only a curious sense of disembodiment, as though he was watching actors on a cart. He felt as though there was a slap at his cheek, that was all, and then there was a warmth that spread from his cheekbone down his neck to his shoulder. The knife flashed again, red, as though it was itself angry now, and Gerard felt his nose break, then a dragging as the blade snagged on bone.

'Stop! Stop!' he cried, but Joce could scarcely hear him. His fist came again, this time thudding into Gerard's shoulder, and the boy wept with the certainty that he was about to die. 'Mother Mary! Sweet Jesus!'

'Where is it?' Joce demanded, his breath rasping in his throat. 'I'll kill you, you little toad, for trying to steal from me. *Where is it*? No one else could have got into my house. Where have you put all my pewter? What have you done with it?'

Gerard felt rather than saw the knife flash towards him, and in his terror, he fell before it could hit him. 'It's with the Swiss! Don't hurt me again! Wally did it! He sold it to the Swiss on the moor.'

Joce stood over him, confused. He was so filled with rage against this thief who could steal all his carefully hoarded pewter that he felt he could burst, but at the same time he was overwhelmed at the thought of all the money which could be lost. He kicked Gerard once in the flank, then the leg, then the shoulder, short, brutal kicks meted out with an unrestrained fury.

'Cheat me, would you? You little shit, I'll kill you!' he hissed.

He raised the knife to stab a last time, but as he did so, he heard a voice bellowing, 'Hold, felon! Murder, murder, *murder*!'

There was a man on a horse, and he was cantering towards Joce. The great hooves looked enormous, and, struck with a fear for his own safety, Joce darted away, running for the safety of some trees nearby.

'Sweet Jesus!' were the last words Gerard heard as he slipped into the welcoming darkness.

They arrived at the grotty little chamber that comprised Emma's home and stood outside. Baldwin eyed it grimly, the Coroner with reluctance, thinking about the fleas inside. It was Simon who finally marched up to the door and pushed it open on its cheap leather hinges.

'Who are you?' Cissy looked up and demanded.

It was a small room, smoky, ill-lit from the small window high in the northern wall, and although the reeds on the floor were not too foul, there was an odour of decay and filth. A pile of straw with a cloth thrown over was the bed for the children, who snuffled and wept together like a small litter of pigs.

'I am the Stannary Bailiff. Are you Nob's wife?'

'Oh, God! What's he done now?'

Simon grinned at the note of fatalism in her voice. 'Nothing, Cissy. But I would like to talk to you about the murders.'

'Very well, but keep your voice down. I don't want to upset her any more. It's taken me ages to calm her this much.'

'Of course. Just this, then: your husband said that Hamelin came here with money. Do you know where he said it came from?'

'He said he had sold a debt to Wally. One of the monks owed him a lot of money. A bad debt. Wally bought it.'

'Did he say who owed it?'

'No.'

Baldwin interrupted them. 'It makes no sense. Why should Wally have bought a debt he couldn't have redeemed? If the owner of the debt was a monk, there was no legal means of recovering the money?'

Cissy gave a long-suffering sigh. 'You officials; you *men*! All you ever think about is simple things, like straight lines. Maybe Wally wanted to give his money to help Hamelin. Little Joel was ill, he was dying. Maybe Wally always wanted a child of his own and couldn't bear to think that the child would die of starvation.'

'It's a leap of faith with a man like that Wally,' Coroner Roger said cynically.

'Is it?' Cissy said. Then her jaw jutted and she faced him aggressively. 'You say that when you don't know the man? How dare you! I knew Wally for two years or more, and he was always polite and kindly. Never raised his voice to women, never caused a fight. When he got drunk he sat in a corner and giggled himself to sleep. Hah! And you reckon he was a violent, cruel man? I think that's rubbish. He was quiet, shy, even, when he saw that old monk, but we know why now, don't we? We've heard Wally had something to do with the monk's wound. Well, I think Wally felt the shame of that, and I don't think he'd have hurt another man in his life. So there!'

'My lady, would you serve as my advocate, should I ever be accused of a crime?' Baldwin murmured, and Cissy preened, grinning.

Simon said, 'Tell me, before Hamelin was killed . . .'

At these words, there was a high, keening wail from the corner of the fire, and Cissy rolled her eyes. 'Did you have to say that? I've only just got her to quieten down, and now you've started her off again.'

'My apologies. But can we ask some questions?'

'Hamelin! Hamelin! He can't be dead! Oh, Christ! Why him? Why us? What have we done to deserve this?'

Cissy shook her head. 'You want to question people, you find someone who can talk without crying. Come back later. Better still, don't bother.'

'What of you? Can we talk to you?'

'Why has he died?' Emma burst out. 'How could someone do it to a man like him?'

Simon was struck by the woman's ravaged features. If he had been asked, he would have said that she was at least forty years old, and yet he was sure she was not much more than half that. It was the toll that bearing children had waged upon her, the toll of little sleep, of fear that her youngest might die, of her husband being taken from her so cruelly and without explanation.

'I am sorry about your husband,' he said with as much compassion as he could.

Cissy tried to hold Emma back, glaring furiously at the men. 'Won't you leave us? This girl is in no position to—'

'Cissy, give me grace! I want to help these men if they can find the murderer of my man! Why should I sit here snivelling while he who has caused my misery dances and sings, knowing he is safe? Let me put the rope about his neck if I may!'

'Do you know anything of your man's death?'

'All I know, I will tell you,' Emma declared with force. She gently removed Cissy's arm from before her and walked to her stool, sitting and composing herself as best she might. It was terrifying to have three such men in her room, but she drew strength from Cissy, and from the memory of the sight of her man's body.

'Gentlemen, Hamelin arrived here the night before last because he wanted to make sure that our son was well and hadn't died. The last weeks have been hard for us. Joel has been suffering because we couldn't afford good food. Then on Friday Hamelin arrived with a purse of money which he said Wally had given him.'

'I told them,' Cissy said.

'That money saved Joel's life,' Emma said with determination.

'You say he saw you the day Wally died,' Simon said. 'Did he say anything about Wally's death?'

'Only that he saw the Brother Mark up there. Hamelin hated Mark for taking our money and gambling it away. It was because of Mark that he became a miner. He saw Mark with Wally that morning, arguing with him, and then Wally set off eastwards and the monk came back to Tavistock. Hamelin followed after him, and went to the tooth-puller, Ellis, to have a tooth out. Then he came back here to me.'

'Do you not think he might have killed Wally to rob him?' Baldwin asked quietly.

'No! If he would have harmed anyone, it would have been that fat monk. No one else.'

'What of the night before last, then?' the Coroner asked.

'He came home to see how Joel was, as I said, and while he was here, the watchman arrived and told him to go to see the Abbot in the morning – that would be yesterday. As soon as he had risen, he left me to go to the Abbey.'

'This watchman – who was it?' Simon asked.

'We didn't see him. He told us the message and said there was no need to open the door.'

'Did you recognise the voice?' Baldwin asked.

'No,' she said with a frown. 'He didn't sound familiar.'

'Were there many routes your man could have taken to the Abbey?' Baldwin enquired thoughtfully.

'No. He would have gone along this alley, across the road, then into the next alley. That would take him straight to the place. But he didn't get there, did he?'

'I doubt it,' Simon said. 'He was ambushed on his way.'

'By the man who gave him the message,' Baldwin muttered.

Joce could hear them. God! How many were there? He crouched low, his knife in his hand, listening intently, and it sounded like the whole of the King's army had come to try to catch him. He still gripped his dagger, and held it out in front of him as he cautiously pressed his way onwards, trying to evade the men, but desperate to return down to the town where he would be safe.

He must clean his hand. The acolyte's blood had stained him all the way up to his wrist, and he could see specks up his arm. That was from his cut to the lad's nose, he thought with a flash of pleasure. There was something good in having punished the bastard like that. He might live, but he'd never forget Joce Blakemoor, Joce Red-Hand.

It was a complication he could live without, though, the thought that the lad might survive. Joce had kicked him hard: maybe he had broken his neck? A cracked rib could kill as easily as a sword-thrust, and Joce had managed at least one good stab with his dagger in the shoulder. Not enough, though, he reckoned. The boy had been fit and healthy, well-fed and strong. He could take a more severe punishment than that which Joce had handed out.

Would Gerard's word stand? Joce was inclined to think it would. If the boy lived to tell his tale in court, that was the end of Joce. Not that it mattered. Without the pewter, nothing mattered. He had no life in the town, no money. Nothing.

He had no choice. Before anything else he must avoid these men looking for him. Cautiously, he made his way along a narrow gully, listening for shouts and knocking as search-parties banged among bushes and ferns to see if he was hiding. It was like a great hunt, with beaters scaring the quarry onward. With animals there would be a line of huntsmen, with dogs or bows, or perhaps men on horses eager to give chase, but here the reason was more mundane. The beaters were hoping to push him forward, up the hill, and out into the open moorland beyond. There he would be easily visible.

That way was madness. He would need a mount to escape to the moors. Instead, he searched for a gap between beaters, and carefully made for it. The line was extended, but the gap between each man was fluid, and it took him some while to spot where he could go. There, a space between one youth and a forty-year-old peasant who looked like his head was built of moorstone.

Joce crawled over to a thick bramble patch and scrambled through it, feeling his woollen clothing snag and pull. Thorns thrust into his hands and knees; one caught his cheek and tore at him, and more became tangled in his hair. He had to bow his head and clench his fists against the pain. He couldn't, he daren't make a sound. The beaters were too close.

With a shock of horror he heard a dog. His heart stopped in his breast. Every facet of his being was concentrated on his ears and it seemed that the slavering, panting sound was deafening, smothering all other noise, even the steady whistling and banging of sticks. Then there was a clout across his back as a heavy staff crashed into the bushes above him, and he could have shrieked as a set of furze thorns were slammed into his back between his shoulders.

There was a louder panting, and he opened his eyes to see the dull-witted eyes of a greyhound peering at him, mouth wide, tongue dangling in a friendly pant. A man bellowed, and the dog curled into a fist of solid muscle, then exploded forward, shooting off like an arrow. Joce felt as though his heart had landed in his mouth, it burst forth into such powerful thumping.

Then the noise was past him. To his astonishment, the line had washed over him and now was carrying on up the hill. He was safe!

He carefully crawled from his hiding place, pulled off his coat and knocked as many bramble and gorse spikes away as he could, while walking swiftly down the hill towards the town. Once there, he could fetch clothes and a horse.

His blood was coursing through his veins with more consistency now. Yes, he would escape from this damned town. Over the moors on a horse, perhaps, or south, to the coast. He would be free again.

Sara had left her children with a neighbour while she went to buy bread, and she was there, outside the baker's when she heard the raucous blast of a horn. Hurrying along the street, she came to the road where she could see the bridge, and there she saw the men bringing a body back from the hill. They trailed down to the bridge, and slowly crossed it before making their way past the Water Gate and on around the town.

There was another blast from the horn, then a harsh bellow. 'Havoc, murder! Help! All healthy men, collect your arms and help catch a murderer!'

At Sara's side a woman gasped, 'My Christ! The poor boy!'

Others had already stopped to stare, watching as the small group, Sir Tristram on his horse at the head, and four men carrying the stretcher of stout poles with a palliasse bound between them, made their way to the Court Gate. All could see the blood and pale features of the boy.

'What have you done to the lad?' came an angry voice from the crowd.

Sir Tristram whirled his horse about. 'Don't bellow at us, man! This is none of my men's doing. One of my Host saw this fellow being attacked, and we are up the hill now, trying to find the culprit, so any among you who are fit and healthy, grab a weapon, and go up there. We need all the help we can muster. Come on! All of you, up that hill and find this bastard before he kills someone else!'

Coroner Roger, Simon and Baldwin were walking back from Emma's alley when they saw the men carrying the stretcher.

'We found your man, Sir Coroner,' Sir Tristram said with heavy amusement. 'Although I fear he won't be of a mood to help you yet awhile. He is a little punctured just now.'

'Sweet Jesu!' Baldwin burst out, and then he whirled around to Sir Tristram. 'Why did you do this? The boy was no threat to you!'

'We did nothing. My man was riding eastwards towards the moor, thinking that the lad might have tried to escape,' Sir Tristram said, waving the stretcher-bearers on towards the Abbey. 'He saw a man striking this lad, kicking him and then preparing to give the fatal blow. He shouted and raised havoc, and the bastard ran away.'

'Did he see who it was?' Coroner Roger asked eagerly.

'Alas, he doesn't know the local folk,' Sir Tristram acknowledged. 'By the time the rest of my men responded to his call, the scoundrel was flown. He could be anywhere. Still, I have left my fellows up there to see if they can find him. It's the best training for war, hunting a man.'

Baldwin felt sick. He could remember how knights had spoken about hunting down his comrades from the Knights Templar after their destruction. It was repellent, this idea of treating men like so many deer or hares.

Gerard had suffered; it would be a miracle if he lived. Baldwin had seen the thick flap of skin cut away from his cheek, the smashed and all-but cut off nose, the slashed ear that dangled from a small flap of flesh, the bloodied shoulder and flank. After so many wounds, any one of which might grow gangrenous, the lad would be fortunate indeed to live.

'There they are!' Sir Tristram exclaimed, pointing.

Following his finger, Baldwin could see a thin line of men working their way up the hill east of them. There was no sign of their prey.

The Coroner saw this too. 'I shall have to organise the Watch to help them. Christ's Ballocks! As if there wasn't enough to do already!'

Baldwin nodded. 'You go, and I shall see whether I can entice a little information from that poor wreck of an acolyte.'

Studying his coat and tunic in among the trees that stood at the side of the road, Joce was forced to accept that he'd be viewed a little oddly if he were to appear like this in town. He'd be better off leaving his coat behind.

He could hear the horn blowing, and when he stared over the river, he saw that Sir Tristram was shouting for more men to help. It made Joce grind his teeth with impotent rage. If he could, he would charge over that bridge and hurl himself at the tarse! Who did the arrogant sodomite think he was? The new conscience of the land, the new hero? From all Joce had heard, he was nothing more than a reiver himself. There were enough of them up there on the border, as Joce knew perfectly well.

Then he saw a saviour. There, standing near the bridge, as Sir Tristram's men rode onwards, was Sara. She would help him: she wouldn't be able to stop herself, he thought smugly. He stepped onto the road from his cover and walked across the bridge, his coat carelessly flung over his shoulder. Once there, he made straight for her.

'Hello, Sara.'

Her face blanched. 'What do you want?'

'My love, all is well now,' he murmured as soothingly as he could, 'since that blasted fool Walwynus is gone, I need have no more fear.'

'Fear?' she repeated dully. 'You wouldn't talk to me after the coining, and now you talk of fear?'

'It was Wally. I told you afterwards, I had hoped you'd understand,' he said sadly. 'Wally came and threatened me, telling me to leave you alone, not to play with your emotions. I was scared.'

'I . . .' Sara swallowed, her face a picture of confusion. 'But you said you beat him.'

He laughed shortly. 'Does any man like to admit that he's been bested? No, my love.'

'You said you wanted no more to do with me, that you'd deny your own child.'

'No, never,' Joce said firmly. He stepped forward and took her elbow, guiding her on, keeping his eye upon her the while, stepping up the lanes, away from the main roadway, away from the Abbey, and down an alley which led to the back of his house. He could enter without being seen. 'How could I reject my own child? Impossible.'

But confusion was already turning to anger as Sara recalled their last two meetings. She shook her arm free. 'No! You're not going to take me in the back here, like a slut. You swore to wed me, and that means I have the right to enter by your front door.'

'Darling, please come with me just this once,' Joce said, smiling. 'It is a whim of mine.'

'Don't treat me like a fool!' she threatened him. She was rubbing at her elbow where he had gripped her. 'If you're serious about honouring our vows, and are not going to deny me again, and if you will support Ellis as well, if he is accused, then I shall enter your house, for the sake of my children, as your wife. But I shall *not* go in the back door so that you can deny seeing me in the future. Ah, no!'

'Stop rubbing your arm, woman. Come! I merely wish to see my horses.'

'Then you can, once we've entered by your front door. Or is this all merely a jest to satisfy some cruel amusement of yours?' she asked.

'This is no jest, I assure you, Wife.'

She said nothing. Her hand was at her elbow still. As he watched, she picked at the material, and pulled a face as she realised that it was covered in mud. 'Oh, look at that. My best linen shirt, too. What have you been up to?'

He could say nothing. Suddenly he felt as though the blood was draining from his face as she took him in, her features at first sharp and irritated, and then subtly altering, until they registered pure horror. 'My God!' she whispered. 'It was you, wasn't it? You tried to kill that boy!'

His arm was up and at her throat in a moment while he fumbled for his knife, but he was too late to prevent the scream that burst from her. She kicked at his feet, and he stumbled, and then she had broken free. Two men appeared from his gateway, and he stared at them dully, before bolting back the way he had come.

He made it to the bridge without anyone catching him, and then he found himself confronted by a traveller on a tired old nag. Without pausing, Joce ran to the man's side. The nag side-stepped, rearing his head, and Joce caught the man's foot, thrusting upwards viciously. In a moment the rider was up and over his mount, falling on the other side with an audible crunch as his shoulder struck the cobbled way. It took no time to shove one foot in the stirrup and lift himself up into the saddle. Kicking the beast's flanks cruelly, Joce urged it into a slow canter.

No one else had a horse behind him, but now he was committed, whether he wanted it or not. The road south was at the other side of the river. He could attempt to ford it further downstream, but that would be hazardous. No, he was better off trying to cross over the moors.

In any case, this was the way he should be taking, he realised. What had the lad said? That Wally, the *shit*, had sold the plate to some foreign bastard on the moors. That was what Gerard had said, and he'd said it in the extremity of his pain, when he was trying to save his life. Surely that was what Joce must do now, then. Find these travellers and retrieve his pewter.

With that resolve, he whipped the reins across the flanks of the horse and forced it to go faster.

Joce would go up by the main roadway, for none of the line of beaters would expect the murderer to be behind them. Then he would ride to the first mining camp and ask about strange-speaking foreigners and whether anyone had seen them. And if the foreign bastards refused to give his property back to him, Joce smiled coldly, he would kill them. Without compunction. He had tried to kill twice today already, with Gerard and then Sara, and he was keen to succeed the third time.

Simon waited until Baldwin had followed the stretcher through a doorway, and then wandered down to fetch an ale. Mark was sitting as usual on his little stool in the doorway to his salting rooms.

'Bailiff! Who was that?' he called out, staring after the stretcher.

Simon walked over to him. 'That poor acolyte Gerard. He was caught and attacked by someone on the other side of the river. We don't know who it was, but we'll get him.'

'It wasn't me, Master Bailiff! I have been here all day. And an exciting one it has been too.'

Gratefully taking a mazer filled with an excellent spiced wine, Simon leaned against the doorway. 'Look,' he said, 'if you were to learn of a monk who'd been stealing from the Abbey you'd want to punish him wouldn't you?'

Mark eyed him curiously, then drained his cup. 'Of course. No question.'

'So what has been happening here, then?'

'Nothing that would excite you, I daresay, Bailiff, but for a crowd of old women like we monks, it was quite thrilling. Young Reginald was discovered sprawled before the altar this morning, quite beside himself. Old Peter spoke to him last night, but it didn't improve Reg's mood. Poor fellow's been put to bed in the infirmary to recover.'

'You have not yet lost your sense of freedom, have you?' Simon said suddenly.

'What do you mean?' Mark's eyes narrowed slightly.

'Monks who have been brought up to the Abbey are more cautious in their speech, especially with relative strangers – by which I mean any outsider, like, for instance, a Bailiff.'

'Aha! I have lived too long in the secular world, you mean,' Mark said, picking up a jug and refilling his mazer. He waved it at Simon, who held up his hand in mild protest. 'True, I can see further than the end of my nose, which makes me stand out a little. I mean, look at Brother Peter! A worthy, kindly enough man at first sight, but in reality, he has a terrible desire for knowledge about other monks. He cannot help but sniff out any little secrets, purely with the aim of satisfying his own inquisitive nature. If he had been apprenticed to a master like my old one, he'd have had that nosiness knocked out of him soon enough! Then there's Augerus. He is less pious than he should be, but he has known only the cloister. How can a man respect the religious way of life if he can remember no other?'

Simon was tempted to remind Mark that his own faults included gossip and imbibing too freely, but restrained his tongue.

Mark continued, 'My own strength comes from the knowledge of the outside world and the way that real people live. To me, there can be nothing more sacred than this convent, because I have seen how people live outside. That,' he sighed to himself, but giving Simon a sharp glance, 'is why I revere this place so much more than some of my brother monks do.'

Simon said nothing but meaningfully raised an eyebrow.

'I don't suppose it matters now,' Mark said. 'I have seen Gerard about at night. I feel sure that he was the thief, although I imagine he passed his stolen goods on to someone else.'

'Did you speak to him about his stealing?'

'Good God, no! I told the Abbot, though. And now, well, his guilt is proven, isn't it? Why else should the boy have committed apostasy, if he wasn't torn apart by guilt? Or unless he wanted to make off with his profits, of course.'

Chapter Twenty-Six

Baldwin entered the room to find Peter standing at the side of the bed on which Gerard had been deposited.

'How is he, Brother?'

Baldwin was struck, not for the first time, with the thought that a man with so extensive an injury to his face should not have survived. During his time as a Templar, both in the Holy Land and afterwards, Baldwin had seen men who had suffered less violent, less apparently lethal wounds, and yet they had died in hours or days, but this man had clung on. True, he had become an object of loathing or ridicule, but he was living, nonetheless. To Baldwin, it proved that he had a strong character and will to live. Many others would have scorned life and sought death.

Peter appeared to read his thoughts. He gave one of his odd, twisted smiles. 'Perhaps he will be as fortunate as me, eh, Keeper?'

Baldwin was embarrassed and looked away, but Peter's voice continued gently.

'If he has an urge to live, he will live, with God's good grace. If he doesn't, or if God decides that he is ready for heaven, then he shall die. Whatever God wills, so be it.'

'What are they?' Baldwin asked, glancing at some bowls sitting on the floor near the lad.

'Egg-white for cleaning his wounds, warm water to slake his thirst, a little strong wine for my comfort, and a cushion for my old knees to pray upon, or to rest my head when I grow too tired to hold my head up.'

It was tempting to leave the man there alone with Gerard, but Baldwin did not quite trust him. There were no other chairs in this little infirmary, only two more beds; all three in plain view of the altar which was the salvation of all those who could glance upon it while they suffered. Baldwin planted himself on one of the other beds and waited.

They had both been sitting in silence for some while when Gerard began to moan softly, his voice snuffling and adenoidal from his ravaged nose. Peter at once leaned forward and rested his hand upon Gerard's, but the boy didn't seem to notice. He groaned several times, muttered like a man who was deeply asleep, and every so often, whimpered like a dog in pain. It was pitiful, and Baldwin felt his flesh creep to hear the agony of a poor fellow so young, damaged so severely for no reason. And then there was a sudden pause, and he spoke again, this time clearly.

'I can't take any more, Augerus . . . I won't steal any more . . . Joce, go to hell. I *won't* do it any more!'

Baldwin felt his heart almost stop in his breast. 'Did you hear that?'

Peter left his hand on the boy's, and glanced upwards as though praying. 'I did. And may he rest now that his heart has confessed, even against his will.' He slowly, painfully, came to his feet. 'With your permission, Sir Knight, I shall go and tell the good Abbot about his Steward.'

'Did no one suspect him?' Baldwin wondered aloud.

'Some of us did, yes.'

'Then in God's name, Brother, why didn't you tell anyone?'

Peter smiled and sat again, resting his hands in his lap with a serene expression. 'Why should we do that?'

'If the man was guilty of stealing—'

'God will know. And God will punish that which He feels He should. It is not my place to accuse or seek another's punishment.'

'You knew?'

'Aye. And I tried to make the boy see by my own example that it was pointless and silly, but he wouldn't listen to an old fart like me. Besides, I think that there was some coercion used. Perhaps he had committed some more minor crime, and Augerus sought to make him obey his commands to prevent his secret being discovered. That, I think, is most likely. I don't believe this boy is peculiarly evil.'

'What sort of hold could Augerus have had on him?' Baldwin asked.

'Some trifling matter, Keeper. A youngster is always hungry – perhaps it was merely the naughty theft of a bread roll, or some pieces of sausage from the *salsarius'* room? Who can tell? A minor offence like that might have been discovered and the evil, older man used it to bend the younger to his will. Make no mistake, the older will be evil. Not this poor child. And now,' he added, climbing to his feet, 'I must warn the Abbot. We know all about the thefts in the Abbey. Although there is one detail I am keen to understand.'

'What is that?'

'How he managed to steal the wine. Surely that was a wonderful thing to do. And just think of all the Abbot's good spiced red wine. I could certainly be persuaded to bribe the lad for that secret, eh, Keeper?' he said, and winked.

In a moment he was gone and Baldwin sat back on his chair. 'Well, boy, you still have many secrets which others would like to learn,' he said wearily.

As Simon left Mark, he gave in once again to the old feelings of despair. The Abbot was right to doubt his abilities. He was nothing more than a fool. Useless. He had no idea who had killed Wally or Hamelin. His enquiry was going nowhere, and so was he. There could be no surprise in the Abbot's decision to replace him with another man better able to investigate crimes. Almost anyone must be better than him, Simon thought bitterly.

Just for a moment his mind returned to his wife. Meg would take the idea of leaving their house very badly. She would not say anything, of course, she would be entirely loyal and supportive, but he knew she would hate the thought of going from Lydford. They had been very happy there.

Just then, he arrived at the Great Gate. From here he could see the scarred monk leaving the infirmary, and he walked across to him.

'Not now, Bailiff, please!' Brother Peter said hastily.

'What is it?'

'Gerard has just told us who was guilty. It was Augerus who persuaded the lad to steal.'

'Yet not who killed Walwynus?'

'No. Walwynus was alive when I left him, and when I returned after seeing the shepherd, he was not at his house. I came straight back to the Abbey. I spoke to my friend the groom and drank ale with him because Augerus and Mark were away and there was no refreshment.'

Simon nodded. Are you sure of that?'

'Aye. Why?'

Simon gave him no answer, but stood deep in thought. Obviously the only reason for the lack of drinks was the absence of Augerus and Mark. Ellis had said that Mark had returned and was already in the Abbey when he went to shave some heads later. Perhaps Mark had gone elsewhere, not straight back to his storerooms?

He was about to enter the infirmary when he saw Mark waving to Peter, and Peter hurried over to the *salsarius'* room. The two spoke for a moment, and then Peter made straight for the Abbot's lodging. Mark immediately locked up his room and crossed the court to the infirmary, and entered by the door which Peter had just left.

Simon suddenly had a strange idea . . . then dismissed it. Surely, he thought, he was leaping to foolish conclusions. To clear his mind, he walked to the trough near the stables and sipped water from his cupped hands. After wiping a little over his face to refresh himself, he stared down into the water.

Wine! Simon had ignored the theft of the wine, at first because the Abbot had told him to leave it alone, and later because there were so many other things for him and Baldwin to consider, with the murder of Wally and Hamelin, but there was still that central problem of the wine. Who had taken it – and why? For some reason he recollected what he had seen when he was leaving the Abbot's presence that first time, when he had just begun to suspect that Abbot Robert had lost his faith in him: a syphon.

Simon was still standing and thinking when he heard shouting at the entrance to the court. Looking up, he saw Ellis. At his side was an attractive woman, and he had his arms about her waist, while her head rested upon his shoulder. Ellis pointed to him meaningfully.

'Christ Jesus, what now?' Simon muttered to himself, and strode forward. 'Well?'

'Bailiff, this is my sister. I couldn't tell you her secret before, but she is happy to tell you herself now.'

Simon glanced at her. 'Lady? I don't need to know if it will embarrass you.'

'Embarrass me?' She stared at him, her face empty for a moment as she recalled the last minutes she had spent with Joce. A sob threatened to burst from her bosom. All her hopes, which had been crushed on the day of the coining, then briefly fanned to life again today, had at last been shattered in horror as he attempted to throttle her. 'My Lord, Joce swore his oath of marriage to me, in secret, purely so he could enjoy my body. Then he denied that oath in public, shaming me, and calling me whore. Today I saw him in town, and he assured me that he was my husband, that he would protect me and my child, but then he tried to kill me! He took me by the throat, see?'

Simon could see the red marks of fingers and a thumb. 'Good Lord! Why?'

'He wanted me to walk with him to his house. I think he wished to fetch fresh clothes, because he had fallen or been thrown from his horse, but I wouldn't go with him. I have some pride left, even after his deceits!'

'What happened then?'

'He ran from me because two guards saw me being attacked by him at his back doorway.'

Simon nodded. 'And where did he go?'

Ellis answered. 'He knocked a man from his horse and stole the beast, riding up the road to the moors.'

'Then he shall be caught by Sir Tristram's men,' Simon stated.

'Won't you fetch him?' Sara asked.

'I have other pressing matters,' Simon said as gently as he could.

'Did you know that Joce beat Wally on the day after the coining?' Sara interjected quickly. She was determined that the Bailiff should know. Seeing Simon's quick interest, she told him about Joce's words. 'He said he had beaten Wally because Wally told him to leave me alone. Perhaps he did more than beat Wally, though?' she finished.

Simon nodded doubtfully. No one had seen Joce up on the moors, so far as he knew. Ellis had said that Wally had been in a fight that morning. Maybe it was Joce who had beaten him. Joce himself showed no sign of having been thumped. Could he be so professional that he could protect himself against a strong lad like Wally?

'I am grateful you told me this,' he said, signalling to a passing novice.

'Find Sir Tristram for me, lad. I think he is in the guest house still. Tell him that Joce Blakemoor has taken a horse towards his men.' Turning to Sara, he added, 'I shall tell the knight about his escape. Sir Tristram will find him and bring him back, never fear.'

She nodded fretfully. 'I had hoped *you* would fetch more men and seek him out.'

'There is no need,' Simon said. He could see Sir Tristram, who descended from the guest rooms with a pot of wine in his hand.

'Well, Bailiff? What is so urgent?'

Simon explained briefly. 'This man Joce must be caught.'

Sir Tristram threw him a contented smile. 'Fear not but that he shall be back here this evening, whether dead or alive!'

Simon left him then, as he bellowed for a fresh horse, and made his way up to the infirmary. At the doorway, he stopped, looking back.

Sara and Ellis still stood in the same place, Ellis with his arm about his sister's waist, she with her eyes streaming with tears for her lost future, while Ellis merely gazed about him dumbly, like a man who had known that the world was cruel, but who had still hoped for better. He looked entirely crushed.

Joce slapped the reins over the horse's flanks, whipping the old beast onward, even though the brute was faltering.

'Fucking thing!'

The owner must have ridden this nag miles already. It was so frustrating! All he needed was a good animal to get him away, and here he was astride this broken-winded, knackered bag of bones. It was only good for the tanner's yard.

'Hurry up or I'll slay you,' he hissed, kicking as hard as he could, wishing he had spurs.

They were almost at the moors now, and they hadn't passed any sign of the men yet. He was hoping that they might have continued along the line of the trees, in which case he should have a clear run to the Swiss travellers, but even as he hoped this, he saw someone else on the road ahead, another rider.

The horse was close to collapse. Rather than see it expire beneath him, he yanked on the reins to slow it, then stood, panting a little.

If only that bitch had gone in with him so that he could have changed his clothes. Then he wouldn't be in this state. Silly cow! He could have killed her inside, away from prying eyes, and got a fresh change of clothing, before escaping. Now, all because of her, he had to hide until he could steal a change of clothes and get rid of these tatters.

He trotted into the security of a small clump of trees near a cross, listening as the sound of hooves approached, but then they stopped. 'Well, friend, are you going to come out here, or do I have to get you out?' a voice bellowed.

Joce froze at the words. He didn't recognise the voice, but there was unmistakable menace in the words, and to match them he heard the slithering sound of steel against wood as a sword was drawn.

'I was only concealing myself in case you were a ruffian,' he declared, allowing the horse to walk forth. 'I am no villein.'

'Joce Blakemoor?' the man asked, peering at him.

'Aye. That's me.'

'I'm Jack, Sergeant to Sir Tristram! I remember you, Joce Red-Hand!'

In a moment the sword was whirling through the air towards his head. Joce fell back against his horse's rump, then slipped his weight to one side, avoiding the first thrust and slash, but then his own sword was out and he could parry the next blow.

'Attack an innocent, will you?' he roared, and turned his blade as Jack's met it, slicing it down into Jack's thigh. The Sergeant screamed, and his horse danced away nervously even as Joce's backed, but Joce thrashed it with the flat of his sword. It stepped on reluctantly, and Joce whirled the sword about his head, swinging it at Jack's neck. Jack brought up his own, but Joce could feel that the man's strength was ebbing, and then he saw why. He had severed a blood vessel in the man's thigh, and there was a spray of arterial blood pumping. Joce smiled, and snarled, then brought his sword round again, beating at Jack until Jack failed to move in time. There was a soft, shuddering contact through Joce's arm, and his vision was blurred for an instant as blood fountained, and then he saw that Jack's headless body was still mounted, but the hands were empty. The sword was fallen.

Joce wiped his face free of the blood, and reached for Jack's horse's reins, but the beast was maddened with fear. The smell of blood, the terror of death, combined to make it insane, and it bolted, running straight for Tavistock, the body lurching in the saddle. Joce swore as he watched it as it gradually sagged to the right and toppled to the ground. All he felt was rage, pure fury, that he should be thwarted again. He needed that mount, a strong, fresh horse that would take him farther.

Joce wearily pulled his horse's head around until it faced east again. Beating it with the flat of his sword, he urged it into an irregular canter, eyes skinned for more enemies.

Baldwin was still sitting on the stool watching the boy when he heard footsteps approaching. He felt no need to rise, and merely nodded to Mark when the monk entered and bowed at the altar.

'Brother.'

'Peter told me he was here. How is he?'

'Weak.'

'Perhaps he will survive – but he looks terrible.'

Baldwin could not argue with that. 'It is unlikely that he can live.'

Gerard was stirring again. He grunted, then shouted out, 'Joce, please, no! Don't kill me!'

'That,' Baldwin said, 'appears to be proof of that man's guilt. I had not suspected that Joce could have tried to do this.'

'A town's Receiver attacking an acolyte. It is almost unbelievable.'

'As is the idea that a Receiver should try to force an acolyte to steal plate from the Abbey,' Baldwin agreed. 'I wonder why he felt he could do that?'

'Has he been arrested?'

'No.' Baldwin stared sorrowfully at the figure of Gerard. Now that the blood had been washed away by Peter, Gerard's wounds stood out more more horrifically. His nose was notched, almost cut in two, while his ear had been taken off. The obscene flap of cheek had been cleaned and rested back in place, but Baldwin doubted that it could remain. That cheek would remain a hideous scar for the rest of the boy's life.

'You go and rest, Sir Baldwin. You look very tired,' Mark said understandingly.

'That is very kind,' Baldwin said, but then he grew aware of more feet ascending the stairs. 'Simon? Did you learn anything?'

'I think so, yes,' Simon answered. He shot a look at Gerard, relieved to see that he was alive. Facing Mark, he said, 'I am glad to have seen you again, Brother. I was thinking about the day when I had seen the Abbot and saw you at your room.'

Mark smiled but his face was largely blank. 'I don't think I understand.'

'You will. I had been so tied up with the murders, I forgot all about the theft of the wine. The pewter being taken, and the dead miner – both seemed so much more important. Yet of course they were no more important. A man who is prepared to steal from the Abbot of a place like this, would be prepared to commit any crime.'

'I could hardly disagree in principle,' Brother Mark said politely, 'but the theft of wine is surely very different from stealing pewter from the Abbey's guests. Anyway, we know who the thief was: as I told the Abbot some days ago, it seems certain that the thief was Gerard.'

'*You* told the Abbot?' Baldwin exclaimed. 'I thought Peter must have told Abbot Robert.'

'I don't know why you would think that. Heavens! Peter tell the Abbot something like that? I shouldn't think so. He prefers to keep secrets from others, not blurt them.'

'Perhaps he feels other men's secrets are their own to keep or divulge,' Simon said pointedly. 'And the master of a thief might decide to surrender him in order to save his own hide.'

Mark gaped. 'You think to accuse me of controlling the lad? You suggest I was his accomplice?'

'Simon,' Baldwin interrupted hastily, 'Peter and I were here when we heard Gerard declare Augerus was the man who persuaded him to steal; Augerus and Joce Blakemoor.'

'I am sure Augerus was,' Simon said. 'Guilty of taking the pewter and having Walwynus carry it away to Joce, more than likely. But I will say this: Augerus was *not* guilty of stealing the wine. Was he, Mark?'

'I couldn't say, Bailiff.'

'No? Then let us consider the matter. The room where the Abbot kept his wine is quite large, and there are only tiny windows, aren't there?'

'Yes. I certainly couldn't break in through one.'

'No. Augerus, of course, if he wanted to steal the Abbot's wine, would merely have taken his key and filched what he wanted. Except if he entered by unlocking the door, everyone would know it was he who had stolen the stuff. He couldn't do that. So if Augerus had done this, he would have made it more obvious, and would have shown a forced door or window to cover his crime. But another man wouldn't have keys. Such a man might decide to get in anyway, but how would he get the wine *out*? The barrel remained inside, yet it was emptied, as though a party had been going on inside there.'

'It is a mystery,' Mark offered.

'No. All the man needed to do was let an accomplice get in, then pass him a tube under the door, and let the wine run from the Abbot's barrel, out under the door, and into a fresh one. It wouldn't be very neat – there would be wine spilled all over the floor – but substantially more of the wine would make it. And then the acolyte could be retrieved and no one the wiser. Especially if you had someone like Gerard, whom you could blackmail.'

'Blackmail?'

'Yes. You knew he had stolen things. Perhaps you caught him

red-handed and forced him to steal for you as well.'

Mark shook his head, but he had grown deathly pale. 'I would do no such thing.'

Simon continued relentlessly, 'And then you killed Walwynus. You were seen. Ellis saw you – so did Hamelin. He told his wife. Was that why Hamelin had to die as well? Did you know he saw you up there?'

'No! My God in heaven, this is all nonsense!'

'Then you had best tell us the truth,' Simon said. 'Because if you don't, I swear I shall take all this information to the Abbot myself and accuse you.'

'How could you think I would do such a thing as steal from the Abbey?'

'You took the wine, didn't you? You made a point of showing me where your syphon tube was, coiling it before me after I saw the Abbot, as though you wanted me to be quite convinced that anyone could have got hold of it.'

Mark allowed a small smile to pull at the corners of his mouth. 'I did show you that, yes, but only so you could see how anyone could have got in there. Look, all I did was share some wine with Augerus. We had been in town that evening, and when we returned here, we went to his master's undercroft and tried some wine. We didn't think much about it. Augerus was going to refill it with other wine, and if the Abbot noticed, he'd simply say it was a bad barrel. He's done it before.'

'The barrel was empty,' Simon reminded him.

'Yes, well, the Abbot had been away for some weeks. We had gone there a few times. It was so tempting. That wine was excellent. Much better than the horse's piss we usually get in here. And one morning we woke up and heard the Abbot was coming back . . . Well, the night before we'd had a few more drinks than usual, and when we went to the undercroft to top up the barrel with some cheaper wine, we realised we'd emptied it. The tap was open and wine was puddled all about it.

'Augerus panicked. I said we should fill it with some rough stuff that had turned to vinegar, and tell the Abbot that it was gone off, but Augerus said that the Abbot could always tell a good wine which had gone off compared with a bad wine. He kept insisting that there was nothing to be done other than we should show that the wine had been stolen. It was his idea to prove that there had been a clever thief by leaving the door locked. Either someone had taken the keys from him, or they had entered without keys. Whichever was true, he reasoned that it would be a mystery.'

'And that this boy would probably be blamed, although he was blameless,' Baldwin observed.

'Blameless? When he robbed people inside the convent, to the risk of the convent's reputation?' Mark said pointedly. 'I should not feel too much compassion for someone with that guilt on his conscience.'

'On the day Wally died,' Simon said, 'you were up on the hill. You spoke to Wally. You were seen there by Hamelin and Ellis.'

'Yes. I spoke to him.'

'Come on, man!' Simon exploded. 'You were the last man seen with him. Do you tell us you killed him?'

'No! I was there to demand that he return the things he had taken from the place. He denied it all, of course, but I knew that he was a thief.'

'Did he continue to deny being involved?'

'No. He said, "Oh, so Brother Peter has told everyone, has he?"'

'What do you think he meant by that?'

'Peter had been his accomplice, of course.'

'What then?'

'Wally said that he had nothing now. A part of the profit had gone to his colleagues and his own share had gone as a gift to Hamelin. He said he didn't want to profit from something which could hurt the Abbey.'

'Did he say anything more?'

'Only that he supposed it was the cut which had led to people finding out. He was quite phiosophical about it. He said that he had taken four-sevenths of the money for the pewter instead of the agreed half. I rather think he considered it was a judgement on himself for cheating an associate.'

'It doesn't make much sense,' Baldwin said.

'No,' Simon said. 'You were there, you took a stick from Hamelin's store to show that he had committed the murder, because you wanted him silenced after all the embarrassment about your not paying him back the money you owed him.'

'This is ludicrous, Bailiff! Why should I kill Wally?'

'Simple. He had stolen from the Abbey, and you knew about it. There could be nothing more intolerable to you than the thought that someone would harm the reputation of the place. The Abbey is now your sanctuary, isn't it? Often those who take on the cloth later in life are more protective of their Order than those who wore the habit from an early age. How did you find out about Wally?'

'It was Peter. I saw him many times, walking about the place. One night I couldn't sleep, and I saw him at the Abbot's lodging, staring down into the garden.' Mark shrugged. There was little point in concealing his knowledge. 'I have never much cared for Peter. He seems to think his looks mean he should be treated with favour compared with the rest of us. So, I went and looked myself, and saw that Wally was there, leaving the garden with a small sack in his hand. I thought Peter must have given him something. Then, when I heard about the pewter being taken, I was struck with horror at his crime, and I was determined to show his guilt. I went to see Wally, it is true, but I didn't have a weapon of any sort. I told him he had to bring back the pewter or I would tell the Abbot what I knew, and he went. That is all.'

'You didn't wait for him?' Baldwin interrupted.

'There was no point. He said it wasn't there with him. I left him to fetch it. I intended bringing it back to the Abbey and giving it to the Abbot. The thief would surely never dare to commit his thieving again once he knew that his thefts had been solved, but I was prepared to give him some time.'

'Why were you prepared to give him time?' Simon demanded.

'He had been in a fight. His eye was closed, and there was no need for instant action. I was content that he would comply. That was enough for me.'

'But the pewter didn't reappear,' Simon said.

'No,' Mark said sadly. 'Wally died, and the metal was not found. I thought that was a judgement on him by God, and I was content to leave the matter in His hands.'

'What of Hamelin?'

'I know nothing about his death.'

'Even though you hated him?' Baldwin pressed him.

'I didn't hate him, as you put it. He was an embarrassment, a reminder of the sinful life I once led, but that was all.'

Chapter Twenty-Seven

Art looked out from the cart's back as it rattled and thumped over the moors.

'Are you all right, boy?' Rudolf asked.

'Yes, Master.'

'Don't call me that, boy. We're all freemen here. None of us is owned by a master. That was what we Swiss fought for at Morgarten. Now you are with us, you are safe.'

Art heard his words, but they were so momentous that he found it hard to believe Rudolf. 'I can work my way, sir.'

He saw the flash of teeth, but there was no answer. Art was partly terrified of this calm, tanned foreigner, but he was also filled with admiration. The man seemed so confident and assured. So too was Joce, Art thought, but Joce was cruel, often for the sake of it, while this Rudolf with his funny accent and voice had shown no desire to beat him yet.

The man who had caught him brought him straight to this Rudolf, who questioned him carefully, but plainly decided that there was no harm in him, and passed Art to his woman, who undressed him and gave him a fresh, clean, overlarge tunic and gown while his own clothes were taken away and beaten in the waters of a stream. While the clothes were being dealt with, a youth gave him a big wooden bowl filled with large pieces of meat in a rich, peppery gravy. Art devoured it with gusto, running his fingers around the bowl to collect the last vestiges.

Then the Bailiff and the others arrived. Art cowered in terror, thinking that they had come to take him back, for all knew how powerful Joce was, but Anna had passed him in among the women with their children, pushing him down until he squatted, invisible, in their midst.

It was a miracle that he had not been found, but then he could hear most of the conversation, and it was plain that they weren't after him as he feared, but instead were still trying to learn what had happened when Wally died. It almost made him want to cry out in relief.

He was safe, he thought. Joce would find another young servant boy to abuse and beat, and Art would take up his new life as a sailor. Soon, very soon, he must make his fortune. All sailors did, he understood. As he was considering the advantages of this, he heard a muttered curse from Rudolf, and looking back the way they had come, he saw the distant figure of a man walking quickly towards them.

For some reason a feeling of awe and hatred welled up in his breast, although he had no idea at this distance whom this walking man might be. There was just something, in his gait, or the set of his head, or simply the aggressive stance in which he stalked forwards, as though he was attacking the roadway in order to subjugate it, that gave his identity away.

'Sweet Jesu!' Art whimpered.

He could see it all now. Joce had refused to accept his going. Joce wanted him back, would drag him, screaming, to the house, and once in there, Art knew that all the pain and indignities he had suffered before would be as nothing. For running away, he would be forced to endure the cruellest tortures his master could conceive.

Art gave an inarticulate cry and drew back into the security of the cart.

Rudolf glanced at him in surprise, then jerked his head. 'Your master?'

'Yes!' It was little more than a whisper. Art's eyes were fixed upon the steadily approaching figure.

'You are safe with us,' Rudolf said calmly.

'He will kill me!'

'No.'

Joce was in earshot now, and he bellowed at the top of his voice, 'Hold! Stop those carts!'

Rudolf, hearing his command, muttered in German to Welf, 'The bastard thinks he can order us around like English peasants!'

'I said stop the carts! I must speak to you!'

To Joce's relief the cavalcade drew to a halt, the men and women separating and the men forming a line at the rear of their column.

He was bone tired now. The horse had collapsed near Sharpitor, and he had been forced to make his way on foot after that. At least he'd been in luck so far. He wondered whether Jack the Sergeant had been the last of a line of men searching for him, because after killing him, he had seen no more evidence of a man-hunt on his trail. Perhaps he had escaped after all, he thought. Certainly this stranger with the thick accent seemed to pose no danger. If anything, he looked a bit stupid.

'You are welcome, sir,' Rudolf called, emphasising his accent. It was always useful to be able to deny comprehension when necessary, he found. 'How may we serve you?'

'May I crave your generosity? I have been robbed, and my food and water were stolen. Could I share a little of your food with you?'

'Certainly, sir. It is poor fare for a gentleman. Still, you are welcome to share what we have,' Rudolf said.

Joce smiled, although he was thinking that this man was a fool. He would eat with them, drink with them, and then, when all was dark and these ignorant foreigners were asleep, he would take the pewter. Perhaps someone might wake – well, if they did, Joce would enjoy setting his blade across the man's throat. It would be pleasant to kill again. There were many of them, and only one of him – but that didn't concern Joce. He knew he was more than equal to them.

* * *

Coroner Roger lunged at the runaway horse and hauled on its reins, almost unseating himself as the wild animal pulled him and his own horse along. 'I have it!' he roared gleefully as he drew it to a slower pace, then to a canter, leaning over to pat the beast's neck, wiping some of the foam and froth away.

'This is my Sergeant's mount,' Sir Tristram said with icy calm.

'Is he the sort of man to lose his horse?' the Coroner asked, but even as he spoke his eyes caught sight of the stain. 'Blood.'

'Christ Jesus!' The blasphemy was deserved. All along the horse's flank was a great gout of blood.

'I fear your man is dead,' Coroner Roger said soberly.

'Up there! Ah, by the devil's cods, he must have got past all the men! Jack was up there as a last line to stop him. If he cut Jack down, he could be anywhere.'

'Not anywhere,' Roger said thoughtfully. 'There are not that many paths from here. And the ground is quite damp. Let's see if we can find out where he has gone.'

They left the runaway horse with another of Sir Tristram's men and made their way back up the hill. The hoofprints were clear enough, for the horse had galloped wildly, each steel horseshoe cutting deeply into the soft, well-cropped grass, and they had no need of a tracker. They could ride at a gentle canter until they came to the body.

'Dear God!' Sir Tristram said with disgust.

'It's your man?' the Coroner asked.

'Yes. That looks like Jack's body. But where's his head?'

Coroner Roger jumped lightly from his horse and left the corpse, walking along the hoofprints until he came to a place where the blood lay thickly. 'Here it is,' he said, picking up Jack's head. He set it with the body and gazed east. 'That's his direction. He's going to Ashburton.'

'Then let's be after him!' Sir Tristram grated. 'I want *his* head.'

* * *

Simon and Baldwin entered the Abbot's lodging after him, and while Abbot Robert roared for his Steward, the two sat in chairs near his table. When Augerus hurried inside, he was instantly sent out again to fetch wine. Meanwhile the Abbot instructed a messenger to collect Brother Peter.

That monk, when he entered, found himself being gazed at by the stern quartet of the Abbot, Baldwin, Simon, and Mark; the latter wore the most savage expression of them all, as though, Peter thought privately, he was determined to outdo all the others in righteous indignation.

'My Lord Abbot, you asked for me?' Peter asked, with apparent surprise. He had been warned, but their expressions were fearsome.

Augerus entered behind him, and now stood contemplating him with some surprise, a tray of cups and wine in his hands.

'Wake up, Steward!' the Abbot snapped. 'Serve us. Brother Peter, I have had some alarming news. It is said that you knew who was stealing from me; that you have known for some time.'

Peter sniffed, his brows lifted. 'It is true that I guessed, as you know, but I couldn't swear to know for certain.'

'How did you guess?' the Abbot demanded, his face darkening.

'My Lord Abbot, as I told you before, I saw Gerard and also Wally, taking goods. Thus when I spoke to Wally, his part was known to me, and he swore he'd fetch back the pewter.'

'Brother Mark has said he thinks you were helping the thieves. Is this so?' the Abbot rapped out.

'No, it most certainly is not. I knew he was about, and for a short while I did wonder whether *he* could be involved, but now it seems . . .'

'You decided he was not?' Simon prompted.

Peter glanced at Mark with an apologetic smile. 'It is hard to imagine someone less suited to clandestine work. He would always be too drunk later in the evening to be able to perform any quiet or secret operation without discovery.'

'He was able to perform one,' Simon said.

'Oh, stealing the wine, yes,' Peter said dismissively. 'That was simple enough, though. Mark likes his drink too much to be able to leave it alone, and it was easy for him to persuade Augerus to get drunk with him one night, and then, when Augerus' wits were entirely fuddled, get him to open up the undercroft and permit him to taste the wines.'

'You knew of this?' the Abbot said.

Peter shrugged uneasily. 'I thought you yourself knew. Otherwise I shouldn't have spoken. It is a matter for Mark and God. Not me.'

The Abbot slowly turned and stared at his *salsarius*. 'I shall wish to speak with you, Brother,' he said heavily before facing Peter again. 'You say that Augerus let him in to drink my wine?'

'I saw them.'

Augerus felt Abbot Robert's eyes turn upon him, and hastily gabbled, 'I am sorry, my Lord, but if I did let him in, it was because I was too drunk to realise! I could scarcely have wanted to let him in to take all your wine.'

'Four times in a week?' Peter murmured in surprise. 'You must have been extremely drunk, Augerus.'

'Is this true?' the Abbot snarled. 'You went to enjoy private parties in my undercroft each night?'

'My Lord, I don't know. All I know is, I woke up one morning and Mark there told me that I must replace all the wine from one barrel because he had finished it, and you had announced your imminent return. Oh, my Lord, don't scold me and punish me for weakness – rather, punish the man who brought me down.'

'What have you to say, Mark?' the Abbot said.

The monk noted the absence of the fraternal title. 'My Lord, I cannot lie to you. I did enjoy your wine. But that is all I have done, and I did tell you about Gerard. I couldn't bring shame to this Abbey. I believe that Gerard was not alone in stealing. I believe he had an ally within who helped him pass the pewter out to Wally.'

'That is something that troubled me,' Simon said. 'How would Gerard have come to know Wally? Surely someone would have needed to introduce them? And then, how would Gerard have gained access to the lodgings here? Would he not have found the doors barred and locked?'

'Yes,' the Abbot said with a frown. 'In your drunkenness, you must have left the doors open, Augerus.'

'Perhaps that is why Mark insisted on ensuring I was drunk, my Lord,' Augerus said with a shocked expression. 'He wanted to give Gerard access to the rooms so that he could pass the stolen things to Wally.'

Simon chuckled. 'This is a fine muddle, my Lord. But we do know some facts. First, that Mark can be persuaded to accept a drink of any sort.' He ignored a huffy grunt from the *salsarius*. 'Second, that it would be easy for Gerard to get in here, if he had an accomplice inside your lodgings. We also know that the thefts were tied to Wally's death, and that Hamelin also died because of the thefts.'

'Why?'

'Hamelin had been given the money, but I think that the money was a secondary motive. If his killer had found it, he would have kept it, but the money itself wasn't the reason for the murder. I think he had to die because he saw Mark up at Wally's house that day. But Ellis saw *two* monks. We know what Mark was doing, he was trying to force Wally to bring back the pewter, but what about the other man? We know Peter was on the moors – but what if there was a third? Perhaps Hamelin saw him too. And which other monk was not in the Abbey that day? Augerus.'

'But I *was* here!' The Steward looked indignant.

'The groom said he could get no ale that day. We know he couldn't go to Mark, but all monks would surely come and ask you for some, if he wasn't about. Yet no one could find you either.'

'It's not true!'

'Hamelin was killed in case he spoke later,' Simon continued sternly. 'You murdered him, leaving his wife a widow and his children orphaned. How could you do that?'

'My Lord Abbot, what can I say?'

'In God's name, just tell me the truth!' the Abbot stormed. 'You have thrown away your honour and integrity and become no more than a felon! You captured an innocent boy and forced him to do your bidding, didn't you? Why?'

'I was scared!'

'Scared of what?'

Augerus began weeping. He knew it was pathetic, but that was how he felt. Feeble and useless. For many years he had been a capable servant, but now all was lost, and all because of his fear of the man who had bullied him as a schoolboy.

'Joce Blakemoor was at school with me, and he beat me. Broke my nose until it gushed. He came to me some time ago and said that he would cripple me if I didn't help him. He needed money badly, and I didn't dare argue. He said he'd make me look worse than Peter. I couldn't stand up to him. He was always bigger than me.'

'You could have told me,' the Abbot said.

'He swore he'd kill me if I said a word to anyone.'

Simon said, 'You must have known he couldn't murder you without suffering the consequences.'

'What would the consequences matter to me? I'd be dead, wouldn't I? You speak as if he's a rational man! He's not, he's evil. He could be a novice demon. The devil's own acolyte.'

'You forced Gerard to steal.'

'Only a little. I had to do something,' Augerus wailed.

'And harmed his soul as well as your own!'

'Is there no one among my Brothers whom I can trust?' Abbot Robert demanded.

'You can trust me, Abbot! Please, don't send me away. Joce'll have me killed, and—'

Simon gave a low, scornful laugh. 'You are sad and fearful now, Augerus, but you brutally murdered Wally, didn't you? Why did you do that?'

'You have said, to get back the pewter or the money for the Abbey,' Augerus said, shaking his head as though sadly.

'No, I don't think so,' Simon said. 'Baldwin and I have already heard that Wally diddled his associate out of a tiny part of his share in the proceeds of the crimes.'

'A tiny part? It was a whole shilling!' the Steward expostulated.

'I think,' Simon said with a faint smile, facing the Abbot, 'that that is your answer. The first murder was for one shilling. The second was for less; it was purely to protect the murderer from the consequences of his first murder.'

'No, my Lord Abbot! You can't believe the strange stories told by this Bailiff!' Augerus babbled. 'Are you going to convict me on *his* word? Please, I beg, let me—'

'You shall have to live out a penance,' Abbot Robert said, ignoring his plea. 'I shall consider it. In the meantime, you shall remain under guard. You can go to the church and begin to pray to God for His forgiveness. When your brother monks are called to the church, you will lie across the doorway so that all can step over you. You, Augerus, are contemptible!'

After eating the food Rudolf brought to him, Joce sat down and talked to the Swiss in a carefully genial manner, waiting for a suitable moment to mention the pewter. If he could, he wanted to learn in which wagon it had been stored, but somehow the foreigner didn't understand English well enough. Every time Joce tried to direct the conversation back towards the town and tin, or pewter, Rudolf began to speak about the mountains in his homelands, or the freedom which the men of the Forest Cantons enjoyed. Every man free, none a slave.

All the while the carts sat so close. They had the look of being well-filled, their wheels sinking and creating ruts in the path, and Joce longed to go to them, to hurl their contents to the ground, to destroy, to torture or kill, but mainly to find that metal. He *must* find it! It was his guarantee of free passage and a new life.

As the light faded, and twilight quickly overtook the moors, he watched the travellers carefully. It seemed to him that the folk were avoiding him, other than Rudolf himself, and he sat a little too far from Joce for the Receiver to be able to grab him with any confidence of keeping hold as well as drawing his dagger. He was tempted to try to move closer, but somehow he felt that Rudolf would notice and could consider it to be a threat. In preference, Joce might reach to pull off a boot. A man without a boot, he reasoned, looked ungainly and unthreatening. He could lean forward once the boot was off, as though peering inside it, and then throw it at Rudolf, distracting the man, and while he was catching the boot, or pushing it away, Joce could draw his dagger and put it to Rudolf's throat. That would give him a chance to demand the pewter, and then he could take a horse and ride off.

But he knew that it was madness. There were so many men here. Any one of them could stop him, could grab at him as he tried to mount a horse, or could wrest the pewter from him. He needed a better plan.

At the sound of horses, Joce saw two of Rudolf's men stand and stare back the way he had come, west, towards Tavistock, but he kept calm and sat quietly, listening intently. There were only a few riders, that was obvious. The ground didn't vibrate as it would with ten or more heavy mounts, and the rumble of hooves was dissonant, a broken noise, in which almost every hoof beat could be discerned. Two, maybe three horses, no more, he reasoned.

They took little time to reach the travellers.

'Who is your leader?' came a hoarse voice, and Joce felt his belly lurch. Sir Tristram? What was that duplicitous arse doing up here?

Rudolf stood. 'You are looking for someone?'

'A man on foot who came past here today, probably late,' Sir Tristram said. He noticed Joce sitting – now that Rudolf had moved away, Joce was alone. 'Who are you? Are you with these travellers?'

Joce rose to his feet and faced him. 'I am the Receiver of Tavistock, Sir Tristram. You remember me?'

Sir Tristram was tempted to snatch his sword from its scabbard and sweep his head from shoulders. 'Of course I remember you. Have you seen a man coming past here?'

Joce shook his head. 'No, no one.'

'That is odd, then isn't it?' Sir Tristram said. He spurred his horse forwards. 'We have had an exciting day today. A young novice, Master Gerard, from the Abbey, was savagely attacked and lies close to death in the Abbey. Then we learned of a girl who was threatened by a man who tried to strangle her, and just now we found my Sergeant dead just a little way from Tavistock, his head taken clean off his shoulders. And the man who did it came this way, first on a horse, then on foot. We came across the horse further back that way. Yet you saw no one.'

'He must have turned north or south.'

'Did you know that Jack saw you at the argument we had in the town? He said he recognised you. Said you were the leader of the Armstrongs. He called you Joce the Red-Hand.'

'He was dreaming,' Joce laughed.

Coroner Roger smiled blandly, and then pointed to Joce. 'Your sleeves are stained, man, as is your tunic near your dagger! You are the . . .'

Before he could finish his words, Joce had moved. He shot across the grass and grasped Anna about the waist, turning with her even as he drew his knife. Instantly he faced the men with the dagger at Anna's throat. 'If any one moves, she dies,' he snarled.

He had forgotten the two crossbows. There was a hideous thump and grating friction at his shoulder. He felt his whole upper body jerk, his arm losing all power in a moment, and the knife flew from his hand even as his shoulder seemed to explode. As Anna staggered and fell to her knees before him, he was only aware of the sudden eruption from his shoulder: his tunic snapped away, ripped and shredded, and there was a violent effusion of blood which sprayed the grass for yards about, a solid mass in its midst. He could see it fly on, a blurred spot in the distance.

A moment later there was a second thud in his spine, and it slammed him down to the earth, where he lay, mouth agape, his remaining good arm scrabbling for purchase in the blood-clogged grass. He tried to speak, to bellow, but no words came. He could feel pain searing his breast like flames: the bolt had shattered in his spine, and fragments of wood and bone had pricked his chest, puncturing his lungs; now the blood was clogging his breath and as he opened his mouth to roar, a fine spray of crimson burst forth, staining the grass anew.

It can't end like this, he thought. There was more astonishment at this than pain or shock. Of all ends, he had never anticipated this. He shivered, and suddenly he realised that his legs were shaking uncontrollably, quivering against the long grasses, and then the spasms spread upwards, to his groin, then his arms, and suddenly his eyes widened.

And then he was still.

When the Coroner returned to the town, riding on ahead of Sir Tristram, who was bringing Joce Blakemoor's body back on a sumpter horse, Simon and Baldwin listened with keen interest to his story.

'So the Swiss men shot him? A kind end to a violent man,' was Baldwin's comment.

'It explains some of the story,' Simon said.

'Yes. We know that the acolyte ran away from the Abbey

because he couldn't cope with the pressure and fear. Augerus had made him steal for him, taking whatever he could from the Abbey's guests, and so he ran away, joining Sir Tristram's men. He hoped to be able to disappear with them. But I suppose when he saw or heard all of us arriving and questioning Sir Tristram, he panicked and bolted, and somehow Joce caught him and tortured him to learn where the pewter was gone.'

'Yes,' said Simon absently, 'except . . .'

Baldwin chuckled to himself. 'Come, there is little enough unexplained! You can be content with the scope of your discoveries.'

Simon smiled, but he was still unhappy at the amount he did not know. The acolyte had somehow found clothing; he had been shaved; he had been helped into the lines of men joining the Host, for he would have been spoken for. Someone must have confirmed his name and details when he applied to Sir Tristram.

And then he suddenly saw in his mind's eye the pleasant, smiling face of Nob Bakere and his wife Cissy. 'I think that we may learn a little yet,' he said.

Leaving Simon's faithful servant Hugh seated at the bedside of the wounded acolyte, Simon and Baldwin walked out through the Abbey's gates and strode into the town once more.

'Where do you want to go?' Baldwin demanded.

'There are some details we should learn,' Simon said, and pushed open the door to Nob's pie-shop.

It was empty apart from the cook and his wife.

'Ah, um. Right, can we serve you gentlemen?' Nob asked, trying to look innocent.

Simon ignored him, but spoke to Baldwin.

'You remember when we came in here to look at sacks? I found a black tunic, and while I dropped it, unthinking, Nob came over and kicked it away from me angrily. At least, I thought he was angry at the time. We often kick out at whatever is near, don't we? When Nob came to me, the nearest thing for him to kick at was the tunic. It flew into the corner. Where is it now, Nob?'

'Oh, I couldn't say. Must still be there, if that's where I kicked it, Master.'

Simon nodded at his cheerful attitude. 'Well, I think it's already burned. Which is a shame, because your son will have to buy a new one. Benedictine habits are not cheap, are they? Apostasy is one thing, but to burn a tunic – that is like burning your boats, isn't it? Oh, Mark is being held by the Abbot, I should tell you, and Gerard is back at the Abbey. Much that was confusing us is now known. All we want is your story.'

'Their son?' Baldwin wanted to hit himself for being so dense. 'I begin to comprehend. Their son is . . '

'Reginald the novice,' said Cissy.

Simon snapped his mouth shut. He had been going to say that Gerard was their boy, and he was glad that he had been saved from making a fool of himself.

Baldwin was frowning intently at her. '*Reginald*?'

Cissy sighed and pointed with her chin to the ale barrel. 'Nob, we might as well have a drink while we explain.'

'All right, my little cowslip,' he muttered.

'And less of your smatter!' she called after him. 'Yes, Master Bailiff. I don't know how you guessed, but our son is Reginald.'

'And he is?' Baldwin enquired.

'Gangly, clumsy, dark hair. Oh, he's his father's son all right,' Cissy laughed. 'Reg is a fool. He got to thinking that Gerard was stealing, so he determined to talk to him and persuade him against his life of crime. Only, when he caught hold of the boy, he missed his hold and knocked him down. Reg was appalled. He was trying to help the boy, and when Gerard went down with a loud thud, he thought he'd killed him.'

'You should have seen his face!' Nob said, returning with the drink and passing pots to their visitors.

'Anyway, Gerard confessed to him, and begged to be forgiven, but asked what Reg would do, and Reg didn't hesitate. He said he'd ask his mum. Me.'

Baldwin lifted his mazer and saluted her. 'And you advised?'

'That he should stay where he was. But he said he feared Mark might kill him. That was what the monk had threatened – that he'd kill Gerard if he didn't do as Mark wanted, and the same if he ever spoke about what he'd done.'

'Yet he told you?'

'He was so lost, the poor child. He didn't know who to speak to, who to trust. By the time he came to us with Reg, he was almost past caring. The only thing he craved was certainty. And so the other possibility we suggested was that he should join the Host.'

'We gave him some of Reg's old clothes to wear, and I personally shaved him bald. I reckoned that would make him hard to recognise,' Nob said with some pride. 'When he went to join the Host, I spoke up for him, and I had paid some others to help, so that was no trouble. We thought he'd be far away by now.'

Cissy's face hardened. 'He hasn't got away, has he? You're not cheating us into telling you what happened?'

'No, Cissy,' Simon said quietly, and told her about the lad in the infirmary and the death of Joce.

'Poor Joce. I never much liked him, but I wouldn't wish that sort of death on any man,' Nob shuddered.

'Save your sympathy, you old fool! It's Gerard you should feel sorry for,' Cissy said scathingly. 'The poor young fellow's near death, from what these gentlemen say.'

'Our Reg won't be looked on with great favour, not once the Abbot knows what he did,' Nob said.

'Oh!' Cissy cried. There was a terrible lurch in her belly at the thought, although she couldn't deny a certain hope that he might be thrown from the Abbey so that he could marry and settle, just as she had always wanted.

'We can only pray that Gerard recovers fully,' Simon said.

* * *

'I need hardly say how pleased I am with your work, Simon,' the Abbot said at breakfast the next morning. He had invited Simon, Baldwin and the Coroner to join him, and he sat eyeing Reginald dubiously as the novice tried to serve the Abbot and his guests with the same professional skill as Augerus. 'You have discovered the secrets of so many with such skill, that even now I scarcely comprehend the full story.'

'I am sure we should never have learned the full facts without his efforts,' Baldwin said.

Simon glanced at Baldwin, who gazed back innocently. 'I am glad you are pleased, my Lord Abbot. I try to serve you as best I may.'

'You have always been a good servant.'

'I am only sorry to have disappointed you so often this year, my Lord,' Simon said with his head bowed.

'What do you mean?' The Abbot looked baffled.

'Simon is convinced you are so miserable with his abject inability to serve you,' Baldwin said, 'that he thinks you wish to remove him from his position. Especially after the mistake of the hammer.'

'What, you mean the coining hammer?' the Abbot demanded, astonished.

Baldwin had thrown out the comment in the hope that he might tease the Abbot into an admission that he was going to move Simon, however the tone of surprise sounded so authentic, he glanced up into the Abbot's face.

'I believed that the coining hammer was the last straw, my Lord Abbot,' Simon said. 'What with the fiasco of Oakhampton's tournaments, and the madness at Sticklepath.'

'Them?' The Abbot waved his hand in genial dismissal. 'Nothing! They had no effect upon me. And you managed to find who was guilty, didn't you?'

'I suppose so,' Simon said. There was a lightheadedness, as

though he had drunk too much of the Abbot's strong wine. Perhaps he had, he thought, but now the atmosphere of the Abbey had lost its menace. It felt calm, friendly and compassionate again.

He need not fear for his post, he need not fear for his money, for his wife's sense of well-being, for her happiness. All was well. All would remain well. He reached forward and poured himself more wine, picking up his goblet with a feeling of renewal, as though he had sat on the edge of a precipice, the soil slipping away from him, doom awaiting him, and the Abbot had saved him, gripping his arms even as he toppled forth into the abyss.

'No, Bailiff. I am very content with you,' the Abbot continued amiably.

'Then what was it you were saying to me after the coining, my Lord Abbot? You appeared to be concerned about my work.'

'Not about your work, no. About the work*load*. I didn't want to keep loading you with more duties, in case you couldn't cope with them all, but you seem to have the shoulders of an ox when it comes to bearing responsibility.'

'I can certainly help with more duties,' Simon said quickly. He dared not refuse any job, not after his concerns of the last few days.

'Good! I am pleased. As you know, I have been granted the position of Keeper of the Port of Dartmouth, and I need a good man to go down there and manage my affairs.'

Simon felt his face fix into a mask. 'You wish me to go there and live?'

'Of course. I need someone I can trust. There is a good little house, I believe, and the duties wouldn't be excessively onerous, but well remunerated. Would you take it on for me?'

In his mind's eye, Simon could see his wife's face, Meg's sadness at having to move home again. He could see his daughter's dismay at the news, having to leave all the boys with whom she had flirted. When he believed that the Abbot was disappointed in him, he had thought that the worst thing that could happen to him was that he and his family might have to quit their house and go back to Sandford, leaving their new friends behind. Now, ironically, due to his success, he *was* to be asked to move – but to yet another place where he knew no one! Meg would be upset, he knew. Edith too.

'I am most grateful, my Lord Abbot,' he said in a choked voice. 'I should be delighted to do that job for you.'

He had no choice.

Over in the quiet morning light of the Abbey sickroom, Gerard the acolyte lay huddled in his bed, his eyes on Christ on the cross hanging above the altar. Brother Peter sat beside him, a goblet of wine for the wounded boy and a cloth in his hands.

'What will happen to me now?' croaked the boy, slow tears sliding from his eyes.

'Ah! Well, I think you will be asked to confess to our good Lord Abbot, and then you will be given a penance of several Hail Marys and the duty of serving my needs. An Almoner always needs a good helper.'

'What of my crimes, though?'

'You were forced into a life of theft – Augerus forced you. He will be made to understand the meaning of penance.'

'And I made you help me leave the convent, just as I forced myself on Reginald's parents.'

Peter shifted uncomfortably. 'Aye, well, let us not dwell too deeply on that. I haven't had a moment to confess to that particular offence yet. I'll do so, though, aye, I'll do it. I'm just not looking forward to the Abbot's face when I tell him.'

'It was good of you – but why did you agree to help me get out? It was a crime,' said the broken voice.

'Aye. I know,' Peter said, thinking again of his Agnes. 'But if you weren't suited to the Abbey, do you see that you might be failing God? What if He truly intended you to be – oh, I don't know – a stonemason, whose skills would show God's glory to a congregation? Perhaps it would be better, if you mean to have a different life, to go and live it, rather than remaining here.'

'I don't think I can live here, not after all I've done.'

'What you mean is, not knowing you'd have to face Augerus every day.'

'Well, I suppose . . .'

'Well, suppose again, lad. He'll be long gone before you're out of this room. He's in a cell now, and he'll not be allowed out, other than during services, until his boat's ready.'

'What boat?'

'The Abbot has decided he will go to the islands. He'll be going to the Abbey's house at the Island of St Nicholas.'

'Good God!' Gerard began to sniffle, and Peter caught his hand and held it. 'Do you think I will be sent there too?'

'Nay, lad. You have done little wrong. Augerus has murdered two men, and forced you to become his slave-thief. He will suffer for his crimes. What have you done? You have been immature and young – but that is because you *are* immature. You will be all right.'

Gerard heard his voice, but the words were washing over him like shallow waves. He could discern little meaning. All he knew was, that the sympathy of this older monk showed that the wounds he had suffered were as truly appalling as he feared. He wanted to touch his face, where the dull throbbing at his nose and ear showed Joce had succeeded in wrecking him, or to scratch at the irritating itch at his cheek and shoulder. He had been a fool, and the memory of his foolishness would be with him every day of his life.

With a sob, he realised he wished that he had in fact died.

The next day, Nob threw open the shutters with a curious feeling of well-being. The sun was streaming down, for once, and with the slight breeze a few leaves blew along the alley outside. It was rare to wake to a clear sky and dry roadway, but today was one such, and Nob whistled cheerily, if tunelessly, as he collected flour from the miller's and some more charcoal, carrying both on his old barrow.

Cissy was already in the shop and lighting a brazier on which to heat a couple of pies for their breakfast, he thought, but then he saw that she had several pies set out beside her.

'Why so many?'

'I'm taking some food to Sara. Her children need all the help they can get,' Cissy said firmly. 'I won't have any arguments, Nob. She is eating for two again, remember.'

'Who's complaining? I'm not saying anything. I was just thinking, though. If she needs some ale, tell her my barrel's always got a spare quart for her.'

Cissy watched him set about cleaning out the ovens, arranging the tinder and some twigs, then striking a spark to ignite them. 'You're a good man, Nob,' she said contentedly.

'Aye, an' you're a good woman. Come here, lass, give us a kiss.'

She dutifully gave him a peck on the cheek.

'Nay, come on, make it a real one.'

'I don't have time.'

'Course you do. An' if you play your cards right, you can have me body as well.'

She clipped him round the ear. 'Later, maybe.'

'Ah, might be too late by then. You don't know what you're missing!' he called as she left the shop.

She was a great woman, he reckoned. Sara would get all the support she needed from Cissy, and so would Emma. Poor woman was almost distraught about her husband, but she'd knuckle down soon enough. She had to, with all her kids. And although she had a few bob now, that wouldn't last for ever. Nob shrugged. Someone else who'd have to come and get free pies. He wouldn't let anyone's children suffer.

He wondered about Sara's claim on Joce. At least he might be able to help there . . . Even if the wedding wasn't official, hadn't been held at the church door, Sara still had a claim. Nob could bear witness to that. Joce had no family, did he?

It was a little later, into the forenoon, that a clerk appeared in the doorway.

'Quick, a beef pie! I am due in the Abbot's court.'

'Master, I have one almost ready for you,' said Nob calmly. 'And I might be able to let you have it for a discount.'

'Discount?' The clerk's eyes sharpened. 'That sounds expensive.'

'It could prove a nice little earner for a good master-at-law,' Nob said dreamily. 'Helping a wealthy widow. A young, attractive, *blonde*, wealthy widow.'

The clerk leaned upon the counter. 'Tell me more . . .' he invited.